# BLOOD ON THE WIND

# BLOOD ON THE WIND

Dawn Kurtagich

RIBBIT
London

Ribbit Books
Instagram : @ribbitbooks

First Edition : March 2024



ISBNs : 978-1-7384150-0-7 (hardcover)

Printed in the United States of America, United Kingdom, France, and Australia

*For those who survive*

*the silence*

This is not a book.

It is the roar of a girl.

# Part I

## Above the Ocean

*"If your dear heart is wounded,*
*my wild heart bleeds with yours"*

—J. SHERIDAN LE FANU, *CARMILLA*

## Ccugoth: The Conjure

Also called "The Finder", Those who favor Ccugoth can discover what is lost, even secrets. Also the symbol to represent the Unclosed.

## Gothol: The Corder

Those who favor Gothol may ensnare the mind, immobalise the body and prevent speach. Because of the quality of this conjure, it has been called "The Puppetmaster"

## Rostar: The Rapture

Those who favor Rostar can make others burn for a kind word, starve for want of a kiss, bleed to prove themselves. The Rapture controls all passion, devotion and desire.

## Targoth: The Soother

Those who favor Targoth are fine thieves. All manner of creature is drawn to their watery ways. Targoth receives what it desires, while soothing the victim. They can heal and harm in equal measure.

## Sorro: The Sighter

Those who favor Sorro, the most common Conjure, see what cannot be seen. Present, past, future. Sorro sees death.

## Varr: The Breaker

Beware Varr, rarest of Conjures, for he that favors The Breaker shall do as they will. Destruction.

# ROAN

# 1851

## *Chapter 1*
## AWAKENING

HE WORLD HAS ENDED.

Roan Evelyn Eddington stirs, opens her eyes.

It is a foggy morning. The sun has not yet risen.

It is raining.

No.

Snowing.

No . . .

Ashes are falling from the sky.

She reeks of fire, of singed edges, of things lost. She is blackened with soot. There are no clothes, no hair. Not even eyelashes. But, her skin is whole. She lifts her hands, examines her arms. Not a scratch, bruise or mar. All around her lie ruins, rubble and scorched walls—

and she screams.

It has all come horribly back to her.

Rapley is gone. She felt him melting away in the flames, just as she felt every nerve in her body scorched beyond all feeling, her bones blackened to charr, before it all went dark.

She looks at the sky. Is he falling down around her? His ashes? She lets one drift into her palm and clutches it to her breast like a lifeline. Prickling in the corner of her eyes. The world turns pink, and she wipes away tears that smear her hand red.

Blood.

Horror overcomes her at the sight, and she scrambles backwards as though she can outrun herself. *What is this?* She scrubs at her eyes again, blinking through the pink haze, and there it is, more red, more blood. She is weeping blood.

Dark rips in the fabric of the world float around her like so many eels. The tears in reality Emma spoke of. Emma. She's gone too. Seamus. Cage. All of them: dead. She had tried so hard to save them all. She had given up everything to do so . . . and it hadn't been enough. Emma had been pulled through one of the tears in the world. Seamus had been slaughtered under Fostos's knife. Cage had been killed either by the flick of Fostos's hand, or the fire . . . and Rapley had been pulled into the flames.

At least Fostos died with them.

Blood and ash comingle.

She is,

once again,

alone in the world.

He awaits her on the mountain. The ram.

She stumbles to her feet and goes to meet him. She is numb. Shell-shocked. A warm blanket lies beside him on the rugged mountain between tufts of dead meadow-grass and slate. The ram, thick musky coat flecked with ash, looks at her with an eldritch gaze, his uncanny slit-type pupil peering deep into her. She hears the Devil's tongue in her mind.

*Remember your promise*, he tells her. *Daughter, mine.*

His voice is everywhere and nowhere, a deep vibration coursing through the gaps in the world, hiding within the veil.

"You said I could save him," she croaks. "You said I would have what I needed."

*I told you truthfully when I said he was right. That he would die on this mountain and be cursed ever more.*

She shakes her head, misses the heavy feel of her hair. Hates that she cares how naked she is. How bare and exposed. "You lied."

*I will never lie to you.* A pause. *And this you know.*

She cannot meet his gaze. Cannot think clearly. Her thoughts are without form or feeling. The ram lets out a snort that plumes in the air, and then he turns and walks slowly on, leviathan hooves clomping over shattering slate.

Roan stares at Mill house, which looks so untouched from this distance, and feels nothing. Her rage is gone. Her love is gone. Everything is gone.

Fostos—is gone.

And then.

A flash of movement on the road far below—a figure hurrying into Maudley's carriage. Black horses drawing it away.

Fostos.

Alive after all.

The flicker of terrible, painful emotion that she does not want to embrace. And a childish thought: *It's not fair.*

She does not want to feel, does not want whatever lever was pulled to make her numb to suddenly release the tidal wave she knows it holds back: grief is terrible. Grief is a magnitude of horror she cannot comprehend, a rabid wolf snapping at her heels. No human could possibly endure it.

Is that what she is?

Human?

She does not feel it. Sure, vestiges of logic are there, buried deep within the black voice of her mind, drowning in the loss of Rapley. Rapley was consumed by the flames. Cage was consumed by the flames. Fostos was not. She was not. She and Fostos both made their Unholy bargains so she and Fostos must be changed in the same Unholy way . . . a way she cannot yet fully comprehend. But these thoughts are pale, illimitable whispers, insubstantial and unimportant. More important is the creeping, snapping rabid dog getting closer.

But there is a shield within, a weapon against the incoming despair. Anger is clarifying, purifying—like fire. White hot, her *fury* rises like a phoenix from the ashes of her life, brilliant and bright.

She wants to chase Fostos down now, at this very moment, naked and unshod. To wring his head clean from his body, to make him hurt in the way he has made her hurt—to see him beg for mercy and then, laughing, deny it. But she senses the danger in the air, some kind of newly formed instinct. She must hide, before dawn brings the sun. The devil did not tell her much when she made her terrible bargain, but she knows one thing for certain: She will not die. Not for a long. Centuries lie before her like the ever-retreating horizon.

She gets to her feet once more, wrapping the blanket over her exposed flesh, and staggers further up the mountain to the slate ledge and the dark space beneath it where she and Rapley fell in love. The same place they discovered was a hidden entrance into catacombs, to secret tunnels that lead deep into the mountain and, finally, twisting up and down and back on themselves, to the innards of Mill House. The caves where, centuries before, Fostos made his ill-fated bargain with the Beast—a bargain that began a cascading effect through time and which led, eventually, to her birth. To all this darkness and pain.

She knows that unless she stops him, it will continue on, and on, and . . . on *in aeternum*. Forever.

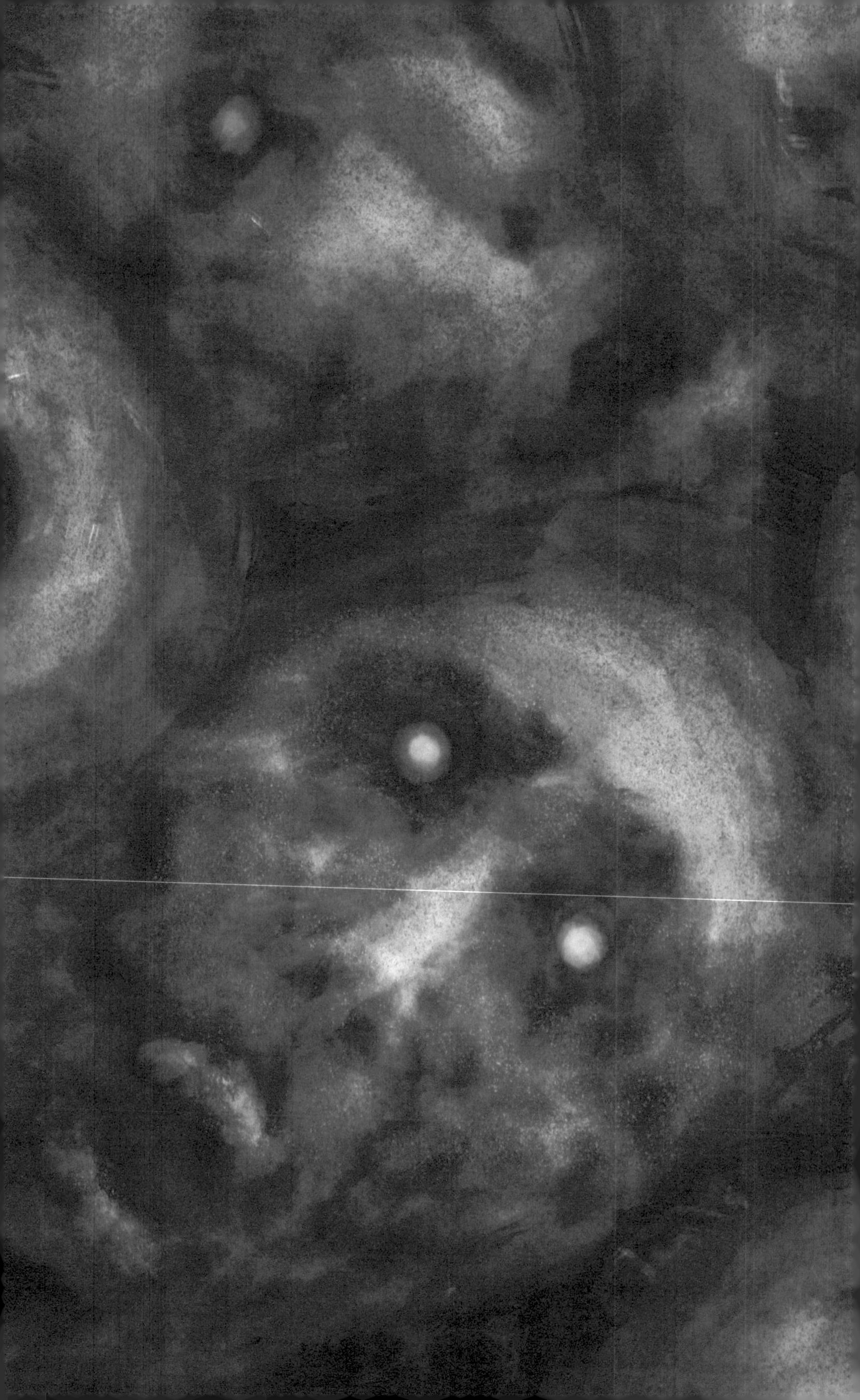

## *Chapter 2*

# HAUNTED

T IS A KIND of agony, walking back into Mill House, darting the slate teeth of a mountain gone quiet, navigating air clear of mists, and stepping back into the cool foyer of a gneiss house no longer haunted. She pads across the chessboard marble-and-slate stones and up the creaking stairs, trying not to look at the place that has, despite everything, been a home. Safety in isolation, her father once told her. Well, she is alone now. *Pant Tywell* is alone now.

The only things that remain are ghosts. Torturous memories—both in their pleasure and pain. The red room, the yellow room, the blue room, all of it so intimate and familiar, Emma cursing the "*innominable*" rain, Seamus laughing as he told her about the habits of serpents and bugs, his delight at all Cage was teaching him—the happiest boy she had ever known. Roan pauses near the top of the stairs, looking tentatively around, hoping and fearing that she might glimpse his rotted ghost. But there is nothing. Just a yawning emptiness that she finds difficult to bear.

Something moves over her foot and she starts back.

A small crimson snake stares up at her, waiting.

"He's not here," she chokes, angry prickles in her eyes.

Another snake slithers from a crack in the wall, inching closer.

"Don't bother," she snaps, hiccupping over the words. "He's dead!"

More snakes reveal themselves in the lobby now, all of them drawn to her, all of them seeking something lost.

She chokes on a sob and kicks out at the crimson snake, which skitters away. "*I said he's dead! Seamus is dead, don't you understand, you stupid useless beasts?*"

Her voice echoes through the house, reverberating through cavernous, empty spaces. The snakes all freeze, watching her. At long last, the only sound is her furious breathing.

After a long time, she opens her mouth.

"Emma?" she calls, voice wobbling. "Seamus? Cage?" Her voice breaks. "*Rapley* . . ."

*Nothing.*

For the first time in a long time, she misses her parents. She misses her mother before she changed, before she knew what Roan really was and grew mad with the fear of it. She misses her father. Even misses his stern lecturing in the cramped secret cellar of their London home—

That's it. The idea comes to her like a flickering flame, fragile in the impenetrable dark.

She could go home. Back to London, back to the house, back to the concealed cellar where her father had kept her hidden for so many years, schooling her in the Devil's Tongue. Maybe the answers she sought had been there all along . . . She had left in a hurry after finding his corpse, taken the letter clutched in his hand and fled, sure that if she were to be discovered, she would be considered complicit in some way. She hadn't stayed to look around, which she now sees was foolish in the extreme.

In her small room, surrounded by snakes, she goes through the motions of making herself respectable. Pulling on cotton stockings, pantaloons and a linen chemise, lacing her boots. Front-opening corset, petticoat, skirt and bodice. The movements are mechanical, practiced. The crinoline is broken, so she leaves it behind. All of this seems somehow a pantomime. How appropriate, she thinks with bitterness, that all her clothes are mourning wear. She can smell Rapley in the flounces of the skirt even now, and her hands shake when she presses the fabric to her face. There are subtle hints of Emma and Seamus there too, flaming hair and green fields, mildew and old food.

She has never wanted to not be so intensely. The skin of her shoulder is knotted and scarred from where Cage branded her. She has a reckless impulse to cut it out of her, but resists. She needs all her strength.

Roan takes nothing but clothes, a pelerine and the book, which she puts into the deep pocket of her skirt and buttons closed. Everything else, including the much-read letter from her father, which drew her here in the first place, she leaves behind. They belong to another girl. A dead girl.

When she leaves Mill House, snakes trailing behind, she does not look back.

She reaches the *Pen-y-Gwryd* tavern in the village late into the night, but the fire is still lit within the hearth, smoke pluming from the chimney like dragon's breath. The noise of merrymaking and the lilting of a lithe flute filter through the smoggy windows. She should avoid people. Instinctively she senses this. But she needs food and drink–she has never been this hungry—and then a ride. Getting to London on foot will take too long. Now that she has chosen her next steps, she feels their urgency. The snakes have decided it best to leave her to her business, it seems, for she is alone.

She pushes open the door, flinching at the smell of boiled meat and cabbage, a simple cawl, the stink of ale on muddy flagstones and the old stench of sour male sweat. She ignores the faces that turn to gawp at her, the halted conversations as she steps up to the bar. The woman behind the counter has a thin, sallow face riddled with lines much like Mrs Goode's, and she eyes Roan suspiciously, wetting her lips with a darting pink tongue. They are the only two women in the tavern.

"Water," Roan croaks, placing her shaking, ash-smeared hand on the bar.

The woman glances at it, squinting with suspicion, and Roan removes it.

"Water," she repeats, and after a moment, "Please."

The woman mutters something in Welsh, which is greeted with a yelp of laughter from behind Roan. "You can't get something for nothing," she says in English. "You have money?"

Roan hasn't even opened her mouth to reply when a rough hand grabs at her bonnet and pulls it from her head. "Look at this, lads. She's clean bald."

Another man calls something else that Roan doesn't catch, but she grabs for her bonnet, which rips. Her fingers itch with a familiar prickle of power.

*Pick him apart, easy as chicken.*

"Well now," the man spits, throwing the hat onto the bar. "I'll buy you an ale, if you're nice."

Conjure marks flicker onto her tongue. They would be so easy to speak. The itch rising up her throat is hard to ignore.

*And why should you?* A delicious voice purrs.

But she remembers the last time she spoke the Devil's Tongue, releasing Varr into her veins, the caustic sulphur of it lodged in her gums, the burning heat of it in her skin, the way her tormentor—Cage—had risen off his feet, hanging in air that held its breath, and how she had almost killed him. She had nearly broken the world in the process.

Gritting her teeth, she grabs the ripped bonnet and shoves past the man who falls back with an exaggerated flourish. She has to get out of here before she kills him . . . kills them all.

The night air is cool and fresh, but Roan's stomach growls, clenching so fiercely that she doubles over.

A touch on her back has her yanking her body away. It is the woman from the tavern. She is holding out a husk of bread and a tankard of ale.

Roan grabs both, ripping into the bread with her teeth and watching the woman warily.

“They mean no harm,” the woman says. “Not really. Still, you should leave before they come looking. A woman alone, a stranger, come from that Mill House . . . that’s looking for trouble.”

Roan shouldn’t be surprised that the woman knows where she’s come from. She wonders how much gossip Jenny supplied about them over the months before it all went wrong.

The bread is ashy in her mouth, stodgy and tasteless, but she forces herself to swallow and nods. The woman looks her up and down once, twice, and then goes back inside, shutting the light away with her.

Roan takes another savage bite of the bland bread and gulps down the ale—also tasteless. She is mid-chew of the third bite when her stomach clenches in protest, sharp knives of pain running up her body like jagged lightening. She collapses in the dirt and wretches, her body forcing the meagre meal from her in sickening clumps, and her eyes stream bloody tears.

Her stomach clenches painfully again, but she throws the bread far away from her, eyeing the tankard that she dropped. A terrible thought . . . did the woman give her poison? She glances at the tavern door, listening to the raucous noises from inside. Maybe it had been one of the men. Is she dying? Are these her final moments? She doesn’t much mind this possibility, but is irked that it should be done with such pathetic ease.

A horse whinnies nearby. Three are tied to the hitching post, saddled and ready. She senses their unease, but it doesn’t matter. A crash from inside the tavern and a yell of protest draws her attention and she listens, one cluster of distinctive voices clearing into focus.

" . . . going to get her. Get some answers about what exactly they're doing up there."

" . . . witch's business," another agrees, riled up.

" . . . isn't natural," the first continues.

Time to go.

Roan steals the black horse, hoping that its size and colour will aid in her escape and hide her in the dark.

"Ey !" one of them yells, noticing her pulling the reigns free. "She's stealing the horses !"

She mounts with surprising ease, clinging on as the horse rears up, trying to throw her, hooves kicking out at the man, who yells again, and then she is galloping down the road, the book slamming against her thigh, skirts flapping around her hips in the wind. She is very glad that her crinoline was broken, for she is riding astride like a man—just as her father taught her.

Behind, she hears the men from the tavern mount their own horses and race after her.

Roan rides hard. She doesn't stop, not even when the sound of the men chasing her have long fallen silent, nor when the horse begins to froth, his flanks quivering dangerously. She doesn't stop even when the sky begins to lighten on the horizon and her skin begins to faintly prickle. It is only when the horse gives a terrified whinny, stumbles and crashes to the ground in a cloud of dust, taking her with it, that the momentum comes to an end.

She falls some five feet away from the horse, rolling across the dirt track until she hits a jagged rock, tearing her arm and sending the book flying from her pocket. She gets to her feet, staring at the wound . . . which begins to knit itself back together. She watched, dimly horrified, until her skin is whole once more, nothing but a smear of scarlet to show she was hurt at all.

What has the Beast turned her into ?

It is a moment before she picks up the book and turns to the horse. It is panting on the ground, blood pooling from wide nostrils. The terror in its eyes should make her feel something. Guilt. Despair. Disgust or grief at what she has done. But the blood spilling from the animal sends an irresistible scent into the air, one that answers the desperate call in her own veins. It is a snake around her throat, a fire in her lungs, and she pounces on the beast with savagery, teeth ripping into its neck with crisp finality. There is no thought in the action, only instinct. A draw and pull as easy as breathing. Blood, thick and salty, fills her like she thought the food at the inn would, like water should—a basic rightness. She can feel the failing heart of the horse pumping life into her own body, knows she is stealing it, until at last, it stutters, hiccups, and dies.

The moment is unreal. She stares at the gore on her hands, wipes it from her mouth, gapes at the carnage she has wrought of the poor animal at her feet. The blood is sticky as it tries on her skin, but it is also . . . warm. Inside. She feels whole again, strong again, alive again. Why should blood revitalise her more than water ? Why should she weep blood and not tears ? Why should her skin knit itself together like spider webs sewing sinew to sinew, flesh to flesh ?

*You are truly a monster now*, the voice in her mind coos. *Daughter, mine.*

The air is warming fast. A sense of danger rises, pricking at her senses. Her skin is tingling now. She must hide. From the men chasing her, from the light.

But where ?

With a desperate cry, she pushes the horse off the road, surprised at her strength, and drags it far from the path, behind bushes of yellow gorse and towering purple heather. Then, hating herself, she disembowels it, cracking the ribs apart and burying the gore in a hole she digs with her hands, nails scraping away earth as though it is nothing but the finest ground spelt. Then, with a final glance towards the lightening horizon, she closes herself and the book inside the carcass and waits for night to come again.

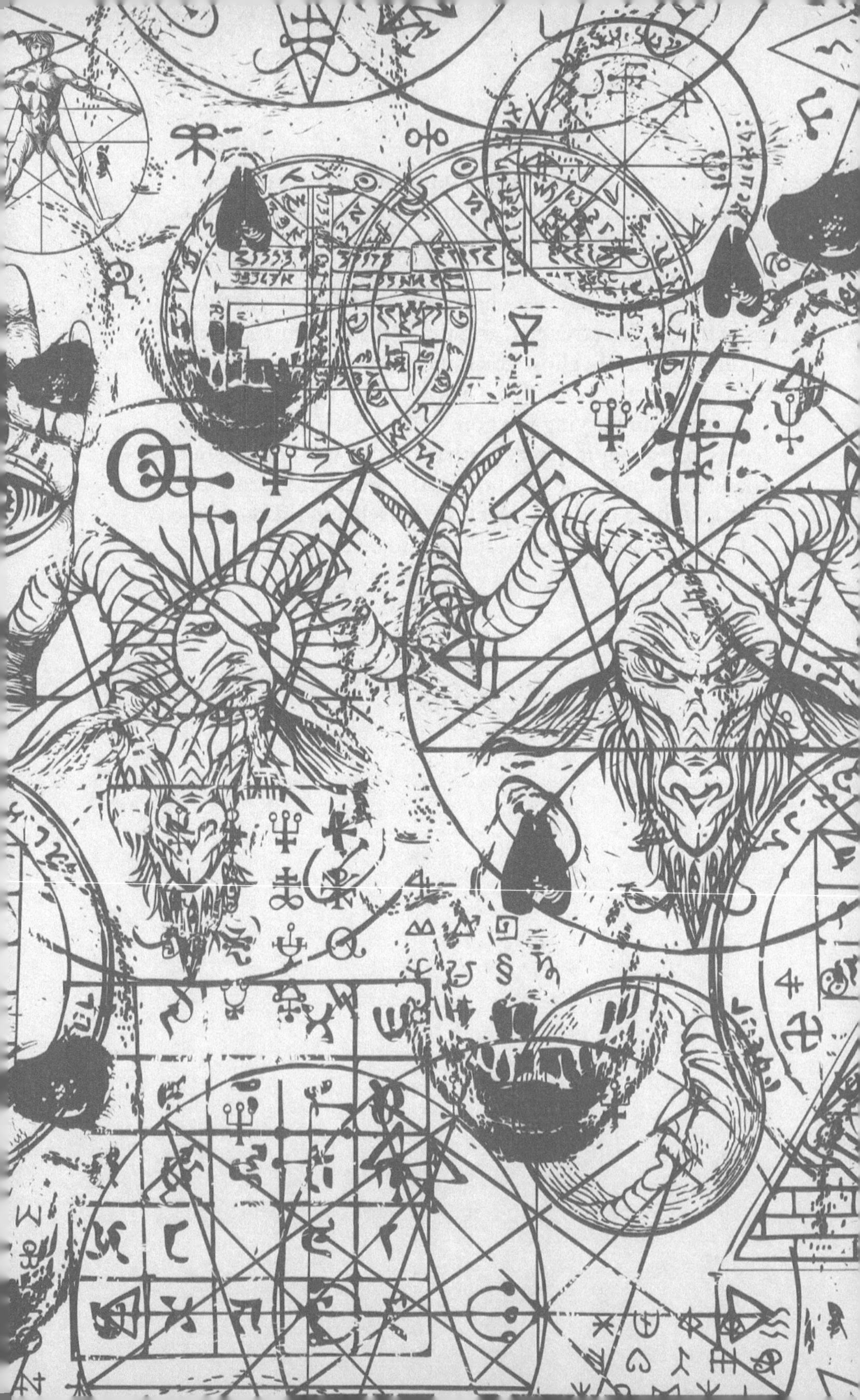

## *Chapter 3*

# THE CELLAR

OAN CAN BARELY restrain herself by the time she reaches London.

Every time someone passes her, their cloaks brushing her hands, their breath ticking her cheek, their eyes darting across her face, scrutinising what they find there, she feels their presence like a physical blow. The blood in the city is a roar in her ears, a thickening desperation in her throat, and her stomach cries out for it—a famishment she has never known. Even during those long days in Mill House with rotten meat she refused to eat—which had later turned out to be human flesh—she has never before known starvation such as this.

Again, the obsessive refrain: What manner of creature has the Beast turned her into? What has she bargained for with her infernal deal? The deal, which is a lie. For Fostos still lives. It galls her, rising in her stomach like poison, like bile. Would that she had some small measure of power over the Beast, she would show him what it means to betray her. Her impotence is a bitter cawl.

The blood in the city is a heartbeat in her throat, insistent and alluring. But she will not give in. If she can no longer be human, then let her at least not be a monster. She will not to be the thing the Beast made into. She is strong enough to resist. She does not need the blood in the veins of the people around her, for did the Beast not give her innumerable years in exchange for her favour? She can and *will* survive without it. The craving is just a manifestation of her rage. Of her curse.

She comes to the townhouse some hours after sunset. How peculiar that it looks the same, given everything that has happened in the intervening time. Surely it should be in ruins, black smoke choking the sky, devastation all around? Anything to mirror the turmoil inside her own body and mind—the ripping, yawning hole inside where Rapley, Emma and Seamus used to be. Where *she* used to be. How can it look so stoic and clean, so adamantly unchanged? How can those mundane walls be standing sentinel behind the same iron gates when she feels as though her entire being has been torn away?

Not even a year has passed since she fled London to find the mysterious Dr Maudley, leaving behind the body of the man who raised her. She is in no doubt that the constable would be very interested in her version of events should he get hold of her, that he may even attempt to lay blame. After all, she is her father's biggest secret. She doubts whether anyone remembers that, once upon a time, Arthur Eddington had a daughter. By the time she was nine, he had taken to keeping her in the cellar, and soon no one remembered the brown-haired child who laughed and danced in the front garden. Or, if they did, they did not speak of it.

Their silence created her as much as her father did.

She clenches her teeth at the injustice of it and steps forward. There is no way to know if the house has new ownership. Perhaps her father left it to her in his will and she will find it empty, waiting for her to contact a relevant solicitor. What, in such a case, is the allowable elapse of time before it is sold on? Perhaps it is already to be auctioned off, sitting in some brokerage catalogue, waiting for the fall of the gavel.

Roan goes silently to the back door by the kitchen and tries the handle. It swings open with a haunting whisper. When she attempts to step inside, however, she finds that she cannot. There is no physical barrier, nothing barring her path, yet when she leans forward, something leans back, denying her entry, as though some fleshy wall, invisible to the naked eye, has been strung across the doorway. She pushes and shoves, fighting the force, imagining some trick of the Beast keeping her from the answers she is now certain are in the cellar, but it will not give. She gives one furious cry and collapses against the limestone architrave, breathing heavily.

She doesn't know how long she sits there, breathing, cursing, hating.

"Good day?"

Roan starts. A pale woman in her fifties with washed-out eyes and a wan quality that is somehow familiar stands in the doorway, peering down at her. She gives the impression of a partridge.

"Are you alright, child ?" Her voice is gentle, concerned.

Roan did not expect to meet anyone, let alone someone with kindness in their voice. She scrambles up and away, averting her face, biting back tears that she now knows will fall red.

"Child ?" the woman says, stepping forward. Again, such kindness, such sympathy.

"I used to live here," Roan admits, her voice small, unsure why she is telling the truth. She means to lie. Means to apologise and leave. Means to tell any story. But her heart is so sore, and she had thought she was home.

"You're the daughter," the woman breathes, and Roan snaps her head to stare at her.

"You knew about me ?"

The woman nods. "We thought you'd died long years since. There were whispers about it. But then Arthur . . . and the paper . . ." She shakes her head, taking Roan in. "What happened to you ? Your hair ?"

Roan raises a shaking hand to her head. The hair is growing back it is true, and much faster than is normal. In only a matter of days a soft fuzz of growth, downy and new, is growing there. She catches sight of her hands and hides them in the folds of her skirt. There is still horse blood and earth caked beneath her fingernails. How must she look ?

"Did someone hurt you ?" the woman asks gently, and Roan cannot reply.

*I have hurt myself.*

"Well." The woman looks her up and down then nods briskly. "I think it best you come inside and tell me what happened. No one knew what to do with the house when it was unclaimed, no one could find you, so it was sold off. I've been keeping it clean by request of the executors, but I suppose it is rightfully yours. The money was put into a trust, I believe. Let us have tea and discuss what to do about it."

She steps back, gesturing for Roan to come inside. Roan shakes her head, about to protest, when her arm falls through the invisible barrier as though it never was. She stares at her hand, then up into the frowning face of the woman. Whatever was blocking her way before is no longer there. She gets to her feet and follows the woman inside, peering with confusion at the architrave as she passes.

Everything is the same. Her father's green armchairs and upholstered Bergères sit in the corner, the same books line the oak bookcases, the same paintings, regal and indifferent, hang upon the flocked damask wallpaper. Here, his alabaster sculptures, there is polished card table. Even the round baluster of the staircase holds memories for her—and is unchanged. She touches the newel post, and it is as smooth as it ever was.

"It must be strange for you," the woman says, gesturing at one of the chairs. Roan takes a seat, aware of her gore-stained clothes and how awful she must smell, and continues to peer around. She ignores her own stench and instead takes in the array of intricate smells that trigger memories and feelings that are, for the most part, unwelcome.

"I met you once," the woman says, "when you were no taller than my waist. A quiet girl, I recall. Do you remember me?"

Roan shakes her head, though there is something familiar about the woman. She fidgets with the stiff folds of her skirt.

"My name is Mrs Amelia Aintree. I live across the road. When we met I was with my late husband, George. Your father invited us for a supper. The lamb was very good, I recall. Your father served a delightful claret. Perhaps you remember my husband, George ?"

"I'm sorry, Madam. No."

A silence falls between them Roan regrets very much coming inside. The smell of Amelia Aintree is growing in potency, a soft milk scent overlaid with the sour floral smell of perfumed sweat folded into starched linen.

"I have the obituary," Mrs Aintree says, standing to retrieve a folded paper from the sideboard drawer. "I thought it respectful somehow, to keep it here."

She hands the paper over to Roan who takes it quickly, folding it over her fingers. She reads the small entry quickly several times over. *Arthur Gordon Eddington . . . a sudden loss . . . a list of colleagues and friends. And then: he is survived by his daughter, Roan Evelyn Eddington, who has been sent to Medwyn Mill, Gwynedd, and there placed under the guardianship of Dr A. Maudley until she reaches the age of maturity or marries.*

Roan looks up, startled. "You knew where I was ?"

Mrs Aintree frowns. "What do you mean ?"

Roan gestures at the paper. "Mill House."

"But . . . you were there ? Oh, but my dear, I wrote ! I wrote to this Doctor Maudley. I enquired after you, asking after your wishes for the property. I received a reply from the doctor stating that he had not seen you."

Roan blinks, her mind befuddled. "You wrote to Maudley ?"

"Well, of course, dear. No one could find you !"

"And Maudley . . . said I wasn't there ?"

Mrs Aintree nods, looking more concerned. "You mean to tell me that you have been in Wales ? All this time ? That he lied to me ?"

She nods. "Yes."

Mrs Aintree looks offended. "Why on earth . . . In his letter he speculated that you must have run off with a lover or that you were perhaps also dead."

Maudley had wanted to keep her at Mill House. Had wanted to prevent her from leaving. For Fostos. Perhaps he had well and truly lost his marbles long before she even arrived.

She closes her eyes. It is galling to be so helpless. To know so little.

"Did he hurt you ?" Mrs Aintree says delicately after a long, drawn-out silence. And when Roan doesn't reply, she says, "Where is he ?"

"Dead." Her voice is flat. She is holding her breath, trying to keep Mrs Aintree's scent away from her clawing hunger.

If only this woman will leave her alone. She needs to visit the concealed cellar and does not want it found by any except her. How can she possibly explain the Conjure marks scratched into the walls, windowsills and bedpost ? How can she explain the volumes of dark tomes or the bloodstains from countless, brutal hours of Conjuring at her father's behest ?

Mrs Aintree's scent is becoming distracting.

"Beg pardon," Roan mutters, her teeth clenched tight. "Might you have some water ?"

Mrs Aintree gives a start. "Of course ! I apologise. Let me attend to refreshments. My maidservant is next door, but I'm certain I can manage."

She gets to her feet and hurries from the room, much like a partridge, taking the worst of her scent with her, though some still clings stubbornly to the air, thick and difficult to ignore. Roan allows herself a painful breath, unclenching her fists and getting to her feet. She rips the obituary from the paper, folds it over to conceal the theft, and places it on her seat. Perhaps she can sneak away unseen, hide herself in the cellar until Mrs Aintree decides she has left, and closes the house up for the rest of the night. That would be ideal.

Roan hurries to the staircase as quietly as she can, pausing to check that she won't be seen, and then rushes down to the basement, tucking the obituary into her pocket next to the book.

The entrance to the cellar, which sits below the basement itself, is concealed on the back wall behind panelling designed to seamlessly blend into the wainscoting on either side. Roan steps through and closes it behind her, then waits, listening. She hears nothing from above and thanks whatever pitiful deity would dare watch over a damned creature such as herself, for mercy. Then, cursing, she draws a Conjure symbol for concealment in the air over the door, and seals it with a sulphurous breath.

She should not be able to see the shadow-cloaked staircase leading into the bowels of the house, just as she should not have been able to navigate the midnight dirt track with the horse in Wales. Yet, she can. Another reminder that this change, whatever it is, has aligned her with the dark elements of the world, the yawning blackness of the underbelly of things, carrying her even further away from the light. And so, not using a lamp, nor needing one, she descends alone.

The further she descends, the more she feels. Familiar, cool stone envelops her. Dim hints of brimstone and sage linger in the air. The takes the last step and enters the small space that had been her existence for so many years, and sits on the rickety bed, staring around. All the same.

No windows.

No light.

Just the bed, a small table and chair where her father would sit and transcribe his notes as she lay, sweating and spent, after long hours of speaking and reading the Devil's Tongue, her fingers blackened with dark magic, the hems of her nightdress smoking. That, and the small bookcase where the most infernal books sit, incunabula of every wretched kind, watchful, biding their time.

*Oh, dark daughter,* they seem to whisper. *Oh, beloved. Welcome home.*

She feels them more keenly than she ever has.

Roan runs her fingers over the marks gouged into the bedposts, the desk, and the sides of the bookcase, feeling their still-potent power. She had been no more than ten years old the first time she had carved a mark with her own hands, using a small knife for peeling apples, longing for Adam, even two years later.

She had been asking herself the same questions—why had he left? Where had he gone? Would he ever return?—when she had cut herself to the bone, startled by the drops that spattered the sheets in a sudden burst of scarlet. The fever that followed had nearly taken her life, this she was certain of. She had vague memories of her father sitting at her bedside, his face grave as he sponged sugar water into her mouth, and wiped her flaming forehead, muttering beneath his breath.

"Would I had perished," she mutters darkly.

There is no use in nostalgia. She needs answers. Dismissing her fear of removing the books she had always been forbidden to touch, she pulls them, one by one, from the shelf, searching every page for a clue. They are vile things. Daemonia, grimoires, syllabaries, codex's, Unholy dictionaries, all manner of cursed texts and rites. As she goes, she piles them onto the bed. She finds her baptism certificate in the back of the fourth volume. It lists her father and mother as witnesses. Lists her baptism name as Ruth. She scoffs and throws it down on the pile and keeps searching.

She finds a hand-written journal that she flips through without reading—time enough for that later—but she does confirm her father's self-possessed, delimited writing. She finds a torn letter in the last book, tucked into a concealed pocked of the spine. Unravelling it, she discovers a familiar sigil, a C and a cross. She's seen it once before . . . with Cage.

Crucisvigil . . .

Most of the letter is gone, but three words remain—*is almost ready.*

What is a Crucisvigil letter doing in her father's house? She tries to remember everything she learned from Cage before he died. Crucisvigil was an order of ancient monks, formed when they discovered one of their own, Fostos, had made a deal with the devil. Their aim was to find Fostos and defeat him, the same aim as hers. Cage had been at Mill House to kill her, essentially, and kill Fostos too. He had tortured and branded her until she, in an uncontrollable act of Conjuration, had almost killed him. And somehow, impossibly, Emma had fallen in love with him.

Was her father working with Crucisvigil to find Fostos ? If that was the case, why had he sent her to Mill House ? Surely he knew, as Crucisvigil did, that the mill sat atop the very catacombs where Fostos's original deal was made ?

And mine too, she thinks bitterly.

Surely her father knew there was a chance he might still be there ? Or had he assumed that Fostos had moved on centuries before ? Was she sent there as a sacrifice ? As a weapon ? To what end ?

She had hoped for answers, but there are only more questions.

Roan finishes searching the small space, tearing everything from its place and examining it closely. At last, she is forced to concede that the six books, her baptism certificate and the Crucisvigil letter are the only treasures to be found. She adds the book from her pocket and the obituary to the pile, then ties the bed sheet around them in a makeshift bindle, then strips her ruined clothes off.

She dresses in items she left behind in the small chest at the foot of the bed, wishing she could wash herself first, then sits on the mattress, looking around.

Her mind finds its way to Rapley, as it always does in moments of quiet. Adam. Rapley. The boy, and the man. Friend. Lover. Family. Lost.

"*Girl of the rocks*," he had called her once, when she had shown him her power. When he had looked at her with fear and fascination.

And then something happens.

A face appears before hers in the darkness, a whisper and no more, materialising in shades of white, grey and blue. Smoke in the shadows.

It is Rapley.

# *Chapter 4*
# FIRST BLOOD

"Adam—"

Shocked, Roan reaches for the ghost of Rapley, but her hand passes straight through his beloved face.

"Adam !"

He opens his mouth—she can see his lips form the shape of her name, but there is no sound. She hiccups a sob, yearning so deeply for him that her heart lurches as if it were possible it could be broken further.

Behind the apparition, a face leers, white teeth spread in a smile as he gazes at something unseen in the distance. Buckingham House stands tall behind this figure. Andrew. *Fostos*. He is here . . . in London. And Rapley is with him.

He says her name again, a desperate longing in his eyes.

"Hold on," she breathes quickly, "I'm coming—"

But he is gone.

It worked . . . the infernal spirit wheel *worked.* Rapley is with Fostos . . . which means he hasn't passed on. Hasn't gone wherever spirits go after life has ended. He's trapped, bound to Fostos like chattel.

Roan lets out a roar of outrage, feeling the Conjure prickling at her fingertips. With effort, she bites down on her teeth, forcing herself to control the fire within, swallowing it like bile. Her stomach clenches painfully, and she bends double, retching.

She shuts her eyes and forces herself to count until the rage and the sickness passes, and then she smiles with the new realisation. Rapley isn't gone. Rapley is still out there, waiting for her to find him. Waiting for her to free him. She will be able to see him again, talk to him, tell him that she—

She does not let herself finish the thought. Instead, she gets to her feet, lifting the sheet of books and hurries to the cellar exit. She glances back once, taking a final look, knowing she will never return. She does not reverse her concealment conjure as she exits. Let this room be hidden for eternity, buried like a little girl who was once called Eve.

Roan is already at the top of the stairway banister, about to hurry from the house for good, when Mrs Aintree rounds the corner at some speed, a sentence half on her lips, and collides with her.

Roan inhales a full-scented gasp of surprise.

"I looked all over for you," Mrs Aintree cries, taking Roan by the shoulders in warm, plump hands and shaking her. "This is how you repay my kindness?"

Something in Roan's face makes the woman pause, and Mrs Aintree drops her hands, stepping back with a look of perplexity.

"I'm sorry," Roan whispers, the book-filled sheet forgotten as she drops it to the floor and steps purposely forward.

Mrs Aintree gives half a startled cry that is instantly silenced as Roan pounces, her teeth growing sharp moments before they sink into the soft flesh of the woman's throat. Roan is barely aware of her body as it crushes the woman to the floor, barely aware of her hands as they hold down Mrs Aintree's arms, which fight feebly against her, barely aware of anything at all except the pump and flow of rich, thick blood cascading down her throat, copper tang and cherries. Mrs Aintree's wrists break and she gives a gurgling cry. Pitiful, mewling.

This is nothing like horse blood.

This is satiation she has never known.

Ecstasy she has never known.

Purpose she has never known.

It is an intoxicating, enveloping embrace.

It is the first time she has felt whole since she made her deal, and the world is red-tinged and hazy, plump and slow. She is swimming in warmth and nothing matters, not even her grief. All that exists is the pull and swallow and the fading heartbeat deep inside her prey; the diminishing *wump*, *wump*, *wump* is the most alluring sound she has ever heard.

She comes back to some semblance of herself when a yell from outside breaks the silence followed by a shrill whistle that splits the air.

"You there !"

Another whistle.

Roan turns, sees that the front door is standing open, revealing her to a night watchman who stands, lamp in hand, on the road outside. He is staring at her and blowing his whistle, a piercing cry into the night. Roan jumps to her feet, grabs the sheet of books, and flees. She runs past him, even as he yells for her to halt and then gives chase, quickly followed by three policemen who round the corner, each of them yelling for her to stop.

She doesn't. She runs with new life pumping in her veins, new vitality flowing in her muscles. Mrs Aintree's life is aiding her own. She has never felt so strong. Every tiny hair on her arms feels the cool night as a caress that tingles ; even her eyelashes seem to kiss the air. She smirks when she glances back and sees that the men are falling behind, until a fourth appears on horseback, gaining ground.

She turns into an alley, but the other end is blocked. Cursing under her breath, she looks for another option, but there seems only one : to go back. But she can hear the hoofbeats on the road clattering nearer and knows she will not make it in time. They'll catch her. She's cornered.

Instinct takes over. She grabs at the wall, noting with surprise that the brick crumbles beneath her fingers, and she climbs. She must look like a floral spider, scaling the building in her skirts, she muses distractedly, only half surprised at her newfound strength. After all, she bartered for the power to defeat Fostos, and she saw what he was capable of.

When she reaches the top of the building, she flings the makeshift bag over the ledge and hauls herself over.

For good measure, she removes her bonnet and flings it over the side, watching it drift down into the alley.

The Peeler dismounts, walking over to the discarded hat. He picks it up and stares around, looking up and down the alley, but never up to the roof where Roan stands watching him. Why would he, she thinks wryly? What policeman would expect a woman on foot to climb a building?

She forces herself to stop listening to the faint thumping of his heart, to stop smelling the sour tang of his sweat, picks up her sheet, and vanishes into the night. Why, she wonders, if she fed on the life of poor Mrs Amelia Aintree only moments ago, is she still so hungry?

# ROAN

# 1852

## *Chapter 5*
## The Babe

HE HUNCHES IN THE shadows beneath the bridge, the cool night air like a balm against her fevered skin. She cannot survive much more of this; the pain is exquisite. A tearing, rending agony that rips up her back and through her pelvis. Her legs shake as she staggers to a halt. The contraction comes again, blinding, breathtaking, and she wants to cry out—but won't. Her child will not come into the world on a scream.

She realized she was pregnant only four months ago, when the sickness and the hunger had been so overwhelming that she killed an entire family as they left their Kenwood home. Mother, father, and two small children, one of which had fled down the road, too terrified to scream. If he had run into the house he would have survived—she knew now she couldn't enter a dwelling without permission—but he had seen it, no doubt, as a trap with no exit. She chased him down, a repulsive grin on her face, hating that, no matter how she lied to her self about it, she enjoyed the hunt.

It was remarkable, she thought, how little people noticed. When she reached the child, she swept him up and clasped him to her chest, crushing his little body, lips pressed to his neck, teeth already sunken deep, and a woman passing smiled indulgently at her.

"Full of terrors at this age," she said sympathetically, and passed on with a chuckle.

Later, when Roan lay in an alley beside their bodies, sated and hating it, she felt the thing inside her give a little kick. It was more of a fluttering. Butterflies and bubbles. The horror of the realization had been more all-consuming than her actions the previous evening. She was with child. And she had to kill it.

She had spent a few weeks debating with herself about it. It was, after all, Rapley's child too. Did she have the right to kill it without his knowledge. She had lost Rapley, Seamus, Emma . . . and now, could she lose this child too ?

But what manner of child would it be ? A demon, no doubt, for it had been within her when she made her bargain. Would it not be Unclosed as well ? And most likely worse.

Still . . . she could not move her hand to kill it. Varr would have done the trick, a Conjure mark for bleeding, for detachment, for release. And she did not, and did not, and did not.

While she grew heavier, she made plans. She purchased a property—a spit of brick built into an alleyway from a seedy businessman who asked no questions and handed over a deed with no questions. In this narrow alley-shelter she kept the books she had taken from the cellar and the book from Mill House. She sought out other tomes and volumes, any book or pamphlet that mentioned magic, Unclosed beings, creatures, or Fostos. If there was even a single sentence contained within the book, she took it. She created rules for herself: She would only feed once every three days, when she was so hungry that she could no longer hold herself back. She would be discreet. She would be careful.

Now, the urge to push is strong, and though she has made it this far, she knows she can walk no further. Her child will come immediately, in the brackish, rotten water of London's underbelly.

She pushes, crying out for Rapley in her mind, knowing that he will not come, that he cannot. It takes a long, grueling time, and she leans against the archway, her fingers digging into the stone, leaving claw-marks behind.

When at last the babe comes, Roan cradles it to her chest. It does not cry, but takes tiny gasping breaths, testing its new eyes in the midnight air. She removes her shawl and wraps the child, surprised by the jolt of feeling in her heart when she sees that it is a daughter.

"I'm sorry," she whispers into the child's ear in the gentle, confiding way only a mother knows.

And then she feels it. The burning thirst. It has been three days since last she fed, and her daughter smells of fresh, new blood. Hunger rises like wolf hackles and her teeth sharpen, ready for the killing blow.

But the pain comes again and she barely manages to hold onto the babe. When her placenta comes, she presses her mouth to it, drinking deeply from her own birth organ, her own blood, sickened and sated all at once. Then she bites away the chord and throws it into the river, hating herself.

Shaking, Roan attempts to walk, but her vision wavers and she grabs at the wall with her free hand to steady herself. The babe snuffles into her neck, seeking a breast.

Roan's own stomach growls once again. She must find more blood. And soon.

On her shoulder, the babe slumbers, hair now dried to reveal soft red curls.

❧

St Catherine's Church stands dark and silent across the road, but beyond the front windows a light flickers. Roan cannot take her eyes from the imposing black door. Is she really going to do this ? Leave her child in the care of the nuns ?

*Better than with you*, a truthful voice inside her says.

*Fostos is out there*, another voice reminds her, and she flinches with the ferocity of her rage.

She had found him in the hubbub of London at last and followed him until three days ago when her birth pains had slowed her and allowed him to escape. And here she is, wretched, with a hollow belly and a helpless child. An *innocent* child with no connection to her sordid past. With no connection to the Beast, her agreement, nor Fostos.

"You'll be safe here," Roan whispers, peering into her daughter's face, surprised by her affection. "And maybe, loved."

It is easy to cross the road and climb the stairs. It is even easy to lift the knocker and let it fall.

The nun who comes to the door is young, with a kindly, open face.

"Do you come to confess—"

Roan opens her shawl, revealing the babe.

"I see," the nun says, stepping back. "Come inside."

Roan wants to say no, that she has changed her mind, that it is all a terrible mistake, but she can't. What kind of life would her daughter have, with her for a mother ? The Beast would find her. And what then ? More tricks. More games. And what of Fostos ? What of her revenge, which sits like acid in her stomach ?

There is no choice.

Roan's eyes fill with blood tears, and the young nun screams and scrambles back, banging into the door as she flees. It swings shut.

An older nun comes then, the Mother Superior, Roan assumes. The Abbess. She eyes Roan up and down with sharp, knowing eyes.

"Begone, Creature," she says, signing the cross. "Here you do not belong."

"Please," Roan whispers, opening her shawl once more to reveal the child. "She's an innocent. If she stays with me . . ."

The older woman stares, distaste evident in the curl of her lip and rheumy gaze. But then she glances at the child. Her face softens and she opened her arms. Roan is shaking as she hands the bundle over. The nun turns away, reaching for the door.

"Wait—" Roan's voice wavers. "Her name. I stitched it into the shawl in the corner there." She reaches into her pocket and removes three sovereigns, offering them in her palm.

When the nun does not move to take them, she steps forward. "Please. It is all I ask."

The Abbess takes the money.

"And when the child shows her nature ?"

Roan considers, hoping that the day will never come. "If ever there is a need—if the child should reveal a darkness—leave a blood stain on the stone lintel, there, and I will come."

The Abbess regards Roan coldly, then nods and closes the door behind her.

"Raplen," Roan whimpers, and as she staggers away, tears of blood stain her cheek red.

# Part 2

## Upon the Ocean

*"Could I desert her—could I say to her, 'My dear girl, when you were full of health and beauty, I loved you, but now that sadness is at your heart I leave you?'"*

James Malcolm Rymer, *Varney the Vampire*

# LEN

## 2019

## *Chapter 6*
## St Bartholomew's Alley

HE RIDE TO LONDON is slow and torturous. Five years trapped in Mill House is nothing compared to the helplessness of watching Zoey staring out of the window, immobile, tied to the seat with a belt like luggage. It's because of her Conjure, and mine, that we were able to leave at all. It's because of us that her best friend, Poulton, is himself again, instead of the mad, possessed creature he became in the bowels of that accursed house. The creature that tried to kill us both.

Even now, I don't trust him.

He too sits solemn and quiet, without his belt, staring out of the window of the train, watching the slanting rain pound the earth like scalpels. The world is grey and bleak outside, an unreal monochrome film reel.

I touch Zoey's hand, not knowing if she can feel it. She doesn't respond either way.

"So, what's the plan?" Poulton asks after the conductor comes around asking for tickets and I have to root through Zoey's bag for money to buy some. Best not to leave a digital trace.

I fold my arms. "We'll start in London. Roan has a house there. She used to, anyway. I don't know if she kept it. She gave me the address a long time ago, but I never needed—or wanted—to go."

Poulton's eyes jump to Zoey and back, and I know what he's thinking. Are we really going to carry Zoey around London on my back like a rucksack? Is this going to work? What have I done? And then, a frown with a hint of accusation: this is your fault.

I look away.

I should never have let Zoey Conjure that much, knowing that the blood cost would be too high. She can't walk or move because of it, the price she is paying for our freedom. I should never have let this happen.

"Okay," Poulton says. "Okay."

It's not much, but it's a start.

❦

The house is narrow; barely enough space for the double doorway, built in what used to be St Bartholomew's alley. It is dwarfed on either side by towering office buildings. The style, smoggy brick and outdoor sconces, predates both and I can imagine Roan's stubborn refusal to sell the property to developers. Or maybe they didn't want a sliver of space barely worth a door span.

"How do we get in ?" Poulton whispers. It's late, past midnight, and this neighborhood is deader than dead. Still, three people lurking outside offices in the middle of the night isn't exactly what we want people to notice. "Do you have a key ?"

I shake my head. Roan didn't leave me anything.

I hate doing this, but I want to get Zoey inside and warm, so I reach forward and shove on the lock, cracking it through the wood. The sound is a scream in the night following by the clunk of metal falling.

"Fuck," Poulton mutters, but he steps into the house at my gesture.

I glance around, but there really is no one here, so I take Zoey in after him. Poulton finds the light switch, and thankfully the electricity is on. Roan must still pay the bill—a good sign. She's alive out there. Somewhere. Or maybe this building is linked to the one next door, and no-one has noticed. One small bulb hanging from a chord in the ceiling illuminates the long thin room that contains a single bed with floor to ceiling bookshelves built around it, a small table, metal chair, and a narrow toilet and sink in a separate room off to one side.

I go over to the bed. It's musty and moth-eaten, clearly unused for more than a few years, but it's soft and Zoey groans when I put her down.

"Better ?" I whisper in her ear, kissing her cheek.

She nods, the only movement she can do on her own.

"What about the door ?" Poulton says.

The lock is busted, lying on the floor. The hole in the door gapes onto the street like a scream. I fit the lock awkwardly in place, held there by the splinters of wood that haven't entirely broken. I pile a stack of ancient looking tomes in front of the door to keep it from swinging open.

"It'll have to do."

Poulton takes the chair and places it in front of the door as well. It's not much, but I guess it makes him feel safer.

I scooch past him and sit beside Zoey on the bed, lifting a moth-eaten blanket over her and tucking it in. "I'll find us something to eat, and then I'll start looking."

"Looking for what?" Poulton asks, taking in the rows of books. "Poetry?"

"Clues. Stay here. Make sure nothing happens to her."

He gives me a look that says *really?* And then I'm out of there.

I steal some guy's Chinese food.

*Like old times.*

I hate going back to this, but Zoey needs to eat, and so does Poulton. I'd do worse. Besides, he looked like he could afford more. There's no drink so I casually stroll into a 24-hour Spa and pilfer a two-liter bottle of Pepsi. We need the sugar. No one stops me. Maybe I should steal a new blanket too . . . only, where from? Ridiculous. Beggars can't be choosers, and there are more important things at stake than a holey blanket.

I head back to the house, placing the bag of food on the mattress next to Zoey to fish inside. There's an order of boiled beef in black bean and oyster sauce, a polystyrene box of spring rolls, a plastic tub of chili shredded beef, two foil boxes of special fried and noodles, and a bag of prawn crackers.

"I'm not hungry," Zoey mutters, turning her face away.

"Please," I say gently. "For my sake ?"

She looks at me for a second, then nods. I feed her gently, and she eats with careful patience. Does it feel different now, I wonder, but dare not ask. To eat without feeling the rest of your body ? To swallow into a void ?

We manage two spring rolls and some special fried rice between us. Poulton devours chili-shredded beef and special fried noodles, sitting away from us by the door, then downs a quarter of the bottle of Pepsi.

"Thought you didn't eat," he mutters at me, never quite meeting my gaze.

I get up to clear the food away. "I eat like anyone. I just need to do it less often."

"Freakshow," he mutters, then lies down in my place next to Zoey.

I want to protest but there's only one bed.

"Is this okay ?" he asks, gently resting his head on the pillow. She nods, and I see his entire body relax.

She smiles and closes her eyes and in moments they're both asleep. I watch his arm next to hers and wish it were mine.

Swallowing down my envy, I look around the tiny space, letting myself really take it in for the first time. So, this is where my mother wanted me to come if I ever needed her. This hovel in the world—not even a real house, just a bunch of bricks built into an alley. I imagine her stashing each and every book on these shelves, bringing armfuls over the decades, reading them, turning the pages, sliding them into place. A childish thought : did she put the bed here for me ? In case I needed to rest ? Did she know I would be weary and heartsick when I finally decided to find her again ?

But she's not here. Doesn't look like she's been here in decades.

Still. I know she would have left me a clue.

I just need to find it.

# ZOEY

## 2019

## *Chapter 7*
## Camera Obscura

'M JUST A PAIR of eyes now.

What I wouldn't give for my camera. Even a pencil and a few leaves of paper to write down what I'm thinking to get it out of me. These thoughts. These hideous feelings. They're stuck in me, clinging to the tender inside of my skin, an itch inside my brain I can't reach. Bugs crawling inside of me. Eating me from within. I'm so desperate to pull them out with hands that no longer work, fingers that no longer feel.

Is this my forever?

I watch Len searching her mother's old books, frantic in her efforts, imbued with a desperate and determined hope. A hope I don't feel. I see Pole watching me out of the corner of his eyes. They are hollow, and he is skinny. I see the guilt and shame etched on him like tattoos, his burden for all the things he did in Mill House. I know he needs comfort. Needs forgiveness. It blares out of every one of his pores like Conjure blood. But I'm unequal to it. I just want to sulk. I need this self-pity. I just want to scream *leave me alone! Stop needing so much* . . . Is that too much to ask for?

They tiptoe around each other, never acknowledging the elephant in the room. Len gets the food we eat and rarely touches it. Pole eats it, scowling. He watches Len feed me with an expression of . . . what? Pity? God, I hate the idea of that. Of him pitying me.

I look around the tiny space and I blink my eyes, a tiny "shhh-clck!" shuttering in my mind. I pretend I am the camera. The camera is me. I'm dissociating from my life because I am just the lens. I am just the chemical film and the shutter and the aperture. Cameras don't feel anything. They are hard plastic, metal, glass, rubber, circuit boards and batteries.

They just record.

Len hunched over another book. *Shhh-clck!*

Poulton biting a hangnail. *Shhh-clck!*

Dust motes floating in the air above my face. *Shhh-clck!*

*Shhh-clck!*

*Shhh-clck!*

*Shhh-clck!*

It's almost enough to keep me sane.

# LEN

## 2019

## *Chapter 8*
## MEMORY LANE

HE BOOKS HAVEN'T BEEN touched in years. Of that I'm sure. They're old, all of them leather-bound and some even gold-filigreed, but fragile. I pull one from the shelf, scanning the spine, then flipping gently through the pages. My mother told me that if I ever needed to find her, this would be the place I could discover how to do that. But I was angry, too angry to stay and listen to the how of it.

And now that I truly need her help, I wonder how I'm going to find her? What clue she left for me. Will I recognize it now, after so long? Is that clue here at all, or am I searching for something that crumbled long ago? Maybe, after everything I said to her, she decided not to leave anything for me at all.

Still, I have no choice. If I want to save Zoey I have to keep searching. So I climb onto the narrow ledge of the second story bookshelf and pull free another book, skimming the pages. Another, another, another. Some are grimoires that drip with Conjure magic, and I shudder when I open them, faint scent of brimstone and sulphur tinging my nose. Others are journals written by unnamed people. Many of them are local handbooks, and three or four of them mention a feral woman or female ghost creature that haunts the local woods, bogs and holloways. *The Witch of Skye* is a pamphlet fifty pages long devoted entirely to this apparition. Dozens of pointless tomes that reveal nothing. I'm on the point of stopping, of climbing down the ladder to check if Zoey and Poulton need anything, when a smaller volume catches my eye. No filigree, and no hard binding—just soft, supple leather with no inscription. I shouldn't have noticed it ; it's nothing special. And yet it is. Something about it calls to me.

I slide it free and open the first page and stop, my breath catching.

What . . . this . . . *what is this?*

Page upon page of handwriting on thin, smooth paper, ink bleeding from sepia to black and back again, as though the author wrote these at different times. Some of the handwriting is neatly paced, other parts are scratchy and frenetic. Partway through the book I stop on a page where three words jump out at me.

*St Bartholomew's alley*

I go back and read the paragraph.

*I have found old St Bartholomew's alley. There is a narrow building here. So, this is where she said I would nd sanctuary, and her aid if I needed it. I will remain here while I figure out the next part of my hideous journey. I don't know what to do. My life feels like a lie. My life is a lie. And yet I cannot escape it.*

My handwriting.

My words.

But I have no memory of writing them. I have no memory of ever having been here. I flip back a page to see the date on the entry: 6th December 1888 . No mention of a key or how I got into the building, but there is no doubt in my mind.

I've been here before. A hundred and thirty one years ago, when I was twenty-six years old.

I've read books. I've watched films. Fantastical stories of immortals with endless memory, the capacity to recall the tiniest detail: The most incongruous facial expression, the exact color and texture of a garment, the top notes of a perfume from their mortal lives hundreds of years before. Fabulous abilities, these immortal creatures have, for recall.

Not me.

I remember snapshots of things from long ago, but they're like a dream within a dream. They are the shadows of shadows, the whispers of echoes. Could I tell you the color of the bell bottoms I wore in nineteen seventy-nine ? No. Could I tell you the number one song on the charts of nineteen fifty-four ? With Google, certainly.

Even so, could I have written an entire diary and visited this very house, and have not the slightest recollection of it ? I close my eyes and try to remember my life, but as always, there are only murky impressions, mists and ghosts and shadows. So much is missing.

The only other immortal I know is a monster. My mother. Whether she has the memory of the immortals of the silver screen, I don't know. But me? I am simply a human who doesn't age and doesn't die—and who doesn't remember.

I turn back to the front page and see three Conjure symbols etched into the inner lining. I read them to myself, my lips forming the guttural words without effort, as though by muscle memory.

It happens in a strange torrent, like a floodgate opening. Like a tornado forming, a wound bleeding. Memories, images, sights, sounds, colours, tastes—

all of it

c

a

s

c

a

d

i

n

g

into my brain

until I grip my temples, trying to contain it all.

Zoey's voice from a distance. *What's wrong with her? Pole! Check what's wrong! Len? Len!*

The book, taken from my hands, no longer necessary.

*I don't know, Zoey. What should I do?*

*Len!*

By the time the flow stops, I remember it all. Every painful moment.

Colours.

Smells.

Sights.

Feelings.

*Everything.*

Including the Conjure I cut into myself and the book . . . my journal. My story.

Poulton is kneeling beside me on the upper platform of the bookcase looking awkward. His hand is hovering an inch from my arm as though he's reluctant to touch me. I lean away from him.

"What the hell was that ?" he hisses in my ear. "You scared Zoey half to death."

I get shakily to my feet, just to move away. I need to be away.

"I'm okay," I call down to Zoey, though my vision is still spinning and my bones feel like they are breaking. "It's nothing."

"Don't lie to me, Raplen," Zoey snaps. "I might not be able to move but I can still see, you know."

"I'm, okay," I mutter again. "I'm okay."

"What happened ?"

I swallow, hanging onto the bookcase for support. "I just inadvertently released a Conjure over myself."

"A Conjure ?" Zoey says sharply. "What kind of Conjure ?"

I look around for the book. Poulton is holding it without interest, watching me.

I gesture for it, and he puts it in my hands, again not touching me. It's like holding my own organ.

I climb down the ladder to Zoey's level, Poulton behind me, and sit on the bed.

"Explain," Zoey says sharply.

I sigh, close my eyes, try to get my bearings. I feel very full, my head pounding with unwanted intruders. Memories forcing themselves back into place, digging in and reasserting themselves.

I belong here, they rage, shoving in their glassy spikes.

"I need a minute."

Zoey is patient, but unforgiving. She watches me every second of the long minutes that it takes for me to settle. To feel close to okay. Poulton too watches from above, legs dangling over the platform.

"A long time ago," I manage at last, "I was in a place where everything I was carrying inside me felt too heavy. So, I Conjured my memories into this book."

"You *what?*" Zoey breathes.

I shake my head, remembering. "I just . . . didn't want it anymore. I wrote it all down and bound it with three containment sigils."

Zoey glances at the book and back at me. "That's impressive Working," she says reluctantly. "But . . . why? Why erase yourself and hide it here?"

I could never explain and she could never understand.

"I'd forgotten . . ." I whisper, voice strangled. "So strange, it all coming back like that."

It feels as heavy as ever.

"So . . . you remember your life now? All of it?"

I nod, swallowing. Hating myself. "Yes."

"Good. Then start talking."

My stomach clenches. "What do you mean?"

"I mean," Zoey says, as though talking to a small

child, “that it’s high time you start telling us about your past.”

“Zoey . . . I—”

Her face changes and she scowls. “If I could take your hand I would. But I can’t even do that anymore. You owe us something, Len. You owe us information. Why do you think your mother can help me ? Why did you bring us here ? What’s the point ?” She adds the last part bitterly, almost to herself.

Poulton’s legs stop swinging and he goes still, watching me warily.

“I . . . can’t.”

“Raplen,” Zoey says, a warning note in her voice. “You owe me this.”

I get to my feet, pacing the small space, panic clawing up my throat like weeds. The walls are too close and the pages of the books are screaming and the air is too thick and I can hear Zoey and Poulton’s blood singing in their veins and it’s too much. They’re watching me too closely and their judgment and their questions and their need press on me like walls closing in.

I can’t breathe.

“Len.” Zoey says my name, urgency in her voice.

“I—I can’t.”

And before either of them can say another word, I’m out of there, running through the night, trying to escape memories I wish I hadn’t been fool enough to unlock.

IHS

# RAPLEN

## 1860

The St Catherine Years

## *Chapter 9*
## Midnight Friend

APLEN SAINT CATHERINE IS eight years old the first time she sneaks out of her bed after dark.

Nighttime is for prayers and then sleep. So sayeth Mother Superior, and so enforces Sister Mary Margaret and Sister Mary Catherine.

But Raplen has never been like the other girls at the Foundling Home. She rarely needs the gruel they slop onto her plate or the husks of bread handed out for tea. Nor does she need as much sleep as the other children. Lying in her cot, night after night, listening to the sleepy noises of the other girls used to be tolerable. She would count how many breaths Nancy took before the clock chimed the hour, she would hold her air and listen to the gurgling bubbles of stomachs digesting. She would listen for the shifting sighs, the hiccupping cries ; the whispered calls of "*mama*" . . . Now, she has heard it all many times over and it has become a kind of torture. At five years old, she is more than ready to find out what lies beyond the confines of the church.

Slipping from her bed, she sneaks across the cold flagstones to the closed dormitory door, listening for the sound of approaching footsteps. She closes her eyes and breathes low, trying to distinguish between the scent of the little girls behind her and the muskier notes of the nuns beyond the door. Nothing reaches her but the dank smell of mildewed stone, moldy wood, mossy window laches and the faintly receding reek of London beyond the walls. She glances back at Nancy, who is so far hidden beneath her blanket that Raplen can barely make out her mop of unruly hair. Safe.

Reassured, she hurries out into the corridor.

The church at night, she discovers, is far more interesting than during the day. There is a hush that isn't exactly sleepy—more like expectant—and the arching stone corridors have a magnitude in shadow that they lack when smoggy sunlight flits through the windows, exposing all its edges. In shadow, the church seems almost alive. She wonders if she should try to sneak into the underground hot springs, the ones only the nuns are permitted to use . . . but she does not know the way.

The Walkaway is a tunnel corridor that connects the nunnery, where the girls live, with the main church and monastery, where the boys and monks live. Half buried underground, the Walkaway allows meager slivers of sunlight through high windows that peer out at the graveyard that connects the two sides. On Sundays, the girls are led through in a straight line, nunnery to church, below ground, like grubby things to be hidden away from the public. St Catherine's is, after all, on Church Street, central to the borough. "It wouldn't do to have dirty children squawking away all day like uncontrollable birds," the Abbess once said, when Florence dared ask why they could only play outside once a week after Church service. "On Sunday afternoon, the patrons expect to see where their donations go. To clothe and feed the unwanted." Her lips pursed and Raplen heard her mutter, almost inaudibly, "Makes them feel righteous."

During funerals, the children sneak into the Walkaway to stare at the feet of the men and women gathered to mourn. They make a game of it. Which lady's skirts will brush against the window? Which gentleman will turn away to wipe a tear, unaware that, at his feet, a dozen children watch him cry. There are other games too, all of their own invention. Racing each other back and forth along the length of the tunnel, jumping from shade to sunspot, shade to sunspot, earning points for speed and accuracy. Boys against girls or blondes against brunettes. The Walkaway is their playground.

At night the Walkaway has a sinister feeling. Moonlight cuts the shadows like a blunt knife, and even Raplen's breath seems to echo. She tells herself to be calm. Nothing can get her. She has never believed the dire warnings the nuns deliver daily, about hell and damnation. About demons that devour little girls who don't follow the rules. It all seems so ridiculous. And convenient.

*Your defiance will be your Achilles heel*, the Abbess always tells her, but she can't help thinking that she is the way she is, and if it's good enough for God to have made her this way, then it should be good enough for everyone else too.

At the end of the Walkaway, Raplen finds the rickety door to the short stairwell that leads outside unlocked, and she ascends into the graveyard, hardly able to keep herself from screaming with delight that she is free. Everything about the night is so . . . alive. The whispering trees seem to be giving her secrets, the smoggy sky seems a veil about to part like stage curtains and the empty cobble-streets are glittering with just-fallen rain. This is the best moment of her life.

Raplen winds her way through the gravestones, inching further and further from the nunnery, picking lichen from the sandstone and flicking it away like feathers. Beyond the grounds that belong to the church stand buildings packed so closely together that they choke on each other, their chimneys tired after spitting out the smoke that makes the air smell gray. Raplen can smell it all. She can even smell the people in their beds, hot breath bubbling around their heads. She closes her eyes and listens, letting her ears pick out the tiniest sound. A rustle of dry leaves as a small creature burrows, the mournful cry and shush of an owl taking flight, even the low hum of the river miles away.

The older graves are her favourite, leaning and neglected, faded and crumbling. She sneaks flowers from the newer graves, just one or two at a time, and places them on the oldest, glad that someone is remembering them, like that is somehow important. Like being acknowledged, even in this small way, is enough to keep their spirits around. She likes to imagine that they hover nearby, invisible and watchful.

She is at the graveside of *Leonard Faulkner 1682 — 1749, From dust I came, to dust I am come,* when something moves in the shadows.

Raplen goes very still.

"I won't hurt you." It is a woman's voice, and a woman follows, stepping out from one of the taller tombstones like a shadow peeling off a wall. Her hair is as deep as a raven's wing, and her skin as white as the moon. "Don't be afraid."

Raplen raises her chin. "Not."

The woman smiles. "Of course you're not. What's your name ?"

"Raplen."

The woman makes a curious sound like she is choking, and wipes quickly at her left eye. Her hand comes away with a blush of red on the skin.

"What's your name ?" Raplen asks. It seems only fair that she knows too.

"I'm Roan."

"That's a funny name."

Roan glances around. "Aren't you supposed to be in bed, Raplen ?"

"Not sleepy."

"No." The woman considers her, and then says, "I don't get very sleepy either. There's far too much to do."

Raplen twists her fingers together, glancing at the Walkaway door. "I'm not apposed to go outside."

*Confession is a balm for the soul.*

"I won't tell anyone if you don't mention that you met me here."

Raplen thinks very seriously about this for a moment, wondering if it would be considered a sin to not tell someone something she knows. Is it a lie ? If nobody asks her, then it isn't, she decides. Besides . . . this seems like a fair trade. So she nods.

"Can you read ?" the woman asks, nodding at the gravestone to her right.

Raplen runs her finger under the lines and slowly reads, "Thou shalt go to thy fathers in peace ; thou shalt be buried at a good old age."

"That was very good. And numbers ? Do you know your numbers ?"

"Yes," Raplen says again, though she hopes she won't be tested.

The woman—Roan—touches a darker gravestone that is taller than the others and has angel wings on top, picking at it with her nail. "Sometimes I come to the graveyard at night, just like you."

Raplen doesn't tell her new friend that this is her first nighttime foray. "Do you have someone in a grave to visit ?"

"No. But the dead make good company."

Rapley laughs. "That's because they can't say anything back !"

"Their best quality."

Roan turns and walks further into the graveyard, heading for the gnarly old yew tree right at the back where the gate is all twisted. Raplen follows her, pulling lichen off graves as she goes.

"Why doesn't anyone come and clean the graves ?" Raplen asks. "They have someone do every job in the church, like Sister Mary Margaret washes the communion set and Sister Mary Francis collects the linen—but nobody cleans the graves."

"No one remembers the dead," Roan says, then smiles down at Raplen. "Except you. Because you're special. And observant. And generous."

Raplen scoffs. "You just met me."

"You can tell a lot about a person very quickly if you learn to really look."

They reach the yew and sit side-by-side, backs resting against the knotted bark. Raplen listens to the night, forgetting that she has company and should learn to converse. But when she looks at her new friend, her eyes are closed and there is a little smile on her face, so Raplen closes her eyes too and simply listens.

"If you like," Roan says after a long, long silence, "I can come back some other time."

"It's Friday," Raplen says. "You could come again the next time it's Friday."

"That sounds good to me."

Raplen nods. She waits for a moment, but there seems to be nothing else to say, so she gets to her feet and dusts off her bottom. "Goodbye."

Roan smiles. "Good*night*."

Raplen is so full of joy when she sneaks back inside that she doesn't see the shadow in the antechamber. But the shadow sees her.

"Raplen Saint Catherine."

It is the Abbess, Mother Superior. As she leans forward, her face comes into the light of the single candle on the windowsill, and she does not look pleased.

Raplen's stomach jolts. "Yes, Sister?"

"You are not allowed to wander at night. You know the rules."

There is no excuse she can make. Chamber pots mean she can't use a need for the privy as an excuse. She considers saying she needed to go to confession urgently, but that would let Sister know she's been in the Walkaway, and she wants to keep the extent of her wandering to herself. Besides, the Father doesn't take confession this late, and were the Abbess to check, she'd be caught in the lie and everything would be so much worse.

"I couldn't sleep."

"Solitary confinement for three days in the sick room."

"But—"

She wants to protest, to beg for any other punishment, extra chores, food rations—anything except being away from Nancy.

The other girls pick on Nancy when Raplen isn't around. Once, a year ago—when Raplen was in solitary for calling the evening sausages bags of misery—the girls had frozen Nancy's hair into her morning bucket while she slept. They thought themselves so funny, hissing with laughter as Nancy sobbed, holding the bucket above her head. Raplen had cried with rage when the Abbess had promptly shorn off a foot off Nancy's hair to get her free, taking the bucket—and Nancy's frozen hair—with her.

Two month later, Raplen had her revenge. She stole the same scissors from Sister Mary Abigail and cut every single girl's hair down to their ears until Mellie had woken mid-sheer and started screaming. Nancy had been horrified, of course, but later confessed a terrible and sinful delight at the sight of twelve nasty little girls jumping up and down, screaming as handfuls of their pretty hair fell through their fingers.

Now, Raplen can see in the raised brows and the hard set of the Abbess's mouth, that arguing will only make her punishment longer.

"Three days," the Abbess says again. "No food, only water and your Bible."

"Yes, Sister," she says dully, and follows the sister to the back of the nunnery, praying that those gibfaced me-aters will leave poor Nancy alone.

Ecce faciem et figuram ejus per quem omnia

# LEN

## 2019

## *Chapter 10*
## HELPLESS

"ON'T MOVE."

Zoey's head snaps in my direction, and then she sees the look on my face and after a beat of silence she laughs.

"You're an utter bitch !"

I rinse the cloth in the bucket and wipe her arm again. It's good to see her smiling. The first few times I stripped her naked and began the slow process of cleaning her body, she couldn't meet my eye.

Her laughs die into snickers. "You know, if I was more sensitive you'd be in a lot of trouble."

"How so ?"

"Teasing a cripple ? Not cool."

My smile falls. "Don't call yourself that."

"Why not ? *I'm* allowed to. You're not."

She watches me with an unreadable expression. It's half provoking, half considering.

"Why do you do it ?" she says eventually and, God, I knew this was coming.

I lift her arm and wipe her armpit, wishing I could tickle a laugh out of her. "Do what ?"

"Come on, Len. Don't be obtuse. Why do you do *this* ? Why do you stay here, day after day, looking through these endless books, washing me and feeding me and brushing my hair and carrying me to the toilet . . . doesn't it get old ?"

I raise my brows. "You'd prefer Poulton do it ?"

"That's not what I mean and you know it. Why bother with my maintenance. And why won't you talk about your journal ?"

The night I unbound my memories, I ran for miles. When I stopped, I puked, and found myself on the other side of the bridge. When I finally went back, Zoey was in a fitful sleep and Poulton was fuming—and I haven't discussed it since, despite endless pressing.

"And here we were, having a grand old time," I mutter, circling the bed and lifting her other arm to wash.

"*Raplen.*"

I glance at her and away. This is not what I want to think about let alone discuss.

"You hungry ? When I'm done I'll steal you anything you want."

Zoey sighs, closing her eyes. "You're so stubborn."

We finish the bath in silence, Zoey looking pointedly away. I've just taken out a jumper I liberated from a Primark in Westfield Shopping Centre when there's a knock at the door. Poulton's sweat has become distinctive to me and I call for him to come in.

He's flushed, but something like triumph settles on his features. "I got the razor," he says, pulling it from his sleeve and holding it up like a trophy. "Never knicked anything before."

"Sorry to make a criminal out of you," I say, taking it from him. "But they can trace your bank card of you draw cash. We just finished."

"Right."

Poulton goes to sit on the bed next to Zoey, taking her hand. "You smell better at least."

"You don't."

He snorts and she's giggling again.

"I'll get us money soon," I say.

"How ?" Poulton asks, but I just climb the ladder to the upper platform and begin leafing through my mother's books again.

I wake disoriented to Zoey's screams.

The alley house rings with them, fit to crumble. I scramble up from the floor of the platform, where I rested my head only moments before, and leap over the railing, landing hard. Poulton is already at Zoey's side.

"What is it ?" he's saying, panicked. "What's going on ? Is it a spell ?"

Zoey does nothing but cry, her body immobile but her head twisting from side to side. A sheen of sweat glistens on her body, the veins in her neck distended.

"Where does it hurt ?" I ask brusquely.

She screams again, head whipping about.

I grip her face to make her focus. "Where does it hurt ?"

"Legs," she gasps through clenched teeth. "*Legs !*"

"What should I do ?" Poulton says, a hysterical edge to his voice. "What should I do !"

"Painkillers," I snap. "Now."

He looks from me to Zoey to me again then rushes out the door, leaving it gaping open behind him. I shut it quickly, placing the chair in front of it again to hold it firm. The last thing we need is someone calling the police.

I hurry back to Zoey, who is now gasping in frantic wheezes, but no longer screaming. I lift her legs onto my lap and begin to rub them firmly.

"Can you feel this ?" I ask, a flicker of hope rising in me. Please . . . *please*.

She shakes her head, her eyes wide and terrified. "No. Len . . . what's happening ?"

I rub harder. "Do they still hurt ?"

"I can't bear it," she gasps. "It's killing me !"

I lay my hands on her legs and try to picture the Conjures for mending—but I don't know them. Nothing comes. The Devil's Tongue is a tool of destruction, not of healing. I close my eyes and try to imagine what Selene would do, but I can't grip it. I move Zoey's feet around, stimulating blood flow, but no matter what I do, she feels nothing except the pain.

"Please," Zoey gasps, "please make it stop."

Eventually, all I can do it hold her while she sobs.

After a long, agonizing time, her cries quieten to soft moans. "Tell me a story," she whispers. "Tell me *your* story. Please."

And I do.

# RAPLEN

## 1867

The St Catherine Years

## *Chapter 11*
## Tombstone

NOTHER FRIDAY NIGHT, AND Raplen is now fifteen.

The last ten years have been better for her midnight friend being here. The secret has been sustaining, a blanket against the bitter coldness inside the walls of the convent. Selfishly, she delights in having something that is hers alone. They often don't speak, but sit and walk together cleaning the gravestones or smelling the slumbering city.

Raplen had once asked Roan why she kept coming.

"You asked me to," Roan says simply.

It has occurred to Raplen that the woman must be like her in some way. She smells like her, is sleepless like her, but . . . there are differences too. Roan looks just the same as she did ten years ago, she feels as cold and as unchanging as the stones in this graveyard. Maybe less so. At least the graves grow moss and chip and weather during stormy days. Roan is like marble that never diminishes.

But Raplen doesn't ask for fear of learning answers about the nature of her own strange maladies—like the insomnia. She thought that maybe as she got older the things others found so easy would become easy for her as well—the regular eating of food, lengthy sleep, a normal sense of smell—which she had learned from Nancy was a dull sense rarely honed or appreciated. She found that the opposite was true. She rarely slept at all now. Only needed to eat a couple of times a month. Smelled everything around her like a painful map of life that she was unable to switch off.

Roan understood these things. Made a game of it.

"Whoever smells the farthest scent wins."

They would sit on a grave, comfortable with the dead, and let their noses find the tendrils of the faintest scent-trails, chasing them on the wind.

"Man on the docks," Raplen murmured, "stepped in dogshit."

The river, she knew from lessons and from what Roan had told her, was over a mile and a half away. Though she had never seen it, she knew it well. Knew the different seasons of the water, the ships coming from various ports across the continent, the men and woman with stalls that hocked bread, cheese, meats—cooked and not—and a variety of fruit and sweet treats. The watermen had a distinctive smell. She was thankful that the waters themselves no longer reeked of human waste—improved these last three years by the addition of large sewers by a gentleman named Bazalgette, who despised the stench as much as the next person but had the means to do something about it. Now people's water privies no longer ran directly into the dead waters, which meant that the legendary beauty of its shores could be enjoyed once again. All this Raplen had learned from Roan, and she listened with a ravenous appetite, promising herself that one day she would see these things with her own eyes.

Now, she grins and turns to her midnight friend, fairly certain she has won the game.

But Roan is still smelling.

"A horse," she says at last, "stabled in Upper Shadwell near the pools . . ."

"You jolterhead !" Raplen says, laughing.

"You're foul," Roan says, wrinkling her nose.

"Well, you are ! I'll wager you made that up."

Roan's face loses its grin. "I'll never lie to you."

Raplen watches her friend for a long moment, wondering if this is true. And if it is . . . dare she ask ?

"Why do you come to visit me every Friday ?"

Roan looks at her seriously. "Because if I didn't, I'd be doing much worse."

Raplen has often received enigmatic replies like this, and has tried to push further, but she knows that when Roan has been pushed too far she will shut off and leave. Once she didn't return for two Fridays in a row. When she came back, she said she was sorry to have caused worry and there would be no repeat of the absence. On her word. Still, Raplen doesn't want to push harder.

"The sun will rise soon," Roan says, smelling the air, tasting it.

"I'll see you —"

A pitiful crying breaks into her goodbye.

Raplen stares at Roan. "What was that ?"

The cry comes again.

"Best leave it alone."

"Leave *what* alone ?"

This time the cry is more of a whine.

Roan's expression is cold. "Don't interfere."

But the noises are so pathetic that Raplen gets up and follows them to the hedges bordering Church Street. A small brown body is wriggling in the girt beneath the laurel.

"A dog !"

The puppy can be no more than a couple of months old.

"Yes," Roan says. "You should leave it be."

Raplen lifts the mewling creature into her arms, smearing dirt all over her nightgown.

"Oh, dear. Look at you," she coos, and the puppy goes silent, snuffling into her neck. Raplen giggles.

"The mother may be nearby."

"Not with it this skinny," Raplen says. The pup is all ribs. "I'm going to keep it."

"They won't allow it."

"'What you do unto the least of my brethren, so you do unto me.'"

"I think that referred to people."

"I'll find another passage, then. They won't refuse if I make it a Christian kindness."

Roan eyes her, a smirk on her porcelain face. "You're devilish manipulative."

"Come with me," Raplen tells the pup. "And get warm. There, now."

She turns and makes her way to the Walkaway door,

knowing that if she turned around, Roan would already be gone.

❦

Sister Mary Catherine looks down her nose at the puppy in Raplen's arms like it's a slug on her pottage.

"Where did you find it?"

"In the graveyard."

Her eyes sharpen. "Why were you in the graveyard?"

"I was going to confession when I saw him through the Walkaway window."

The sister sniffs. "Best put it back."

"He'll die."

"Then it is God's will."

Raplen steels herself. "'Are not five sparrows sold for two pennies? And not one of them is forgotten before God.' Luke twelve, six."

The sister blinks. "We cannot keep a dirty mongrel in a convent, child. This is a Holy place."

"But God said, 'Whoever is righteous has regard for the life of his beast, but the mercy of the wicked is cruel.' You are not cruel, Sister?"

Sister Mary Catherine sighs and pinches the bridge of her nose. "We will take the matter to Mother Superior and she will decide."

Raplen, trying not to grin, follows Sister Mary Catherine as the girls titter and talk in the dorm, the day's schedule utterly thrown off. Raplen knows she will likely be punished for that, but if she can get them to keep the dog, it will be worth it. She kisses the puppy's head.

*Please*, she wills the Universe. *Let us keep him.*

Raplen has to quote Psalms 50:10-11 and repeat Proverbs 12:10 and Luke 12:6 before the Abbess grudgingly agrees that the "thing" can be housed in the shed outside. The children, she insists, are responsible for its care—providing food, water, and cleaning away any waste. Raplen agrees, pleased to have won a boon for Nancy.

When she is dismissed, she runs back to the dorm where she hands the dog to Nancy in triumph.

"Tombstone can stay."

"What kind of a name is Tombstone?" Anne says, wrinkling her nose.

Raplen shrugs. "I found him near one, so it fits."

Nancy hugs the puppy to her. "It's perfect."

"We'll have to put him out in the shed at night with a blanket," Raplen says, "and we'll all have to save some of our food to give to him."

The children don't care at the moment, but Raplen knows that rumbling bellies will change that soon enough.

"I'll give him some of mine," Nancy says. "I'll do it gladly."

Raplen whispers in her ear. "He can have all of mine."

Nancy, who knows Raplen's oddness with food, grins and nods. For the rest of the afternoon, the sisters allow a rare play day, and the children—including the boys from the monastery side—let Tombstone chase them up and down the Walkaway until they all huddle at the far corner and fall asleep.

After darkness falls, Nancy says a tearful goodbye to the sleepy pup, and Raplen walks him out to the shed with an old blanket. She settles him down inside with the scraps of her dinner and a bowl of water, then locks him inside so he doesn't try to follow her back.

His whines as she hurries away are enough to break her heart.

Tombstone becomes the centre of their small world, bounding from one child to the next during play, and even during lessons. Never has a convent been so lively. Sister Agnes locks him in the communion cupboard on the third day "for some peace", but his pitiful howls distract the children so badly that she gives in and releases him. His delight at his recovered freedom teases a reluctant grin from Sister Agnes, who watches his little bottom wiggle with obvious pleasure, and when Tombstone settles in Nancy's lap and goes to sleep, she announces that the beginning of lessons in future be devoted to physical education in order to expend the energy from the little animals—and the dog. Even the sour Sister Gertrude grudgingly pets Tombstone now and again, and Raplen even catches the Abbess feeding him a little lamb under the dinner table one evening. Tombstone brings lightness to the austere church—a lightness that everyone seems in particular, if unknowing, need of.

The biggest change is with Nancy. Gone are her silent melancholies, her haunted eyes, the pinched look of worry in her lips. Her cheeks flush with a delicate pink that Raplen can't help but marvel at, and when she visits her midnight friend on the first Friday after his arrival, she spends more time tending to Tombstone than she does listening to Roan.

“Thank you,” she whispers to him on the thirteenth evening as she puts him to bed. “Thank you for making Nancy so happy.”

He circles his blanket and then settles down with a sigh. Tomorrow, she will sneak him an extra egg or two.

On the morning of the fourteenth day, Raplen can sense something different when she gets out of bed. Her breath is frosty white and lingers longer than normal in the frigid air. The other children are huddled in tight balls beneath their thin blankets, trying to conserve as much heat as possible. Rather unusually, she had fallen deeply asleep some time in the early hours of the morning.

A cold, sinking feeling sits in her belly as she rushes from the dormitory, through the Walkaway and out into the graveyard and the shed. She knows before she opens the door that something has gone terribly wrong.

But, no—he's there, asleep on his blanket, and she closes her eyes and sighs.

“Good morning, boy,” she says, crouching down beside him. “You worried me— ”

He smells wrong. Sounds wrong. He sounds . . . like nothing at all.

She reaches out a shaking hand and touches his cold, rigid body, and lets out an anguished cry when she finds him frozen. No . . . . no. This can't be real. This can't be happening. With shaking fingers, she lifts him up and presses his cold body to her chest, rubbing his fur, trying to warm the life back into him.

“Come on, Tombstone. Come on.” She shakes him, a little roughly. “Come on !”

Stepping out into the frigid air, she lays him down on the frosted grass and pushes on his ribs. “Please, please . . .”

His eyes stare blankly at nothing.

He is so tiny.

He is so still.

Something rises up in her, despair and anguish, yes, but also a dark rage she has never felt before. Nancy had him for two weeks—no time at all. How dare the cold steal him away? How dare the sisters force her to keep him in a shed, instead of inside, tucked safely next to Nancy, or Anne, or Agatha, or her. How dare he be taken so soon?

Something on the edge of the fingertips of her mind makes itself known—a possibility that wasn't there before, like a rope begging to be taken—and she grabs it with both hands. And pulls.

Something slithers from the nothing of the other side and into the tips of her fingers. She almost lets go it is so cold. But then it rushes up her arms and bursts from her body. Tombstone is standing before her, yapping and trying to jump up, happy to be reunited. The real Tombstone, the physical Tombstone, still lays cold and dead at her feet.

The death rope in her hand is colder than anything she has ever felt, but she does not let go, fearing that if she does, Tombstone will fade away. How is she to get his spirit back into his body? How can she tie him to himself?

She is looking around, trying to sense something—anything—that can help her stitch Tombstone to himself, when a pressure closes around her heart and begins to squeeze. She drops the death rope and Tombstone is gone in a hiss of shadow. She falls to her knees, gasping for breath, but the pressure does not let go, crushing her like a giant fist around her heart. She gags, trying to breathe, but dark spots patter her vision.

*So*, she thinks, as the world shrinks and darkens. *This is what dying feels like.*

# ROAN

## 1867

## *Chapter 12*
## I See You

HE MAN STILL SMELLS of the prostitute he used, beat and refused to pay. Roan has been following him at a discreet distance for several streets now, waiting for him to meander down a quiet alley. She knows he will at some point, whether it's to find another unsuspecting woman, or to relieve himself after a few too many ales at some squalid public house.

The faint heat of the day is seeping out of stone buildings and she shudders when it touches her skin. It's the only way she can comfortably endure sunlight. She took it for granted when she was still human, before the pact that had made her into—whatever she is now.

The man stumbles and catches himself on a wall, scraping his palm. His blood sings and Roan's teeth sharpen. She is getting better at suppressing the blind need, but sometimes it catches her unprepared and she stops walking. Stops following. Closes her eyes.

The man coughs, rights himself, and moves on. Roan breathes through her mouth for a few heartbeats before she follows. Another five hundred yards and he slows and turn into Emerald Court. She enters behind him, ensuring that no other person is in the emaciated alley, a mere two-dozen inches or so across. The man scarcely fits.

She is on him before his drunken brain can process what is happening, and dead moments after it has. She wants him to know what's happening, to suffer as the women he abused had suffered. It is her small contribution to the balancing of scales. The thought that she can injure, scare, feed from, and kill innocents like Fostos had . . . is abhorrent. She still seethes when she remembers that Maudley was a party to that violence by feeding his wards Fostos's victims. She might be a night creature, just like Fostos, but she refuses to be the same as him.

It is Friday night, and her thirst is sated for now. Safe then to go to her daughter at St Catherine's. She can trust herself not to be tempted by the mortal blood singing in her fragile veins. Of late, Roan feels proud of how strong she is getting—of how well she is resisting the call of the blood. She is proud too of how beautiful and strong and good her daughter has grown. Raplen is fifteen years old ; a young woman.

She is on Church Street when she feels something ripple on the air.

Power. Familiar power.

Roan breaks into a sprint, and is in the graveyard in seconds, hiding behind an ancient yew. There, by the shed, her daughter crouches over the body of the little dog she found only two weeks before. Roan might think she is weeping if not for the ripples of shadow in the air around her. She is a stone cast into the middle of a dead lake, her body causing the tides in the air as though repelling it.

Roan can sense the dead stirring all around her.

She watches with horror as Raplen opens her arms as though she means to take flight, and a shadow is ripped from the ripples, a small, dark thing that distils, after long, agonising moments, into the spirit of the animal that lies dead at her feet.

The puppy makes a movement like it wants to bark—like it is barking—but Roan hears no sound. It is preternaturally quiet, as though sound has been syphoned off the world. Raplen laughs and Roan doesn't hear that either.

What is Raplen doing? What Conjure is this? Roan has never heard of a Conjure to raise the dead before—it does not exist. She hoped—had dared to believe—that her daughter would be free of the Unclosed curse. Rapley saw the dead. They were drawn to him. They tormented him. But he could never raise them like this. Is this some corruption of the Conjure, an already corrupted magic?

That she would be normal. She must have known, she realises, that Raplen was different, what with her nocturnal wanderings . . . but she had chosen not to see. But now she cannot help but see.

She feels the chords of cursed magic in her own body tighten, the familiar heat rising on her skin as her own Conjure responds to the Conjure in Raplen.

*No*, she thinks. *It can't be.*

Whatever Raplen is doing is drawing out the Conjure from Roan. Is awakening it from the deep slumber she sank it into years before.

*No. NO !*

Varr, the Breaker, the most destructive of the Conjures, rises like a terrible phoenix and Roan's dress begins to smoke at her ankles. She isn't doing this . . . Varr is waking of its own accord. Roan shuts her eyes and tries to pull Varr back but, like a querulous child, it will not be quelled. She sees with terrible clarity the Beast watching her, Unholy eyes and proud, ancient horns, the same as all those years before.

*Daughter*, comes the low, tremendous voice. The voice of the mountain. It shakes the world. *Daughter mine.*

She speaks through gritted teeth. "You can't have her."

Varr continues to rise, flowing like molten river, until it has encircled Raplen, who collapses, choking and gagging on the airless night. Roan can feel her Conjure siphoning the life of her daughter, attempting to smother it like a flame in a jar. To quell it—to kill it.

"No," she groans, straining to pull it back.

It only pushes harder, and Raplen gasps, collapsing as she clutches her chest.

With a monumental effort and an otherworldly scream, Roan forces Varr to retreat, speaking cursed Conjures on a tongue that tastes of ash, pulling the Conjure back into her body. The tips of her fingers burn with agonising fire and the Conjures scorch her mouth, but slowly—too slowly—Varr breaks away from Raplen and withdraws back into her body.

Roan runs faster than she ever has until she is on the other side of the river and Raplen is half a dozen miles away. Even now, Varr flickers and grumbles, eager to seek Raplen out, drawn to her like a loadstone.

On the banks of the Thames, Roan paces, blowing on her blackened fingers with brimstone breath. What just happened ? Why did Varr rise without her control ? Why did it attack and try to kill Raplen ? And what was Raplen doing ? Necromancy . . . necromancy is not a Conjure magic. It is something else.

"I think I was waiting for you to come," Roan says when Selene steps up beside her.

"You're causing ripples," Selene says, just as she did the first time she stumbled upon Roan at the river.

Nigh on sixteen years before this moment, Roan—filled with self-loathing and a deep, abiding hatred—had knelt at the banks of the Thames after midnight, and coaxed Varr, the Breaker, to rise in her flesh. It rattled her bones, acidified her sinews, and she had coaxed it to destroy the *thing* that was growing inside of her.

Born of her love with Rapley, yes, but born too of a Cursed mountain and doubly-cursed parents, she felt—*knew*—that this child could never be anything good. It was a thing, a creature, and an evil vessel. She was doing the world a favour by ridding herself of it.

And so Varr had woken, tasting the air like a lewd lover, tongue stretching out demonically in search of destruction. When she turned the destruction upon herself, it bolted, shying away. She had forced it upon herself, directing it first at her stomach from the outside in, and then goading it from within her.

"Just kill it," she grumbled through her teeth. "Kill it !"

Selene had found her there, bent over and cursing the night.

"You're making ripples," she had said then, and taken Roan into her home.

Selene was a Water witch, a Soother, drawing her power from the Thames itself, and channelling it into her Conjure. She used it to heal. To heal. Roan's astonishment when Selene told her this could have bowled her over, had she not already been crouched on the floor in the corner of Selene's workshop.

"The child may yet be good," Selene said, warming water in a copper pot on the fire. "There is no real black and white, this or that, to the world. There are shades of grey."

Roan had scoffed at that. She had seen shadow upon shadow upon shadow, and had long since stopped looking for rainbows.

"You should give it to someone who will guide the goodness from her."

"Who is good in this world ?" Roan mumbled.

"If the child shows, then you can do something. But give it a chance to choose a different life. A life you might have chosen for yourself."

"The foundling home, perhaps."

Selene nodded, pouring the water over tea. "That would be fine."

"Then I will be free of it."

She turned a sharp eye on Roan. "You should put Varr away for good. Lock it up, tightly bound. There is no good from that."

"What about shades of grey ?"

"Varr is not confused. Varr does not compromise. It takes. It breaks. Control it if you must. Suppress it if you can."

And she had done exactly that.

Now, almost sixteen years later, the women look out over the water in silence.

"My daughter is causing ripples," Roan clarifies at last.

Selene looks at her warily "She's shown ?"

Roan nods stiffly.

"Which Conjure ?"

Roan sighs. She feels strangely weary. "None that I've seen. I don't think it is a Conjure. Not in the way we know them."

She turns away, but Selene puts a hand on her arm. "Tell me."

"Some sort of . . . necromancy."

"She sees death ? Sorro, then."

Roan shakes her head. "No, it's not Sorro. She doesn't merely see death. Not ten minutes past I watched her raise the spirit of a dead dog."

Selene watches her, searching her face. But she has come to know Roan these last sixteen years. She knows that Roan does not lie.

"Necromancy," she agreed. "No, that is no Conjure I have heard of. But maybe there are others we haven't discovered."

"Perhaps. But it felt different. And there's something else."

"Tell me."

"Varr woke. I had no control over it. It responded to Raplen's power and it tried to quell it. To quash it." Roan looks at her and feels herself falter. "It tried to kill her."

Selene folds her arms, her long scarves rippling in the cool wind. "I'll see what I can discover. Maybe something was mentioned in a book. Maybe I overlooked something.

In the meantime, watch her and make sure she doesn't make a mess any bigger than she already has."

Roan nods and watches Selene vanish into one of the winding alleys, flowing away like water itself. Roan isn't certain of what's happening, but she is certain that her Friday midnight visits with Raplen are over. She closes her eyes and wonders why it feels as if she is dying.

# RAPLEN

## 1867
The St Catherine Years

## Chapter 13
## Solitary Confinement

HE DOG IS STILL dead when Raplen can breathe again. Tombstone's spirit is gone, and she thinks maybe she dreamed it. She cannot hold in her anguish any longer, and she bends forward and weeps. It is only when the tears are slowing that she realises she is being observed. She spins around with a gasp.

The Abbess is standing at the door to the Walkaway, her eyes wide with both horror and fury. Beneath that, Raplen realizes, she doesn't look all that surprised. As though she has been waiting for something like this all along. Not a dream, then.

"Get up."

Raplen does.

She follows the Abbess into the convent house, her cotton slippers padding silently behind the clomp of the Sister's boots. The rest of the children are awake now, and as they pass, she shakes her head at Nancy and whispers, "I'm sorry."

Several years ago, solitary confinement was refined. The Abbess had first heard of the idea, she once told Raplen, from a Quaker friend who had written of the practice in Pennsylvania whereby confinement was prescribed to the unruly. She had been intrigued by the calming effect of the treatment, and how penitent the confined had become. She had elevated the idea of "solitary" and of "confinement" a great deal since Raplen had last been forced to endure the punishment. It was no longer the sick room of the convent where the doctor sometimes comes to look at a case of pleurisy or suspected consumption. Now, solitary confinement was a wooden box with a short door where food and drink could be slid underneath.

As the Abbess closed Raplen into the box, which had no bed or bench, the light all but disappeared.

"You will pray for forgiveness," she hissed. "You will pray that God can save your dark soul from eternal damnation."

Raplen closed her eyes and wondered if she truly was wicked, simply for wanting to save the life of a dog.

The long hours alone gave her time to think about what had happened. What she had done. It was some kind of witchcraft, surely. And witchcraft was evil. The Bible said so. Raplen knew her Bible well, knew many verses by heart. "*Do not turn to mediums or necromancers; do not seek them out, and so make yourselves unclean by them.*" Was she unclean? Was she a medium, or a necromancer? She had more questions than answers. She had no idea how long the Abbess would lock her away for, but she did know that the moment she got out, she was going to ask her midnight friend to get her answers.

❧

"You shouldn't be here," Raplen whispers, when Nancy kicks a hunk of bread through the gap beneath the door.

"Jane's on kitchen duty. She said they don't bring you anything to eat."

It was true. The Abbess hadn't let Raplen have food in two days. Not that it mattered.

"You know that's fine," Raplen says. "I don't need it, but you do."

She pushes the bread back out, but Nancy forces it in again.

"It's not right. It's not charitable to starve someone."

It was the lack of drink that was affecting Raplen the most, but she wasn't about to tell Nancy that. She knew that if she did, Nancy would contrive a way to sneak her water, and then she'd surely be caught.

"Please," Raplen whispers. "Please, Nancy. I don't want you to get into trouble."

"I'm careful," Nancy says. "As you taught me."

A spasm seizes Nancy and she coughs loudly, trying to hold it in and failing.

"Nancy, go !" Raplen whispers urgently. "Go, now !"

But it's too late.

"Nancy," says Sister Mary Catherine. "God expects better from you."

Raplen is angry enough to smash the wooden walls of her prison to pieces. If only she were strong enough. Instead, she listens helplessly as Nancy is led away.

Time passes excruciatingly slowly in what Raplen has taken to calling "the hole", and then it seems to stop entirely. She silently rages, wishing she had made Nancy leave sooner. Wishing she knew what Nancy's punishment was. She assumes that Nancy has also been locked away, alone and afraid. Otherwise she would have tried to visit again, tried to bring Raplen food and water. As it is, Raplen has been fed twice during her punishment and given water on seven separate occasions. She is released on what she thinks is the twelfth day, but turns out to be the ninth.

The world is so bright that it hurts. She is taken to her bed by one of the sisters—she is too tired to know which—and instantly falls asleep. She dreams of ghost dogs and the cobbled streets beyond the convent walls. She dreams of a life free from the confines of the church, and when she wakes she wonders where such a life could possibly be.

Nine days. Her midnight friend has come and gone, and she will have to wait another five days to see her again. Raplen has never missed an appointment before. What will Roan think ? Will she feel abandoned ? Will she feel slighted ? Will she not return ?

None of the other girls will talk about Nancy, and Raplen begins to panic. On the tenth day, she walks right into the Abbess's office and closes the door behind her.

"What have you done with Nancy ?" she demands, her hands balled into fists. She really thinks that if she doesn't get a straight answer, she might lose her composure.

Nothing else matters except Nancy.

"The bond the two of you share is unnatural," Mother Superior says.

Something snaps. "I demand to know where she is !" Raplen yells, and her voice echoes eerily through the stone.

The Abbess sighs and leans back in her chair, steepling her fingers. "Nancy was punished for breaking the rules. She's recovering in the sick room.

Raplen spins on her heels and heads for the door.

"You'd do be well to remember your place," the Abbess warns. "You have been cared for by this church since your infancy. I have no problem with letting that burden fall on your own shoulders. Nancy's as well."

Raplen stiffens, but keeps going, closing the door quietly behind her when she leaves. It's true that the nuns have raised her. That they have shown actual "care" is a laughable notion. Fed her, yes. Clothed her, yes. Kept her from freezing to death, barely. But care ? Surely there is more to the world than duty and cold regard ? Nancy's love has shown her that it must be so. Nancy's constant kindness, her unending care and friendship are the example to which she compares everything else. Even her midnight friend has shown more regard for her wellbeing than any nun in these "charitable" walls.

Maybe it's time to discover what lies beyond the Foundling House gate.

Nancy is lying on her side on the sick bed. She is fast asleep, but rouses quickly when Raplen sits beside her. As soon as Nancy's eyes fall on her face, she bursts into tears.

"Oh, Raplen," she cries, clinging to Raplen's nightdress and pulling her closer. Her hands are shaking.

Raplen rests Nancy's head on her lap and strokes her hair.

"I thought they would never let you go," Nancy whispers, her tears warm on Raplen's skin.

"I would have broken out to find you."

She laughs, but the tears keep falling. "I'm so relieved."

Raplen rubs Nancy's back, and her friend flinches violently. "Are you not well ?"

"No, I am. I'm quite well."

Something sick and grotesque squirms in Raplen's belly. "Show me your back."

Nancy sits up with difficulty. "No, Raplen. Leave it be, please."

"They *beat* you ?"

"I broke the rules."

Raplen feels her anger in her teeth like a heartbeat. "I'll kill them."

Nancy grabs her wrist as though she believes Raplen really means to do it. "No ! No, don't do anything foolish. Let us just forget this ever happened. Please. For me."

Nancy looks so earnest, so terrified, that Raplen reluctantly agrees. She is learning, though. She is learning that the Abbess has finally found a way to control her.

Nancy is the perfect muzzle.

# ZOEY

## 2019

## *Chapter 14*
## Green-Eyed Serpent

I want to touch Len's hand so badly that, for a moment, it surprises me when I can't. Trapped in this cage of bones and listening to Len talk about her deep love for Nancy, a perfect, pure girl from her past . . . The enormity of my rage surprises me.

It should scare me, but it doesn't.

"I wish I could comfort you," I whisper, my anger turning into a quiet exhaustion. "I wish I could hold your hand."

Len reaches for mine and grips it. I don't feel a thing, but force a smile anyway.

"What was the punishment ?" I ask, trying to keep the tremble from my voice. "What did the Abbess do ?"

"I—"

"This is so pointless," Pole says, stomping down the ladder from the upper level. "All these books and nothing to read. You know half of them are in Latin or French ?"

He sighs and sits down on the end of the bed. He's beginning to smell. I should say something but who am I to nit-pick ? It's not like he has the luxury of bed-baths.

Len lets go of my hand and stands, moving to the ladder. She'll be buried in the books soon, and I'll have lost her again. I wish I could get up. I wish I could ask her the questions I want without tiptoeing around them. Why did you love Nancy so ? What happened to her ? Did you live together, growing old, running along the banks of the Thames, a fantasy of a life together until she died of old age ? Did you watch her wither away while you remained the same, a perfect porcelain doll ? Is that what will happen with us ? Will you sit by my bedside, tied to a useless creature, until I wither away too ? Do you love me as much as you loved her ? Will you leave me ?

But I can't do any of that.

Because I know that Len doesn't want to talk about her past. Doesn't want to talk about Nancy. I see her resistance in the tension of her body, the way she flinches when I ask her to keep going, the shadow in her eyes when she looks back. I see how she clenches her jaw and squeezes her eyes shut in the middle of the night when she thinks I'm asleep. I can almost hear the grinding of her teeth, even over Poulton's snores. She doesn't want to think about this.

But I must know. It's torturous to know, and I have to know. I need to have every little detail of her Before. I long to claim it somehow, to witness it. Nancy is a new obsession. I wish there was a photo.

I consider asking Len to draw me a picture, but that seems too cruel, even for me. Even though my desperate obsession is like fire inside me. When Len leaves the house, which she does late each night, I find myself lying awake, imaging everything she has told me. Imagining St Catherine's church. Imagining Church Street and the graveyard, the yew tree and the Walkaway. And Nancy . . . always Nancy.

Poulton lies down next to me and heaves a sigh. "I'm so *bored*. Aren't you bored ?"

"A bit," I admit, and see Len tense. "But there's not much for me to do anyway."

"That's my point. Like, shouldn't we be going to a hospital or something ? This mad search for a ghost thing is doing my head in."

Len is quiet, and I frown. Before she found her old diary, she was so sure that the answer was here. But since she broke the Conjure, she hasn't mentioned her certainty, hasn't mentioned the next steps, hasn't even thought to reassure me.

"Len has a plan," I assure him. "She knows what she's doing."

"Yeah," he mutters. "Like a monkey on crack she does."

I want to defend her, want to trust her. But my anger is a sharp fang in my mouth and I bite down on it.

Pole sighs and rolls onto his side, looking down at me, head perched on his hand. "I suppose I'd better get us some food. I'm getting good at knicking stuff," he says with resignation. "Fancy anything in particular ?"

I can't be arsed. "Chippy ?"

"Chippy it is." He kisses my cheek, tartar on his breath, and heads for the door.

Len hands him a twenty-pound note as he passes. We don't know where she got the money from, but we've both silently decided not to ask.

"Get a toothbrush," I call. "You fucking stink !"

He laughs and waves, and Len closes the door behind him.

"I should keep looking," Len says after a moment.

She doesn't want me asking her to continue her story. It's obvious. But is it because Nancy's absence is too painful ? Is it because, after all these years, she still loves her ?

# RAPLEN

## 1867

The St Catherine Years

## *Chapter 15*
## The Proposal

HE NEXT FRIDAY NIGHT, Raplen waits in the graveyard until sunrise, watching for her midnight friend and keeping a wary eye out for Mother Superior. Neither of them come. When dawn peeks over the houses across the street, Raplen knows that she has seen her midnight friend for the last time. Either the Abbess did something to send her away, or Roan decided that Raplen's missed appointment was too great a slight to forgive.

Either way, Raplen blames the church.

On Saturday, during morning chores, Raplen pulls Nancy away from the sink where she, Joanie, and Rebecca are washing the cutlery and crockery.

"Eh ! No slacking off and leaving the rest of us to do all the work," Joanie snaps.

Rebecca looks equally ready to call for Sister Mary Margaret.

Raplen rolls her eyes. "*Pshaw* ! No need to wake snakes ! I shall do both of your laundries next wash day."

Joanie grins. "Have at it, ladies. Ain't no business of mine."

Raplen hurries her into the deep and narrow alcove near the kitchen where the spare washday supplies are kept.

"What is it ?" Nancy asks.

Raplen notices she is still favouring her left side. "I want to leave the Foundling House. And I want you to come with me."

Nancy blinks at her, then laughs. "Have you lost all reason ? Leave ?"

"Yes. We can't be more miserable out there than we are in here. At least out there it would be us, alone, doing what we please. Living the way we want to live." Raplen takes Nancy's hand. "No longer at the whim of the nuns."

"I don't know," Nancy says. "We have shelter here. Food. Everything we need."

"We have a dungeon whenever they think we've broken some arbitrary rule, we have barely enough blankets, we have scorn and derision. What can we expect here but starvation and a batty-fang ?"

"Not arbitrary, Raplen !" Nancy whispers, pulling her hand free. "Not arbitrary. Sin is sin. God's law is God's law. I was told to keep away. I stole bread and I gave it to you."

"You stole it from yourself, that's hardly a sin."

"I deserved the punishment. And . . . yes freedom is tempting, but freedom is worth tuppence compared to a night in the gutter. I was three when I was found. I remember being terrified of everything. At least here we're safe."

Raplen scowls and mutters, "For how long ?"

"As long as possible. Now let me go back to my chores before I get into trouble again."

There is no barb in the words, but Raplen feels them nonetheless. Whatever Nancy may think, Raplen is responsible for her suffering. She bites her tongue and lets Nancy go.

The following week, Raplen and Nancy are doing the washing for Joanie and Rebecca as promised when sister Mary Catherine comes to fetch them.

"We haven't done anything wrong," Raplen says quickly, glancing at Nancy.

She has, in fact, done plenty wrong in the last seven days. Every night, instead of cleaning the tombstones or rearranging the flower distribution on graves, she's been venturing off the church grounds. The first night she only took a single step. One foot on the cobbled street, to test it. Would God strike her down ? Would someone shout and call her back ? But nothing bad had happened, so she had stepped out. A single step away from the convent walls, and the furthest she had ever travelled. The next night she had taken several more steps, each night adding more and more, until last night she had made it all the way to the corner. If not for Nancy, she would have left right then and there. The world was before her, hers to grasp. It would have been so easy.

"I know," Sister Mary Catherine says. "Mother Superior wants to see you about a particularly discrete matter."

Nancy and Raplen exchange a nervous glance, but Sister Mary Catherine is impatient and shoos them on.

When they arrive at the Abbess's office, she is standing to the side of her desk and the Monsignor is seated in her chair. Raplen goes cold at the sight of him. He only appears on Sundays for sermons and never comes to the nunnery.

There is a third person in the office—an older gentleman of considerable size dressed in a dark tweed walking suit with a colourfully pattered waistcoat, the buttons of which are stretched taut over a sizeable belly. The sweet stench of bergamot oil is thick in the air. The gentleman's top hat sits on the desk between him and the Monsignor, and he is stroking his whiskers in a way that Raplen finds perverse.

"Come, girls. Stand before the Monsignor."

They do as told, and Nancy curtsies. Raplen does so as well, a moment too late.

The Monsignor clears his throat. "Ladies, this is Mr Geoffrey Rothersham. He is the owner of the Rothersham textile factories, and he has come here today seeking a companion for his life."

Raplen's mouth falls open but she closes it quickly. She sees that Mr Rothersham has noticed, his frown evident even behind his bushy brows. He has stopped stroking his whiskers, at least.

"Mr Rothersham's late wife was also one of our Foundlings, though before your time," the Abbess says. "She passed away six months ago in childbirth and Mr Rothersham is ready to make a new start. He is seeking a Christian wife of impeccable morals to join with him and make a new life together. I have informed him that you two represent the pinnacle of Christian virtue and meekness."

She gives Raplen a particularly hard look and Raplen swallows a snort.

"I shall decide that for myself," Rothersham says, heaving himself to his feet with a grunt. Nancy keeps her gaze averted, a blush rising on her cheeks. Raplen stares him down, hating the way he licks his lips.

He circles them, eyes raking up and down their bodies as though they are prize pigs for slaughter.

"I don't suppose we get a say in this, do we?" Raplen asks at last.

"*Raplen.*" The Abbess's eyes flash, despite the desperation in her voice. "Marriage is a voluntary act in this country, as you well know. But any young lady would be honoured to have such a husband." She lowers her voice. "You would be safe."

Raplen hears the unspoken words. *You would no longer be my burden.*

Rothersham licks his lips again.

"This is farcical. That you think either of us would choose to marry . . . this."

"This one," Rothersham says, pointing at Nancy, and cutting Raplen off. "You are lovely, my dear."

Nancy's breath hitches in her throat, and Raplen tenses.

"I offer you a place in my household," he continues, "as my wife."

"No!" Raplen yells. "Absolutely not, you cussed beardsplitter!"

"Raplen!" the Abbess yells, her face blazing red. "You shall hold your tongue!"

"You can't really think—"

"Enough!" Raplen has never heard the Abbess so incandescent before, and is startled. "Quit this room at once. You will be dealt with most severely."

Raplen can't contain her rage, and she feels something horrible rising inside. Something not unlike the death-rope she felt hanging in the air before her with Tombstone. She spins on the spot and storms out of the room.

It is only when she is halfway down the corridor that she realises that Nancy has not followed.

# ROAN

## 1867

## *Chapter 16*
## Dear Raplen

*ear Raplen,*

*I must forgo the possibility you will ever read this letter; nevertheless, love compels me to do so. Although I have attempted to do well by you, I have repeatedly disappointed my hopes. I deemed it necessary, given my nature, to leave you in the care of the nuns, in hopes that their presence would be sufficient to prevent a life of darkness, to shield you from the Conjure and the touch of the Beast, with which my own follies have burdened you.*

*What I was witness to in the graveyard persuaded me that it was wrong to assume Holy ground would suffice to contain your Unclosed nature. But one thing is certain: my presence only exacerbates it. Something in your Conjure attracts mine, waking it without my consent, stirring it to quash yours. I cannot risk your life for my endearments. For my desire to know you.*

*The light you have brought into my life has led me to neglect my oath. But I am a creature of darkness, and in the darkness I must remain.*

*Your mother,*
*Roan.*

# RAPLEN

## 1867

The St Catherine Years

## *Chapter 17*
## Me and You, Just Us Two

ister Mary Margaret has Raplen pulling weeds from the small cobbled outside area near the privy that the children call the "bubbler", because it has a water fountain in the centre that they imagine once spouted glorious crystal streams into the air, but which now sits dry as a bone—a receptacle for dead leaves and mulch. Raplen rips the weeds from the paving with a particular force, tossing them aside with disgust.

Imagine, marrying that old man! Imagine it, she thinks, being subjected to his heaving, clammy body, night after night, to his droll, condescending conversation, simply for the security of his wealth. Simply for a place? No. *No*.

She pictures Nancy in his bed and chokes on a sob.

No . . .

Clenching her fists around a painful nettle, she squeezes her eyes shut and forces the image from her mind. It is too painful. She cannot bear it.

"That's enough for now," Sister Mary Margaret says quietly behind her, and when Raplen gets to her feet, she hurries back inside so that the sister won't notice her grief. She collapses onto her bed, muffling her head in her pillow. The other girls are at lunch, but she cannot eat.

Some time later, she feels a soft hand on the back of her head.

"You can't marry him," Raplen whispers into her pillow.

"I know that."

Raplen turns to her sharply. "You swear it ? You won't marry him ?"

Nancy smiles, some of the color returning to her cheeks. "I swear it."

Raplen lets out something between a cry and a laugh, and falls into Nancy's arms. Nancy giggles at the force of it.

"You'll be the death of me one of these days, Raplen. You're too strong."

Raplen releases some of the pressure, but doesn't pull away. Her nose is full of the scent of Nancy and there is nowhere else she wants to be.

"We have to get out of here," she whispers. "Nancy . . . we have to."

There is a beat of silence before Nancy whispers, "I know."

The plan is simple : they will leave when everyone is asleep. Raplen wakes Nancy at the witching hour, when she knows they'll have a solid interval before any of the sisters begin their morning duties and prayers. Nancy shivers violently as she puts on her day dress, whether from cold or fear, Raplen isn't sure. She motions for Nancy to keep her shoes in her hands and to bring the blanket from her bed. Raplen does the same, and together they sneak past their sleeping companions. Raplen pauses at the door and looks back at them. She has done this every night for seven years, and this time is the last.

They make a stop at the kitchen and Raplen puts a week's worth of bread and cheese into her blanket, tying it into a rudimentary bag. She takes an empty flask from the shelf for good measure. She has no desire to steal, but she and Nancy need a little help getting started. Besides, the convent will have two fewer mouths to feed.

They lace their shoes onto their feet at the entrance to the Walkaway, and then hurry for the graveside door. Nancy hesitates, but after a moment she squares her shoulders and walks out, her chin high, claiming their future. Raplen has never felt so proud. Just as she is about to follow, Raplen is startled by a shadow at the other end of the tunnel.

The Abbess watches silently from the umbra, moonlight glinting in her eyes.

She and Raplen stare at each other for a heartbeat, and then Raplen has disappeared into the night.

Shaken by the Abbess's presence, Raplen insists they run several blocks, only letting them stop to breathe when

Church Street is far behind them. Sunrise is in a little under two hours. They need to find somewhere safe to rest.

"I can't keep going," Nancy gasps, putting a cold hand on Raplen's arm. "Are you sure this is the right ? We could still go back."

"No, we can't."

"We can. No one has to know what we did. We can return the bread and climb into bed. Maybe we should—"

"The Abbess saw us leave."

Nancy pales. "What ?"

"I saw her watching us from the end of the Walkaway. It's done."

Nancy stares at her, eyes wide and terrified, and then she collapses against the side of a building, her breath coming heavy and fast. "Oh no . . . oh no . . . "

She slides to the ground.

Raplen kneels in front of her. "We don't need them. They were going to marry us off to old men one by one, and then what ? We'd never see each other again. This is better. I'll take care of us."

Nancy looks around, and now Raplen can see what she sees : the enormity of the world, and just how fragile and exposed they really are. What do they know of survival ? Outside of the week's worth of bread and cheese—and no water source—they have nohing. Nancy's fear is contagious, and panic rises in Raplen's throat—but she quells it. What good will it do if they both lose their marbles ?

The scent of fish catches in her nose. "Come on," she says, standing up and offering Nancy her hands. "We have to go."

Nancy looks left, back the way they came, then right, to where Raplen is leading them. There is a choice here, and yet no choice at all. The Abbess saw them. She looks up and Raplen can see the trust there. And, she hopes, the love.

Raplen and Nancy take to sleeping in Hyde Park. On their third morning of freedom, Raplen leaves Nancy tucked onto a bench and, once again, ensures she won't move.

"I'll be back as soon as I can," she says, rubbing Nancy's arms. Nancy is tucked into both blankets and still frigid with cold.

She nods miserably, eyes screwed shut. "Be careful."

"I will."

Some miles away Raplen finds a bustling street market. It is a teeming mecca, a swarm with tented stands, haggling patrons and hills of produce. A group of boys no older than ten or twelve catch her eye. They are loitering casually down one of the many alleyways, some of them smoking like little dandies, others hocking and spitting like cattle. She follows their gaze and notices another boy near the orange stand. The seller, a rotund man, calls out to passing patrons—"Seville oranges ! Orange flower water ! Jam ! Lovely sweet jam ! Sweet Chinas, four a penny !" His voice was nearly drowned out by the baker's cries of "Eight loaves a shilling !" and the butcher's yowls of "mutton, four shillings three !" In all the raucity, the orange merchant fails to notice the boy kick out at the leg of his table. Raplen however, does.

The oranges, vials and jam jars crash to the floor, and several perusing women shriek as they are deluged with sticky sap and heavy fruit, which bounces off them like rubber and rolls along the cobblestones this way and that.

The merchant yells, and the boy—a picture of innocent incredulity—scrambles to help him catch his wares.

The watching boy-gang move seamlessly through the chaos and each pluck whatever they wish from the surrounding stands, casual as you please. Several loaves of bread taken here, a bottle of sherry pilfered there, a handful of sweetmeats swiped and hidden in pockets. Every seller's eye is on the commotion. It's almost laughable how easily they have done it. Raplen can't help but be impressed.

The boy who kicked the table leg finishes helping the merchant right his stand and is given an orange for his trouble. He thanks the rotund man and walks away, a cheeky grin on his face. The other boys are already gone.

Raplen follows, intrigued.

The casual confidence of the swindle impresses her. The seamless flow of their con is mastery itself. But Raplen is good at not being seen, and the boys don't notice her watching them as they slip into imprudently unlocked houses like wraiths, pilfering whatever they please. She sees glints of silver flash as they disappear into pockets and under caps. They hit three different houses before she lets them go, sure that she has seen enough to pull off her own little heist. She doesn't feel as bad as she thinks she ought to. These people have more money than sense . . . she won't take too much.

Except when she attempts to enter the house through the same back door she watched the boys cruise through, she can't cross the threshold.

It is as though an invisible barrier has been strung against the entryway, and no matter how Raplen pushes her weight against it, she is not permitted entry. The boy gangs made it look so easy.

Raplen abandons the door and tries the window instead. The same invisible force keeps her out. She stares, confounded. Had God done this ? Decided she had taken one too many liberties and finally made Himself known ? She backs away with horror, feeling as though she's been burned, as though she is carrying some terrible infection in her bones, and she flees down a side street before anyone notices her Otherness.

She wanders the streets, trying to make sense of it. Nothing for it but to try again. This time she hits a house on the eastern side of the slums, a poor house that'll no doubt have nothing of value inside. She'll go in, look around, and leave. Just to prove she can.

She is met with the same resistance as before.

Whatever this is, she cannot enter.

She tries over and over with different dwellings, and it is only when she breaks into the factory on Cleve's Road that she realizes that maybe the places she has no way to enter, for whatever reason, are places someone calls "home". She wanders the factory floor in the dark, smelling the residue of the day's work, and considers what made the convent different. Perhaps she has admittance to houses of God, but not the houses of ordinary people ? But then why her ? Why can those boys, those pick-pocketing gangs, climb into houses at their whim, and she cannot ?

It's maddening.

Before sunrise, she heads to the church near Sloane Street—the one with the high steeple and colorful glass windows. She pauses at the door, her hand on the door handle. If she is expelled even from God's house, then she must be wicked indeed.

She pulls the door open and steps inside.

No barrier. No invisible hand keeping her out. She doesn't linger. Nancy will be waiting, cold and hungry. She will be disappointed that Raplen has returned with no food and no drink. She eyes the holy water basin a few steps away and glances around. No one is here to watch her rip off a Holy house, so she pulls out her flask, and dips it into the water, flinching when it fills slowly and loudly, bubbles shouting on the surface.

When it is full, she screws on the cap and backs away, her eyes darting in every direction. At least Nancy will have water to drink tonight. And not the sewage they have to skim on a daily basis, neither. But Holy water. Clean water. Blessed water.

Raplen grins as she closes the door behind her.

Amen.

❦

Raplen has something that the boy gang didn't: her death rope. She uses her strange talent to raise spirits in the air around her, startling a milliner so badly that the woman fairly flees the entire shop, screaming down the street about witchery. Raplen takes two bonnet caps and pelerines and skips away feeling that she could truly own the world, or steal it, for Nancy—should she choose.

They are not the only women to seek sleep and safety in Hyde Park by night. Most are pick-pockets like her. Some prostitute. Raplen keeps Nancy away from those, even though she understands. Some women work in the match factories, but don't earn enough for room and board as well as the drink they require to numb the pain in their jaws. They are all of them displaced.

Raplen knows that Nancy feels the same. That she questions if they have done right. She can see Nancy struggle to keep warm, to let go of her fears, to trust that Raplen will always protect her. But Raplen can't help feeling different. She can't help but feel free.

"I think you should stop," Nancy whispers one night when the world is hushed and dark around them. The crickets sing in the grass to an empty sky. "Stop stealing. It feels so wrong. I don't think I can live with it any longer."

"We need to steal to survive. Just for now."

"I can't, Raplen. I feel tainted."

Raplen falls silent. "I'll earn a wage, then," she says at last. "I can find employment. I saw fliers . . . the matchstick factory is looking for workers. Will that make you happier?"

"Yes."

"Then it will be done."

Months later, Raplen and Nancy huddle close under their blanket, their breath commingling together in the air. Around them, in the various nooks and crannies of the old factory building, the other homeless of the area talk in hushed tones and settle in for the long, cold night. Under the blanket, however, they feel alone—as though they are the only two people on earth.

Raplen wishes it were so. She yearns for a world empty of everyone except the two of them. She often sits late into the night, watching Nancy sleep, imagining walking on a sandy beach, the kind seen in paintings, the warm baking their skin, a frigid night nothing but the vaguest of memories. She imagines that they'll run into the sea hand in hand, laughing as the waves overtake them.

They had spent the day together, delivering matchbook subscriptions. Nancy insisted on accompanying Raplen on her rounds, and in the end she had been grateful for the help. Again, Raplen had encountered that invisible barrier strung over the doorways of the grandest and lowliest houses. Nancy, seeing Raplen's hesitation, had taken the packages into the houses herself until, on Baker Street, a woman had requested their entrance and Raplen had discovered that the barrier had lifted. It didn't take long for Nancy and Raplen to learn that Raplen could not enter a dwelling without first obtaining the permission of the dwellers. So, as the day progressed, Nancy would ask if she and Raplen may enter, and upon an assent, Raplen would find the way unbarred.

Now, Nancy shivers and huddles closer under the blanket.

Raplen reaches into the pocket of her dress and pulls out a sweet cake she stole earlier in the day and a small taper candle she pilfered the previous week from the church. Thieving has become easier on her conscience.

"What is this ?" Nancy whispers, touching the cake reverently.

Raplen grins. "Happy birthday."

"It's my birthday ?"

"Yes. Sixteen years old today."

"But that means we missed yours ! And the New Year too."

"We were chased from Hyde Park on New Year's," Raplen says. "And my birthday isn't special."

Nancy takes her hand. "Yes it is. Yes, it is."

Raplen smiles. "Well, Happy Birthday to us both, then."

"What's the candle for ?"

Raplen pushes it into the top of the cake, and Nancy giggles. "You are mad, do you know that ?"

"Sister Mary Catherine told us about it once. A German festival called *Kinderfeste*. On the birth day of a child they would have a cake and place candles on top of it, lighting the same number that equalled the number of years the child had been alive, plus one for the hope of a birthday the following year. They'd keep them lit all day, then blow them out before eating."

"How peculiar !"

"I stole some matches from the factory today," Raplen says, holding up the matchbox.

"Are they not evil ?" Nancy whispers, leaning away.

"It's chemistry—science. Friction lighters are better than flint. Watch."

Raplen pulls a match from the box and strikes it against the side. It fizzes violently and Nancy squeals, earning them both a grumpy reprimand from a sleeper somewhere beyond their blanket cocoon.

Raplen lights the candle and blows out the match, and the warm glow between them is luxuriously warm.

"I don't want to blow it out," Nancy whispers, her breath making the flame dance.

"I don't want you to either. But the light will draw the others."

Nancy smiles and blows the light away. The scent of burning is a comfort, even as the meagre heat dies.

"Soon I'll have enough for us to rent a room together," Raplen whispers. "And then we can light a hundred candles if we want and leave them burning all night."

Nancy reaches out a hand in the darkness. Raplen feels it on her cheek. "How is your toothache ?"

"It's fine." A lie. The pain is unbearable some days, and work in the matchstick factory is long and exhausting. But Nancy need not know this.

"And the headaches ?" she presses.

Nancy looks so worried that Raplen smiles, leans forward and kisses her.

She doesn't mean to do it, but now it is done. Her stomach drops away from her at the feeling of Nancy's soft lips against her own. There is a beat of terrible silence, and then Nancy is kissing her back.

Raplen has never been as happy as she is in this moment, Nancy pressed against her, their lips and their tongues colliding, their breaths heavy and fast. Passion and love, a heady mixture. Raplen can scarcely breathe.

And then Nancy pulls violently away.

Raplen breathes, "Nancy—"

"This is a sin," Nancy says, her voice as brittle as glass. It cuts Raplen deeply to hear her so distressed. "This is evil ! This is a sin !"

"How can it be ?"

Raplen reaches for her hand, but Nancy rips the blanket from them and clambers to her feet.

"Do not touch me ! You are unclean !"

Raplen stares, unable to speak. Nancy has never looked at her with such an ugly expression before. Nothing about the world makes sense any longer.

"Let's . . . let's get some sleep," Raplen manages, though her heart is pounding and breaking inside.

Nancy inches away from her, lies down on the gathered newspaper, and curls into a tight ball facing away.

Raplen stares at her back for a long time, still holding the cake and the candle, not knowing what to do.

Raplen sleeps near dawn, her exhausted mind and body no longer able to exist in a reality where Nancy is repulsed by her. She falls into painful dreams where Nancy runs away from her on the beach, disappearing into a violent ocean and never coming back.

When Raplen wakes, Nancy is gone.

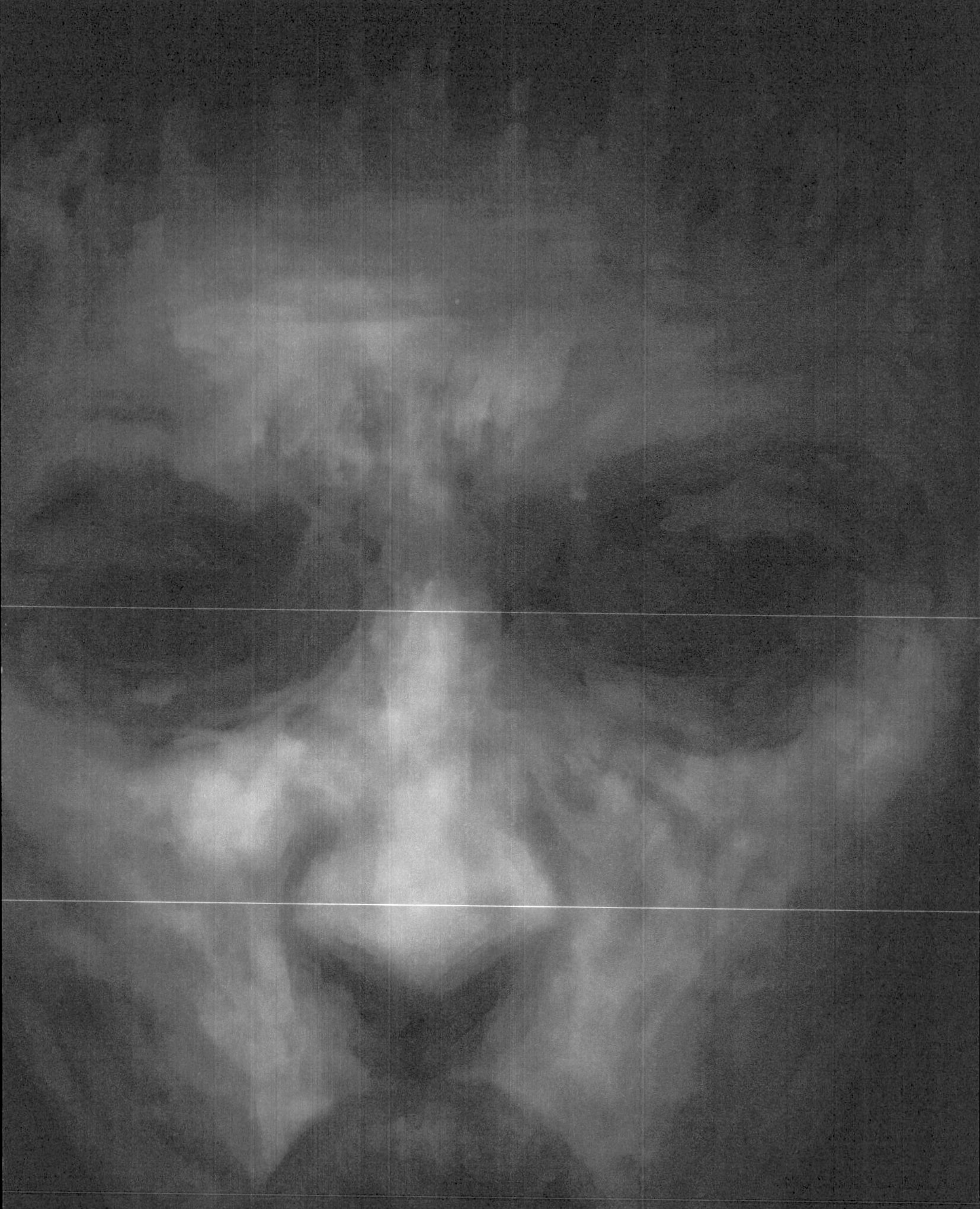

# ZOEY

## 2019

## *Chapter 18*
## STIRRING

"SHE WAS JUST . . . GONE ?" Something inside me is snaking to the surface, but I don't want to look too closely at it. I wish I could lean in, take Len's hand, stroke her long red hair, *feel* her. Everything is tied to movement. Every breath, every glance, every impulse—everything that is human and that is life is linked to your muscles, your sinews, your bones and your skin. Touch, warmth, *sensation.* We are more than just a mind. I am more than this . . . *computer.* I know it's wrong to feel this way, that I'm still me, but I can't help it.

Len looks far away, as though she's still back there. With Nancy. She doesn't answer my question, and the silence drags on. Inside I am twisting into contorted shapes, yearning for *more*. Poulton sits on the upper platform, watching us but not saying anything. He raises his eyebrows at me and shrugs.

"How long were you on the streets for ?" I ask Len instead, hoping to draw her into more neutral territory, fighting my desire to pull the story out of her—all of it, all at once. The snake in me coils and waits.

Len sighs and rubs her face like she's weary. "It felt like a long time. The streets make everything harder, longer, more desperate. My whole life became about finding places to sleep, getting us water and food—keeping Nancy safe."

"Did you ever want to just stop ?"

"Of course. I wanted to give up every day."

"But you did it anyway."

"It was better than the alternative."

"Are you sure ?" I ask it tentatively, but she still turns to glare at me.

"Yes."

Poulton gives me a warning look, but I plough on. "I don't know... A warm house ? A safe place ? Food and water ? Isn't that what you wanted for her ? Isn't that what St Catherine's offered ?"

Len's eyes flash and her tone becomes waspish, her teeth bared in a horrible grimace. "At the expense of her freedom ? To sell herself into a phony marriage with that bastard of a human ?"

"Of course not," I murmur, my cheeks burning.

Len hisses through her teeth and turns way, pacing the small space like a caged animal. She's all pent-up energy, all reckless motion—and a spike of anger pricks at my mind.

*She takes it for granted.* The snaking voice in my head doesn't quite feel like my own. *She takes her body*, *her liberty*, *her freedom for granted.*

And another voice. *She flaunts it.*

"I don't want to talk about it," Len says, voice low and constrained, as though I had pressed her for more. But I do want to press her for more. I want all of it and I want it right this *second.* I wish I could shake it out of her by force.

"Len—"

"Why do you want to unpick my past?" She rounds on me, seething. "Isn't it bad enough I lived through it once and then again when I broke that Conjure on the journal?"

The tiny flicker of anger inside me flares into a full flame. "I just want to know what it was like for you, that's all!"

Len paces again, like I'm not even here. "All these Victorian ideas about the charmed under-people," she mutters, shaking her head at the ceiling. "Wealthy authors would come to the slums, stand in shit for a few seconds and then write sensationalized versions of our lives, while the middle class demonized us for being lazy. I worked in matchbook factories for hours, until my fingers bled and I began to feel the phossy jaw eating away at my bones, the blisters bursting in my cheeks, swallowing the pus and the decay until I could barely stand it. Lucky me for I have my mother's cursed my DNA, so I could regrow the tissue and start again." She turns furious eyes on me. "Do you know what it's like to rot, inside out, day after day, month after month?"

"Len—"

"The other women weren't so lucky. I watched the suffering around me and wondered why I was ultimately immune. Hundreds of anonymous matchstick women thrown away by a capitalist history that didn't care about them."

I don't need to ask about her body's healing properties. I've seen it for myself. I still dream of it, I still see it when I don't want to, in flashes—Poulton stabbing her in the chest at Mill House when he was possessed. The way she collapsed, then pulled the knife from her own body, coughing up blood. Her nonchalant : *I hate it when that happens.* The way I saw her skin knit itself back together like a tacky movie.

A small silence. "But Nancy didn't work there ?"

"Of course not ! I worked so she didn't have to."

Again, the impulse to take her hand. To be closer to her. To pull her into my body and feel her skin against mine. And the other urge . . . the urge to spit at her. To slap her face. To hurt her like she is hurting me.

Because Len adored Nancy. It's so blindingly obvious that it sits like acid in my stomach. It's simple and it's true. And I hate myself for asking. I hate myself for wanting to know more, because I am inflicting this on myself. And, yes, as selfish and shitty as this is : I hate Len for loving someone else.

"I'm sorry," I murmur, trying to be gentle, trying not to think, *what about me* ? "It sounds horrible."

"People didn't know a thing back then. It was twenty years until the matchgirl strikes, and by then I was long gone. Nancy went back to the Foundling Home," she says, sighing and rubbing her thighs. Her long copper hair falls over her face.

"Did you follow her ?"

*Tell me. Tell me everything.*

Len glances at me and her eyes are darker than I've ever seen them. She rubs her thighs furiously and then gets to her feet.

"*Did* you ?" I press.

Len shoves the chair away from the door and briefly glances back. "I'll be back later. We need more supplies."

Then she's gone, door wide open behind her.

"You shouldn't have pressed so hard," Poulton says, leaning against the railing. He looks better since he washed his hair in the sink. "You pushed too much."

The snaking, seething mass inside me rears up, all the static energy bursting and useless in my bones is burning me alive. "Get me her journal," I tell him. "Bring it down."

"Wait, what ?"

"I said bring me her bloody journal, Poulton !"

He swallows. "Zo . . . I don't think that's a good idea."

"Are you my friend or not ?" I snap.

I can hardly believe what I'm saying, giving him an ultimatum, using his guilt, but I am so *angry*. I feel like I could kill something.

Good girl, something inside coos, purring.

"Make. A. Choice," I say, unfazed by his horrified, wide eyes.

He swallows again, then reaches for the small leather book on the bookcase and brings it down. As he passes the door, he glances out into the street, then closes the door against prying eyes, as if Len could be right outside.

"I really think this is a bad idea," he says, putting it on the bed.

"What exactly do you expect me to do with it ? You're going to have to read it to me."

He steps away. "I really don't want to get in the middle here—"

"Oh, really ? Like you didn't want to get in the middle when you tried to force yourself on me at Mill House when you were drunk ?"

He turns a horrible shade of grey and looks nauseous. "Zoey—"

"Or did you not want to be in the middle when you stabbed my girlfriend ? You are in the middle, Pole. So why don't you try *helping* me for once in your life ?"

"For once in my life ?" he says, clenching his fists.

We stare at each other for too long, and then he turns to leave, storming for the door. But at the last moment he turns back.

"For once in my life ? Like the time I brought you supplies to Mill House when you chucked our plan out the window ? Like how I cut school and left my whole life behind to come get you ? Like the time I helped you study all night for your Year nine sats ? Like the times I lied for you to your mum or Greg ? Did you ever consider what I went through in that mountain ?" He's yelling now. "That something evil was inside me, scratching at my skull wriggling in my brain, making me do things and think things and see things I would never—I'm only here because of you ! You fucking brat !"

I burst into tears.

He's right.

All this time, all I could think of was my own pain. My own loss. My own anger. But he went through it all with me. My impulsive choices led to this, and look what it's done to all of us.

"I'm sorry," I sob. "Poulton, I'm so sorry. I just . . . I just hate everything so much."

He takes a breath, purses his lips, and looks at the floor. And then he bends over to hug me. "You need to stop taking it out on me," he murmurs into my hair.

Now that the tears have finally come, I wonder if they'll ever stop. "I know."

He pulls back and picks up Len's journal. "Right. Let's do this, then."

# RAPLEN

## 1868

The St Catherine Years

## *Chapter 19*

## I Can't Help but Love You

ANCY HAS BEEN GONE for several hours by the time Raplen wakes. She can barely smell Nancy's fading scent. The other homeless people in the factory are going about their day, unaware that the world has changed forever.

Raplen spends hours wandering the street, calling Nancy's name. She asks every person she passes if they have seen her.

"Please, have you seen a young woman with pale hair and a blue dress wandering the streets ?"

Each time they shake their heads and move on, sometimes they cross the street to avoid her, but she follows, begging them to help her. By the late afternoon, Raplen is distraught. She collapses in the doorway of a grand building and tries not to pull her hair from her head, her mind screaming that this is all her fault.

*This is evil. This is a sin. Do not touch me ! You are unclean.*

And then she realizes that there is only one place that Nancy would have gone.

Raplen runs the entire way. She doesn't stop. Even so, it takes more than an hour to cover the near two miles to St Catherine's. The entire way Raplen's mind is racing. What if Nancy didn't go back to the Foundling Home ? What if she simply went in any direction that was away from Raplen ? What if she got lost ? What if she was attacked ? Nancy doesn't know London, not really. She is protected by Raplen—she hasn't seen the horrors of the street the way Raplen has. What if she got trampled or fell in the river ?

It is already dark when Raplen raps on the convent door. It is Sister Mary Catherine who answers, her face flushed with indignance.

"What do you mean by—" She breaks off when sees Raplen.

"The Abbess said you'd be along. We expected you sooner."

"Where is she ?" Raplen asks desperately. "Where is Nancy ?"

Sister Mary Catherine's lips purse. "She isn't here."

"Don't lie to me !" Raplen yells, slapping the door frame.

Sister Mary Catherine sighs. "She isn't here, Raplen. That is the truth. She was married this afternoon and is now with her husband."

Raplen's breath leaves her in a choke. She cannot survive this. She will die from this. She turns away, but the world dips and wheels and she stumbles, almost collapses. Sister Mary Catherine catches her and sits her down on the outside bench.

"Come, child. Sit."

Everything is buzzing. "She . . . she's . . ."

"Married. Yes. Mr Rothersham was sent for and they were married in the chapel not three hours ago."

"Where has she gone ? To his house ? Where does he live ?"

Sister Mary Catherine hesitates.

"Please, sister ! *Please* !" She bursts into a fit of tears. "Have mercy on me," she whispers.

"You know, you never should have left. Neither of you."

Raplen sniffs, scrubbing her face. "I know it."

The sister sighs and removes a card from her pocket where Mr Rothersham's name is printed neatly above an address.

"He left this."

Raplen takes it in shaking fingers, then kisses the sister's hands. "Thank you, sister."

"You know that the Abbess will never allow you to return to us."

"I know."

Feeling like her entire body is bruised along with her heart, Raplen walks away, the card clutched in her fist.

There is no chance of knocking on the door and asking to speak to Nancy. This Raplen knows instinctively. She was there when Rothersham came to try to buy them the first time. She might as well have been a fly or a gnat bothering him. She cannot bear to remember the way he circled Nancy, examining her, licking his lips as he imagined all kinds of indecent things he planned to do to her—may have already done to her.

Raplen clenches her jaw and eyes. No.

Instead, she goes into their back garden, scaling the gate, and she watches and waits. A candle is placed in the upstairs center window and Raplen gasps when she sees Nancy there in fresh white night gown, staring out.

Raplen scales the wall, using the stones and trellis to ascent to the upstairs window. She is strong and lithe, surprising herself with how easy this is. Nancy is no longer by the window. Raplen peers in. Nancy is sitting on a big, plush bed, twisting her fingers together. She is alone.

Raplen knocks softly, and Nancy starts and turns to the window. When she sees who it is, she rushes over and uses the sash pulley to open the window. She leans out, directly into Raplen's one-armed embrace.

"Raplen," she whispers, like a prayer.

"You stupid girl," Raplen murmurs into her hair, her tears falling again. Nancy is already crying. "Stupid, stupid, stupid."

"I had no choice."

"You could haves stayed with me," Raplen says, pulling back. She adjusts her grip on the iron gutter and peers into Nancy's face, searching for damage. "Are you all right?"

Nancy closes her eyes and leans her forehead against Raplen's. "I am now."

Raplen smoothes her hair behind her ear. "Why did you run away?"

"You know why."

"I thought I lost you forever."

Nancy doesn't say anything for a long time. Eventually she whispers, "You have."

Raplen jerks back. "No. No ! I've come to steal you away." She laughs, or chokes, or sobs—or a little of all three. "I've come to tell you that I am going to keep you. I'm going to fight for you. I won't stop."

Nancy looses a choked sob and kisses her, leaning so far out of the window that, had Raplen not been holding her torso, she might have lost her balance and fallen.

"I love you," Nancy whispers against her lips. "I love you, and so much more . . . but it's wrong. It's a sin."

"Don't say that," Raplen begs. "Let me in. Let me in and we can talk about it."

Nancy pulls away. "No."

Raplen's stomach drops. "Nancy . . ."

Nancy shakes her head. "You must go."

Raplen realizes then that she has no power. And Nancy knows it. Without Nancy's permission, Raplen will never get beyond the window.

"Nancy," she says, "let me in."

Nancy steps away. "No. I love you, and I would choose you, always, but I will save us both from damnation."

A bang from the other side of the room startles them both.

"So this is what I have wed." Rothersham is standing in the open doorway, his face red and heaving, his lips curled back from yellowed teeth that are bared in a snarl. "Vile cunny !"

"Nancy, let me in," Raplen says desperately, not looking the glint in Rothersham's eye.

"Witch," he spits, advancing on Nancy and overturning a chair in the process.

"Husband—" she begins, but his fist flies fast, slapping her with a thunderous blow that sends her careening across the room.

"Nancy !"

Nancy gets to her knees, but Rothersham isn't done. Raplen screams her lungs raw, throwing her body against the open window, but the invisible force that keeps her out doesn't budge. She might as well be throwing herself into a wall. She loses her grip on the gutter and falls to the garden below, but she's back up and scaling the wall in moments.

"Nancy !" she screams. "Let me in ! *Let me in !*"

Nancy looks at her and shakes her head, blood flowing from her nose. Rothersham kicks her in the stomach and she spits blood. Raplen can feel the edges of her mind fraying with desperation. She claws at the air, screaming curses at Rothersham, yelling things that have no meaning and also mean : *get away from her* and *I will kill you.*

No one comes.

Rothersham kicks, punches, and beats Nancy until she is so bloody that Raplen can no longer see her face or hair clearly. Her night dress is soaked and torn. Still Rothersham beats her, and still Raplen screams and pushes and claws at the barrier.

"Let me in ! Let me in ! Nancy ! Let me in !"

He goes on kicking her long after she has stopped moving, until he is panting and sweating on the floor, leaning back as though he has had an exerting walk.

Raplen is hoarse now. Her fingers are bleeding from gripping the iron gutter so hard. It is dented from her fingers. She is waiting, waiting, waiting for Nancy to take a breath.

Everything in the world has narrowed to the single point of Nancy's chest.

"Let me in," she is murmuring without sound.

"Away with you," Rothersham says, and there is a slight turn to his mouth that suggests a grin, even as he spits the words. "Witch."

"Let me in. Let me in. Let me in. Let me in."

I have found

Bartholome

narrow build

where she sa

sanctuary, and

it. I will re

figure out the

hideous journ

what to do.

lie. My li

I cannot esca

# LEN

## 2019

## *Chapter 20*
## Never, Never, Never . . .

HERE THEY ARE, ON the bed, Poulton's head bent over my journal, my words in his mouth. *My* words. *My* past. *My* secrets. My pain. He is dishing them out, gouging them from the pages I bled them into, right into Zoey's waiting ears. But I know this wasn't his idea. Of course, it was hers.

Rain water drops from my hair, my lashes, my nose, and I can't process what I'm seeing.

"He killed her," Zoey whispers, and when she looks at Poulton she catches sight of me dripping in the doorway.

She leans her head back into the pillow, neck muscles rigid, her mouth open in a little "O" of surprise. "Len . . ."

Poulton pales, closing my diary and placing it onto the bed between them. He stands slowly, facing me.

My heart beats in my ears, a roaring ocean, and everything turns dark at the edges, like the world closing in, losing its shape. I press my hand to the doorframe and breathe.

Zoey and Poulton have invaded my memories, betrayed my trust, ripped open my pain and peaked inside. This is all Zoey. Poulton is too uninterested. Zoey had all but demanded to know the rest before I left—and so she took it. Worse, behind Zoey's guilty expression, the biting of her lip, is something else . . .

The glint of defiant triumph.

I breathe.

At last I turn to go, but stumble. I turn to face the wall, pressing my face to the stone, trying to contain everything. Trying not to explode. Trying not to feel this. Why did I have to remember ? Why did I have to read that Conjure ? Why did she have to steal this ? It's a violation.

Zoey's voice is tentative, far away. "He . . . he killed her."

Poulton says something—I don't catch what. Then Zoey's muffled voice. "Go. Go check on her. Poulton, go !"

But I am stumbling away. I hear Zoey calling my name, then a hand on my arm. I shove it roughly aside and Poulton is crashing to the floor, overturning the chair, the books scattering across the short corridor and sliding under the bed.

"I'm sorry," Zoey says desperately, and Poulton scrambles up again, backing away.

I realize that I'm panting now, my chest heaving.

"Len, please," Zoey says, desperately, "I had to know. It felt like you were hiding things from me !"

"It wasn't yours to take !" I roar, surprising us both. "It was mine !"

I have never wanted to hurt someone so badly.

"We're together," Zoey counters, and there it is again : that defiance.

I need to get out of here.

I turn and I flee, ignoring Zoey's yells behind me. I just run. I run and run and I don't know if I'll ever go back. I walk without direction and without much thought. I hate this feeling. I hate these memories.

Nancy . . .

How could I have forgotten ?

Her face, bright and alive, fills my mind.

Nancy laughing as we ran along The Walkaway. Her expression when I told her Tombstone could stay. Her heartache over his loss. I remember frigid nights when she climbed into my bed and fell asleep holding my hand. Her terror when she stood in the Abbess's office listening to Rothersham's proposal. Her stubborn refusal to let me in the room, the look of terror on her face when he took away her light.

I failed her.

What if I fail Zoey too ?

The night deepens and I find myself on streets that were once familiar. They have grown up and filled in since the last time I was here. Semis cluster together beneath tired trees, shops boxed over and dripping with graffiti. A woman standing in the doorway to a dimly lit corner shop open unusually late eyes me with suspicion. I smell the Conjure on her. She is Unclosed too. It is faint—a diluted or corrupted connection, but there. I must be a beacon to her, having read the Conjures in my journal so recently.

She grins as I pass, her teeth yellow and black.

"Evening, pretty."

I hurry faster.

"What's the rush ?" she calls, cackling.

Newly unlocked memories of the blood-soaked years I spent with my mother crowd in. I remember them with horrifying clarity, like little slivers of glass in my eyes.

I've changed since then. Become more human. I met Zoey.

My heart swells at the thought of her, and breaks. She betrayed me, yes, but she also saved me. Saved us. Can I really allow the consequences of that Conjure be that she never moves again ? I always knew I would do anything to save her.

I won't let her pay for my mistakes. Not like Nancy.

But to do that, I have to go to places I swore I'd never go again.

I get back to St Bartholomew's Alley in the early hours. Zoey and Pole are asleep, but startle awake when I open the door.

"Go back to sleep," I murmur.

"What the bloody hell was *that* ?" Zoey snaps.

I can feel her anger seething in the air. No doubt she has been simmering since I left.

"I had some thinking to do."

"Yeah, well you'd better start explaining. Pole, get off me."

Poulton sits up and rubs blearily at his face. He looks perfectly content with my absence, I think wryly, though he doesn't ever meet my eyes.

I shut the door and pile the books on the chair in front of it.

Zoey rolls her eyes. "Poulton, get *off* me !"

Poulton stands and yawns, shuffling over and edging past me to the chair. He moves the books and sits down.

I sigh and go to sit on the bed beside Zoey and take her hand, but she's no mood to be placated.

"Where the hell did you go ? I was worried."

"I'm sorry."

"You're sorry," she says flatly, and there might as well be steam coming out of her ears. I can feel the anger radiating from her, growing in size.

I lift her hand to my lips, kissing the soft skin there. "Zoey . . ."

"I'm . . ." She swallows, watching me. "I'm sorry too. About Nancy," she clarifies.

The hesitation catches my attention. The bitter twist of her mouth catches my attention.

"I loved her once," I admit, caressing her fingers. "I can't change that. She was so like you. You both have this . . . this radiance. This light. You carry it with you wherever you go and you shine it on the people around you."

Zoey scoffs, looking away.

"It's true. You're hurting now, rightly so. You sacrificed everything for us." I pause. "It isn't fair."

"So, yes. I loved Nancy a lifetime ago. But you're what matters to me now. You."

Poulton makes a sound in his throat very much like a gag, but I ignore him.

She searches my face. "I want to believe you . . ."

I lean over and press my lips to hers, tasting her softness, inhaling her scent. "You," I whisper. "The Conjure

I released made me relive it. It was fresh again, that's all. You're my priority, and I'm not going to fail you."

"Then tell me what's going on. Where did you go ?"

"I really did just need to get some air. To process. Seeing you there with my journal . . . I didn't expect that."

Zoey clenches her jaw. She will not apologise, and I almost laugh. So stubborn.

"I've realized something," I continue. "I think I've known for a while. It's why I've been delaying."

"Okay . . ."

I take a breath. "We can't stay here. The clue that Roan left for me isn't here. Or if it is, I don't know how to find it. It's been so long that she might have removed it—I don't know. The point is, I don't know where to find her. But the journal reminded me of a way that I can bring her to me."

Zoey stiffens. "Not a Conjure ?"

"You let me worry about that."

"There's something else, isn't there ?"

I brace myself. "I need to take you somewhere safe."

She frowns, searches my face again, her eyes going back and forth between my eyes. "Whoa . . . no way. No way you're going to leave me somewhere without you."

I squeeze her hand even though she can't feel it. "I can't take you with me."

"Bollocks !"

"I have to do this alone."

"You just don't *want* me there," Zoey yells, her voice cracking. "But I'm coming with you ! You can't throw me away !"

I stroke the hair out of her face. "Zoey . . . I can't bring her to me if you're there."

Her lips quiver, eyes filling with angry tears. "I'm a burden. The wart on your arse."

"No. Never. *Never.*" I kiss her forehead and she lets me. I kiss her cheek, her other cheek, her eyelids, her eyebrows, her nose, her chin, and finally, her mouth, whispering, "Never," each time. Her lips part and I press into her, tasting her, yearning for her.

I wish things were different.

"You just won't like what I'm going to have to do," I whisper into her lips.

She looks away, clenching her stubborn jaw again.

"Roan won't come out unless... unless I provoke her. She's a creature that doesn't want to be found." I look up at all the books she's collected over the decades, the rows and rows of cursed volumes. "I have to force her hand."

I touch Zoey's cheek but she leans her head further away, neck muscles taut with fury.

She closes her eyes and refuses to look at or speak to me for the rest of the night.

Poulton pretends to be asleep in the chair, but I can see him smiling.

Momento Mori

# ZOEY

## 2019

## *Chapter 21*
## A Game of Choices

Y DREAMS ARE FULL of inverted crosses, dark corridors stretching on into the night, the taste and texture of snake meat in my teeth—a hunger beyond endurance. I'm running, terror leaching into my bones, and then I'm falling, down, down,

d

o

w

n

into icy, haunted waters.

Chalk sigils scrawled onto stone, the blocked wing of a terrible, living house, a giant and infernal water wheel etched in Conjure marks, a hunting room hung with skulls, all inverted, demonic, black spaces where eyes used to be full of a strange, sentient cunning.

I am sitting beside Len, gripping her hand, listening as Poulton bangs on the door. It is the middle of the night, and he is not himself. Except it wasn't Pole banging, was it ? Because he was down below, with the wheel, haunting those darkened spaces of the dams.

I turn terrified eyes on Len. "Who is it ?"

Her eyes meet mine, brilliant and terrified. "I think you mean what is it . . ."—

"Look at this !"

Poulton slams into the room like a tornado, waving a newspaper around, waking me. My forehead is drenched in cold sweat, the eerie taste of Mill House still on my tongue.

"Can we lower the volume," I mutter. My head is killing me and I'm still annoyed with Len for wanting to dump me somewhere.

Poulton hands the paper to Len. "Read it to her."

Her expression darkens as she reads. "Oh."

Pole scoffs. "Yeah, oh." He turns to me. "Your parents are looking for you, Zoey. It's all over the news."

My stomach falls away from me. "Oh . . . shit."

Len frowns. "If they find you, they'll cart you off to A&E and have no idea why you can't move."

"Yeah, well maybe it's time for that," Pole says.

"No, it's not. They wont let her out of their sight and how will Roan help her then ?"

"If you can even *find* Roan," Pole mutters. "You've been looking through these books for weeks, not telling us how a sodding poetry party is going to help her !"

Len bares her teeth at him. "If you want to help, maybe don't touch people's private things. Might find yourself with broken fingers."

"Well then they can fix my *broken fingers* at the same time they're giving Zoey an MRI."

My head is going to explode.

"Doctors and medicine aren't going to help a magical injury, you idiot !" Len snaps. "They'll just run tests upon useless tests, then decide she's bonkers, lock her up and leave her to rot."

"Isn't that what you've done ? Zoey isn't exactly thriving here, is she ?"

I take a breath and yell, "Shut up ! Shut up both of you ! Have either of you even thought to ask me what the bloody hell I want ? No ! I'm just the invalid, who cares what she thinks !"

They both look at me, stunned.

"I'm sorry," Len says, lowering the paper. "You're right."

"What do you want ?" Pole asks.

"I don't want to go home. I don't want to see my mum or Greg or Dexter. What I want is to be better. And if there is even a chance that Roan can help me, then I want to find her."

"Zo . . ." Pole says gently. "Your mum is really worried. I saw her on the telly at the news agents. She's beside herself."

"I'd rather have them worried and with hope than see me like this and not be able to do anything. I'd rather apologise to them when I can walk again than go back to them like this."

"But—"

"Mum will know this is from Working, Pole," Zoey says, fighting back tears. "She'll know this is the consequence of my actions. She'll know it . . . and I can't face her. The pain and disappointment. The blame."

For the first time in my life, I'm glad my Dad has no idea who I am.

"Are you sure, though?" Pole says quietly, imploring me with his gaze to reconsider.

I know I'm dragging him along again, but it feels like the only real choice. Part of me wonders if he wants to go home, to put all of this behind him. To get back to school and exams and the life he put on hold for me. I wouldn't blame him.

"Yes, I'm sure." I look at Len. "You said you knew Roan could help me. How can you be so certain?"

Len's face registers some brief flicker of feeling, and her mouth opens, but she bites down on something she wants to say. Then she closes her lips and sighs. "I just do." After a moment of awkward silence, Len clears her throat. "We can't stay here. We can't risk being caught."

"You were going to leave me somewhere," I mutter, bitterness rising in my throat like bile.

"Yes."

"Get on with it, then."

# LEN

## 2019

## *Chapter 22*
## A Delicate Delivery

T Catherine's hasn't changed, but the city has grown up around it, choked by a cement jungle gone wild. It used to be the tallest thing in the neighborhood, but now sits dwarfed between buildings that touch the sky. Standing there, it seems so sad and small—so utterly forgotten.

They've paved over the cobblestones, and patched that over many times by the looks of it. The buildings have been built so close that the churchyard  is tucked away in a series of alleyways, a hidden pocket. The park is smaller, the gates having been moved in at some point in the intervening time, or perhaps I'm misremembering, and it is littered with empty plastic cups, crisp wrappers, and other rubbish of a careless and jaded humanity. An old woman sits on a bench feeding fat, one-legged, disease-riddled pigeons.

Some decades ago, I learned that the convent—which I was surprised still existed—had begun taking in women affected by Conjures, a sanctuary for those made victim to the devil's tongue. Maybe the Abbess—my Abbess—had seen to it after I left. Maybe it was a natural conclusion for a place of holy worship, to accept the damned. They accepted me, after all.

I knock at the wooden door, aged but the same.

A young nun opens it, her eyes downcast. "How may I help you?"

"We seek sanctuary. A resting place.'

The nun looks up at me then, takes in Zoey strapped to my back and Poulton standing behind. I can see her looking for the signs of Conjure, for the taint of magic.

She nods at length. "We accept only women into the inner sanctum. Your friend will not be allowed to stay."

"We just want to say goodbye."

The smell inside is the same. Mildew, wood-rot, and something ancient rising from the stone like the echo of ghosts. At any moment, surely, Mellie will run past me laughing, or Sister Mary Catherine will send me out to pull weeds, scowling at my brash nature. I spot a small stone carving of a snake near the ceiling that I don't remember, and a feeling of derealisation settles over me. Everything is so similar, but there are changes that settle uncomfortably in my stomach. The steps are worn lower, the windowsills have been replaced, the windows themselves seem much smaller. It is hard to believe that, at one time, this tiny space was my whole world.

The nun leads us into the main hall, where the Abbess used to sit and read the Bible or light a candle for observance. She allows us to take a seat in the old pews and I try not to shudder, try not to bolt for the door. Poulton helps me unclip Zoey and lower her down into a seated position.

"You brought me to a church," Zoey mutters, her waspish whisper echoing around the room. "Are you mad ?"

"That's what I'd like to know," Poulton mutters, sitting next to her.

I sit on her other side, tucking her more securely into the sleeping back so she doesn't fall over. I don't like being here either, but there is no other acceptable choice.

"These nuns take in women who have been afflicted by the Conjure. It's a place of healing."

Zoey lowers her voice further. "It's a *convent.*"

I smile. "It's St Catherine's."

She blinks, processing. "Wait . . . St. Catherine's ? *Your* St Catherine's ?"

I nod, watching with amusement as she peers around with sudden interest. Past and present colliding.

I look around too, trying to remind myself that my time here was another lifetime. A whole new generation of women live her now—several generations have passed through since I was a girl in these halls . . . since I stood bloody on these flagstones before the Abbess's cold gaze. It isn't the same place.

Zoey looks around and some of the venom dissipates from her voice. "Do . . . do they know ?"

I shake my head. "How could they ?"

"This is stupid," Poulton mutters. "We should have taken her home."

"I said no," Zoey snaps. "And if you tried I would have bitten your face off. I can still do that."

Poulton laughs, rolling his eyes. "Developing a taste for cannibalism now ?"

Her mouth twitches as though she wants to smile, but it lasts only a moment. She frowns at me. "How long do I have to stay ?"

I hesitate. "I don't know. When I find Roan, I'll come back for you."

"But how long ? Weeks ? Months ? Years ? Decades ?"

"Zoey, I really don't know. I'm going to do this as fast as I can, but I don't even know if she's in England."

She closes her eyes. "Shit. I'm going to grow old in a convent."

"*No.* I won't let that happen, okay ? I—"

The young nun returns with an older woman in tow, the clopping of their shoes echoing on the stones. This is the new Abbess, no doubt.

"A convent is a lovely place to grow old in," she says, eyes twinkling with humour.

Zoey reddens. "Oh, I didn't mean . . . "

"Don't worry, dear. We're deeply misunderstood. My name is Abbess Crane. This is Sister Wren. I understand you need shelter."

Zoey glances and me and I stand. "Hello, mother. My name is Len. I'm sorry to drop in without warning, but we need somewhere safe for Zoey."

The Abbess looks me up and down and suddenly I'm eight again, scolded for being caught out of bed at night.

"Have we met ?"

"No, sister."

She looks at Poulton. "We don't allow men to stay, even if they are under age."

"No, it's just Zoey that needs a bed."

"And her injuries ?"

"A Conjure."

The Abbess nods. "She was the vessel ?"

"She worked the Conjure."

Her eyes flicker to Zoey and back. "I see." A pause. "There is a bed. For how long will she need it ?"

"I don't know. But I can send money in time."

The Abbess smiles. "We don't require payment. Only trust."

I swallow and lower my voice. "I trust you. In time, she might."

The Abbess considers me with sharp, blue eyes, and then she nods curtly. "Very well. Welcome to the Sisterhood of the Sparrows, Zoey. Best say your goodbyes now, and we'll take you to your room."

The Abbess and Sister Wren leave us alone, their footsteps clopping away again. I wonder if they choose those shoes on purpose.

I touch Zoey's hair. "You'll be safe here."

"I'll be bored here. Out of my mind."

"And what about me ?" Poulton asks. "You can't expect me to go back home without you. They'll never let me sleep for asking where you are. I'll probably be arrested."

"I'll get you money," I tell him. "You can stay in a hotel nearby. But lay low. We don't need any attention right now. I'm sure they'll let you visit Zoey."

"No."

We turn to look at Zoey.

"What do you mean, 'no' ?" I ask.

"I mean, no. Poulton will not be staying in a hotel and coming to visit me like I'm in some palliative care home. I want him to go with you."

Poulton and I share a rare glance, and then burst out laughing.

"No way," I say.

At the same time Poulton says, "Yeah in your dreams."

"Len, give me a minute with him, will you ?" Zoey says, exasperation dripping from her tongue.

I get up and dawdle to the other end of the room, even though I can hear every word they say echoing across the walls.

"Pole," Zoey says gently. "Please. I need you to go with Raplen. She's doing something dangerous. She hasn't said what, but I know she's going to a dark place. I can see it in her eyes. She looks . . . haunted. You heard what happened to Nancy. She's going to need you to keep her in the light. To keep her . . . herself. I'm begging you."

A beat of silence, and then Poulton says stiffly, "Wait. Am I fucking hearing this right ?"

"Pole . . . "

"You want me, knowing how I feel about you, to go with the witch who stole you from me ?"

"I know, I know . . . I've been selfish, and I've been a brat, and I've taken you for granted, but we need to find Roan. I wouldn't trust anyone else with this."

"Fuck, Zo."

"Do you really want to wait this out watching rubbish on the telly in some grotty hotel ? You heard that nun. No men allowed."

Poulton sighs. "I don't know how much use I'll be. She never listens."

"You don't know how persuasive you can be. How good you are. Just stay with her. Promise me."

A long pause and then a groan. "Shit, Zoey. Fuck's sake. Fine. I promise. But I don't promise I won't strangle her myself."

"As long as you don't stab her in the chest with an ancient knife, I'm good."

They both laugh, and Poulton mutters, "Well now you're asking for asking too much."

I pretend to be considering a painting of the Virgin Mary when Poulton comes over. He doesn't look at me, just flicks his thumb over his shoulder to tell me Zoey wants me now.

I sigh and make my way over.

"Your turn," Zoey says when I sit down.

Her sleeping bag slips on the pew and she begins to slide off it with a yelp of surprise.

I grab her and put her back into sitting position, tucking her into my side. "Well, I'm going to miss our adventures of you preventing me sliding onto the floor like a meat sausage," she jokes.

I grin. "Me too."

Our smiles fade into the silence.

"You have to take him with you."

I almost make a snarky comment about how he's going to keep me on the straight and narrow when she leans her head on my shoulder.

"He's going to need you, Len," she whispers. "He's lost in this. He's so lost he doesn't even see it. You have to keep him safe. Keep him safe and bring the both of you back to me."

I didn't expect this. I turn to face her, taking her cheek in my hand.

"I love you more than you know," I tell her. "I love you more than anyone."

I see the thought flicker on her face.

"More than Nancy, yes. I do."

"Please don't hurt Poulton," she whispers.

I close my eyes for a moment, letting the implication sit with me. "Okay."

I kiss her, breathe her in for the last time, and then stand and head for the door.

"Come on, then," I mutter after I've passed him, wondering if my mother felt this way, a hundred and seventy seven years ago when she left me behind in this very same convent.

# LEN

2019

## *Chapter 23*
## Rirrom

OULTON IS SILENT WHEN we leave, but I can sense his want to go back. I'm not much better myself. Leaving Zoey is hard enough, but leaving her here . . . I glance back and say a silent prayer that she will be safe. Her cure, or the hope of it, is out there somewhere. So out there I must go. I just didn't expect to be doing it with company.

We walk for several miles to the nearest underground.

"Where are we going?" Pole asks on the platform.

"I need to get you something before we can start."

"Get me something?"

"I have to make it."

"Okay . . ." He glances at me sideways. "Why?"

"So I don't eat you."

The train arrives in a scream of noise, drowning out his shock, and we get on without further talk. Poulton keeps his eyes on me and a seat firmly between us. Why did she have to make me promise to bring this kid with me ? He has no idea the danger he's in.

The shop is still in Hawes Alley. It's like time hasn't moved since the seventeenth century. An old sign with a woodcut witch announces *Wares, Scares and Con-jares.*

I push open the door and a little bell tinkles as we step inside. The whole place smells like bitter rue, angelica, and rosemary. Protectives. Poulton coughs and waves a hand in front of his face.

"Bloody 'ell. Don't they ever clean ?"

I ignore him and head into the first of seven rows of wooden shelves. They've moved everything around so it takes me a while to find the amulets.

Poulton picks up a jar with a white rat floating in formalin. "Some corner shop."

"It's a supply shop for Conjurers."

He rolls his eyes. "Obviously. Do you need to Conjure Roan like a rabbit out of a top hat ?" He scoffs at his own joke and puts the rat down.

"This is for your benefit."

"Mine ?"

"You'll need protection before we start."

"Are we going into skanky bars and nightclubs ?"

"You really don't listen, do you ?"

"So you don't eat me," he says, half laughing, half eyeing me.

"Exactly."

He steps back from me, head retracting like a turtle, mock afraid. "Okay, Hannibal Lecter."

I move aside several large athames and dig through a small box of silver trinkets.

"You promised Zoey you wouldn't hurt me."

"Maybe you do listen," I mutter, rifling through endless talismans that feel wrong.

What I'm looking for isn't here.

I leave Poulton gawping at a necklace with a naked figurine dangling from the chain, and head for the counter at the back. No one is manning it so I walk around to the back room. Something stops me at the entrance.

I look down. No salt. No visible barrier.

It's a home. Of course.

I've spent so long in Mill House and then at Bartholomew's Alley, I forgot the one simple law of my nature. No access granted to homes without permission.

"Hello?" I call, hoping someone is nearby in the orange glow beyond. "Hello?"

A tall man comes around the corner with his chin up and eyebrows raised. He has a tawny gaze underpinned by dark purple eye bags and a crooked nose that lends him a corvid air. He glances at me, down at my feet, and then grins.

"Unusual to see one of you during the day."

"Yeah. I need something and I can't find it. A little help?"

"Item?"

"*Rorrim* amulet for my friend out there." I nod towards Poulton, who is now sniffing a candle dipped in herbs with a crow's foot sticking out of the side.

"Protection from?"

"Me, mainly."

He grins, sly. "We don't produce them anymore."

"Why?"

He shrugs bony shoulders. "Change of focus."

"You mean a change of pressure from outside donors? Vampires don't like you selling their meals protection against them."

"Something like that."

I grit my teeth to prevent me doing something I'll regret. "Fine. Then I need an unworked amulet. Something wearable."

He eyes me up and down again, sliding his tongue over his teeth. "You'd have to work it yourself."

"I figured."

"Never seen a Conjuring vamp."

I fold my arms. "There's a first time for everything. You have something?"

He reaches into the greasy, stretched-out collar of his shirt and pulls free a silver cross on a black thong, undoes it and hands it over. I close my hand around it, letting my senses explore the cool metal, searching for any enchantment that may have been concealed. Aside from a vague sense of greasiness, I find none.

I had it back. "How much?"

He runs his thumb over it thoughtfully. "For the price of silence. No need to go spreading around that we no longer trade in certain items . . . "

I narrow my eyes at him. "Why would—" and it comes to me. "You're supplying those who come for the protection amulets to . . . interested parties."

"A man has to make a living," he says, putting the cross on the counter and eyeing me with amusement.

I snatch the cross and shake my head, disgusted. I'd forgotten just how sordid this side of London and humanity can be.

It's only when I've dragged Poulton away from the shop—him protesting that he absolutely *needs* to get the amulet with the naked woman or he'll perish a lonely death—that I realize the cross was cold when the man in the shop gave it to me.

Whatever he was, it was not human.

Maybe not even alive.

---

"Who even shops at that place?" Poulton kicks at pebbles all the way down St Olave's Avenue. "How do they even keep themselves open?"

"I'm sure there are plenty of normal people who shop there for their silly little love-spells. Besides, you'd be surprised how many Conjurers need supplies to make their spells work. Not everyone is as powerful as Zoey."

"Or you?"

"Or me. Bloodlines are diluted. Some deals made with Unholy creatures don't pass on to the next generation, and some deals are made with lesser demons who haven't any real power to imbue."

Poulton stares at me. "What do you mean Unholy creatures? Plural?"

"'When Lucifer fell from heaven, he did not fall alone.'"

"I'm not sure I really want to know more."

"Probably best."

"No, I think it's probably best if I do. I just don't want to." He shakes his head and mutters, "I'm starting to seriously consider if I'm getting out of this alive."

"You will. And once I've worked this cross for you, you'll be a hell of a lot safer than you are now."

"So where do we go to Work it ?"

"We need to find an area in an already corrupted part of London. I don't want to do any damage. I think I know a place."

I take him to a dingy hotel in Soho called PIPER. I stayed here about decade ago and it reeked of dark magick. It was so potent that, despite a rare instance of needing sleep, it eluded me.

We get a twin room so that Poulton can sleep. He climbs into one of the twin beds straight away and faces the wall.

"Should have got that amulet," he mutters under his breath.

"It was Worked to make you want it. An Unclosed Rostar put a desire spell into the plastic."

He turns to look at me, the whites of his eyes fully visible. "*Seriously* ?"

I nod. "Yep."

He grumbles something even I don't hear and turns away again, dragging the blanket over his head.

"I'll get us some food," I tell him. "Anything okay ?"

"Pizza."

I sigh. "Pizza it is."

"And coke."

"Don't you ever eat a vegetable ?"

He grumbles again and hunkers deeper into the blanket.

"Don't move. I'll be back." I hesitate. "And Poulton ?"

"Yeah ?"

"Once I start the Conjure, don't interrupt me," I warn him. "Not for anything."

"Fine, whatever."

I shake my head and lock the door, trusting that he's not stupid enough to leave without me.

---

We eat the pizza in silence. He scoffs his down like a man drowning and I realize with a pang of guilt that I haven't fed or watered him in a while. I offer him the rest of my pizza and he nods, mouth bursting with cheese, pepperoni, and bread, adding mine to his own. When we're both done, he groans with pleasure and wipes his face with the back of his hand.

"Thanks. Needed that."

I nod, not mentioning that I had to steal them from an understaffed Dominoes three roads over and then slide into an alley and climb the wall to escape the indignant employee that would have to remake the order.

It's hard to admit that theft and evasion is invigorating.

*Like mother like daughter*, I think bitterly.

---

The Conjure is so easy to think, so easy to speak, and so easy to use.

The noxious poison of it flows like silk between my fingers, making me shudder. I scratch the marks into the cross with my fingernail, muttering under my breath, trying and failing to keep Zoey from my thoughts.

Did my mother feel this when she left me behind? This . . . heartbreak? This miserable longing? This regret and guilt and shame?

Cycles and circles, the universe mocking us all.

I grit my teeth and force Roan and Zoey and Poulton away. Nothing else matters except the Conjure. Nothing is as important as Poulton's protection. From you, a tiny voice reminds me.

I continue to mutter the Cursed tongue under my breath, feeling the intoxicating stink of it, until I feel the urge and necessary pull for my sacrifice. A binding. With trembling fingers, I reach into my mouth and grip my back molar. I squeeze my eyes shut, swear under my breath, and then rip it from my jaw, root and all. It comes away with a revolting crack, and a gush of coppery blood floods my tongue. I spit the blood onto the cross, and then mutter—resentfully—the Conjure marks for binding, protection, fusion, and fire.

I hold the cross and the tooth and blood in my rigid palm, feeling the heat of the Conjure working, and when I open my hand, a new amulet sits gleaming in the moonlight. Imbued with the blood of my body, the pain of my intention and, fused to the center, the tooth of my sacrifice, it is finally complete.

I grimace as my tooth begins to regrow itself. From what stem, root, or source, I have no idea. In minutes, nothing excepting an ache in my jaw and the tang of blood on my tongue, might reveal that anything out of the ordinary has occurred.

It's been a long time. I almost don't hear the singing of human blood anymore. The closest I've come was smelling Zoey's anemia in Mill House. I shudder at the memory and push it away.

"I'm regretting this already," I mutter.

Poulton glances at me. "Well, you wanted me to have the stupid amulet. Better to see if it works. I don't suppose we'll always have a hotel to run to."

"Unlikely."

"Then, I stay." Poulton lifts the cross and eyes it with a curled lip. "This is seriously gross. Why the tooth ?"

He still doesn't know what this is all about.

"A piece of me was needed," is all I say. "I've never had an audience."

Not strictly true. Roan and I were each other's blood-soaked audience for years , the two of us a death-knell on the streets of London. But by then I didn't care. I was lost in my own grief. This time it's different. And for some reason, I do care about what Poulton thinks of me.

"So how does it work ?" he asks, sliding his hands into his pockets. The silver cross glints against his t-shirt and I really, really hope my Conjure worked.

"I find a target."

"Okay . . . "

It's so strange doing this again. Remembering this again . . . The last time I was in this area, everything was different. I'd been living on the streets, skimming sewage water just to have something to drink, stealing food for Nancy so she wouldn't starve, always looking for the next safe space. Back then the buildings were far fewer. It's like the city just grew up all around me when I wasn't looking. Have I been sleepwalking so long ?

"Haven't you been back to London since then ?" Poulton asks incredulously, and I realize I must have said something of my thoughts aloud.

"No. Bad memories kept me away for the most part. By the time Roan and I parted ways, the world was changing. London had too many terrible memories. I just wanted to get away. I stayed around long enough to stow my diary and put the Conjure on myself, and then I left."

"Where did you go ?"

"We need to test that amulet."

"So, what do I do ?"

"Maybe just stay back, okay ? Follow me at a discreet distance. And when it happens . . . don't make a sound. And . . . don't breathe too loudly."

He looks bemused, but nods and stays put as I walk down the road, looking for a target that won't be missed. The last time I did this, I had a type. Men who hurt women. I suppose I ought to stick to what I know, so I head for the clubs. The streets are bustling, full of young people already mostly drunk. Girls in short skirts and high heels, leather jackets and cakey makeup. Men with leering grins and loud guffaws. Catcalls, cigarette smoke and secret gropes and the tangy under-scent of sour vomit.

I mill around them, wade through them, searching for someone, waiting for a mark to catch my eye. Their scent is heady and intoxicating, sweat and skin, and underneath it the steady hum of a hundred different heartbeats. Like hummingbirds.

He's in the alley between two nightclubs. He's thirty, maybe forty, and sober ; holding onto a girl no more than sixteen, who is so drunk—or drugged—that she's stumbling, head lolling onto his shoulder. He's heading away from people, into the dark back-ways where rubbish will be piled high come morning and she'll wake—or not—with no memory of what he's done to her.

"I should go home," she mumbles, leaning heavily against him.

She's lost a shoe. Her bare foot is filthy with grime. Her right pinkie toe is bleeding.

He yanks her along faster, not bothering to be gentle anymore.

I follow them like a shadow.

My own shadow, Poulton, is surprisingly quiet.

It's now or never.

The couple turns left into a dead-end. I follow, and watch.

He presses her into the brick wall, and she groans and tries to push him away, hands clumsy, arms weak. He buries his head in her throat, hands grappling with the bottom of her dress.

I give into the thing that is always with me, simmering under my skin like a sting.

When I grab him and throw him off her, she slumps into a pile of rubbish bags and begins to snore.

He spits blood from his mouth. "What the *fuck*?"

I stand in front of him and let my senses take him in. Feel my bloodlust rise after so long. Run my tongue over sharpening teeth and then—

He's mine.

The skin breaks, easy as butter. My teeth pierce his jugular. It's messy like always, but more so from the years unpracticed. The feral thing inside me growls and drinks, draining him even as my hands grip onto his shoulders—too hard, breaking his clavicles, crushing his scapula, pulverizing the top of his humeri.

He gives a feeble wail that heightens my excitable blood lust, spurring me onto a wild frenzy, and I break off at the moment his heart gives out, head thrown back in the purest ecstasy I've felt in decades. I almost groan aloud.

He crumples to the floor, empty and gone.

The thing inside me purrs, stretching her limbs in a luxurious yawn of awakening.

A tiny sound behind me catches my attention. I snatch my head in that direction, my eyes finding a boy.

Poulton.

He is staring at me with wide, terrified eyes, his mouth open in a grimace of horror.

I bare my teeth at him, warning him to stay back. I inhale, and smell . . . nothing. He has no scent. Not even mine.

"You're fine," I growl. "I don't smell you."

He looks queasy.

Turning back to the man, I kneel and rip open his shirt. Then I use my nails to carve a Conjure mark—Roan's Conjure mark, Varr—into his hairy chest .

Behind me, Poulton vomits, the splatter of it echoing into the night.

I'm covered in blood, so I take off my top and make Poulton give me his jacket. I zip it closed and put the hood up. He is shaking but that doesn't matter. What matters is that I have left the sign for Roan. I have begun to leave my trail of breadcrumbs.

"Let's go."

He follows me, pale and silent, as we weave through the oblivious crowds. I hope I am far away by the time someone finds his body. I don't want to hear the screams.

*Come out, come out*, I think. *Wherever you are.*

"I nearly legged it," Poulton admits later, when we're sitting in a chippy, the neon lights buzzing brightly above us like a determined fly.

"Why did you stay ?"

"For Zoey."

I nod, fiddling with my coke. After the blood, it's going to be hard to feel satisfied by human food again.

Poulton isn't eating either, and I can't really blame him. He's seen what I'm truly capable of now. I'm surprised he can bear to look at me.

"How is this going to help ?" he says, his voice small. "How is killing people helping Zoey ?"

"It's the only way I know to get Roan to come out."

"There has to be another way," he says desperately. "There has to."

"I used to think there was," I admit. "I tried it before. It didn't work. Only this did."

"Can't we do a finding spell ?"

"How do you suggest we do that ? We need a Finder, like Zoey. Zoey's is Ccugoth. Do you want her to Conjure again and lose more ? Her sight ? Hearing ? Her life ?"

"You know I don't," he snaps. "I just don't think *killing* people is the answer."

I feel my hackles rise. "So I should have just let him rape her ?"

"No, but you didn't have to kill him !"

"*Keep your voice down*," I hiss, glancing at the man in the kitchen. "Or do you want to get arrested ? I told you that I would do anything for Zoey and I meant it. You didn't have to come with me. You could have gone home. You chose to come." I put a chip in my mouth and chew, not tasting it. "But I'm very happy to do this without you. You can leave anytime. I'm more than happy to walk this road by myself."

Poulton shoves his chips away and folds his arms. "You make me sick."

"Then we're even."

A heavy silence falls between us and I'm tempted to just get up and leave.

"You needed the tooth for the binding," he says after a long silence. "You needed it because you wouldn't eat yourself. That's how it protects me, isn't it?"

I eye him. "Not as stupid as he looks."

He looks like he wants to hit me. Or vomit. I sigh and lean forward.

"What would you suggest?"

He glances at me, scowling. "Like you care."

"Don't be a child. If you have a better idea, then spit it out."

"You said you tried something last time. To get Roan's attention. What was it?"

I lean back in my chair, shaking my head. The neon lights are bugging me. "I told you it didn't work."

"Well maybe it will this time. If it doesn't, we can go back to . . . your way."

I watch him. His earnest, fervent integrity, his young, pig-headed belief. "Fine. We'll do it tomorrow night."

"And another thing," he says defensively. "I know you stopped your story for Zoey's sake. Because you're scared she won't love you if she knows it all."

Wish he'd punched me after all.

"But I think you better tell me the rest. If I'm going down this road with you, I deserve to see where it leads and how dark it gets."

# RAPLEN

## 1868

## *Chapter 24*
## Blood Thirst

OTHERSHAM IS ALL THAT matters now. The cold calmness that falls over Raplen when she realizes that Nancy's chest will never move again is a sort of relief. The world has distilled into two things.

Her.

Him.

He has not left the house since it happened. People were summoned. The body was moved. Raplen watched it all from the shadows, a pair of eyes in the night. Rothersham checked for her, of course, wondering where the witch-fly had gone, but he could not see her. They wrapped Nancy up and took her away and Raplen did not follow. Nancy wasn't here anymore. Perhaps they would return her to St Catherine's as a bad investment. Let them bury her. Raplen is certain Rothersham believes himself done with the unpleasant business.

And yet he does not leave the house.

Days follow nights follow days. Servants come and go, letters come and go, deliveries come and go.

And he does not leave the house.

It is only on the fifth day that she realizes that he is afraid. Afraid of her. Afraid that she is waiting. Maybe he fears she really is a witch.

But Raplen is patient.

One evening he comes to sit at the window with a lit cigar and a glass of brandy.

"I know you're there," he says. "Witch."

Raplen doesn't move, doesn't give any indication that she can hear him from her perch on the roof.

"Come out, come out, little witch."

She smells his cigar smoke, hears the squeak of his lips on the crystal glass, the gurgle of his gullet as the brandy goes down, the sigh of his breath. She is learning to listen very well. Her ears are becoming as astute as her nose.

When he finds no indication that she is still there, he chuckles under his breath and closes the window. She can hear that his heart has slowed from the nervous race that gave away his fear before to a confident murmur. He is as he was again: assured of his safety and superiority.

He orders his carriage the following evening, well after sunset. He hums a tuneless melody through his evening ablutions and dress, stomping around the house as though there isn't blood on his hands. As though his conscience is clear. Is Nancy the first he kicked to death? Did his last young wife, a St Catherine's girl, meet the same fate?

He is seen out by a frail housekeeper. The carriage door opened for him by the driver with a little bow and top hat. So much respect. So much decency. So much wealth. He is dressed in a silk evening suit, no doubt heading to the opera or some other proper place that Raplen is likely never to see. That Nancy certainly will never see. It is easy for Raplen to step onto the back footboard and cling onto the toprail. Neither the driver nor Rothersham notice their extra passenger, but the horses skip a step and toss their heads, smelling a predator among them.

When the carriage takes a shortcut through a alley, Raplen moves, climbing from her perch onto the hard roof. The driver glances back and sees her.

"What the rattle !" he yells, "Get off there, you ! This ain't no free ride !"

She doesn't move, so he slows the horses to a stop and climbs down from his topseat.

"I'll summon the Constable—"

She leaps from the roof, snapping his neck in one fluid motion. Her strength surprises her, in the measure that she can be surprised now, but she doesn't stop. The carriage door begins to open, the white glove of Rothersham's hand resting on the handle. She pulls it all the way open and slips inside, pushing him back onto the seat.

"You—"

But she is already on him, her nails making ribbons of carnage out of his skin. He tries to swat her away, but she is stronger. So much stronger than Nancy was. Nancy's last look fills her mind and she screams and bites at his face, ripping his cheek clean away, spitting it to the side like offal.

And then the smell of the blood hits her in a new way.

She can't resist. Her teeth change, sharpen into fine points like they never have before, and she bites down into his flesh and drinks deep from the wounds.

This blood is heady and exquisite. Nothing she has felt before has ever compared to this. When his heart begins to slow, she pulls back and watches, her feral eyes meeting his, reveling in his horrible gore.

"Witch," he whispers, gurgling the word so softly that no one except her could hear it.

She leans closer and whispers, "Yes."

❦

The Abbess glides through the shadows of the chapel on silent slippers, heading for the antechamber on the North side. It is well after midnight, and the girls are asleep. She must be as quiet as a specter. But even her steps disturb the air, and the *ssh*, *ssh*, *ssh* of her apron echoing softly off the walls.

Raplen is there, waiting, a wraith in the darkness. How she must look, drenched in blood, hair and skin bathed in the gore of a killer. The Abbess startles with a sharp indrawn breath.

Raplen smiles, the sharpness of her teeth softening. "Welcome home?"

"Raplen?"

She steps into the soft glow of the Abbess's candlelight and waits for a response. The Abbess stares back, not altogether surprised.

"Nancy is dead."

The Abbess nods.

"You don't seem all that shocked. You knew he was a killer, then?"

She shakes her head. "All whom you love will die."

Raplen feels something, then. Her dead heart stirs for a moment.

The Abbess sighs and places her pricket and candle on one of the benches, sitting down beside it. She looks old in this light. Older.

"I want to know who found me. Who brought me here when I was an infant?"

"I knew you would come for answers, sooner or later."

"Give them me, then."

"She was like you. The girl who brought you. Blood on her lips, like yours now. Blood falling from her eyes. A creature of the night."

"Why did you never speak of it?"

"Because I hoped I was wrong about you. About your nature. I can see now that I was not."

Raplen closes her eyes. The beautiful numbness is fading and she is fighting it with all she has. She doesn't want to feel. She can't survive it.

The Abbess takes a breath. "'*Leave a bloody mark on the stone lintel*,' she said, '*if there is ever a need. If the child should ever reveal her true nature.*'"

Raplen opens her eyes. "She left a message?"

"I should have thrown you in the gutter for the dogs to eat."

Raplen's voice hardens. "Show me the lintel, old woman."

The lintel is in the stone arch over the iron gate at the entrance to the graveyard, near the yew tree where she used to meet her midnight friend. It seems obvious now that the girl she played with for all those years is the very same girl who brought her to the convent in the first place. Maybe she knows Raplen's provenance. Maybe they share a provenance—siblings, cousins, something. Maybe she can point Raplen in the right direction.

The Abbess closes the gate behind Raplen, drawing across the iron bar.

"Evil will follow you wherever you walk. You were only safe as long as you stayed within the confines of the church." The Abbess hesitates. "Maybe not even then."

She turns and walks slowly back inside, leaving Raplen alone on the cobbled street.

Raplen uses one of the sharp spokes of the iron gate to cut open her hand, then smears a bloody mark on the stone lintel.

And she waits.

# LEN

## 2019

### *Chapter 25*
## My Body Is a Cage

HE STREETS ARE AS quiet as the dead. St Catherine's sits in shadow, every light within extinguished. It's just gone 1 am.

"We could go in," Poulton says. "See how she's settling in?"

"No."

I use a rusting tin I found in the gutter on the way here to cut open my hand and smear my blood on the stone lintel.

"Why is it always blood?" Poulton mutters, his lip curling.

"Because blood is life."

"Okay, Dracula."

"Shut it."

"What about Zoey? You coming in?"

"No, and neither are you."

"Bollocks I'm not."

"Do you really want to do that to her again? Make her say goodbye all over?"

He hesitates so I use the pause to drive my point in further.

"It's not fair on her. And it's not fair on me."

"I just want to make sure she's safe."

"She is. She's with nuns for God's sake."

"Yeah, I suppose," he mutters, looking over at St Catherine's with longing.

"We should find somewhere for you to sleep. I'll give this three nights, and if Roan doesn't show, we do it my way. Agreed?"

"Fine. Agreed."

I walk away from St Catherine's, just far enough that I'm not tempted to run inside and get Zoey out of there. Just far enough so I can see the lintel in the darkness, my blood a horrible reminder of the futility of this whole plan. I've been here before.

I glance at the darkened window of St Catherine's. I don't want Zoey to see me like this. Not after I've done the one thing I promised myself I would never do again.

Become like my mother.

The monster.

# RAPLEN

## 1868

### *Chapter 26*
### MOTHER

IGHTS PASS DAYS PASS nights, and no one comes.

Raplen doesn't know how long she waits, but eventually the stirring of her grief is too much for such stillness. Her stomach is a cavernous hole and the same impossible yearning is burning in the hollow of her throat. So she leaves, deciding to forget the past in its entirety and give into the darkness that has been swallowing her up since Nancy died. Damnation upon the person who abandoned her. Damnation upon it all.

She doesn't know which is stronger, the inescapable grief, her utter, complete sense of loss—or the thirst. Whichever it is, it is of no import. It is, she decides, too much to reckon with. Too much to live with.

In a hollow in the underbelly of London, amid the rats and the putrid sewage of the gentry, Raplen Saint Catherine attempts to take her life.

Her body is a cage. The pain is a cage. Her life is a cage.

When the knife, pilfered from a careless butcher off St Martin's Lane, does its deadly work on her wrists, she leans back against the cold, stone wall and waits.

An hour or an eternity later, she is still breathing. Still mourning. Still alive.

When she looks down, her wrists are bloodied, but whole. There is no split seam of flesh anywhere in sight. She blinks through the rain, confused, and rubs at her skin, but there is no wound. It is certain.

She cuts again.

And she heals again.

She cuts and cuts but the life clinging to her body refuses to be shucked off.

As the moon grows higher in the stormy sky, she *screams.*

When she jumps from the top of the newly erected lions in Trafalgar Square in the early hours of the following morning, the sun rising pink over the limestone buildings, her bones shatter on the flagstones—

—and then crack themselves back together.

It is there, watching her blood pool upon the ground about her rumbling body, that it occurs to Raplen that she is being punished for the sin committed against Nancy's murderer. Her victim. Could it be that God wished for him to live after such a transgression ? Or was Nancy right when she said that their love, hers and Raplen's, was itself sinful and damnable?

She doesn't want to believe it, but can find no other explanation.

When her body is done the work of keeping her alive, Raplen drags herself to her feet and decides that if she cannot give in to her only true wish—to be free of this life—then she will give into the other.

She walks north.

The second man to die by her hand is one who knows violence. He is beating a streetwalker in an alley near the workhouse on Corwallis Road. She smells the blood. Hears the pitiful screams of the prostitute.

Very well. The thought is bright and unfettered. *If I cannot unshackle myself from the world, then I will wreak my vengeance upon it.*

His blood is sweet as nectar. It sings inside her.

And so, each night, she chooses a man of violence to devour, cleansing the world of the Nancy-killers one at a time, losing herself piece by small piece.

She loses track of the number. And the nights.

*Evil will follow you wherever you walk.* The Abbess's words are a taunt in her mind.

And a lullaby.

And then, on one not particularly memorable night, Raplen feels something new.

She is holding a whimpering man by the throat, her nails firmly planted in his flesh, his warm blood coating her hands, when there is a new sensation in her body. It is a buzzing hum in the hollow of her throat, like wasps tuning their wings. Like bees thrumming their protective rhythm. A sense of alarm climbs her neck and she frowns, seeking out the source, like following a compass, eyes darting about for the cause.

Slowly, the feels the location and she turns, realizing that she is not alone.

Behind her: a figure.

She blinks, the blood haze of her hunt clearing her vision enough to see. There, standing tall and still in the shadows with an unreadable expression.

Her midnight friend.

At last.

*Chapter 27*

# MOTHER, MONSTER, ME

HE MAN IS WHEEZING now, a high-pitched keening rippling from him, like a wounded animal. Raplen only has eyes and ears for her Midnight Friend.

"It was you," she says, dazed. "You took me to St Catherine's."

Roan watches her, eyes oddly bright in the shadows, and says nothing.

"It *was* you, wasn't it?" Raplen presses, and the man in her hands screams, low and guttural. She doesn't know if she wants the answer, but she needs it.

Faster than Raplen can blink, her Midnight Friend is by the man, breaking his neck with one quick twist of her wrist.

The look on Roan's face is terrible.

"Who are you ?" Raplen asks, surprised that her hands are now empty and fast growing sticky and cold. "My sister ? My guardian ?" She pauses, suddenly tired. "Some demon sent to torment me ?"

"Careless," Roan mutters, "Leaving your corpses all over London."

"In alleyways," Raplen says nonchalantly. "Under bridges. No one cares."

"You'll be noticed sooner or later."

"I do not care."

"Well you should," her friend snaps. "Have you not read a history book ? They burn creatures like you."

Raplen laughs, hollowly. "And what creature am I, since you know so well ?" How she had yearned for her mysterious graveyard friend to come and give her answers. Now it hardly seems to matter. She turns to leave. "You don't know the first thing about me."

"You're wrong." The voice is quiet, but Raplen hears. "I know the very first thing about you."

Raplen pauses. Turns back. "What ?"

"I know your first breath. Your first cry. Your first embrace."

Raplen goes cold, shaking her head. "No..."

"I know your first moments."

"Liar."

"You come from me, Raplen. You're mine."

Raplen shakes her head. No. No, this is wrong. "You're . . . but you . . . you're no older than I am !"

"Looks can be deceiving."

"I don't understand."

"There is a lot to tell. If you will listen."

Raplen closes her eyes, suddenly exhausted. "I am so tired."

"You need to feed."

Raplen scoffs. "And be burned for the creature I am ?"

"I will teach you how to clean up your messes. I should have done so, long ago."

Raplen considers Roan for a long, silent moment. And then, eventually, she nods once.

"Teach me then, Creator. Monster. But know that I hate you for your hand in what I am."

Her friend nods, as though she expected nothing less. "Just call me Roan."

"You will always be Monster to me."

There is a cursed child in London, progeny of Boan Eddington. Should she be dispatched?

CY

# Part 3

## Within the Ocean

*"If you want to overcome the whole world, overcome yourself."*

—Fyodor Dostoyevsky, *Demons*

# ZOEY

## 2019

## *Chapter 28*
## A Flock of Sisters

HEY CARRY ME INTO a more permanent room.

It takes four of them to do it. They all have stupid names. Sister Swallow. Sister Wren. Sister Pea. Sister Finch. Each of them at the four corners of me. The bed is fine. I can't feel it, so I don't really know. But it doesn't make a scratchy grass sound when they dump me on it, so I guess that's good. The room itself is also fine. A cloister with no windows and an ogival door. I might as well be in a limestone cave. There's a small table with a porcelain jug and dish in one corner, so I guess someone will wash me now and then. I have to be grateful for whatever I get. I'm trying not to be bitter.

Len and Pole off adventuring and me, here, with a bunch of nuns and nothing but endless time to rot in my own juices. None of the nuns say anything after they dump me on the bed. They just leave, heads bowed under their stupid head dresses. After a few silent minutes the Abbess comes in. She knocks at the door, which is nice I suppose. Pretend privacy.

"My name is Abbess Crane," she says. Her voice is thick and deep. Warming, somehow.

"Cute," I say, looking away.

"Cute ?"

"The whole bird thing. So far I've met a wren, a pea, a finch and"— I pause to scoff— "a swallow. No tits ?" I ask, looking back at her.

"Sister Tit will be along in due course with some food. I'm sure you'll get along famously."

I roll my eyes, laughing. "*Fuck.*"

"You are very welcome here, Zoey. But I hope you'll show our sisters the same respect they will show you."

I swallow and try not to spit my rage at her. This isn't her fault.

I force myself to nod. The only thing I can do. I wonder if they'll gag me and put me in a cellar if I refuse to shut up. If I swear at them and curse their existence.

Probably.

The Abbess sighs. "You've been through a lot. Your friend Raplen explained some of it. I expect there is a lot more to the story."

My "friend" Raplen. I wonder if being gay is a sin to them. Likely. Suddenly I feel very exposed and very unwelcome. These women could literally do anything to me. This could be one of those American conversion camps and I wouldn't know it. I remind myself that Raplen trusts these women. That she loves me, and wouldn't have left me somewhere unsafe. That she basically grew up here.

I glance around, wondering if this room was once hers.

A young nun appears in the doorway. She keeps her eyes averted and her head bowed.

"Ah, Sister," the Abbess says, nodding. She gestures. "Come in, child."

The young woman steps into the room, but still doesn't look up.

"This is Sister Robin," the Abbess tells me. "She's going to be your companion while you're with us. She's very much looking forward to getting to know you."

I seriously doubt that. But then Sister Robin glances up at me and smiles, her cheeks flushing pink, and I realize it might be true.

"Hi," I manage. My voice sounds feeble and not very welcoming to my own ears. "Er, I'm Zoey."

"Hello."

She drops a little curtsy like we're in regency England, but I'm oddly charmed. But then I scowl. I am determined to hate this whole thing.

"Sister Robin is our youngest nun," the Abbess says with a hint of pride. "Around your age, actually. She's shown great promise and dedication. I shall let the two of you get acquainted."

The abbess leaves and an awkward silence falls between us as we listen to her footsteps clacking as she walks away.

Sister Robin closes the door, plunging the room into surprising darkness. She lights a candle from her pocket, lets it burn for a few seconds, then drips a little of the wax on the table before pressing the candle into it to stick it down. The light, meagre though it is, is a comfort. It pushes back some of the gloom. With no windows there's no way to tell the time. Maybe that's the point.

Sister Robin sighs heavily. "The abbess doesn't like me to talk very much." The shy, retiring girl is gone, replaced by . . . someone normal.

I feel myself relax. "Why ?"

A shrug. "I'm comparatively new. I have to earn my words, so to speak."

"That's pants."

"It's a sisterhood of earned respect."

"And the whole bird thing ? Is your name really Robin ?"

She smiles. "We adopt new names. A way to free ourselves from our previous lives."

"Why though ? We are who we are."

"Sometimes the lives we were born into hurt us or change us so deeply that a symbolic freeing of ourselves, of accepting a new family, is healing. Besides, there's power in choosing who you're going to be. It's important. We have a sort of ceremony for the renaming. A mark of respect."

I think about it. About what Len and Pole and I have been through. It seems like a pretty thought to be able to mark the changes with a new name, giving up the one I have now. It would be nice to give up this powerless girl and choose one who is in control. But that's a fantasy. Besides . . . what about my surname ? My father's name ? Could I give that up ? I think about what my father went through himself, Working so much that he lost who he was—even the *memory* of who he was. This is sort of like a voluntary version.

I'm glad, now, that my father is so far gone that he doesn't even know who I am, let alone what had happened to me. His blood price is sparing him from mine. And I have to be thankful for that.

"I understand," I say slowly. "I understand wanting to be someone else."

Sister Robin nods. "Shall we get you cleaned up before Sister Tit comes with your meal ?"

I nod, giving myself over to her care. It's a little easier than I thought it would be, now that I know that she might also understand a painful past, but I still feel ashamed when she sits me up.

She takes my clothes off with gentle care. They haven't been changed since . . . I can't exactly remember. There was no opportunity. I catch a whiff of mould—and something linked to Mill House in Meddwyn—and flinch my head away.

"Did I hurt you ?" she asks quickly.

"No." I swallow, shaking my head. "It's just . . . just memories. Ones I'd rather not have."

"I understand."

"How could you ?" I snap suddenly, the venom in my heart bleeding into my tongue.

She smiles, gets up and retrieves the basin on the table. Shame rises in me, but I don't apologise. I just sit in silence and watch as she brings the bowl over to the bed and begins to sing. She sings as she dips the washcloth into soapy water, and she sings as she washes the grime from my skin.

"*Autumn comes, the summer is past, Winter will come too soon.*

*Stars will shine clearer, skies seem nearer, under the Harvest moon.*"

"That's nice," I mutter.

"It's about the last chance to gather crops before winter sets in, and the melancholy that comes with saying goodbye to summer."

As she sings the second verse and dresses me in a clean nightie, I close my eyes and let myself grieve my summer, which also seems to have passed.

Sister Tit, an elderly nun with drooping jowls that very much remind me of saggy boobs, brings me vegetable soup and bread. Sister Robin takes them from her with a little bow, and brings them over to the bed. She gives Sister Tit the wash basin with the dirty water, closing the door again when the older woman leaves.

"It's dehumanizing," I mutter bitterly, when Sister Robin begins to spoon the soup into my mouth. "Being bathed like that in this bed. It was humiliating enough when Len did it and she was my—"

I glance away, scowling. Sister Robin spoons another mouthful of leak and potato slop into my mouth.

"Don't you people believe in salt ?" I grumble around the bland mess.

"I can get you some," Sister Robin says, making to stand.

"Don't bother." I pause. "It's fucking humiliating to be cared for by other people when I'm so young. It's humiliating to be a burden. I wasn't always this way," I add, needing her to understand. "I used to be like you. Normal."

"What's 'normal', anyway ?" she says.

I consider her, wondering how much to tell her. Len said that this sisterhood was formed to heal women injured by magical means. Surely then, she knows of and has seen far more than I could shock her with. It would be nice to talk about it with someone who wasn't there. Still . . . it feels like exposing my innards.

"I had to use a powerful Conjure to save us from a very bad situation, and the blood price was this. I lost my body." The way my father lost his mind.

Morbidly, I wonder which is worse. I decide my situation is, because at least dad doesn't know he's lost anything. Or maybe, I think perversely, he's actually in there, locked behind a stranger's eyes. Screaming for anyone—for me—to see.

Sister Robin frowns. "I've never heard of a blood price before."

"It's something I grew up with. My dad taught me about it. Every time we Conjure, something has to be sacrificed. For him, it was pieces of himself—his memory. For me, I had to tell the truth. If I lied, then I'd have to and give up blood to compensate. I should have known then that a Conjure big enough would cost more than my blood could pay for." I pause. "Maybe my losing movement is to do with my blood."

"Why should you have to pay a blood price? I've seen plenty of women Conjure without that."

I learned the very reason at Mill House.

"It was my ancestor, Hermione Smith. She Conjured over herself and her son that no one born of her line could Conjure without repercussions. I think she hoped the magic would fade from her line and she'd be keeping us safe. All she did was hurt us."

"People do things you could never believe them capable of when they think they're protecting the ones they love."

I nod. "True. I broke myself to save Len and Pole. I was ready to die for them, but this . . ."

"People also do amazing things every day in order to keep living. So will you."

I remember munching on rat and snake on the mountain and know she's right. I wonder what she's seen to make her so sure, but don't ask.

"And Len?" Sister Robin asks. "Why did she leave you with us?"

A surge of bitterness washes over me. "Because I'm a burden and nothing more."

Intellectually I know Len left me here so she can move faster to get me the help she thinks I need. But emotionally, I find myself hating her just a little.

*She abandoned you so easily*, a voice purrs. *It pained her not.*

"You will never be a burden here," Sister Robin says firmly. "We're a family. No-one is left behind."

# LEN

2019

## *Chapter 29*
## Some Kind of Hybrid

E SPEND A COLD and irritable night in an alley down the road where I can still see the blood-smeared lintel. Poulton mutters something about me being insane and then huddles into himself. I return his jacket.

"You need it more than I do," he says bitterly, his teeth chattering.

"I really don't."

"Um, yeah you do. You look like a final girl."

"A what?"

"You look like you escaped a slaughter house."

"No one's going to see me in this alley. Take it."

He curls his lip. "You got dried blood in it."

'Take it or freeze to death. We've got nine hours at least until the coffee shop next door opens."

He pulls another of his faces, but takes the jacket and slides it on, gagging every two seconds like he just ate a pigeon.

"Can't we just wait in a hotel ?" he moans.

"And how will we know if Roan appears ? This was your idea, genius."

"Well, *I* could wait in a hotel."

"Be my guest. But if Roan shows up and you're in a hotel, I'm leaving you there."

He grumbles something about me being high maintenance.

"You're the one who needs a hotel," I mutter through gritted teeth. "I didn't even want to do this."

"No, you just want to *kill* people."

"I don't want to. But I have to get Roan's attention and I know this will work."

"How ?"

I turn back to the lintel and mutter, "Because it did before."

"What happened after she came back for you ? Did you stay with her for long ? Did she teach you to clean up your messes ?"

"Yes," I say grimly.

Poulton gets as comfortable as he can and looks at me expectantly. "Well ?"

I sigh sharply. Might as well carry on. It's going to be a long and useless night. "I was so haunted, so grief-stricken . . . and so bloodthirsty. I followed where she led. I fed on people with abandon. Roan was good at finding monstrous people. There never seemed to be a short supply."

I cast my mind back to that terrible, uncomfortable place. I can still smell the smog in the air, feel the grime on my skin, the coppery tang of warm blood fast-cooling in my throat, the way it clotted quicker than I wanted. The pure ecstasy of perfect satiation.

"The most efficient way to get rid of a body was using a fire Conjure. She taught me the words and the symbols. I was surprisingly detached from the whole thing. Sometimes there wasn't time to destroy a body after a feed and they were discovered. I didn't care. All I wanted was the next kill. I was a mindless creature." I swallow, hating this. Hating my life and my choices. "I think we were both running from something. We didn't talk. Not about anything important. Whenever she'd try I'd leave. Once, she tried to say something comforting to me on the roof of a building. It was a full moon. The city looked almost beautiful. I jumped off the edge, shattering my body on the cobbles below. She had to come looking for me days later."

"Sounds like you got your crazy streak from her," Poulton mutters bitterly.

"You wanted to hear all this."

"I don't *want* to, freakshow. I *have* to. Though, I will admit jumping off the edge of buildings sounds cool."

"Hm."

"Anyway, if you're so good with fire, why don't you make one so I don't freeze to death?"

"You have a corpse handy?"

"Yeah. Mine, soon." He blows into his hands. "Why did you stay with her if she made you miserable. And if you didn't ask her for the answers you'd spent so long wanting?"

"I don't know," I mutter. "Misery loves company. And I did get answers out of her. I discovered what I am."

"Which is ?"

"She made a deal with the devil while she was pregnant with me to escape the mountain in Meddwyn. She found a way out just like we did. Hers came at a cost too. She didn't know I existed. So I couldn't blame her for that."

"What difference does it make if she was pregnant ?"

"The deal . . . I don't know. It transformed her somehow. It's why she craves blood. And I was inside her, so I suppose something happened to me as well. But I'm different because I can survive on human food. Like some kind of hybrid."

"But not her ? She's fully . . . vampy ?"

"I suppose so."

"What about the deal itself ? What did she offer ?"

"I didn't ask. Her soul ? Maybe that's what makes you change."

"You didn't think that was important information ?"

"You have no idea," I snap. "No idea the kind of pain I was dealing with."

"Yeah," he mutters. "The kind that makes logic fly out the window, apparently."

"Poulton, you don't want to do my head in right now."

"Amulet," he says, holding up the cross and my tooth in it.

"Puny human," I say, baring my teeth.

"Least I have my soul."

"She didn't trade my soul."

"That you know of."

I look him up and down and then laugh. "Okay, point to you. Know-it-all."

He grins. "I might not be a hundred and yonks bloody old, but I have a perfectly developed frontal lobe."

I raise my eyebrows at him.

"Logic center," he says, tapping his head. "Amongst other things."

"Not one for humility, are you ?"

He scoffs. "So why did you eventually leave Roan ? You must have done, or we wouldn't be here."

"We hunted together for a long time. And then one day something changed."

"What ?"

"I hurt an innocent."

# RAPLEN

# 1898

## *Chapter 30*
## The Soother of Gravesend

APLEN HAS LONG SINCE stopped reading the papers. She does not know the date or the time. Life is merely a series of nights, a series of kills, an endless parade of blood and death. Nancy has all but faded from her mind.

It is to be a kill like any other. The code of killing those who preyed on others has begun to wane over the years, and tonight their sights are on a man simply because he is cleaning chimney stacks after dark.

He is thin, but robust and fit with long, lean muscles and thick, raised veins on his arms. He is grimy and unkempt, but his blood sings sweetly in the air. Raplen has never had a chimneysweep, and now that she has seen him, she must taste him. Her desire becomes a sharp focus and cannot be denied. With no reason to argue, Roan does not.

"Good evening," he says when he's extricated himself from the chimney. His eyes are a shocking blue in the soot-smeared face. He is quite obviously perplexed to find a lady on a rooftop at this hour, but he removes his hat and gives a proper salute none-the-less.

Raplen sees the precise moment he realizes he's in danger—a flicker of recognition as she approaches. What is it, she wonders dully, that gives her away ? Her eyes ? Her teeth ? Her tongue, as it darts out to lick her lips ? Clearly panicked, he glances behind her and to the right, and she should realize something is wrong. But she is thirsty—it grows and grows with each kill—and it is insatiable. She has already ripped his throat messily from his neck, a satisfying rending of man to meat, when she hears the tiny, "Oh !" and a yelp of fright followed by a dull thud from the street below.

It is enough to make her pause.

Roan tries to stop her. "Don't look," she says, laying a gentle hand on her shoulder.

But Raplen has to look. Has to see.

A little girl lies on the cobbles beside a coal hole carelessly left open.

"We must leave," Roan says gently, tugging on Raplen's arm.

They should have gone then. Left the bodies for others to find.

But the girl moves.

And Raplen hears her tiny heart thunder in a broken chest. Smells the young blood spilling onto the street. Cannot ignore the feeble little cry.

"I have to help her," Raplen says, breathless, and launches herself from the roof. She lands two feet from the girl's head and hurries over.

Even though the child lies broken and dying, her breaths an exhalation of tiny bloodied particles, she tries to move away from Raplen, terrified by the creature that took her—what ?—brother ? Father ? Friend ?

"I'm sorry," Raplen moans, her heart thumping with something she has not allowed it to feel for a long time. "I'm so sorry."

Roan lands beside her and takes her arm. "Break her neck."

"No."

"Do it fast, and let us leave this place before others arrive."

Raplen yanks her arm away. "I said no ! I have to save her."

"She's dead," Roan growls, teeth bared. "Be on with it and let's go."

"Please," Raplen says, turning to look her mother in the eyes for the first time in years. Her voice breaks on the word. "*Please*."

Roan growls and shoves Raplen out of the way, reaching for the child with clawed hands.

Raplen pulls Roan back by the hair and crouches over the child, protecting her like a feral lion defending a cub.

Roan makes to go around her, but Raplen shoves her away with a desperate cry.

"Mother, *please* !"

Roan pauses, teeth still bared in shock. "What did you say ?"

"Mother, *please*. Please, help me save her."

Roan blinks and stands straight, her fight gone. She looks down at the child gasping for breath and back at her daughter—so fearsome, so empty. "She's dying, love," she says gently. More gently than she thought she remembered how to be. "She'll be dead soon."

"I can't let that happen. I can't be responsible for this child's death too."

Roan turns away, clenching her fists. "Every one of her bones is broken, no doubt. Saving her would be . . . a waste."

"If you can save her, do it. Do it for me. I have never asked anything of you."

Roan growls low in her throat, pacing the road. "I can't do it alone. We need a Soother . A powerful one."

"And you know one."

"She won't survive the journey."

"Maybe she will. I think she's strong. We have to try."

Roan closes her eyes, no doubt weighing the recklessness of the options ahead.

"We'll need some kind of stretcher to tie her to. Wait with her while I look. If she dies . . . let me know."

Raplen nods. "Thank you."

Roan grimaces and leaves them alone to their mutual misery.

"I think I can make you feel better," Raplen whispers at the child, who is still staring at her with wide, terrified eyes, even as she chokes on her own blood. "Or at least . . . keep the death angel away."

It has been a long time since Raplen raised the spirit of Tombstone, but she remembers the feeling, which rises as naturally as walking. She finds words on the tip of her tongue, words very like the simple few Roan taught her when burning corpses, always with the warning of their fickle and dangerous nature. They are words she feels she has always known.

The death rope hangs in the air, and Raplen grasps it.

The girl groans as though in great discomfort, but Raplen continues, banishing death from the girl, which had been lingering like shadows over her chest. It withdraws like a wraith from sunlight, and Raplen breathes easier knowing she has staved off the inevitable—for a time at least.

When Roan returns, she has two wooden pallets and the torn remnants of most of her skirts in her hands. She pauses some feet away, dropping the wood and stepping back.

"No . . ." she breathes, and Raplen can sense something changing in the night. Something terrible is curling in the air.

"What is it ?"

"Let your Conjure go," Roan says stiffly, still backing away, and Raplen notices that her fingers are beginning to curl like claws.

"I can't ! She'll die."

Roan closes her eyes, breathing heavily, and growls, "Raplen, stop."

"I won't !"

The air is becoming claustrophobic now, thick and clogged with . . . something. A something without borders or definition. It is like a weighty shadow crawling closer. Raplen senses she is in danger and the hairs on her arms stand on end.

"Mother ?" she whispers.

Roan is shaking now, the tips of her fingers growing black. "No," she growls. "No !"

Raplen watches, holding fast to the death rope, as Roan begins to shake and convulse, battling a seemingly invisible foe—a foe that is within herself. Somehow Raplen can smell the Conjure in her midnight friend, a sulphuric brimstone that singes her nostrils.

It takes a long time.

Eventually, Roan falls to her knees shaking and digs her fingers into the street, nails breaking the cobbles, crying out with a fury that almost has heat. And then the world goes very still, like a held breath.

Roan looks up, and she is drawn, her teeth clenched. "We must hurry. I can't hold it back forever."

Raplen doesn't ask questions. They bind the two pallets into a makeshift stretcher quickly, aware that as every minute ticks by, the child bleeding onto the cobbles might be lost forever, or the power Roan is holding back may waken.

"I hate myself," Raplen murmurs as she gently lifts the girl onto pallets

Roan regards her for a long, silent moment. "Me too," she says at last.

❦

The water witch lives in Gravesend along the Thames. Nestled between the broken boats and fishing ropes sits a tiny tack shop that is easy to overlook. A sign over the door has been etched in Conjure symbols and the warning : price upon entrance.

Roan pushes inside with one hand, the other still holding onto the head of the stretcher, and Raplen follows in with the rear.

"Selene," Roan calls, depositing the girl on the floor and flipping the wooden sign in the window from "open" to "closed".

"If you expect my doors to close to other customers," a sweet voice calls from behind a tapestried curtain, "then you had better be paying for the privilege."

"It's Roan."

"I recognized the scent of your Conjure the moment you walked in."

A young, dark-skinned woman with cunning feline eyes sweeps the curtain aside. She wears an array of skirts over a colorful bodice, black kohl over her eyes and some of her teeth are gold, giving her an otherworldly appearance.

"But I don't recognize yours," she adds, looking Raplen over.

"Save this child," is all Raplen says by way of greeting. "I can pay you."

Selene grins and glances at Roan. "She's like you. But she'll be taken advantage of if you don't tell her not to reveal her desires so easily. The next half-decent Targoth will have her begging for a taste of their kiss and bleeding for it too."

"Will you help us ?" Roan snaps. "Time is short. She's dying."

"Yes. I know."

Selene runs a hand in the air over the girl and glances sharply at Raplen. "Seems you do know a thing or two. But keeping death at bay isn't going to save her."

"So what will ?"

She grins, her gold teeth a mockery. "Sacrifice."

"And your payment ?" Roan asks, her gaze sharp and canny.

"That . . . can be negotiated."

"I'll pay it," Raplen says quickly. "Whatever it is."

"No !" Roan snaps. "I will pay it, Selene. If you refuse I'll snap her neck myself."

Selene considers, running her long-nails over the child's pale skin. "Agreed."

"She isn't to know the price," Roan adds, nodding at Raplen.

Selene steps up to Roan and leans in, inhaling deeply as though taking in the top notes of a particularly delicate perfume.

"Motherhood suits you," she whispers. "So much guilt . . ."

"Enough games," Roan snarls, her teeth growing sharp.

"Fair's fair," Selene says.

"Just hurry up !" Raplen says, glancing between the women, sure that she has missed some vital and horrible meaning.

Whatever the exchange was, she is not to know it.

Roan swallows, and nods. "Get on with it."

"In the back."

They follow Selene through to the room concealed by the tapestry curtain and lay the broken child on a bench to the side of the room.

The ceiling is entirely hidden by an array of hanging herbs that are dizzying. It feels like floating upside down through a heady and sweet meadow. A black rook in a brass cage at the back rustles its feathers and gives a dignified squawk, while dusty jars and bottles containing ingredients that look like sand, sludge, and water sit scattered on shelves that seem to have no discernable order.

The child gives a feeble cry as her broken body settles into its new position.

Selene kneels before her. “First,” she says gently. “Do you want saving, child ? Or would you rather die ?”

The girl glances nervously at Roan, then at Raplen, and back to Selene. “Live,” she whispers.

Selene’s grin is ugly. “Of course you do.”

She strokes the child’s head with something like tenderness, then yanks a few strands of hair from her head. The girl gives a little moan, but does not complain.

“Your turn,” Selene says, smiling at Roan and unfolding her hand, palm up, the strands of hair still hanging from her fingers.

“What do you ask ?”

“Something . . . canine.”

Roan raises her eyebrows and smirks. “So vulgar.”

“Pay up, or leave. And I want the root. No growing back so easily.”

Roan sighs, opens her mouth and rips one of her elongated canines from her gum, root and all. She grunts, eyes crunched closed, and drops it into Selene’s waiting palm, a string of bloody saliva dangling between her mouth and hand.

“Lovely,” Selene says, closing her fist around the tooth with gleeful satisfaction.

“What did you need that for ?” Raplen asks, grimacing.

“Payment.”

“Yeah, but why a tooth ?”

“Don’t you worry your pretty head about it.” She turns, a bounce in her step, opens a small cork-stoppered jar and drops the tooth inside. She keeps hold of the hair.

Roan presses another ripped portion of her skirt to her mouth and mutters, "Get on with it."

"First, I need your little sweet thing to remove her Conjure."

Raplen glanced between the women. "She'll die."

"She'll come pretty close. But until you remove it I can't work my own Conjure and neither can your . . . mother."

"You never said anything about you Conjuring," Raplen says defensively.

Roan removes the material from her mouth. The hole where her tooth used to be is ghastly. "Would it have mattered ?"

Raplen thinks about it. "No."

"Then remove your Conjure so we can get along."

Raplen focuses her energy and withdraws the Conjure, feeling her spirit hiccup and expand outward as though wanting to leave. She unbinds the death rope from the child and watches it dissipate—and death draw close once more.

"Hurry," she mutters, feeling the Conjure marks on her tongue and in her mind fading to smoke.

Selene eats the hair in her hand—choking it down with a sip of a cloudy liquid poured from a vial carefully unstoppered moments before the drinking—before holding her hand out to Roan, eyes closed. Roan glances at Raplen, grimaces, and waves a hand over her arm. The skin splits in a seam from crook to wrist, and blood gushes forth, coating the child and Selene in red. A thundering noise shakes the room and the table begins to vibrate as though protesting the breaking of one of nature's most absolute laws.

Raplen gasps, jumping back, staring from woman to woman. She wants to crawl into the earth and never rise again.

"What is that ?" she yells over the din.

"Blood magic," Roan mutters, lip curled in distaste. Her skin is already re-knitting itself.

Selene begins to growl Conjures beneath her breath, every word more guttural and feral than the last, until she sounds more beast than woman. On the table, the little girl begins to pant, then to moan, then to scream.

"Is it working ?" Raplen asks through gritted teeth.

But Roan is chanting too, the same horrible, wretched words, and the hem of her skirts are smoking. There is a darkness in her eyes and her mouth is full of blood and shadow, and for the first time in Raplen's life she knows what it means that Roan embodies the darkest, most deadly of all the Conjures. Varr : the Breaker. On Roan's lips the world seems to bend and break, the room around them contorts into something not quite right, reality pulsing out of shape.

The girl's body creaks and shatters, her screams rend the air as bones and sinew bend and knit themselves back into place. And as her bones heal, Roan's break.

Selene's words choke on liquid that rises from her throat, brown brackish water coming like a strange tide, waterfalling from her lips, even as she continues to gurgle the Conjures.

Raplen stumbles back until she is pressed against the wall, and it too is damp with water. The room is roaring now, the floor beneath their feet shuddering fit to splinter and Raplen is certain that the child will die and take Selene and Roan with her.

She senses her Conjure rising in response, feels the dead pressing in.

Roan shoves out a hand, fingers splayed. Stop, her panicked gaze says. Do nothing.

And her fingers snap, broken backwards at the joints. Her sclera bleed fully black, her mouth full of rising shadow that pools in the air above her head, and when her spine breaks she looses a scream like Raplen has never heard. A scream that shudders through them all, and a scream that provokes something to scream back.

Roan never said that this was the price.

"Stop it," Raplen whispers desperately, the chaos around her unbearable, and her voice is lost in the din. "Stop !"

The girl's legs crack back into place in the same moment that Roan is lifted off her feet by some force Raplen can't see or understand, the hems of her skirt smoking so much that she's is sure they'll turn to flame at any moment.

Selene gurgles one last series of waterlogged commands, throwing the Conjure out with the last dregs of water, and everything in the room lifts into the air along with Roan in a slow-motion symphony of terror.

The world freezes—

*hung in the air*
*like a moth caught in time,*
*like a held breath,*
*a clock winding down,*
*stillness personified*

—and then f
a
l
l
s,

# *CRASHES . . .*

and is silent.

The shadows clear from the room like water draining towards the sea. The silence is so loud that it seems to buzz with lightening. Roan lies broken in a mess of blood and water, and Selene gasps in blood-curdling lungfuls of air.

"It is done," she says, coughing.

Raplen gapes at her. "What . . . what was that ? The water . . . "

"The Thames . . . "

Raplen glances at her door, which faces the huge river outside. "The Thames ?"

"She lent her power to my Conjure."

"I don't understand."

"Help your mother."

Raplen glances at Roan, and then at the child, who is blinking up at the ceiling in confusion.

"She's not my mother," she mutters, stepping over Roan to check on the child. "Are you alright ?"

The child swallows several times before answering. "Where am I ?"

"You're safe," Raplen reassures her. "Does anything hurt ?"

She sits up and looks around. "No. Who are you ?"

"I'm . . . " She swallows. Takes a breath. "Do you remember what happened ?"

The child shakes her head, her eyes widening. Her voice is trembling. "No. I don't . . . I don't remember anything."

"There is always a price," Selene murmurs, her gaze sharp. "Always."

Raplen swallows. "Well. That's for the best I think."

"Go now. I've done what I was paid for."

"What about her?" Raplen nods at the child. "What do I do with her?"

Selene gets stiffly to her feet and slowly makes her way to the back of the room. "That wasn't part of the bargain."

She opens the back door, steps into dark room beyond, and closes it behind her.

"We can take her with us," Roan says, grunting as she sits up. Her body is still snapping painfully back into place. She looks like she's been trampled by wild horses, but at least her tooth has grown back.

"No. I can't . . . I can't."

Roan watches Raplen for a moment, then nods, wincing as her fingers crack back into their joints. She wiggles them. "Then I know a place."

Raplen nods, pressure leaving her head and shoulders. "That was . . . that was the water from the Thames coming from her mouth . . ."

Roan nods. "Healing isn't natural to the Unclosed. We are creatures of destruction. Even the most gifted Soother needs elemental power to heal. She's a water witch. She draws on the raw power of the Thames for her Working."

"That's why she lives here," Raplen realizes aloud. "She draws on the power of the river for her own ends. Not just for this."

Roan nods once. "We should go. Best not to linger where the natural law has been disturbed. Selene is perfectly capable of dealing with the aftershocks."

Raplen is about to ask questions, but realizes she does not care to know. Instead, she helps the child to her feet and steals one of Selene's blankets to wrap around her shoulders.

The child takes Raplen's hand and smiles up at her with such trust that Raplen wants to be sick.

What has she allowed herself to become ?

❧

"*Here* ?"

They are standing outside of St Catherine's.

"They'll take her in."

Raplen's rage and nausea rise, each at war with the other. She grips the child's hand tighter. "You brought me back to this hell hole to leave her here ?"

"This is the appropriate place for her. She'll be safe and learn to live a new life."

"They'll marry her off," Raplen says, barely able to control her fury. She feels as though she could rip the place from its roots and burn it all down.

"Maybe," Roan says coldly. "But that would be better than living in the gutter, or worse. With us."

"*No.*"

Roan Steps closer to Raplen and whispers, "Smell her. That young, innocent blood ? How long before you kill her again ?"

Raplen clenches her jaw, even as her mouth fills with saliva and her teeth sharpen to points. She tries not to respond to the girl's blood, but she has a strong heart pumping healthy, fragrant blood through delicate, fragile veins.

Raplen shoves the girl harder than she meant, and the child stumbles forward, almost falling.

"Go in there," she snaps. "Find the Abbess, if she still lives, and tell her that Raplen sent you as payment."

The girl hesitates. "Why can't I stay with you ?"

Raplen's tears rise unbidden and her words stick in her throat. Roan leans forward, eyes terrible and inhuman, and hisses, "Because we'll eat you ! Off with you !"

The girl staggers back, her mouth open in shock at the sight of sharp, canine teeth. She turns and flees into the graveyard and to the wooden door, where she bangs and screams until the Abbess, much aged but still harried, opens.

"They'll eat me !" the child shrieks. "They'll kill me !"

Raplen sees the Abbess turn and spot her, a look of horrific comprehension dawning on her face, before Raplen turns, and flees.

Roan catches up with her in Highgate cemetery.

"I'm done with this."

Roan is silent for a moment. "With what ?"

"With this life. With this monstrosity I've become. With you."

Roan swallows. "You can live any way you choose."

"You're right. I was so caught up in this . . . *blood.* In my grief and my rage and my hate . . . and you facilitated that."

Roan lifts a hand to touch her, but Raplen steps away. "We were both lost."

"You're a monster. And I don't want to be like you anymore."

"Raplen . . ."

"No, Monster. It's over. I don't want to see you anymore."

She takes a breath and begins to walk.

Roan does not follow, not until she is almost out of the cemetery gates. Then, suddenly, Roan is at her side.

"If you ever need me, go to St Bartholomew's alley in London. I'll leave you a way to find me. Just in case."

A bitter, almost hysterical laugh bubbles up Raplen's throat. "I wish I'd never been born. The last thing I'll ever do is look for you."

She will be "Raplen" no longer.

# ZOEY

## 2019

## *Chapter 31*
## Filia Diaboli

A shadow sits in the corner of the room. Vaguely human-shaped, with a conical head, it is tall—towering, whilst sitting, almost to the ceiling of my small alcove-room.

"Hello ?" I whisper.

It is right on the edge of my vision, but definitely there. I have no pile of clothes nor sofa to make a midnight shadow person with my imagination. That corner had most definitely been empty when I went to sleep several hours ago. Now, in the midnight witching hours, it sits.

My lungs freeze when an infinitesimal movement shows that it has turned to look at me.

The room grows chilly, frigid.

My breath comes in white gasps of cloud.

"Who are you?"

A groaning, barely there, issues from the black throat, growing louder and louder until it sounds like a death rattle.

I take a deep breath and whisper, "*Go away* . . ."

And it is gone.

Or maybe

had never been there.

# ROAN

# 1898

## *Chapter 32*
## Conversing with the Deep

T IS NO BOTHER to use the last of her money to board a ship. Roan does not care where it makes birth. She does not care into which corner of the world it is heading. She cares not that it is full of sailors who leer at her and cross themselves muttering about the ill-luck she brings, about the captain sailing close to the wind by having her aboard. She is sorely tempted to point out the paradox of believing that Poseidon, god of the sea, would be both pacified by ships bearing a female name and wrathful for carrying her across his dominion. In the end, she abandons *The Bess* with its superstitious sailors and pays for passage aboard a steamship heading for America. The *SS Northern.*

Mostly she stays below deck, keeping to herself, hidden amongst the stores, enveloped by her misery and the creak of the waterlogged wood and steel around her. When she first felt the pull of Raplen's blood on the Conjure-worked lintel of St Catherine's all those years ago, she hesitated. She stood silently in the shadows, felt her daughter's raging grief, and was paralyzed with indecision. When she followed in her bloody footsteps, she hesitated. What had she to offer her daughter, who was so deeply broken, by way of healing ? What could she, a cursed Varr creature, possibly use as a balm for one so wounded ? She watched as Raplen took step after step further into the darkness, and at last knew there was nothing she could offer. So, instead of trying to help or heal her, she would, she decided, simply be *with* her. As long as she was needed and wanted.

And now she is not.

What a pitiful life she has led thus far. Given in infancy to a man who was not her father, imbued with magick so dark she drove her mother to self-destruction, sent into the hands of yet another man—a mad doctor whom, she learned later, was her brother—and then into the clutches of a beast so foul it tainted the earth upon which it stood.

She is still haunted by the Beast. Still plagued by the sounds of those hooves falling on rickety floorboards, the snort of two distended nostrils ; persecuted by the memory of those terrible, towering horns.

*Daughter, mine.*

She forces the infected memories away, refusing to think of the damage she has done to her love, Rapley, whom she is beginning to forget, and her daughter, Raplen, who has spurned her—as she should.

She closes her eyes and buries herself in the bowels of the ship night after night, until one calm, moonlit night, when the seas are still and the ship slumbers and she senses that it is time. Only then, when even the scent of fertile land is a distant memory, does she crawl from her hiding place.

The moon is a full, jaundiced yellow. The water is a silken blackness beneath her, glinting where the propellers churn the ink, but otherwise it is unfathomable. She should be terrified as she teeters on the edge of the ironclad ship, with nothing but the heaving steam engine for company. She should be horror-struck by the tug of the stones in her pocket, gathered near the London docks and carried all the way for this very purpose. She should feel the shock of regret, of despair, of panic as she steps from the safety of the vessel, out into the heart-rending drop—which is further than she imagined—toward the icy waters below, left behind by the hulking vessel and every soul aboard it. She should even feel afraid when the frigid clap of the Atlantic grabs hold of her ankle and pulls her under.

She does not.

What she feels is the inevitability and certainty that this is the best she can do for the world. For Raplen. And the relief of finally shirking her mortal form, of entering into a hopeful oblivion.

Everything is dark. Everything is cold.

As she sinks, falling into the unplumbed depths below, the pressure building building **building** so that she is sure it should kill her, it occurs to her that she should want to fight. Should want to kick for the surface, for the precious, vital oxygen she thought she needed . . . and that she does not.

It is only when her eardrums burst and a furious pain erupts so intense that she screams silently, and when her lungs are hard, compressed rocks in her chest and the feet rise above her, that it occurs to her that she has not needed to breathe. Has not felt the compulsion to gasp for air. The pressure is so great that it forces itself into her mouth and her lungs, replacing any compressed air remaining with the unforgiving weight of seawater. Micro-explosions inside her body ought to have killed her . . . and have not.

All is ice.

All is dark.

All is pressure.

She d

e

s

c

e

n

d

s

into the nothing of the deep, wide Atlantic—hardly having to try as the ocean, suction-like, drags her ever downward, until, brushing something cold and hard, finally hits the ocean floor.

For a long time there is nothing. Only darkness. Only pain. How long she floats there, she doesn't know or care. When she realized she wasn't likely to die by drowning, she hoped that she'd be crushed by the gargantuan pressure. But slowly, very slowly, the pain in her ears and her skull and her lungs begins to subside. There is a maddening itch as her eardrums regrow, delicate membranes and nerves knitting themselves back together. The tiny blood vessels in her eyes likely burst long ago, but even if she could see at this caliginous, hypothermic depth, where no sunlight penetrates—far darker than any moonlit night she has experienced— she'd be blind now.

She is in the void.

She is the void.

Until the void meets her.

It is a long, long, very long time before something changes.

She feels him as a ripple in the water, a slow-moving current. She can sense his immense size, his breadth and depth, many times larger than herself, several times larger even than the ocean-liner she jumped from.

*I'm going to be eaten*, she thinks, and finds it fitting. For all those she herself has consumed, she will now be the sustenance. At least, with one good chew, it will finally be done. She almost laughs.

The thing circles her in a slow, agonizing loop, and she waits.

Why do you linger in the depths ?

His voice is a knell in her head. An ancient, bone-deep vibration. It scatters her thoughts, obliterates them, to make room.

*Who are you?* Even her mind sounds afraid.

I am the thing in the deep. The slumbering one. The guileless.

She remembers another conversation she had with an ancient creature— one with tall, gnarled horns that curled and rose toward the sky—and recoils.

Why do you slumber here ?

Why lie ? She is at the bottom of the Atlantic. There is no one else to hear her confession.

*I am seeking . . . rest. Eternal rest.*

For one such as yourself, that is near impossible.

*Near impossible. So it can be done?*

All things can be done.

*Be on with it, then. Eat. Fill your belly. Chew me up. Do it now.*

The rumble is so deep it feels like anger, until she realizes the thing—this creature of the deep—is laughing at her.

Her anger rises like a water snake, silent, but deadly. Had she the power, she'd strike at its heart.

*I am amusing to you.*

A creature that does not accept what

it is and seeks its own destruction is amusing to me. Long have I haunted the oceans, and long have I been what I am.

*And what is that?* She spits. *Meaningless?*

I am what I am.

*A predator.*

Yes.

*I don't want to be a monster.*

You are what you are.

Oh, but she is tired. *I cannot change what I am. I cannot even cease to be.*

That is not so. Everything dies.

*And you? Will you die as well?*

He circles her, slowly. So slowly. And it is good to have company.

I have yet to meet my like. Yet, I also know that I too, will die.

Frustration bubbles inside her. *How can you know this?*

All things die. Nothing is forever. And if they cannot die . . . they can be unmade.

She wants to believe him, this creature of the deep. She wants to believe that he has some knowledge of the meaning of this . . . futility. But if fire, nor drowning are enough to kill her, if the very weight of the world's oceans cannot crush her—then what will ?

*I'm tired.*

Sleep. I will be here when you wake.

She learns much in the depths.

She learns of the void, of nothingness, of darkness. She learns the language of the sea, of wolf fish, lanternfish, blue hake and anglerfish. Of even the smallest forms of life, and their vitality—proboscis worms, sculpins and isopods. Tiny amphipods—tenacious things—continually attempt to feast on her like little underwater flies and she bats their tickling away until, at last, they learn that she is one of them. She is buffetted on the ocean floor by changeable currents that anger her, and the Deep—the name she has given the ancient creature by her side—encourages her to stop fighting.

Let go of your expectations. Of your resistance. Allow the currents to carry your burdens for a time.

So she does.

She relinquishes control. She relinquishes care. And the water seems warmer now, soothing. Inviting. Comforting. It is a blanket around her, a swaying hammock beneath the world. In this perpetual dark zone, there is some meagre measure of . . . peace.

Hydrothermal vents on the ocean floor provide variety. Large fish, six or seven feet long, become her prey. A white octopus mistakes her for the ocean floor and she delights in the feel of his tentacles searching her skin. Then it is gone in a whisper.

Time loses all meaning.

It passes slowly, and quickly, and slowly . . . and she wonders if she will lose all sanity. She and the Deep travel together and talk together and many secrets are exchanged that cannot be put into words.

There comes a time when Roan has learned three vital things. The first is that she cannot change what she is. The second is that there is a way to destroy herself, if she is determined enough to find it. And the third is that she ought to care . . . but not that much.

He does not say goodbye.

One day, he simply moves away from her, his enormous presence receding into the void as though he had never been—and Roan is once again alone and bereft. The ocean is once again frigid.

She runs her fingers through the soft sand below, and turns her face upward. Almost twelve thousand feet of ocean slumber above her head, before the sky breaks upon the world, and she is ready to meet it.

The ascent is slow and painful, draining her of precious energy. The pressure is so great, and she is so accustomed to it—her body now a low-density organism, that it drags her downward like clawing hands and she must fight to break free.

It takes a long time.

There is pain. So much more pain than when she "fell". Many times, she misjudges her speed, and her fragile lungs—hardened like rocks and entirely unused—explode outward. She feels every rending cell. She sinks again in excruciating agony, regenerates, and must try again more slowly.

She consumes the blood of several small sharks, for she is by far the most dangerous thing in these waters. Even the jellyfish avoid her. There comes a time, after days or weeks or—a meaningless amount of time—that she realises she can still, in fact, see. She suspected as much when, after attaining some unknown and lesser ocean depth, the soft spongy vitreous parts of her eye regrew themselves, tickling as they jellied themselves back into form. Sight came as a subtle shift in the hues of darkness, which gradually turned grey, green, and an astonishing blue.

And then—the world she has known for some immeasurable eternity opens up to reveal a perfect, overcast sky. The air feels strange, sharp and warm. So much warmer than anything she has experienced in a while. It is almost a painful pleasure for the salt-slicked creature she has become. There is no sight of land, only endless ocean, calm and unrevealing, subtle undulations of dizzying movement she is unused to. So, she looks towards the sun, at the watery horizon, and picks a direction.

# ZOEY

## 2019

## *Chapter 33*
## What Would You Give

N THE DREAM, I am walking.

My shoes crunch on a pebbled track that runs between towering larch trees, ancient and magnificent. Their stillness is eerie, limbs so intertwined I can't see the sky.

The path winds through endless forest until it opens, suddenly, onto a field draped in blue morning mists. The air is sharp and sweet, flavoured with the scent of sweetgrass and cowslip.

*Filia . . .*

*Diaboli . . .*

A voice.

A whisper.

Undulating through the mist. Both far off and right by my ear.

*Filia Diaboli.*

I turn, my dress swishing like a cackle, displacing mist and morning dew.

The voice, bouncing off the world like an echo.

*What*

*would*

*you*

*give*

*to*

*feel*

*the*

*earth*

*beneath*

*your*

*feet?*

And suddenly my feet are bare, toes pressed to the cold, moist earth. I laugh. I cackle. I scream.

The sound of hooves *c-clomping*, echoing through the field, and the puff, like a gust of angry air, through ovis nostrils. Mule? Horse? Ram?

What would you give? It asks again, closer.

I shut my eyes and wriggle my toes into worm-infested soil.

"Anything."

❧

Robin feeds me a hard-boiled egg, gently salting it after each bite.

"Toast ?" she asks, holding up a buttered slice. It looks home-made, riddled with seeds.

I shake my head, and she begins to peel the second egg.

"Did you sleep well ?"

"Sort of. I think."

"How do you mean ?"

My nose it itching, driving me mad. "Strange dreams," I mutter.

"I used to get the strangest dreams," Robin says, salting the now-peeled egg. "Then I realised I must have been sleeping well, since I dreamed at all."

"I suppose so."

Robin offers me the egg and I take another bite, but my nose is too distracting to think about anything else.

"Could you . . ." I flush with embarrassment, but it's urgent now. "Could you scratch my nose ?"

Robin grins. "Of course !" She scratches my nose, but hits the wrong spot, so I move my head until her nails relieve the hideous histamine needle.

"God, that was driving me mad ! Thanks."

"Don't be afraid to ask for things like that. Maybe I can prop a pillow next to your head at night in such a way that if you have another itch you can get it yourself."

"I'd be grateful."

I eat the rest of the second egg, and then accept the now-cold buttered toast, realising I'm more hungry than I thought.

"So what happened ?" Robin asks when I'm done and she's clearing the plate away. "In your dream ?"

"It was so stupid. I was walking, and all of a sudden I was barefoot, and there were these worms in the earth, and this voice asked me . . ."

"What?"

"Asked me what I'd give to be able to feel the earth under my feet."

Robin smiles sympathetically, her fingers twisting in her black skirts. "I expect it's normal to dream about what we want. I dream about things like that. I mean, not the *same*, but the things I long for."

"At least you can achieve your dreams if you want to," I say, a barb in my voice. "If you dream of becoming the next triathlete champion, you could just practice. If you wanted to swim the English channel, you *could*. I'm dreaming about *walking* for God's sake. It's the first thing babies learn, and I can't do that no matter how much I try. You can still make your own choices."

Robin sighs, gets up and puts the plate on the chair by the door—the chair where I saw the conical-shaped shadow the other night. The chair where I have been seeing some new . . . thing sitting every night since.

"Sometimes we can't do what we want. No matter how hard we try."

It feels like she's talking from experience, but I have a hard time feeling sorry for someone who just got up of their own volition and walked across the room. Someone who can scratch their own itches.

"Pray with me?" she asks tentatively, coming to sit beside my bed again.

I hesitate. "Oh, um . . . I'm not much of a prayer."

"It's an old prayer. Not even in English, if it makes you feel better. I just want to give you a blessing. Let me?"

"Okay . . . "

She murmurs a phrase under her breath, and looks at me expectantly. I repeat the words, they twist in my mouth, foreign and unusual. She murmurs another sentence, a sense of deep reverence on her face. I repeat it, but get it wrong. She says the same line again, and I get it right this time. Another line, another repeat, on and on, until she bows her head with a deep, satisfied breath.

"Are we meant to say 'amen' ?"

"You can if you want to."

"Um . . . amen."

"Do you think that was a load of rubbish ?" Robin asks, leaning closer, elbows on her knees.

*Yes.* "No. No, of course not. Um, thanks. I guess it's something I can do for myself."

"There is something you could do," Robin says after a beat. She's looking at me curiously.

"Yeah ? What's that, then ?"

"There's a place here in the church. A sort of Holy place of healing. I could take you there if you want. See if it helps."

I frown. "What kind of place of healing ? Like a hospital ?"

Robin chuckles. "No. It's a spring. A hot spring. It flows under the church. Has done for a long time, I think. The waters have healing properties."

"Does it work ?" I ask, voice dripping scepticism. "Do the waters heal ?"

"I told you I was in a bad way when I arrived here, didn't I ?"

I nod. "Yes, but you never said . . . how."

She nods in return, looking at the floor. "Scars." She touches a delicate hand to her face. "Bad scars. There was a fire . . ."

I examine her skin closely, wondering if the scars were where she's now touching, on her perfectly smooth cheek, or if it's simply a self-soothing gesture. Do the scars remain, hidden beneath her habit ?

"Did . . ." I hesitate, not wanting to pry but also desperate for more information. "Did it work ?"

She looks up, then, her face bright. "Yes," she breathes. "It was miraculous."

My mind is reeling. Hot spring water healing burn scars ? That seems . . . impossible.

"Would you be interested ?" Robin asks.

"Are you joking ? Of course I would !"

"It's usually reserved for members of the order. Sisters only. But maybe I can speak to Abbess Crane. See if she'll make an exception."

My heart thunders in my chest. Okay, a hot spring is probably the most pseudoscience thing ever. Placebo effect galore. But . . . what if it works ? What if Robin is telling the truth ?

"Please," I say fervently. "Please, Robin, do."

# ROAN

## 1900

### *Chapter 34*
### From the Darkness . . .

HEN HER FEET FEEL the shifting sands of the shore at the same time as her head again breaks the surface, witness to a low sunset, she takes a needless breath and waits. She doesn't know how long it has been, but she knows that she is a different creature to the one who jumped from the decks of the *SS Northern*. She wades onto shore and feels the rags of her once-dress shred and fall from her body, caught like seaweed on the barnacles clinging to her flesh. A sailor stares open-mouthed as she passes, and she stops to regard him.

"Where—" her voice is gravelled as stony coral, terrible as an ocean storm. "Where is this place ?"

He stumbles back from her, falling over a bucket and landing hard on the sand. "*Ar n-Athair a tha air nèamh!* Holy Mother of God—"

His accent is thick and loud in her ears, grating.

She hisses, "*Where am I?*"

His jaw works. "N—Na h-Eileanan Siar!"

"Speak plainly!"

He crosses himself, scrambling backwards. "The Western Isles!"

She shakes her head, trying to shift the saltwater from her ears. "Where?"

"You're on Sgarasta Mhor in Na Hearadh! The Isle of Harris," he adds, when she looks confused. "Lord God in heaven, save me!"

She can still hear the tides. They are calling her home, plaintive cries of *come back . . . come back . . .* "Tell me how to get to London."

He raises a shaking finger and points south. "N-Northton is the nearest village, but you'll have to go east to the Bays and Mànais for the ferryman."

She nods slowly. "Thank you."

When she kills him, a desperate hunger for warm, human blood enveloping her entirely, he can't have looked more surprised. What does he see, she wonders, as the life fades from his eyes?

She hates how good it feels to have his blood running into her body, so different from the cold shark blood and meagre offerings of the creatures of the deep. She had become accustomed to the frigid waters, the endless night of the lower depths, the way her lungs burst and bled, blood bubbling from her nose and ears when she rose too swiftly, the pressure so strong it took all her strength to fight against it. The depths does not relinquish its prizes so easily. How long had she walked the bottomless ? Conversed with the ageless ?

She wriggles her toes into the dark sand, feeling the sun, even as it sets, baking her sensitive monster skin. The burning is almost beyond endurance, but she stands in it, fully present nonetheless. She would, she thinks, kill a thousand men to have this sweet, painful moment again. The days and weeks and months with The Deep have calmed something inside her, solidified it into a resolve made of stone. He was right, after all : She is what she is and cannot help but be. But she can also change it.

She will research ways to kill those of her kind. Then she will find Fostos and do what she failed to do before Raplen was born on that cursed mountain when she lost everything. After that, she'll end her existence once and for all and the world—and Raplen—will be free of her.

And any lives lost in the cause will in time be avenged.

She takes the little money bag from the man's belt, steals his shirt and begins to walk. It takes a while to find the road. It is a long stretch of dirt between endless green plains, but she has walked long distances before. The hardness of the earth beneath her feet takes getting used to. Her flesh, though strong, has been waterlogged for so long that having an unbending plain beneath is dizzying. Why does the earth not yield and sway with the tides in the air ? She feels an inherent wrongness in the solidity of it. The stillness feels like death. The only unchanged thing is the sky. As the sun disappears behind the hills and darkness creeps in, she might still be floating in the Atlantic amongst smacks of jellyfish, staring up and the unfathomable ether.

Plains rise into hills, green bleeds into smudges of purple heather and yellow gorse, and she sees no other human life. Long-wool sheep graze in the distance, avoiding her as they would a wolf, and deer scatter when they sense her presence. She is once again adrift.

It takes several hours before she reaches a town dotted with weather beaten homes. They look abandoned and despondent, greyed and waterlogged by harsh winters.

She keeps walking, though her body screams for more blood. She does not want to take another soul from these people, who seem to have so few to spare. She passes little settlement after little settlement, stopping to ask for the direction to Mànais and the ferryman. The people cower from her, pointing shaking fingers and crossing themselves as she passes. Roan is getting used to being a monstrosity. Some four hours later, when the moon is rising high, she comes to Mànais and barters passage from a sea-beaten man with a stormy face. He eyes her with a canny sharpness when he takes her money, as though he knows exactly where she has been and what manner of unholy deal she has made.

They cross by moonlight. It takes longer than the walk from Sgarasta Mhor, and all the while the sea calls to her. Beckons for her return. She can feel the cavernous abyss beneath the wooden planks like a siren song, Neptune urging her home.

The boat moors in a fishing village called Ardmair, and it is here that Roan learns she was with The Deep for more than two years, and that she is now living in a new century.

The year nineteen hundred has arrived.

❦

At night, Roan haunts the villages, feeding on livestock. She keeps to forests and wetlands, hiding by daylight. Creeping south by moonlight, always making sure to avoid being seen. She is no longer used to humans, if she ever was before. She would rather avoid them at all costs.

But on one moonless night, she is drawn from the shadows by the voice of an old woman telling tales by a fireside. She sounds like the sands shifting at the bottom of a midnight ocean, tiny grains scratching at the heel of the earth.

"Feral as a dog," one woman is saying. Her hair shines silver in the firelight. "My sister's lad saw her with his own eyes, scaling a tree like a panther."

"Probably a squirrel," another women mutters, and the others scoff and laugh.

"Does a squirrel have skin as pale as moonlight ? Hair as long as a matted web and dark as a raven's wing ? Does a squirrel sing the caoineag song ?"

"If you saw the *caoineag*, I'll eat my hat," a third woman says.

"Perhaps it was Beira, Queen of Winter."

Another pipes up. "Or Nicneven, the mother witch !"

The women break into bickers, and Roan sniggers at them from the shadows. It is the most entertaining thing she has seen in many a lonely night.

"I saw her," a small voice wedges itself between the rest, and the women fall silent.

The girl is no more than fourteen, Roan would guess.

"I thought I must be dreaming when first I saw her," the girl says in the same quiet voice. "Pale as moonlight, just as," she says, nodding to the first woman. "And long dark hair. Just as a raven's wing. She was walking among the sheep. I thought it was Beira as well, until I saw her crouch by a sheep and press her face to the shorn wool side, and . . ." The girl swallows. "And drink."

The women fall silent, and Roan's heart skips a beat. She did not know she had been seen. The older woman crosses herself and mutters, "*Baobhan Sith.*"

Roan knows it is time to leave. She has not been careful enough. It is time to move on.

Several villages away, she hears tell of an immortal doctor who claims to know the location of the human soul. What ridiculous things humans tell themselves to sleep better at night. She has put it cleanly out of her mind until, in Edinburgh, she finds a pamphlet pasted to the side of a textile mill that catches her eye and stops her in her tracks.

*Andrew Fost, miracle doctor, claims to have found the location of the human soul! Speaking in Manchester!*

Roan scrutinises the hated face printed on the paper. Fostos is still here, alive, and scheming. Not even bothering to hide. She reads the listed address, then rips the paper from the wall, crumpling it to particles in her hand before continuing on.

She still doesn't know how to kill him, but she can keep him in her sights.

# LEN

## 2019

## *Chapter 35*
## Into the Light

HREE DAYS PASS WITH no sign of Roan. I stare at the stone lintel until the grains in the lime mortar blur together into a mess of nothing. What is it they say about trying the same course of action again and again, expecting a different result ?

"It's time to move on," I tell Poulton on the morning of the fourth day.

He looks up at me blearily. "You sure she would have come by now ?"

"Who knows ? I don't even know if the Abbess was telling the truth when she told me to do this."

"The Abbess ? I thought this was some kind of magic conjure thing."

"Did you hear me conjure anything?"

"No . . ."

"Well then. It's not working. She's not here. We go back to my way."

Poulton looks like he would rather eat slugs.

"Unless you want to keep sleeping in an alley that smells of piss?"

He wrinkles his nose. "Yeah, fine. I'm sold. Can we get some food?"

"I got you a pizza yesterday."

"Exactly. *Yesterday*. And a *medium* pizza. Humans normally eat several times a day, you know.'

Raplen sighs, experated.

'I'm practically hypoglycaemic,' Poulton presses. 'I could really go for a bacon butty and a coffee."

I turn away and look at the lintel one last time, trying but failing to ignore the hollow, raw burn in my throat and the smell of blood in the air as London wakes for another busy morning.

Roan didn't come.

I don't know why I'm surprised. I don't know why I'm disappointed.

"We should check on her," Poulton says, staring at St Catherine's gates. He makes a move towards them but I grab his arm.

"No."

"Geddoff," he snaps, yanking himself free.

"We've gone over this," I warn.

"She's right there," he says, sounding as desperate as I feel.

"I know. But we can't."

We stare at the church for a long moment, and I have to tug his sleeve to pull him away.

"Yeah," he says. "Yeah, all right."

The sooner we get to Roan, the sooner we can get Zoey help. I keep telling myself this with every step that takes me away from her.

"So stupid," he mutters when we're halfway down Victoria Street. He's clutching the sleeping bag I got him from a charity shop to his chest like a teddy bear. It smells of ancient skin cells and mildew and I wish he'd bin it. "This whole thing is idiotic."

"You wanted to try the lintel."

"Not *that*. I mean this whole thing. You haven't seen Roan in, what, a hundred years, and your clever plan is to go around killing people to get her attention ?"

"Pretty much."

"She could be dead for all you know."

For a split second, a flare of anger tints the world red. "She isn't."

"Yeah, how do *you know* ? We could literally be doing all of this and she's a corpse. Which should be listed in the dictionary as *idiotic*."

His voice is a knife in my head ; the bustle of city serpents on their way to their boxy offices is even more agitating. So many human hearts thundering with blood, cortisol, adrenaline. A heady mixture that I'm struggling to ignore like I used to.

"They should add your photo," he mutters. "Look ! There's a Pret ! Let's get a bacon roll, a coffee, *and* a pain au chocolat—"

"Shut it, will you ? Do you ever stop talking ?"

"Yeah, actually. I don't talk to your dead mother."

I turn off abruptly into a quieter side street and then into another alley where the morning rubbish sits sickly sour in leaking bags on the pavement. Poulton hurries after me.

"Oi, hold it !" he yells.

The rush and bubble of all the people, plus my new and very intense desire to divorce Poulton's body from his head, is too much, so I spin and climb the side of the building, heading for the roof.

"Oi !" Poulton yells again. "I can't do that, you know !"

I don't listen. I don't stop. I need to get away.

"Shit," I hear him mutter, when I'm a few roofs over. "What the bloody hell am I supposed to do now ?"

❦

The truth is, Poulton is right. I have no idea if Roan is alive. It just hadn't occurred to me that the reason she hasn't come is because she *can't*. Nausea roils in my stomach like an ocean. It can't be true. Roan can't be dead.

I don't stop to think about it. I shut my eyes and reach into the freezing mists of the After, which always hangs nearby like my own shadow, sweeping my hands through that colourless, frigid air for the death rope. I feel it graze my fingertips and reach for it, gripping tightly. I take a breath, picture her face and whisper, "Roan."

The air hums with vibrations, sending my call into the After, echoing endlessly through the dead land, and ringing back empty.

I open my eyes and exhale a plume of white air, the muscles that were bunched in my shoulders unknitting, cortisol and adrenaline draining away.

Roan isn't in the Dead Lands. She isn't dead.

My relief is a surprise. Why do I care ? Is it because, after everything, her presence in the world is a strange sort of comfort ? To know that there is someone a little like me out there ? Or is it because she is my only hope of saving Zoey ?

I glance at St Catherine's in the distance and feel a pang of yearning.

"I'll save you," I whisper. "No matter what it costs."

I follow Poulton's stale, amulet-protected scent to the Pret-a-Manger down the road and take a seat opposite him.

"Look what the cat dragged in. What are the odds ?" he mutters through a mouth of pastry, a fleck of which flies free and lands on the table between us.

"How did you pay for that ?" I snap. If he drew money from his bank card . . .

"I had some cash leftover from that twenty you gave me ages ago."

I consider him, and nod.

"She's not dead," I inform him.

He pauses chewing, searching my face, then nods. "Right, then."

"Enough games," I say. "It's time to get Roan's attention."

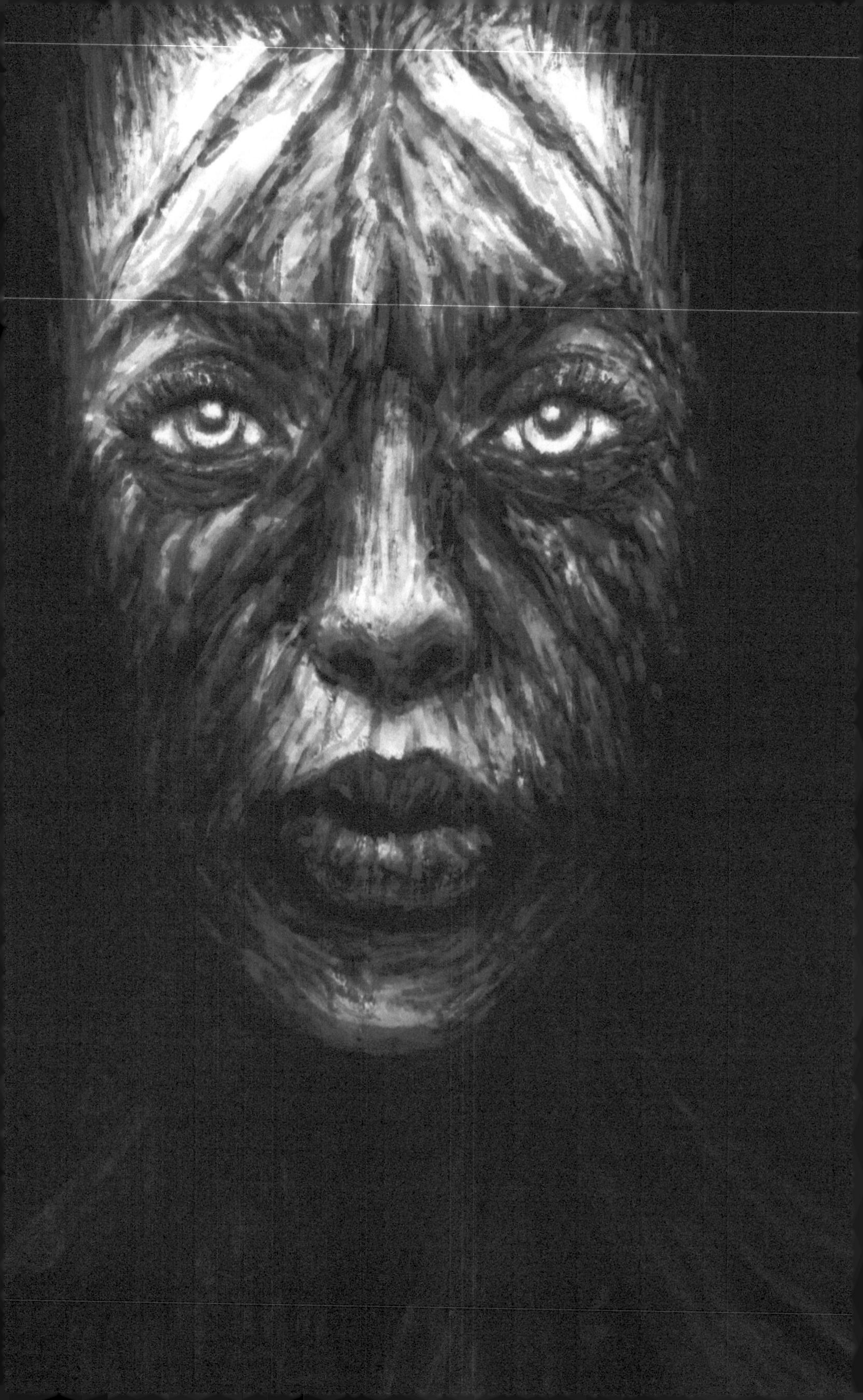

# ZOEY

## 2019

## *Chapter 36*
## A Whisper of Power

HE HOT SPRING SITS below the church. A perfect secret.

The milky water ripples and steams, casting caustic shadows over the cross vaulted ceilings, lending an air of solemnity to the chamber.

"Hardly anyone knows about this," Sister Robin murmurs after she and Sister Pea have lowered me in. "The church was built over the thermae. We don't know exactly when."

The walls are pale limestone with faux pillars and stone ivy chiselled into the brindled surface. Every word spoken echoes around us like butterfly song. I can feel the warm sulphurous water against my face, but my body still feels nothing at all.

If Sister Robin lets me go, I'll drown.

She seems to sense my tension and holds me closer. Her lips by my ear: "I've got you."

I swallow, and she begins to hum, a soft tuneless melody meant to soothe.

"So, you wash here?" I ask, wondering how much filth I'm floating in.

"We are only allowed into the waters once a month each, sometimes less. This isn't for bathing, it's for palliation."

Sister Robin steps further down into the water, her robes billowing around her, until she lies back and floats beside me, one arm under my torso, keeping me up. We drift, head-to-head. Two floating heads.

The thought makes me giggle. I glance at Robin and see that her eyes are closed. I sigh and I float, and I let myself imagine and half believe that this water can fix me.

"It's calming," I murmur. "To lie here and not feel watched or assessed. To sense my weightlessness."

Sister Robin smiles at me, and I notice a tiny sliver of blond hair peeking out from her wet headdress.

"Do you always wear that thing? Even when you sleep?"

She smiles. "Not to sleep. And usually not to bathe in the spring. The sisters can show their hair to one another but . . ."

"Not to outsiders."

"Not to those who haven't been adopted."

"Sounds cultish to me."

She laughs. "I can see why from your perspective. But it's more about trust. A symbol of respect. The day you see my hair will be the day you know you have my trust and my love."

I almost scoff. I don't need or want love and trust. My mind flits to Len and a surge of anger rises. She left me here. She left me alone with a bunch of strangers.

Something slithers across my leg, and I gasp.

"*What* ?" Sister Robin asks, panic in her voice. "Did I hurt you ?"

"My . . . my leg," I choke out. "My leg."

"I was just rubbing your legs to get the circulation flowing."

"I *felt* it," I stammer. But suddenly I'm not so sure. "I think."

We stare at each other for a full five seconds, and then Sister Robin swallows and lets her hand run down my leg, slowly pressing against my skin.

"Do you feel this ?" she asks as her hand runs over my thigh.

I shake my head.

"And this ?" Her hand gliding over my calf.

I shake my head, my eyes filling with tears. I am such a fool.

"And this ?" she whispers, running a fingernail down my shinbone.

So daft. So naive. So utterly, utterly stupid. I shake my head.

"How about this ?" she says, cupping my foot.

And I *feel* it.

Dully.

As though she is touching me through a dense, rubber glove.

But I feel it.

A sob escapes me, and Sister Robin lets me go for a second, shocked. Water floods my nostrils and fills my mouth. She lifts me up and hugs me to her and I cough and choke and sob, until my howls of grief, pain, relief, and a desperate, fragile hope are echoing around us, bouncing off the walls.

Sister Robin holds me.

She never lets go.

❦

Back in my cloister, dressed and dry, Sister Robin tucks me into bed.

"Try it again," I beg her. "Please try it again."

She purses her lips. "We tried . . ."

"Please," I whisper. "Please. Just one more time."

She turns and lifts the covers off my feet. I don't feel it. She begins to touch and massage my feet, then my calves, and then my thighs. And I feel nothing. Nothing at all.

"I don't understand. I felt something in the water, I know I did."

"What were you thinking about when you felt it?"

I try to remember. "I was thinking about Len."

"Your friend who left you here?"

"Yeah." I sound bitter even to my ears.

"So, your love for her?"

I look away. "I was feeling angry."

I expect her to tell me that love and forgiveness and mercy is the path to healing. Instead, she nods.

"Anger can be very purifying. Maybe focus on that and we'll try again next time."

"When?"

"A month."

A searing surge of anger. "I can't wait that long."

*So impatient . . .*

A voice, not my own.

I blink, startled.

"You're impatient," Sister Robin says. "I understand. It is my turn in the spring next week. I'll take you with me, and we'll try again."

"You'd do that for me?"

She smiles. "Of course."

If I could take her hand in my own, I would.

"Thank you, Sister Robin."

"You can just call me Robin," she says. "You're my friend. I'm happy to do whatever I can to help you."

She takes a handkerchief from her pocket and wipes the corner of my eye.

"Focus on what you were feeling before you felt my touch," she says. "Next week, we'll try again."

# ROAN

## 1900

## *Chapter 37*
## The Relic

OSTOS. IN MANCHESTER.

The flyer is old, but the name and the date is clear. Andrew Fost will be in Manchester alongside the apprentice to James Prescott Joules, and J.J. Thompson, speaking about new medical discoveries relating to the brain and the human soul on the fourteenth of the month. Four hundred and fifteen miles to Manchester as the crow flies–and today is the fourth. That's what the man at Ardmair Inn had told her between halting, gasping breaths. Impatient, she had taken his blood into her body and tossed him aside.

She estimates that at a regular walking pace it will take her a week or two. Less if she doesn't stop. So she won't. She has no plan. No way to actually *kill* him. He won't be extinguished by fire, won't be drowned in water–and she can't throw him from a great height. This she knows from experience.

She daydreams about dropping a mountain on his head, watching his skull fracture into a million fragments . . . and then pauses, thinking it over. Alright, so she can't kill him. But maybe trapping him is an option. Keeping him prisoner somewhere for all eternity, away from the world, slowly driving him mad. She grins at the thought. What cage would be strong enough to hold him ? One that could hold *her*. She is her own perfect test subject.

She will keep an eye on Fostos in Manchester as she researches and tests the options for an indestructible prison. How cocky he is, she thinks grimly. Assuming her demise. Otherwise, why use the name Andrew Fost ? Why not hide as he did in Meddwyn ? Unless he means to draw her out. Tempt her into the open.

More likely, he assumes that there are no more of his creations to hunt him. Perhaps he has even made more. In the forty-nine years that have passed since the mill burned, he might have created two more generations of Unclosed children and experimented on them like he did on poor Seamus.

Unbidden, the image of Seamus's rotting ghost rises in her mind's eye. And of Emma, pulled into whatever darkness lay beyond the rips in the world only she could see. Rapley's hand, reaching toward her out of the flames. She still doesn't know what happened to young Jenny. Perhaps she fled to the village. Perhaps she escaped. The less hopeful and more realistic side of her knows that Fostos probably got her too. Drained her blood as he did with Maudley—the brother she didn't know she had. They were all her siblings, of course. She knows that now, in a sick and twisted way. Yet she was always more. Fostos is her father, as he is theirs, but the Beast is her father too . . . on the mountain his horned presence possessed Fostos, writhing together as one in the act of—

She will not think of it.

*Daughter of evil.*

All that is gone now. Except Fostos. And she knows that no matter how long it takes, she will haunt him, follow him, be his shadow, until the moment she knows for certain she can end him—or cage him.

The sailor's shoes were only up to half of the journey. She discards them in Traquair and does the rest of the journey barefoot. It hardly matters. She has learned that she no longer has to fear human injuries. There is freedom in the feel of the stones and sand beneath her feet. She can climb trees during the hottest hours of the day, shielding herself from the worst rays of the unforgiving sun. She knows well that the sun never kills her, but the pain is exquisite. Too much even for her self-destructive personality.

She finds that her toes are strong enough to cling to the sides of the buildings she encounters. She makes a game of it. How high can I climb without my hands ? What can I scale like a spider ? The civility she once possessed has been washed away on salt-licked tides. When you have seen the raw, unforgiving power of the bottomless deep and conversed with its most ancient creatures, there is not much humanity that can endure.

She sleeps rarely, but when she does it is in muddy trenches on the sides of dirt roads, in trees, in hillocks, in caves. She has her fun, picking off a traveller or two, listening gleefully at the terror-stricken cries of their companions as they huddle in their carts and wagons, praying that the fairies do not steal their horses. Her laughter scatters them like cats.

She reaches Manchester city on the twelfth and begins to hunt down updated flyers on Fost's appearance. She wanders Market Street in a daze. She has not seen this many people in one place in a long time. The smell alone is noxious, but the noise is almost past bearing. The black smog that covers much of the city stings her nostrils—she could smell it several miles out—but she appreciates the dim half-daylight it creates.

At last, she comes across a large sign pasted to the side of a brick building. Renowned scientists to speak at Victoria University on the fourteenth. Dr Andrew Fost.

The arrogance. The hubris.

She bares her teeth. The *audacity*. And rips it from the wall and walks away with it.

He comes out of nowhere. A shadow more than a man, black hood drawn high over indistinguishable features, coat flapping as he kicks her in the back and then spins away. She doesn't cry out—has been silent for so long—but releases a ragged breath as she stumbles forward. She turns instinctively, jumping high and back at the same moment to get an eagle-eyed view, and sees that it is a man. Just a man. And at the same time more.

He comes at her again, too fast, his hands flying towards her face, a silver blade skimming the skin of her cheek, cutting peach fuzz. She kicks out, knocking his arm away and hisses, baring her teeth, feeling them subtly elongate into delicate points as they do when she is thirsty.

The man's hood falls back revealing an irritatingly handsome face, dark hair and eyes just as black. He laughs.

"Let's get it over with, shall we ?"

His voice is resonant, like a deep valley draped in winter frost.

"Shall I bear my throat ?" she spits, eyes darting left and right, seeking escape routes.

"That would be helpful."

She swears at him, and dodges left, but he's fast, and she finds him in her path. She changes direction smoothly, but again he follows, his steps matching hers, a strange dance in alleyways.

She grins. "You first."

"Think I'll hang onto my blood a little longer."

"Not your decision."

When he thrusts forward in a sharp, decisive movement, she doesn't dodge the blade. Why should she ?

So when it slides into the flesh of her abdomen she laughs. Then the laughter falters when the blade slips free with a burning slice and her skin doesn't knit itself together. She presses her fingers to a wound hot with blood, feels the clean divide in her skin, and raises shocked eyes to the dark stranger.

He blinks, his expression faltering for a moment, then she's scrambling back, grabbing for a handful of earth and flinging it into his face.

He swears, dropping the blade and scrabbling at his eyes. She scurries away, trying to keep her legs from collapsing beneath her.

By the time her assassin looks up again, she has gone.

❦

The angel of death finds her bleeding out into a sewage-filled gutter in an alley between shop fronts. When she opens her eyes on the grey sky, it is a pair of dark wings that are shielding her from the rain.

*This is it*, she thinks feebly. Joyfully. "I am ready."

# ZOEY

## 2019

### *Chapter 38*
### Phish Food

T IS A CHILLY morning and hardly anyone is about.

I should feel excited about Christmas in the air. I should be walking along Finchley High Street back home, looking for presents, wondering what Mum would like, what Greg might fancy, and knowing that I'm sorted buying Dexter a bunch of chocolate and some Lego. I should be thrilled with the idea of stocking-fillers and tinsel on the tree, of the switching on of the lights, and of the stupid frivolities that most teens get to enjoy. Instead, I'm in a wooden wheelchair older than my grandad, strapped in just in case my body flops out and onto the cobblestones, being pushed along a street I don't recognise by a freaking *nun*.

"I can sense you seething," Robin says, a grin in her voice.

"I'm not seething. I'm . . . stewing."

"In your own amazingness ?"

"In my own rot."

She scoffs and rocks the chair so that I flop about a bit. "Oi !"

A lady pushing a pram glances at us and away as she passes.

"You're on a power trip. Are you sure you should be a nun ?"

"I'm just airing you out," Robin says casually. "If you want to be a bag of rot, I'm not going to deny you that pleasure."

"Cheers for letting me by my authentic self."

Robin chuckles. "The great thing about the sisterhood is that they accept me for who I am. They accept my flaws and my weaknesses. I don't have anything to prove."

"Must be nice."

"Well, don't you feel that way with your friends ?"

I don't answer. The truth is, I used to feel that way. But since the Conjure that put me in this chair, I feel like a burden. And I feel, in a dark and unexamined part of me, that Len and Pole aren't equal to the anger inside me. That they couldn't understand the rage that I feel bubbling under the surface of my grief, like a magma seam about to erupt and destroy everything in my path. And, though I hate myself for feeling it . . . I blame them.

We don't talk for a while. I watch the streets pass by, listening to London waking up. She takes me into a small park surrounded by a high wrought iron fence that passes close to a pond near a copse of overgrown willow trees and positions me beside a bench. She sits down with a sigh.

"I love the morning," she says. "Early, when no one is really awake yet. Feels like I'm stealing time for myself."

"Secret hours," I murmur.

"Yeah, exactly."

"I don't know what I like anymore. Nothing makes sense."

Robin glances at me. "What did you use to like?"

"My camera. I used to carry it with me everywhere." I smile at the memory of the feeling of it in my hands. "I used to say that I couldn't fully understand the world until I'd seen it through the lens of a camera first. Photographs show you what is, not what you wish was."

Robin takes this in, nodding. "Where is your camera?"

"We left it—" A hiccup in my sentence. "Somewhere else." I wonder if the film has degraded in the mouldy air of Mill House. Len had tried to insist we lug it down the mountain, but what was the point? I couldn't—*can't*—use it again. I didn't want those memories, and we were all weak. A small pang of regret tells me that maybe I was wrong to abandon the camera the way Len has abandoned me.

Except she didn't abandon me, I remind myself. Len is searching for a way to help me. Poulton too.

*They left you behind, sweet, useless girl.*

I clench my jaw and shut my eyes against the voice. Not true. Not true.

It laughs as it fades away.

"You said it was a Conjure that made you this way," Robin says after a while, drawing me back out of myself. "Which one was it?"

"Oh, um. It was more than one, actually."

She looks at me, waiting.

"Do you know much about unclosed magic?"

"Probably more than you think. I've seen a few things."

"We were stuck in this cursed place. Locked behind these unending mists . . ." The memory of it I still raw. "There was no way for us to leave, and we couldn't understand why. We ended up finding a huge hidden water wheel that had been spellbound to keep everything there, even ghosts. Anyway, the Conjure was to break the wheel. We broke it and it did nothing, except take away my legs. I still had my arms and my body at that point, though.

"And your friend, Len ? She was there with you ?"

"Yeah."

"Is she . . . Unclosed like you ?"

I glance at her and nod. "She's a necromancer."

"Oh. Oh, wow. That's . . . a powerfully dark ability. It's housed under Sorro, I think. The Sighter Conjure."

"Oh . . . yeah, I suppose."

"I've never seen that kind of magic before though. It's rare."

"She's unique for sure."

"And you're . . . ?"

"A finder."

Robin nods. "Ccugoth, the Conjure. So, you're good with finding secrets." She grins at me, and I feel a little of the heaviness leave my chest.

"Well, I never really learned about this. Len never wanted to talk about it."

"I don't see why not. Keeping things hidden is more about keeping power than anything else. If everything is brought out into the open, it can't be used for control."

I want to argue with her, to defend Len, but my head is all turned around.

"Do you miss it ?" she asks. "The power you had ?"

*Yes.* "I miss being useful."

"You know, some might tell you that we're human *beings*, not human *doings*. Your worth isn't about how much you do."

"That's fucking easy to say when you can do anything you want !" The rebuke flies from my mouth like venom. My heart and head pound with my vitriol.

"That's fair. But it's still true. If I do something or I don't, *I'm* still worth something."

"When can I go back to the spring ?"

"You already took my slot last week," Robin reminds me gently. "You'll have another chance in three weeks when your turn comes around again, and the week after I'll give you my slot again."

"It's not soon enough," I mutter.

Last week we had tried to get the sensation back in my legs again, to no avail. I'm beginning to think I imagined it. I'm beginning to forget what it feels like to . . . to feel.

"What are you really after ?" Robin asks, settling back into the bench like she expects a long answer. Like she's my therapist.

The anger is toxic, rising like poison.

"I want what I lost. My legs. My body. My mobility and my freedom. And I want more. I want my Working without consequence. I want power so that this never happens to me again. I want more."

Robin touches my shoulder . . . and I feel it.

"Sit with the anger," she tells me quietly, her breath warm against my ear. "Sit with what you've lost. Feel your rage."

And I do.

s
e
s
i
It r

It boils.

It bubbles.

It s e e t h e s.

It slithers into my veins like green acid, eating away the parts of me that are human until the only thing left is

hate.

"Let us say a prayer together," she murmurs. "Say what I say."

I close my eyes and repeat her words.

"Relek a vanorok tarrok vol navok."

*Relek a vanorok tarrok vol navok . . .*

Over and over, we say the prayer until it becomes a sort of chant. A lullaby. A mantra. I sit with the words, feeling them roll over my tongue like thick honey, sweet and cloying. Robin, beside me, is an anchor. When she goes quiet, so do I.

Robin leans over and takes my hand.

And when she squeezes it . . .

I<br><br>s<br>q<br>u<br>e<br>e<br>z<br>e<br><br>b<br>a<br>c<br>k<br>.

A knock at my door startles me awake and I feel my stomach plummet when reality distils into the room. I was dreaming I was flying over Mill House, looking down at a mountain destroyed, chewed up by the maw of an unforgiving world. It was exhilarating. I was in total control.

I glance towards the door where Robin's tiny head is poking around the wood.

"You awake ?" she whispers.

I nod, and she comes inside and shuts the door quietly behind her. "Are you up for some clandestine rule-breaking ?"

"The spring ?" I ask hopefully.

I still haven't been able to move on my own again.

Her smile falls a little and I regret asking. Of course it isn't.

"It's almost as good. Maybe better. You game ?"

I hesitate. "I don't know . . ."

"Come on, please ? It'll be fun. The others would love to have you."

"Others ?"

Robin grins. "Want to find out ?"

"Can we do that mantra again ?"

"After, okay ?" She wiggles her head from side to side, enticing, and I laugh.

"Okay, okay, fine."

She does a little dance. "Yay !"

It takes a good ten minutes for her to manoeuvre me into the wooden wheelchair I've come to think of as mine and strap me in place. Without the help of Sister Wren, it's a challenge. At one point I slide clean out of her arms and onto the floor and she has to lock the wheels and hoist me up by my armpits. Robin is smaller than me, but surprisingly strong.

"We do this every few weeks," Robin whispers in my ear as she pushes me down the hall. The wheels sound so loud in the hushed silence of the midnight hall.

"What happens if Abbess Crane catches you ?"

"Well, hasn't happened yet, and I'd prefer to keep it that way, so keep quiet until we get there."

"Where are we going ?"

She's leading me down corridors I haven't seen before. Then again, I haven't seen much outside of my little cave-room.

"You'll see."

We take two more turns and then enter what I can immediately see is the dining hall. Sculpted marble statues of penitent saints reach for an arched, vaulted ceiling, heads bowed in supplication or raised in wonder, whale-eyed and passive. A long table sits in the centre, with one smaller table at the head of the room on a dais, like some kind of sacrificial altar. Congregated around the bottom table sit five nuns. I've seen most of them a few times before, on the rare occasions I am forced from my room, but I don't really know their names with one exception : Sister Wren.

She waves, her plum cheeks flushed with excited colour. "You came !" she says, once Robin has pushed me next to her.

Sister Wren has opened up a lot since I first met her. Compared to the silent, slightly dour woman she was when I first arrived, I'd be tempted to believe she had a giddy twin.

My wheelchair doesn't quite fit under the table, so Wren and Robin lift me into one of the high-backed wooden dining chairs and strap me down like I'm headed for electrocution.

The other sisters watch and say nothing.

"You are hereby sworn to secrecy," Robin says, sitting down next to me.

I glance around, waiting for the punchline. "Secrecy about what ?"

"Every few weeks, we let ourselves have a little treat," Wren says. "And this week, it's—" she reaches for an earthenware cloche in the centre of the table and pulls up the lid, revealing various tubs, frosted over and tempting. "Ice cream !"

"Ssh !" one of the other sisters hisses. "Keep it down, Wren, honest to goodness."

"This is Sister Grebe," Robin says, pointing to a little nun with a mousy face and upturned nose. The girl, no more than nineteen I'm sure, waves and gives me a meek little smile.

"Sister Teal." Robin gestures to a beautiful black woman who seems to be in her early thirties ; she raises her eyebrows at me and dips her chin.

"Sister Jay." Robin points to another young nun who, rather oddly, gives me the metal "rock on" fingers and nods, her tongue poking out between her teeth. I think I catch a glimpse of metal glinting in her tongue.

"Sister Dunnock." Robin nods at the fourth sister who has a closed face with cold grey eyes. She stares at me but says nothing.

"Which do you want first ?" Robin asks.

I eye the chocolate fudge brownie flavour, my whole mouth filling with saliva.

"Fudge brownie it is," Robin says, reaching for it and one of the spoons sitting in a pile. The other sisters sit expectantly until Robin gives them a look. Then they each reach for spoons and a preferred flavour and the awkwardness of my intrusion begins to melt away like the ice on the tubs.

"My favourite is strawberry cheesecake," Robin says, spooning some chocolate brownie ice cream into my mouth.

I'm self-conscious until I realise that no-one is looking at me. All of the women are whispering and eating, swapping tubs and arguing. It's so surreal how real they are . . . like actual friends. I could be at a sleepover right now. The weirdest, most ecclesiastical sleepover ever, granted, but still. It feels almost normal.

"Pass the Phish Food," Sister Grebe says, reaching her arm across the table.

"Ssh !" Sister Teal hisses, gently slapping her hand away. "Not so loud. Besides, you've already had four spoons, you heathen !"

"I want a fifth spoon," Grebe says, smacking Teal's hand away until they're both swatting each other like cats and cracking up.

"Oi, let the rest of us have a go," Wren says, cheeks full of chocolate brownie.

"Abbess Crane is going to flay you alive if she hears us," Robin warns, though she doesn't seem much upset. "Besides, I got two Phish Foods after the debacle last time. Did you bring it, Dun ?"

Sister Dunnock bends under the table and retrieves two new tubs of Phish Food ice cream and puts them on the table triumphantly. "Gluttony is a sin, you know," she says, smirking, and the others roll their eyes.

This is the most unholy bunch of women ever.

Teal grins. "Did I ever tell you two that you're certified geniuses ?"

"No, but now's as good a time as any to start."

"Don't you ever feel like . . ." I hesitate when all the women turn to look at me. "I mean . . . this is a sin, right ?"

They glance at each other and then laugh and I feel my face flame.

"Well, it's not such a stupid question," I snap. "Given you're a bunch of nuns being gluttonous and sneaking around and—"

Robin takes my hand. "We don't deal in shame or guilt."

"That's . . . complete bollocks."

She smiles indulgently at me. "How so ?"

"You're . . . the whole church institution is about feeling guilty and afraid."

"Not us," Dunnock says, scooping a runny spoonful of Caramel Chew Chew into her mouth.

"That's why you wear those head scarf things ? Because you're not ashamed, right ? And that's why you're sneaking out to eat ice cream at midnight, because you *don't* feel guilty, right ?"

Dunnock laughs and glances at Teal.

"The Abbess doesn't like us to consume sugar," Robin says. "She wants us to be clear-headed. That's why we don't have coffee either."

I frown. "Clear-headed for what ?"

"This and that," Wren says, grinning.

"More secrets," I mutter, my face hot.

"It's not that we want to exclude you," Robin says, taking my hand. I wish I could yank it away just to be petty.

"None of you could understand." I turn my face to each of them. I want them to feel my scorn. My eyes burn with tears. "None of you with your health and your youth and your beauty and your bollocks sisterhood."

They all fall silent, watching me. Smiling at me. The venom in my veins could scorch walls.

"Wren came to us blind," Robin informs me after a glance of agreement passes between the women.

Wren puts down her spoon. "I was a broken, angry girl with nowhere to go and no-one to turn to. The sisters took me in and gave me hope. Gave me a home and gave me validation for my rage."

"It took many years for the vision to return," Robin says. "A lot of patience, pain and guidance."

I glance at Wren, at her clear hazel eyes that seem so wide and perfectly healthy.

"All of us have had a fair share of pain," she says gently. "We know what you're suffering."

I open my mouth to argue, but a sound in the hallway makes us all look up. Abbess Crane is standing in the doorway, eyebrows arched and hands behind her back. My heart plummets into my guts. I always bring bad luck.

I don't know if it's just me, but I think I spy a hint of wry amusement in the quirk of the Abbess's mouth.

"Good evening, ladies."

Robin stands and puts her hand on my shoulder. "Abbess. I apologise—"

"It seems more than about time for bed, I think," the Abbess says, interrupting her.

The women gather the tubs of ice cream and the spoons and leave, chairs scraping loudly as they stand. They pass the Abbess with little nods, heads bowed in contrition. Robin begins to unstrap me from the chair.

"Leave her," Abbess Crane says. "I'd like a word."

"Shall I wait?" Robin asks softly, a seam of worry running through her like a stitch.

"That won't be necessary."

Robin hesitates, glances at me, then at the Abbess, and finally leaves. She glances back at me several times, her eyes searching mine for some sign of my preferences. *Should I wait?* They seem to ask. I smile at her and shake my head. I want to see what old Craney has to say to me.

Crane surprises me by sitting down on the seat Robin vacated at my side with a low groan.

"Getting older has its charms," she says. "But not many."

I eye her, waiting for the other shoe to drop.

She closes her eyes and doesn't say anything, and I am deeply weirded out by her relaxed posture—so different from the rigid woman I have known these last few weeks.

"They just needed some fun," I say at last.

The Abbess opens an eye to peer at me. "Oh, yes. I know."

"You know?"

Crane chuckles. "There is not much that happens under this roof that I don't know. One of the perks of being a leader. One of the downsides is that no-one asks you to the party."

My stomach drops at her words and a rising sense of pity makes me want to squirm. Why is she sharing this with me?

*Because you don't belong.*

The voice again, telling me truths I don't want to hear.

"You could invite yourself," I tell her. It's more than I can do.

Even though I don't say the last part, it feels like she heard it. She looks at me with her rheumy blue eyes for a long time, analysing.

"There will be choices for you, Zoey. Choices that determine the rest of your life. All of the women here have faced similar choices. Life is full of them. You still have agency. You still have control of your destiny."

Rage flares in me again. I hardly had a choice about being left here, did I?

Something of my thought process must register on my face, because she smiles and says, "Destiny steps in once in a while to deal a few cards of her own."

"Destiny can bugger right off," I mutter.

Crane laughs, surprising me. "Indeed. I have felt that way many times myself." She sighs. "But as I get older, I learn to flow with the river instead of fighting against it."

"Even if it's going to drown you ?"

"Even then. We must all of us die. In the end."

I turn away, wanting to rid myself of her calm old face. I don't accept that this is who I am going to be forever. Robin has shown me that there is a possibility of cure . . . of reclaiming my life. I fully plan to take that opportunity with both hands.

A repeated motif in the carving on the columns across the room catch my attention. Long winding shapes that surround the pillars.

"Why are there carvings of snakes in your church ?" I ask. "Aren't they the originator of sin ? Tempting eve and all that ?"

Crane looks at me with a peculiarly sharp expression. "Well spotted, Zoey. Yes. Snakes have long been blamed for the original sin just as much as Eve. Lilith, the first wife of Adam, banished into the wasteland ; Eve, second wife of Adam, blamed for all sin and punished for eternity. All women along with her, yes ? And the narrative that tells us this ? A book no more than three thousand years old. In all the hundreds of thousands of years we have inhabited this rock, three of them tell us that women should be ashamed."

She pauses, looking at me with an expression like amusement. A glint or a twinkle in her eye tells she isn't upset, but she's breathing harder.

"And what if," she says conversationally, "God were a woman ? Would the narrative we're told change ?"

"Probably. But, who cares ?"

"If God were a woman, and this Woman-God created man, and then used the rib of man to create woman, would that woman be a tool ? An add-on ? Or would she be sacred ? And if God were a woman, would first sin be a sin—or would it be the first enlightenment ?"

I pause. "Enlightenment, I suppose. It depends on who's telling the story."

"Ah," Abbess Crane breathes, holding up her finger and grinning. "Precisely. The same is true for everything. What narrative have *you* constructed about the women in this convent, I wonder ? Pious. Subservient. Trapped ? Nuns, I heard you call us on your very first evening. Did any one of us ever tell you that was our name ?"

A flush of humiliation washes over me "I don't . . . no, I don't think so."

She folds her hands in her lap, waiting.

"But . . . but you *are* nuns. I mean, look at you ! You live in a church, in a convent, you wear those black habits, you don't show your hair, you pray and you have rituals and . . . just all of it. If the shoe fits . . ."

Abbess Crane smiles indulgently at me. "You are not simple-minded."

I look back at the snakes in the stone, remembering the horror of eating them in Mill House. Wondering, even now, if it would have been better if I'd died up there.

"Time for bed," Abbess Crane says, getting to her feet with a groan.

I sit silently as she unbuckles me from the chair and lifts me, with surprising strength, into my wheelchair. When she's wheeled me to my room, put me into bed, covered me up, and headed for the door, I call her.

"Abbess ?"

She turns to me, brows raised in question.
"Are you . . . Unclosed?"
There's the twinkle in her eye again. "Child. We all are."

# Part 4

## Beneath the Ocean

*"I dread the events of the future, not in themselves, but in their results."*

—EDGAR ALAN POE, *THE FALL OF THE HOUSE OF USHER*

# ROAN

## 1900

## *Chapter 39*
## THE LIBRARIAN

OAN WAKES IN A small room littered with books.

She takes a moment to scan her surroundings, looking for danger, then sits up, wincing as her stomach protests, skin tight and sore. She lifts the blanket. Someone has removed her clothing and dressed the wound. She peeks under the bandages and sees that the skin has been sewn together neatly, though it is still bleeding. What is happening? Countless attempts to end her existence and two years at the bottom of the ocean and she is undone by a knife?

A sound just beyond the door, and she's on her feet, backing away. She assumes that whoever saved her doesn't want to kill her, given the sutures, but she won't take any chances. The assassin had come out of nowhere. She has learned her lesson. And she has something to do before she allows herself to die.

The door opens a crack, and then wider. "Ah, you're awake. Excellent."

A tall greying man in a creased shirt and loose, sloppy trousers comes in bearing a bowl of cloudy pink liquid. He sets it down on the table next to the bed and turns to her with a smile.

"It was close, but I think that wound will start to heal with a little help."

She licks her cracked lips. "Help ?"

He nods at the broth. "You'll need this. Believe me. That was a nasty cut."

She looks around, scanning the room for a way out. There are no windows, only endless books in ceiling-high shelves and piled precariously on the floor—plus the door behind him. He looks easy enough to get around, but with the wound . . . She decides to stall.

"Who are you ?"

"My name is Gabel, and you are currently beside Baronial Hall, at Chetham Library. In Manchester," he clarifies after a pause. "I found you in the gutter."

She licks her lips again. "And you . . . you sewed me back together ?"

He nods. "Relics do untold damage to Unclosed bodies."

She starts and raises her hands defensively, a flicker of weak power rising on her tongue. She doesn't have the strength to hold it for long.

"No need for that," he says, chuckling. He swipes the air as though dismissing a ludicrous sentiment and her power dissipates altogether. "I'm no threat to you."

"You know . . . about me."

"You, my dear, stick out like a sore thumb. Practically pulsing. Come now, you really do need to eat."

Roan curls her lip. "What is it ?"

"A concoction of herbs designed to speed up recovery and a little pig's blood. You'll need to continue an ichor diet, for lack of a better word."

Roan is ravenous, so she takes up the bowl and drinks it down as fast as she can, not expecting much. It's not the same as human blood, but it's enough, and her body accepts it.

"Good," Gabel says, nodding. "I was unsure about your willingness to try animal blood after a richer human diet. This is an marvellous start."

"Why are you helping me ?" Roan says, eyeing him over the edge of the bowl.

"We'll get to that in time," he says kindly. "Rest now, and we will talk when you are stronger."

He smiles at her again, and then leaves the room, closing the door behind him. She hears the click of the lock and realises that she is trapped and exhausted, so she might as well rest.

# ZOEY

## 2019

## *Chapter 40*
## Lies for the Good

"OU LIED TO ME."

I am fuming. Raging. Betrayed. This feels like Len dumping me here all over again. Robin sits in the chair beside my bed, her hands folded contritely in her lap.

"I never lied to you."

"You made me believe you came here because of an Unclosed injury—"

"I did."

"—not that you were Unclosed!"

"If I had told you that I was Unclosed, you'd have closed yourself off. Kept your pain hidden. Refused to allow the possibility of healing into yourself."

"Wrong."

Robin smiles. "You're stubborn, Zoey. Magical working did this to you. You weren't about to trust more magical working."

"You don't know that," I snap. "You don't know me. And it wasn't your decision to make."

"The prayer I had you recite that day after breakfast. Those were Conjure chants."

"You should have told me."

"And I think you knew it."

I want to snap at her, to yell that she is a filthy fucking liar and that I want her to leave me alone. Except . . . maybe I did know. Did I ? I can't tell anymore.

"You said it was a prayer. An ancient prayer."

"It was. It was also a Conjure."

"Was . . ." I swallow. "Was I Working when I spoke them ?"

She nods. "Yes."

I squeeze my eyes shut. "Robin, that's . . . that's messed up ! I told you about the blood price ! You knew the risks !"

"Did you pay a price ?"

I sigh, short and sharp. "No, but that's probably because I didn't lie."

"Oh, you did."

"How do you know ?"

"Because I asked you if you believed the prayer helped you, knowing full-well you didn't. And you lied." She takes my hand. "Zoey, I needed you to see, when it finally came down to it, that you have power. You have power over this blood price—you have power to ignore it. To transcend it. You have the power to heal yourself."

# ROAN

## 1900

## *Chapter 41*
## Gabel

ABEL BRINGS HER THE pig-blood broth five times in a twenty-four-hour period. She drinks, rests and reads the books around her. They are all what her father would call cursed books, and she devours them all. *Aurea Catena Homeni*, *Aurora Consurgens*, *Bibliotheca Chemica Curiosa*, *Septimana Philosophica*, and other alchemical treatises. *Almanach de Liège*, the *Codex Coemeterium*, *Daemonologie*, the *Dictionnaire infernal*, laughing through *De Praestigiis Daemonum*. She tears through books postulating the nature of evil, of creatures in her condition, of the Unclosed itself. There is a small pamphlet devoted to each Unclosed Sign—except Varr. Hers.

She allows Gabel to change her bandages every third day, each time checking the sutures and the progress of the healing. Every time she expresses frustration about how long it is taking, he tells her that it is not a normal wound.

"Tell me about the relic," she says.

"When you're stronger," he always replies.

She finds, to her surprise, that she doesn't mind the isolation. Doesn't mind the small room without windows or escape. She finds that she is happy to be confined. She is safe from the world, and the world is safe from her. This is a harbour in a stormy sea, a cage for a lethal animal.

"How old are you?" Roan asks one evening when Gabel hands her the broth. The bowl is different today—larger. Earthenware. Pleasant to hold.

Gabel sits down on the bed and considers her. "That's your first question?"

She sips, buying herself some time. "It's what I have energy for."

"I am older than I look."

"As old as me?"

His eyes twinkle. "And how should I know when you were born?"

"Because you seem to know an awful lot about me."

Gabel folds his hands in his lap and smiles. "About your kind. The books I keep in Baronial Hall all concern creatures like yourself. Unclosed mortals, immortals who have made deals with deities that have no business being bartered with . . . those born to a cursed life."

"I have a place too," Roan admits, thinking of Bartholomew's Alley. Perhaps she too will fill it with books.

"Protect it well."

Roan drinks the rest of the blood-soup and wipes her mouth with the back of her hand. "Fine, then. Tell me who you are, Gabel of Baronial Hall. And tell me why you're helping me—and the cost."

"They call my kind Nephilim in some texts," Gabel says, picking at a thread on his shirt. When Roan shows no sign of understanding, he adds, "The product of a fallen angel and a mortal coupling. I am both and neither."

Roan laughs. "I see."

"You don't believe?" he asks, his brows raised.

"In angels? I don't believe in anything Holy."

"What do your instincts tell you?"

She considers him, and then remembers. "The wings . . . I saw wings over me. They were yours?"

"You have some Sight, then." He nods. "Good."

"Angels are real," Roan marvels to herself, shaking her head. Will wonders never cease?

"You made a deal with the devil. How could you not have known?"

"The devil, yes. But God? Angels?" Roan tries not to sound bitter. "Seemed too much to hope for."

"You are a black pit," he says gently. "A void. A chasm. An abyss. It is in your nature to see only darkness."

"How fortunate for me."

"Yes," he says firmly. "It is."

Rage gnaws at the edges of her mind. "You mock me."

"Quite the opposite." He gets to his feet and searches the bookcase at the bottom of the bed, finger scanning the spines, though most have no titles. At last he pulls free a brown tome of considerable width and opens it, scanning and turning pages until he finds what he is looking for. He hands it over to her. "See, here."

A woodcut on the page shows a female figure, bare-chested and tall beside the words *Astarte : Carnal love, fertility, war*. Roan considers it, not understanding. Gabel flips the page. Another woodcut. This figure is rounder, fuller. *Lilith : Mother of Demons.*

"Keep going," he says, stepping back and leaning against a bookcase.

More deities follow. *Nyx : Goddess of Night*, *Hecate : Goddess of Witchcraft and Necromancy*, *Brigit : Warrior-Maiden*, *Circe : Goddess of Sorcery*, *Kali : Goddess of Death*, *The Morrigan : Goddess of Destruction*, *Baba-Yaga : The Hag Goddess*, *Medb : Goddess of Intoxication*. More follow. *Medea : Priestess of Hecate*, *Enyo : Goddess of War*, *Sekhmet : Warrior Goddess*, *Cliodhna : Banshee Goddess*, *Freya : Goddess of witches*, *Ereshkigal : Dark Goddess*, *The Erinyes : Vengeance Furies.*

Roan closes the book. "Goddesses ?"

"Women," Gabel clarifies. "Real women who lived and breathed and were extraordinarily powerful. Women immortalised in legend. Women fixed with one common Unclosed witchery."

*No.*

Roan doesn't want him to say it. Cannot hear it. Cannot accept it.

"Varr. The Breaker. The Power contained within you."

Roan stares at him, rage boiling in her veins once more. "You said you didn't know anything about me."

"Your power bleeds off you like steam from a crucible. I can smell it. Anyone who knows what to look for will see it. There are some, I would wager, who can hear it." He pauses, scrutinising her. "Did you never question why you were attacked ?"

"I'm tired of thinking," Roan mutters. "I just wanted to not think for a while."

"Survival requires effort."

"I don't care about survival."

"No," Gabel agrees. "I think you don't." He sighs heavily, pushes himself off the bookcase, and sits down on the bed once more. "Tell me about the attack. What did he look like ?"

"Tall. Broad. Cloaked. The cloak had a hood so I didn't see his eyes. Nothing distinguishing—except the brooch. It was brass with an ornate cross on it."

Gabel frowns, gets lithely to his feet and searches the bookcase once more.

"Did it look like this ?" He shows Roan the page where the same cross is etched.

"That's it."

He snaps the book shut. "Crucisvigil."

Roan goes still. "*Crucisvigil?* They persist ?"

"You've encountered them ?"

Her mind slips painfully back to Mill House, to Emma, poor Seamus, to things she hurts to recall. To Cage and the sigil she had seen him use. Roan remembers Cage well, the burly bully who came to Mill House one stormy night in 1851. The man who tortured her, drowned her, tormented her, branded her . . . the man whom, against all odds, Emma had fallen in love with. The man who, it transpired, was blood kin, and who died in the bowels of that Cursed place.

"Yes, I know them. But the sigil I saw was different."

"Show me," Gabel says. He goes to a small desk near the door and rummages inside the top drawer, bringing over a pencil in desperate need of sharpening and handing it to her along with the book.

She glances at him to make sure she isn't misunderstanding his intention for her to draw into the book itself and sees the urgency on his face. She sketches the sign she remembers onto the first page and hands the book back.

"What does it mean ?"

Gabel sighs. "There are schisms within the brotherhood. Factions. Not all believe in the same values they once did. This sign represents one of those factions. This one," he says, pointing to the sigil in the book, the one on the cloaked man's brooch, "is the closest to the original monkhood. Hunters. Holy Men."

Roan tries not to scowl. "Holy Men can be hunters ?"

Gabel gives her a look she isn't sure she's been given before. One that implies she isn't very clever.

"Bishops and Abbots—even Popes—have ridden to war."

"Fair." Cage certainly wasn't meek and Holy when he drowned and tortured her.

"My encounter with Crucisvigil involved only one man," she says. "And it was . . . some time ago. He was hunting Fostos in a place called Mill House. It was in Wales."

"That pledge remains intact. But they've branched out. They now target any and all creatures, including Unclosed witches and magick users."

"He did not exactly approve," Roan says, agreeing.

"That must be why you were targeted."

"But how did they find me ?"

"They have Finders working for them, searching out others."

"Hypocrites," she spits.

"Had you been Conjuring?"

Roan shakes her head. "I don't remember."

"In any event, they won't stop until they eliminate you."

"That makes us exactly even."

Gabel eyes her. "What drives you?" he asks, his voice a gentle river, nudging her towards a truthful answer.

"Vengeance. Fostos took everything from me. I won't lay myself to rest until he's dead and me straight after."

"If you really want to die, stop eating the soup I bring you. That wound will do the job in a few weeks. But if you want vengeance, truly want it, then eat, rest, and heal. I have a lot to teach you, young destroyer."

# ZOEY

## 2019

### *Chapter 42*
### THE TEMPTATION OF ZOEY ROOT

IT WAS ONLY A moment. But it was everything.

Robin held my hand for three seconds before the feeling seeped out like water running through my fingers. I sobbed, begging it to stay. But it was gone.

"We'll try again," Robin says, tucking me back into my bed. "After breakfast I'll read to you for a while."

"I don't want to be read to. I want that feeling back. Tell me how you did it."

"It was all you."

"You won't tell me until I join your cult?" I snap.

Robin laughs. "Cult? You're onto that again?"

"What would you call it?"

"Sisterhood. Family." She smiles at me in that infuriatingly kind way of hers. "Rest a while. I'll be back."

She closes the door behind her, and I grit my teeth to stop myself from screaming. What were the words she spoke? What were they? I try to rip them from my memory, but they too seem to have dissolved.

"Navok . . . relek . . . *shit!*"

I close my eyes, trying to picture the words in my mind. When she said them they felt so familiar, but now they aren't there.

"Relek . . . tarrok . . ."

They won't come. They just won't come.

Sister Chaffinch, a woman in her late twenties but with the air of someone in their eighties, brings me a bowl of oats. She leaves it on the side table and goes to the door. I don't know how she expects me to eat it, but I hardly care.

She turns back. "Sister Robin will be back in a moment. How are you feeling?"

"*Fuck*ing *shite*."

She smiles. "I used to feel like that too. But the sisterhood took all my pain away. I hope that you find the same peace. Enjoy your breakfast. Sister Condor mentioned that you liked cinnamon, so I added some."

She closes the door behind her before I have a chance to thank her. Maybe she doesn't need it. They all know, then. That Robin asked me to stay, to join the sisterhood. I wonder if Abbess Crane instigated it. Somehow the idea of that makes me feel warmer.

When Robin comes back, she won't let me talk about what happened in the park until I've finished the entire bowl. I eat and swallow fast, not tasting much, eager to get to business. Finally, I feel like there is something I can be doing to help myself. Finally, there is a little agency that belongs to me.

"Okay," Robin says, once I've finished. "Ask me what you want to ask."

"I want you to tell me what that prayer was and to write it down for me."

"You are a powerful young woman, Zoey," Robin says gently. "You don't need the spring and you don't need the prayer."

"Please. Just write down the words for me. It'll give me something to focus on."

Robin sighs and goes to fetch paper and pen. She writes the words out phonetically for me, telling me that they appear differently in their native language. She sticks the page on the wall facing the foot of my bed so that I can see it always.

"This is the actual Conjure language, then?"

She nods. "Yes."

I process this. "Len always refused to teach me."

"Nothing will be withheld from you if you join us. Now, try to focus on directing the feelings you have into your body."

I nod. "And later, maybe you can tell me more about the Conjures and how they work. I want to know what I am."

She smiles at me. "I will always tell you what you want to know, and it will always be the truth."

"Okay."

"Do you want to be left alone?"

"Yeah."

"Alright. If you need me, just yell. I'm close by."

I nod, unable to take my eyes away from the paper.

When she closes the door, I begin to say the words to myself, over and over, trying to burn them into my memory.

I will feel again.

I will touch someone again.

I will get out of this bed and walk again.

And more.

I will be powerful again.

I say the words over and over.

I visualise them.

I see the sounds as shapes that flit by in my mind, dancing like butterlflies.

Relek a vanorok tarrok vol navok
Relek a vanorok tarrok vol navok
Relek a vanorok tarrok vol navok
Relek a vanorok tarrok vol navok
Relek a vanorok tarrok vol navok
Relek a vanorok tarrok vol navok
Relek a vanorok tarrok vol navok
Relek a vanorok tarrok vol navok
Relek a vanorok tarrok vol navok

I wriggle my toes and laugh.

# ROAN

## 1900

### *Chapter 43*
### The Penny Horrible

OAN RUNS HER FINGERS lazily over the books. She doesn't know why she's still here, except that it has been a very long time since she's had an injury, and until she knows more about the assassin who came after her—and the relic he used—she might as well accept safety and learn what she can.

There is an odd sort of peace in this room, with these books. The pages are cursed, yes, she can feel the darkness radiating from them like plumes of sulfur, but they are also a mirror of her own accursed nature and she finds comfort in their presence. The wound is a real inconvenience, but her skin is slowly beginning to stitch itself back together, cell by painful cell. What more can she ask for? Her impatience is juvenile. If not for her vengeful mission to kill Fostos and free Rapley, she would have all of eternity.

She needs to distract herself from the monotony of endless days, so she reads. Gabel's private collection is interesting to say the least. She isn't surprised that he keeps these books away from the main collection. She imagines they might infect the others like seeping ink, slowly changing the mundane into the baneful.

There are texts with instructions for summoning and containing demons, huge tomes about the known Unclosed abilities, histories of occult communities, books covering the demimonde and beyond, texts on demonic planes, angel languages, diablerie, gramaryes, principles of advances thaumaturgy, demonologies, angelology's and more. She pulls a book on Angels out and wonders if she'll find any reference to Gabel, still unsure about how honest he's been about himself, but finds nothing .

St Bartholomew's alley holds the only cursed book she owns and the other smaller books from her father's collection—the ones tainted, in her mind, by Amelia Aintree's lifeblood. Perhaps she will have a collection as vast as this one day. Cursed tomes lining the walls of that spit of space in London, a nest of her own.

She pulls another book from the shelf and flips through it at random. The frontispiece reads *MALEFICIUM*. It is a book, like many of the others, on demonolatry, referencing "magical words of power". She sniggers. The author clearly knew nothing of true value. Not a single mention of what those words are. She can read and speak the Conjure like her native tongue, but she doubts this writer could wrap his stubby tongue around even one guttural syllable. She puts the book back with a curled lip.

A small, unassuming book pulls her eye, magnetic, and she removes it from the shelf. It is a handwritten account of Fostos. She checks the pages for an author but finds none. In it is a series of dates tracking Fostos with gaps in time, some that are decades long. The dates continue for pages and end with his time in Meddwyn, but also far, far into the past. This is not the work of a single mortal lifetime. A note scrawled in the margin of a page reads '*the bloodlines are getting weaker*'.

Roan reads it twice and smiles. She remembers Andrew . . . how unassuming he was. How cocky in the end with his admission of being the Fostos, originator of her accursed life. He killed Seamus looking for a way to find the location of the human soul, to barter back his own, so that he might continue his quest to create a strong Unclosed creature. *The bloodlines are getting weaker.* She roars with laughter at how this knowledge would anger him. When, she wonders, will his debt finally be called in ?

"I stopped tracking him some decades ago."

Gabel is standing in the doorway, watching her.

"You wrote this."

He nods. "My focus for many years was Fostos. Crucisvigil needed to know where he was and what he was doing."

Roan narrows her eyes. "You said Crucisvigil has Finders."

"I tracked Fostos for them, that is all. I am Nephilim, as I told you. I am not Unclosed."

"Holy," she says, scoffing. "A Holy angel."

"Hardly. Just as you cannot help what you were born, so I cannot. We are what we are."

*Be what you are.*

The memory of the ancient Deep's booming presence in her mind.

"Here," he says, holding a thin book out to her. "I thought you might find this one of particular interest."

The title, Satan's Mill, makes her catch her breath. "What is this . . ."

"It is an account of a demonic haunting." He pauses. "At a mill house in Wales."

She looks sharply up at him and he smiles.

"I'll leave you to read."

She opens the first page. *Here I transcribe the heinous tale of Pant Tywell, as related to me by Jenny Thomas, the young servant of the great Mill House in the years before her passing from a sickness of the mind.* Roan runs her hand over Jenny's name. So. The girl did escape. She is glad for this at least. Here her pleasure ends. The account of Pant Tywell's "possession" is fractured and absurd, full of ridiculous assertions and farcical errors. The author asserts demonic orgies and the summoning of the twelve princes of Hell for the bidding of a female witch. Roan cannot help but laugh. A note at the back of the book states that the story is to be turned into a penny horrible, and will be sold at a shilling a part.

The priest-author, whether accurately describing Jenny's impression of the events at Mill House, or taking great artistic licence, portrays Dr Maudley as a learned and brave scholar who brought demonically inclined individuals together for study and was an unfortunate victim. A pioneering man. Roan scoffs and rolls her eyes, remembering how pathetic he was in the end. His ultimate fate : a devouring.

Rapley, the "ungrateful heir" is portrayed as a lazy lout, a greedy money-grabber. No better, she supposes, than her own caricature: the wicked, devil-whoring witch seeking demonic amorous conquest.

She lets her fingers run over Rapley's name, closing her eyes. She misses him deeply, like a wound to the soul, like a breath quickly stolen. In her memory, his face shines like a beacon, his scowl turning into a smile, and then to tears.

*You're too powerful. I love you.*

"I love you," she whispers, a secret vow, a plea, a curse.

There is no mention of Seamus, but Emma is portrayed as a thieving vixen, in pursuit of the attentions of Maudley for her own, unknown ends. Even Mrs Goode is mentioned—a tyrannical woman with no warmth who runs poor Jenny ragged for her own amusement. Yes, Roan thinks wryly. All are predators if you view yourself only as prey.

Roan looks up when Gabel knocks at the door. He is holding a bowl of her blood-soup. She is very hungry.

"I had no idea, when I found you in that alley, that you were the one to destroy Mill House. The 'whoring witch'."

He comes to her and offers the bowl in exchange for the book. She hands it over, glad to be rid of it, takes the bowl and drinks.

"What a farce," she mutters in between gulps. "Jenny was there, but that is not what happened."

Gabel sits on her bed. "Tell me."

She gulps blood-soup, watching him, and then she tells him the real story.

"So Rapley wasn't a wealthy brat?"

She laughs. "Well, he was a little grumpy at first, but . . . no. He was like a storm at the summit. He was lightening and rain and flint and moss. He was . . . he was wounded."

"And you loved him."

A beat of uncomfortable silence, and then Gabel chuckles.

"I always took the penny horrible with a pinch of salt."

Roan blinks, unsure if she is pleased or insulted. "You have the penny horrible too ?"

He shakes his head. "It wasn't worth keeping. But I read it. Entertaining, if you like that sort of thing."

"Best not go into the details," Roan mutters. "I'd hate to destroy your library with my temper."

"Life amuses me, even now," Gabel says. "I am always aware of the changing fashions of different eras. What's portrayed in this paper will be gone tomorrow. This will pass, as all things do. Remember the Goddesses I spoke about ? They were just women imbued with Varr. Like you. And history remembers them as Goddesses." He pauses, contemplating her with an ancient sort of benevolence. "This will pass."

She wishes her own father might have bestowed upon her this kind of care and education. How different her life might have been had he not been so afraid.

# ZOEY

2019

## *Chapter 44*
## Delicious

DREAM OF FLYING.

No, that's wrong. Not flying. Floating. Floating over my old house at night, the sky a bespeckled jewel-scape above, the safe, cosy nest of my bed moon-washed below. The scene changes and I am over the ocean now, the waters a glistening black, a crescent moon sharp in the distance. My fingers are tingling with power, and when I tap them against each other, there is a satisfying crackle. I laugh and my joy is thunderous, crashing like waves.

Delicious, a deep and ancient voice says, washing over my skin like a caress.

I glance behind me, expecting wings, but there are none. And instead, I touch my head, where my hair flows wetly like riverweed, and there feel proud, gnarled horns twisting from my skull like two strong tree trunks.

*Delicious . . .*

When I open my eyes, I am floating near the ceiling of my small alcove room, and my fingers are burning. I touch them, tip to tip, and cackle when I feel my skin, the warmth as real and whole as any I've ever known.

I mutter the Conjure under my breath, feel the rage Robin spoke of filling me up.

There is no effort.

There is no consequence.

There is no blood price.

The power *is* delicious, and I want more.

# ROAN

## 1900

## *Chapter 45*
## THE BURNING SIGNPOST

ABEL LOOKS GRAVE WHEN he comes into her room some days later.

"This was left at the gate." He holds up a letter with a very familiar seal in scarlet wax.

She sits up on the bed. "Crucisvigil."

Gabel's eyes are shadowed. "There's no name, but I think we can assume it's for you."

She takes a breath and accepts the letter, then crack sthe seal and begins to read.

"It's for you," she says dryly.

"Read it."

"'Librarian, we assume the creature is with you. Let us meet it and discuss a truce. With a common foe, a temporary alliance seems logical.'" She scoffs, folding it again. "Charming people. I can't see why you left."

Gabel smiles. "Indeed. Compromise is not exactly their forte. They are . . . earnest, for lack of a better word. They take themselves very seriously. No sense of humour," he says, blue eyes twinkling. "Just like you."

She chuckles and he feigns shock, his hand flying to his chest. "I'm going to have to send for the physician !"

She blinks, startled. "Why ?"

"You *laughed.* Clearly you've taken leave of your senses."

She shakes her head, smiling. "A creature-witch joking in the inner sanctum of a Holy Angel. Who would have seen the day ?"

Gabel grins. "Not me."

Her grin fades. "I'm not sure I trust them."

"Nor should you. But a truce might be to your benefit. They have been hunting Fostos for a thousand years and more. He was once of their order. They understand him and they may know how to kill him. You might be able to, shall we say, "borrow" a relic ?"

A flicker of intrigue comes to life in her breast. If only she'd grabbed the assassin's knife when he dropped it. "*Borrow*," she says, her eyes glinting. "Indeed."

Gabel conceals his grin by taking the letter from her and reading it himself. "I will write a reply and leave it where I know they will find it."

Roan leans forward. "Where ?"

"A secret place."

"Tell me," she insists.

"In time. When I know your thirst for vengeance won't send you blindly into their den."

She grits her teeth, but cannot argue that he hasn't come to know her nature during these last few decades.

"Fine. But I will hold you to it, old man."

He does chuckle, then. "When their reply comes, I will tell you immediately."

She nods, agreeing. After a pause, she asks, "Why did you leave ?"

"Factions began to form within the ranks. Political factions. Ideological factions. It did not feel . . . undiluted. It no longer felt holy."

She nods, considering. She has never been much of a "joiner" anyway.

"Rest a while," he says at last, "tedious though you find it. That wound is almost healed. Let us not undo the progress we have made."

She leans back down again, watching Gabel as he heads for the door, head bowed over the letter, the reply he will send already framing his lips. She is close to something, she senses. Progress. A weapon. A relic.

If she can steal one, she will have what she needs to end Fostos once and for all. And after that : herself.

The meeting place is set for midnight the following evening, at Hunt's Bank, near the sixth arch. It is a mere three minute walk and within sight of the Cathedral. Roan wonders if that is where Crucisvigil are based, and where Gabel dropped off his reply. She is burning with curiosity about what he said, but he will not tell her.

"They will make you wait," he tells her, pacing the room. "They like to watch to make sure you truly are alone. Don't be discouraged."

"Well, how long should I wait?" She does not much like the idea of games.

"An hour. No more."

"An hour?" The gall of it.

"They know you have nowhere else to be," he says, grimacing. "This is the most vital piece in the puzzle. Access to a relic is worth an hour. Biting your tongue and working alongside the people who tried to kill you is worth even the possibility that you get that weapon." He pauses. "And I suggest you do get the weapon. At any cost."

She widens her eyes at him, mock innocent. "Are you, Gabel of Chetham Library, of the sacred Baronial Hall, a *Holy Angel*, telling me to steal?"

He grimaces again. "Whatever is necessary to keep you alive."

She blinks. "Oh." She had not expected what she sees in his face. He cares about her. He doesn't want her to die. She feels guilty that she will, eventually, disappoint him.

"The arches," he says again. "Wait an hour."

"Sixth arch," she confirms. "Within sight of the cathedral."

He nods stiffly. "Nothing to do now but wait."

---

Just before midnight on the day of the meet, Gabel straps a brass cross to her neck. She pulls a face, but he insists.

"It's mine. It'll make me feel safer if you have it."

"Is it special?"

"To me, yes."

She allows him to tighten it around her neck, feeling a faint warmth in her chest.

"And this as well," he says, pressing a gold pocket watch into her hand. "To keep the time."

She grips it, running her thumb over the smooth cover.

"Ready ?" he asks, once she has clipped it to her mended dress and slipped it into her pocket.

"Yes," she mutters again.

The whole walk over, Roan is tempted to look over her shoulder. She does not, however, want to give the impression of fear or paranoia, so she strides ahead, back rod-straight, eyes forward, jaw locked. Let them see her at her best. They will never know how close they came to ending her.

The arches stand near River Irwell, and their swampy tang fills her nostrils with the smell of sewage and riverweed. There are no people around, and for that she is thankful. She is now so used to her blood-broth diet that she does not wish to be tempted by a juicy passerby. It is the first time she has left the confines of the hall in . . . how long ? She isn't exactly sure. A while.

A full orange moon leers overhead, obscured by slashes of low-lying cloud ; it makes her uneasy. The jaundiced light gives everything a sickly cast, and she wonders if this is a bad omen.

*Pull yourself together.*

Despite herself, she paces, glancing in every dark nook and cranny, looking for the eyes that are surely on her. She can sense the presence of several people, but when she closes her eyes to listen for heartbeats, she finds none. The cathedral's western tower stands sentinel over the city and she loses herself in the window tracery.

Minutes pass.

More minutes pass.

When the hour is almost up, it becomes abundantly clear they never intended to keep their promise. This has all been a waste of time. But to what end ? To inconvenience her ? That makes no sense. Her hackles rise and she turns all around, looking for danger. Did they mean to get her alone ? Send in their assassin once again ? What did he call himself ? The Cross.

She is alone.

Suddenly she is very on edge, and when she catches the tang of burning in the air, she grows suddenly cold.

Gabel.

She runs faster than she ought, with her wound not fully healed, and feels the edges of her skin tearing. But she does not care. Something is awfully, terribly wrong.

And she fell for it.

The meeting was never about her. It was about getting her out of the way.

How did she not see ? How did she not realize . . .

Chetham Library is a raging inferno by the time she reaches the gate, a crowd of screaming people gathered in a semi-circle at a distance, most in nainsook nightgowns and bed hats. Their hearts pulse with fear and adrenaline.

Roan pushes past them, heading for the gate, and when a man grabs her arm and attempts to tug her back, she screams in his face. He releases her with a startled cry, arms pin-wheeling.

Flashes of memory assault her as she rushes into the flaming building—memories of scorching hair, bubbling skin, singed sinews ; of Rapley dissolving beside her, his hand turning to liquid and ash in her own. She forces them aside and screams Gabel's name, running through rows of blackened books, rolling smoke that chokes her lungs, until she remembers she does not need to breathe.

*Find him*, her mind screams. *Find him*.

He is in Baronial Hall, in the small side chamber she called home these last few months, half collapsed on the small bed where he tenderly fed her blood-broth and soothed her sharp edges with kind humour. The front of his white shirt is drenched in blood, and more is spilling from his mouth.

"No !" she screams, rushing to him, pressing her hands to his chest where she can feel streams of hot blood beating out, turning cold too fast. "Gabel," she chokes, her vision turning pink. "Oh, Gabel."

"Trick," he gurgles, gripping her arm with feeble strength.

"I know," she gasps, her mind reeling—what can she do ? How can she fix this ?

He coughs, more blood spilling from between his lips. A horrible, rattling inhale through liquid. She can hear his lungs full of bubbles.

"How did you heal me ?" she asks desperately. "How did you do it ? I can save you !"

He shakes his head. "They . . . watching. Leave. Leave, now."

She shakes her head, looking around, but the fire is everywhere, the smoke obscuring it all.

"Take . . . book."

He presses the small volume of Fostos sightings into her hand, his blood smearing across the cover and along the edges of the rough paper.

"Gabel," she warns, choking on a sob and a laugh. "You're an angel. You're not allowed to die."

His words are gasps now, his eyes wide and meaningful. There is urgency in them. “Run,” he pants, gurgling. “Hide. Relic. Kill.”

She is sobbing now, her blood on her cheeks and his pulsing through her fingers. He feels so solid, so strong, but he is fading. She desperately wishes she could hang onto him, keep him here with her, prevent the wisps of his life from leaking away. She is losing him.

“Control,” he manages, convulsing, his eyes still locked on her, “anger.” He grimaces, shudders, then\, paler than she has ever seen him, mutters, “Release . . . Varr . . . goddess.”

And then the spark in his eye is gone and the fire is licking at her back.

The roar of the flames consume her scream of pain and fury and grief.

*Run. Hide. Relic. Kill. Control anger. Release Varr goddess.*

His last instructions. A map to stare at, a road to follow. She plants them in her mind like an anchor, a flaming signpost—and begins at step one.

*Run.*

She grips the book, mutters, “I’m sorry,” and does exactly that.

# LEN

## 2019

## *Chapter 46*
## VARR

OULTON AND I HEAD west as the day dies around us, not speaking. There is profound horror in the premeditation of killing. It's a line that can't be uncrossed. And I'm dragging him into it, making him a part of it, an accessory. I am ruining him, and I know it. But I can't allow myself to ponder the human soul and what damage I could be doing to his.

I also can't let myself think about the *who* of the mark. If I do, I'm finished. I can't allow myself to see them as human. To see their minutiae. Their fashion choices, favourite colours and materials, haircuts and cologne. To think about their families, hopes, ambitions, worries.

I can smell their health complains and that is enough. There, a man's dodgy knees, bone necrotising under skin and muscle, cartilage rubbed away over years of misuse. A woman's cancerous breast, a bitter musk under the vanilla oil in her hair. Halitosis. Seborrheic Dermatitis. Pheromones.

I walk faster and Poulton speeds up behind me. I can't smell him, but I can hear the hammering of his heart. Sense the disapproval. A faint tang of fear.

Am I a monster too? Like Roan? Like . . . my mother?

I lose track of the streets as day becomes night. I turn down one lane and along another alley, round and through, twisting along London's underbelly. Slowly the vibe begins to change, and I realise I have been heading into seedier places, instincts drawing me toward them. Men loiter in pub doorways, cat calling as I pass. One of them reaches out for Poulton, and he gives a startled yelp and jumps away.

*Welcome to my world.*

The men in the pub roar with laugher, calling "Alright, pretty boy?"

He hurries to catch up to me and then stays close. I smell young blood on the tall man hopping the fence of a park I don't know the name of, and follow. Poulton falls behind, clambering over more noisily than is ideal.

But I don't care. All my senses are fixed on the tall, hooded man with a child's blood on him. What has he done? Whom has he hurt? He is wrong, all of him. He feels wrong, moves wrong, smells wrong.

A human predator.

My pulse quickens at the sound of his monstrous heart, a thrill of exhilaration as his cortisol and adrenaline sparks when he realises he is being followed. A wild grin spreads over my face when he glances back, sees only me, and relaxes.

That's when I pounce. I am already drinking from his hideous body when something makes me pause. I look up. Poulton is watching from behind a nearby tree, but that's not what's bothering me. I sense something . . . else. An off-kilter skew to what should be stillness.

Someone is here. I stand, looking wildly towards the park gate.

A dark, cloaked shape is heading in my direction.

Roan ?

I step towards her, hope rising in me like a wild flame.

Roan.

Poulton steps out from behind the tree, right in the path of the hooded figure, just as I realise that this is not Roan. It's a man.

And he's carrying a weapon.

"Poulton !" I yell, flinging out my arms. "Down !"

He reacts immediately, ducking and covering his head as the cloaked figure swings a blade across the space Poulton's head occupied only moments before. A bolt of nausea flashes though me, and then anger.

*What the fuck?*

The knife, or sword, or whatever the hell cloak-man is carrying, looks deadly, glinting an eerie silver under the park lamps. It flashes between swishes of shadow.

I run forward and shove our attacker back, but it's like shoving a brick wall. He hits out with his free arm, catching me across the face ; my head whips back with a rending crack, but there's no time for shock. If I had any doubt before, I don't any longer : whoever he is, this man is here to kill me.

I don't recognise him—his stubbled face and dark eyes hold no familiarity. But he's staring at me with such a darkened expression of hate that he must know me. Or *of* me.

"Who are you?" I hiss, but he's coming at me again.

I kick out, connecting with his ribs, and he stumbles back, swiping with the blade once again. It hums through the air, trailing a high-pitched whisper behind it, as if singing. A lethal hum.

I block his blows until he yells, guttural and animalistic, and kicks out with immense force, his entire body leaning back. It gets me square in the stomach and forces me off my feet. I hit a tree several yards away, splintering the wood.

There's no time to realise he is like me, because he is towering over Poulton now, knife raised high for a killing blow. I don't even call for my power: it's just there, the death rope hanging over my head like a lifeline. I grab it and use it like a lasso, throwing it outward. It loops around the attacker in a death knot, and I tug, pulling him back from Poulton, towards myself.

I am going to end this man, whoever he is.

I draw him closer, all the while pulling the death rope tight. I can feel it squeezing him, suffocating him. He gurgles and fights, but there is nothing for him to fight. He swipes out with his arm, but there is nothing to cut.

I laugh maniacally, pulling, pulling, pulling.

*I am going to choke you to death.*

And then, with one last swipe, the knife slices through my clothes and my skin. The pain is such a shock of brilliant cold that I lose my grip on the death rope, and it unravels.

I collapse under the sudden loss of it, unbalanced. The wound throbs, tender—pulsating. I touch my fingers to the gap in my flesh and it comes away bloody. I'm not healing.

The assassin, panting, wipes his mouth with a scratchy rasp, and raises the knife once more. He looms over me like a clock-tower, his ragged breaths chiming down my last moments.

This is it. This is how I die.

"*Raplen!*"

A cry rends the night.

Roan.

My midnight friend is so suddenly here, so suddenly present, that my arms fall to my side. Mother. Monster.

My attacker doesn't turn, just begins to drop his knife, full force, at the top of my skull.

I see why they call Varr the Breaker. Roan yells, "Cross!" as her fingers bleed black, her sclera bleed scarlet, and the world darkens around her in a thrumming void. She is sucking everything into her event horizon—like a black hole. She is breaking everything.

The attacker stops, turns to face her, his face bleeding white.

"Hypocrite!" Roan spits, her breath heavy with fury. "You made your own deal."

They know each other, I realise. This is happening because of her.

"Not all deals are unholy," he says through gritted teeth. "She must die," he adds calmly, as if my mother need only see reason.

"Over my dead body."

Some of the colour returns to his cheeks, and he actually smiles. "That'll be just fine."

The death rope dangles before me, tantalisingly real, and I grab it in the same moment I sense Roan unbuckle

Varr. We both fling our Conjures out at him, a terrible, unspoken symmetry, and he growls, choking under the pressure of it. Roan is right : this man is not mortal. He has made his own deal.

I clutch the death rope and pull, willing it to kill, to eviscerate, to destroy. Varr rises behind Roan, from Roan, a tidal wave, a horrible void, but this time it is not coming for me. It hums colossally ringing in my eardrums until it crescendos over the knife, which the man drops with a cry. It skitters on the floor, like stones on a boom box, and then—explodes into a million tiny fragments of silver sand.

I drop the death rope in surprise.

"NO !" Roan roars, her hand snapping outward as though she could catch the weapon and save it, Varr diminishing.

The man, released, collapses onto his knees, coughing and choking.

Between me and Roan, over the man who tried to kill me, hanging in the air like some kind of hellish tear in the world, a black space hangs. I stare at it, and then at Roan, who is also seeing it, and then at the man choking on the ground, who doesn't seem to notice a portal to outer space over his head.

Something happens, a weird bending, jarring jolt, and suddenly a figure is tumbling out of the nothing of the tear into the world, a bundle of torn rags and bruised flesh. She lands hard on the grass behind the attacker, lying still.

"You're fools !" the attacker growls, spittle flying from his mouth. As he rocks forward on his knees to spit blood, an amulet not unlike the one I made for Poulton swings forward from around his neck. “You don’t know what you’re doing. The sisterhood will destroy everything.”

My insides squirm with warning bells. Something is very wrong.

“What sisterhood,” I ask sharply. “What sisterhood ?”

“The Sisterhood of the Sparrows will bring about the end.”

“Zoey,” Poulton mutters, hurrying over from his hiding place. “She’s in danger ?”

“Whore of the Catasrophe !” the attacker spits, reaching into his cloak faster than should be possible, and throwing something at me.

Poulton yells, and dives between us.

Even in the millisecond it takes to register what is happening, I think : *Poulton, no !*

The small knife imbeds itself in his chest with a sickeningly dull sound. Poulton cries once, a boyish sound, and falls. I catch him before he hits the grass, carrying him gently down.

The attacker spits at me and flees. Roan does not follow.

Poulton gasps, crying out in pain as I press my hands around the blade, trying to stem the flow of blood.

“You’re so stupid,” I choke.

He laughs, then whimpers. “For once we both agree.” He swallows. “Should have taught me to fight. You need to get Zoey.”

“Go,” Roan says, with a glance at the form spat from the rip in the world, which is now nowhere to be seen.

The street is so mundane it feels wrong.

I hesitate.

"Go," Roan says again. "I'll keep them safe."

"Shit," I mutter, taking Poulton's hand and bending as though to kiss his head. "Keep that amulet on," I mutter quickly. Don't fucking die."

I slide out from under him.

And I *run.*

# ZOEY

## 2019

## *Chapter 47*
## INVERSE

"T'S USUALLY THE SAME dream, night after night."

I feel like I'm dreaming right now, lying in bed telling Robin about my nightly journeys. I am languid and sleepy, cosy and warm in a way I haven't been in ages.

"Tell me about it," she says, leaning forward and resting her elbows on my mattress. The stool she is sitting on slides a little on the floor, wailing.

"There's this voice . . . deep, primal. It asks me what I want. If I want to walk, to be free of consequence, to have power . . . I always say yes—the most emphatic yes I've ever given—and then I'm floating. Floating over cities, over mountains, floating over my bed. But now, lately, I have these . . ." I hesitate, knowing how weird it's going to sound, but Robin nods and smiles for me to continue. "I have these . . . horns. They grow right out of my skull, gnarled and ancient like some kind of twisted granite. And I always feel so . . . so omnipotent. Like I'm a god."

"And the voice ?" Robin asks, her eyes shining with something like intrigue. "What does it sound like ? How does it make you feel ?"

"It sounds . . . sort of scary. Like I'm speaking to the darkest part of the Universe. Like a black hole. Something so vast I can't really wrap my head around it."

"Does it frighten you ?"

"A little. But mostly it intrigues me."

Robin's face breaks into a glorious smile. "I was hoping you'd say that. I have something to show you."

She stands and goes to the wall where my wheelchair is waiting, as though some invisible person is sitting in it watching us. I try to ignore the memory of the nights when I could swear there was someone sitting in it, someone female, with huge horns scraping the ceiling, face veiled in shadows. I shake my head, blinking the memory away as Robin parks the chair by the bed and puts on the breaks.

"Now ?" I say. "It's the middle of the night."

She grins, lifting the quilt off me. "The middle of the night is when the best things happen."

"What about the others ? What if the Abbess catches us again ?"

Robin just grins wider, sliding my legs off the bed and hauling my body up, then moving me across into the chair. She tucks the quilt around my legs and then buckles me into place, knees, stomach, chest. This is a routine we have become very good at.

She pauses after buckling the belt at my shoulder, eyes sly as she looks at me. "Can you feel your toes ?" I roll my eyes in annoyance, but she insists. "No, really. Can you ?"

I sigh and turn my attention to my feet, zeroing in on my toes and the toenails on them. "No."

"Think hard," she prompts, taking my hand. "And remember that voice. Remember the questions it asked you."

I sigh, close my eyes and try.

*What would you give . . . ?*

Even as I think "anything", I feel my toes tingle and warm, as though some stopper has released life-giving blood flow back into them. I choke out a gasp, and Robin laughs, giddy.

"Come on," she says, releasing the break and spinning me around. "It's time."

She leads me through the abbey, which is so familiar to me now, down the main cloister, past the small quadrangle, and through to parts of the building I haven't seen. There is a steep staircase, but she passes it, pushing me into a claustrophobic, antediluvian lift, where she pushes a green loading button and shuts a mesh door that screams as it locks.

*Great*, I think sardonically, *I'm heavy goods.*

Robin meets me at the bottom, slightly out of breath, but whether from her descent down the stairs or from excitement, it's hard to tell.

This lower part of the building is much darker, and it smells wet with mildew. I wonder if we are near the spring.

"Is this where you chop me into little pieces and bury me in the walls ?" I ask, laughing nervously.

"Of course," Robin quips back, and I chuckle.

We walk for a long time, the corridor narrowing and twisting, several branching corridors and hallways running off at several points. I am completely lost. I wonder if I care.

"Are we underground right now ?"

"Yep."

"Same level as the spring ?"

"Lower."

"You're joshing me. Are you lot some kind of secret government department ?"

She snorts. "Hardly. Just be patient, will you ?"

The light bends and twists, emanating from wall sconces that look centuries old. It reminds me of one of those quarries where they blasted slate with gunpowder.

Eventually, Robin pauses at a set of wooden doors, one of which has a window.

"Robin catches me looking. "It's a peekeasy."

She raises her eyebrows at me, bites her lip, and then knocks three times.

The peekeasy opens and a dour face peers out. She examines me with suspicion, then sees Robin and her eyes warm.

A bolt slides free, and the door swings inward with a heaviness I didn't expect.

Robin wheels me inside and the shadows bleed away, spilling from shelves and tomes like a veil lifted at a wedding.

I stare in awe.

It is a library. The largest I have seen in real life—tall shelves rising into the vaulted ceiling in every direction. The shelves are crammed with ancient tomes, most bound in leather or vellum, some with latches and other metalwork. There are also scrolls, piled up one on top of the other, some as thick as tree trunks. The sound of my wheels are almost offensive in the reverent silence. The nun that let us in closes the door and bolts it, then sits behind what looks like a confessional booth, the interior screen facing outward. I watch her silhouette, wondering if she is observing me, knowing that she probably is.

"This is the inverse library," Robin tells me. "Everything we know about the Conjure, about the demimonde, about magic—all of it is here."

She wheels me slowly down one aisle and then the next, and I long to reach out and touch the books. To lift them from the shelves and press my nose to the fragrant pages. It is so beautiful.

"I couldn't show you before. I wasn't allowed to until I was prepared to ask you a question. Until I was prepared to hear whatever answer you gave."

We are at the back of the room now, sequestered between two high shelves near a green leather armchair and a writing table. She sits in the chair and faces me, suddenly solemn.

"What is going on?" I ask.

"You know that we are all Unclosed now. Some of us only have the faintest hint of Unclosed magic in us, others have more. But we're like you. We're all like you. We've all been hurt by, maimed by, abandoned, and lost in the Conjure." She takes my limp hands in her own, leaning forward. "I know your pain. I *know* it." She licks her lips and sits back again. Had there been a window, she might have looked out of it. Instead, she gazes at the books wistfully, tension leaving her body. "Your friend. The one who brought you here."

"Len?"

"She lived here once. A long time ago."

I flush, my cheeks burning like a beacon. "You . . . you know that? But . . . but that was more than a hundred years ago."

Robin looks at me unblinking. "I know. We all do. This place was something else before her. It was a Christian church. An abbey. She Conjured here and it infected the land. The poison grew until nothing strictly "holy" could exist for long on it." She says the word holy like it's something to mock. Something dangerous. "It became something more. Something greater. The women who gathered here after the transition were all Unclosed. They had all been ill-used by men, and hadn't understood their own power. Together they formed a kind of family. A kind of coven . . . and they began to reclaim the power they had been told for so long was not theirs. This is what we are."

I hadn't noticed her get so close to me, but she is, her eyes blazing.

"When I arrived I was fourteen. I had been broken in every way a girl can be broken. I didn't want to live anymore. I couldn't see the point. I couldn't see a way to continue. Abbess Crane refused to let me die. She showed me the strength I never knew I had. My own power."

I feel it now, flowing out of her like nectar, warm and sweet. Inviting. Her Conjure smells like burned sugar.

"Stop," I murmur, struggling to resist her. "Stop manipulating me."

The Conjure stops abruptly, jarring me into coldness.

"I would never!" she says urgently, sliding off the chair and dropping to her knees, my hands buried in her own. "I would never manipulate you. This is me being *honest.* This is me being me. Rostar is the Conjure I favour. The Rapture. I can't help what I am." Her eyes are shining, begging me to understand. "Just as you can't help that you favour Ccugoth, or the colour of your skin. It's what we are."

"I wish you had told me sooner."

"I know. But I had to trust you. The Conjure can be a weapon. And I needed to help you first. I needed to see if you were willing to open yourself up to healing."

I remember the delicious movement of my toes. The intoxicating feeling of floating over my bed. That voice in my ear . . . *What would you give?*

I lick my cracked lips. "You worship . . . the Beast from my dreams?"

My head is reeling, trying to take in the magnitude of my feelings. I feel betrayed and misled, but also intrigued. I understand needing to hide who you are until you're safe. Until there is deep trust. In a way I feel honoured to have come with far with her . . . but I still can't shake the idea that I've been manipulated.

"The Beast is genderless, but we worship her as a Goddess. The dark goddess Lilith, reclaiming her power from the men who stole it from her. We don't submit. We don't serve. We are freedom incarnate. We are power." She takes a breath and releases it slowly. "Remember the feeling in your feet, your legs? Remember that moment when you had some control again? When you could direct the course of your own life?"

I feel the prickle of tears and a swell of raged-tinged desire. "Yes."

"You can have it all. It's already yours. You just have to choose it. I was left to rot once too. Left broken and alone.

But I found my true family. I found the Ram. I found the Goddess. I found *me.*"

"You said you had a question."

Robin nods, gets off her knees and sits down in the chair again. "I will accept whatever answer you give me. If it's no, then I will take you wherever you need to go."

I realize with horrible clarity that this is an ultimatum. Join, or be cast out. Power, healing, agency . . . or abandonment. Again.

"Ask it," I tell her.

"Will you join us ? Will you become a Sparrow ?"

I examine her face, her soft honey eyebrows under the dark veil, her smooth pink lips, her brilliant blue eyes like a summer sky. I search my own feelings for the truth, the answer, the way forward.

*What would you give ?*

I take a breath, and I say, "Yes."

# LEN

## 2019

### *Chapter 48*
### The Price

ALREADY KNOW ZOEY ISN'T here before I burst through the doors of St Catherine's abbey. There is a palpable stillness in the air—a rigid emptiness.

"Zoey !" I yell her name, racing along pews to the back of the church, my boots echoing through cloisters as I rush into the dormitories. "*Zoey !*"

I crash through one room after another, doors banging open against stone walls.

"Zoey !"

There is nothing.

No-one.

The abbey is empty. Completely empty.

There are no nuns, no abbess, no Zoey. No lit candles,

nothing. The abbey has been abandoned. Panic rises in my throat, untamed. I run through the entire building again, screaming her name, hoping that someone will jump out and tell me this is a joke, that I didn't leave Zoey here in danger, that I didn't mess up.

When it becomes painfully clear that there's no trail or trace of Zoey, I run back to the others, my heart screaming in my chest.

"She's gone," I pant when I arrive. "She's gone."

Roan has removed the blade from Poulton's chest and is pressing her jacket to the wound. When he hears the news, he jerks forcefully to sit up, but Roan holds him down. I don't like his pallor at all.

"What—" he says, gasping in obvious pain. "What do you mean, *gone*?"

"The church is abandoned." I begin to pace. "It's empty. I messed up."

"Fostos," Roan mutters.

The pile of clothes I can now see is a girl with brilliant ginger hair that curls around her face. She is shivering, twitchy, and agitated, with purple hollows under her eyes. She has Roan's arm in a vice-like grip even as Roan presses down on Poulton's chest. But there is no room in my brain to wonder where she came from or what is going on.

All that matters is Zoey.

"What?" I snap. "What do I do? Maybe there's a Conjure, a Finding spell. They took her. They took Zoey."

I can hear myself babbling.

"Fostos must have found her," Roan says. The twitchy girl lets out a piercing scream, and Roan gathers her into her arms, shushing gently. "Ssh, it's okay, Emma. I've got you."

"Who ?"

Roan looks up at me and shakes her head. "It's a long story."

My blood is boiling. I don't have time for cryptic answers.

Poulton tries to stand again, but gives a cry, blood spurting from his wound, and collapses, even more grey-faced.

"I went to St Bartholomew's alley," I rage at my monster. "I looked for your damn clue !"

Roan looks troubled. "I removed that years ago. When I'd accepted you would never need or want my help. It was a beacon Conjure that would have alerted me to your arrival. It seemed . . . unnecessary. Dangerous to leave a Conjure so long unguarded."

"So, what, you just decided to give up ?"

Roan hesitates. "I watched you leave your Conjured diary behind. You didn't want or need me. I was only causing you pain. I felt the Working in that charm, how you poured your memories into the leather binding, the fragile paper pages. It didn't make sense to leave a Conjure beacon for someone who may not remember the purpose of it. I couldn't do that to you . . . or myself."

"Dying over here," Poulton mutters, looking rather green.

"Bollocks," I mutter, crouching to press my hands to his chest. "Stupid git."

"Can't argue with that," he gasps, lips tinged blue.

"Help me," I yell at Roan, who is staring off towards the road, absently stroking the crazy girl's hair. She is whimpering, her eyes clamped shut, teeth just as tight.

"Nothing to be done," she says, taking her hand off her jacket so Poulton's wound begins to pour once more. "He's dying."

I glare at her, pressing down on the jacket myself.

Poulton hiccups a terrified sob. "Fuck, Len."

"He is *not* dying, and you're going to *help* me or I swear to God, mother !"

History all over again.

She looks at me then, her black eyes search my face, scattering all over like they're seeking . . . what ?

"*Help me*," I implore. "*Please*."

"Call the death rope," she says after too long. "Hold it, and keep the darkness at bay. It will delay the inevitable until we can find a Soother."

"What about the water witch ? She was a Soother—before, with the girl. Is she immortal ?"

Roan's face closes. "Selene ? She's long dead. There will be another. We need a Finder."

"But—"

"What if Zoey's dead," Poulton asks me, some of the horrible breathlessness gone from his voice. "What if the Conjure injury . . ."

I shake my head, cutting him off. "No. *No*."

Roan looks at me sharply. "She's Unclosed ?"

"A Finder."

Roan's lip twists bitterly. "No doubt Fostos has her."

"Who *is* Fostos ?"

"Someone I've been hunting for a very long time. He's been looking for me in return, but the bloodlines have been diluting themselves for decades. If he had a powerful enough Finder, he could find me and others. Continue his work."

"What work ? What does Zoey have to do with this ?"

"It's a long story—"

"How do we get her back ? That's all I care about."

The night suddenly blares with light and sound as several police cars screech to a halt by the park gates.

"We have to go," Roan says sharply, bending down to gather the whimpering girl at her feet into her arms. "Now, Raplen !"

I try to lift Poulton, but another spurt of blood gushes from his chest beneath my hands.

"Can't," he manages. "Can't."

"Leave him," Roan growls, the girl flopped over her shoulder.

"I can't !"

"You have to !"

Poulton clutches my hand weakly. "Go." He coughs more blood. Too much blood. "Zoey. Find. Keep safe."

"You there !" someone yells, and the park gates swing open. Several uniformed police officers run towards us, the blue lights of their patrol cars flashing dizzyingly over the trees. "Stop !"

"Pole—"

"*Go.*"

"Don't die," I murmur. Then I let go, and run.

There is no chance of the police catching us. By the time they have reached Poulton, we are already more than two roads away.

I stop at the corner of an alley that cuts through to the high street running parallel and close my eyes, listening.

"We've got a stab wound to the chest," a woman says. "Airway unobstructed, pulse irregular. Pressure on artery. Gurney ! Prep saline bandages !"

"Stay alive," I whisper fervently, feeling like I have lost everything I had as a price for finally having found Roan.

We end up in yet another alley. A blind one, this time. It is piled high with rubbish and Biffa bins. Roan sits on a pile of bin bags, cradling the twitchy girl to her body. She clings to Roan's neck fiercely, muttering under her breath.

I don't know what to do with myself, so I just pace back and forth, berating myself for buggering this up so badly. Maybe I can still go back for Poulton. I could use the death rope to keep him alive, rip open the ambulance and get us both . . . where ? St Bartholomew's alley ?

And then what ? I don't have the power to heal, and that injury looked . . . it looked bad.

What if the doctor's can't save him ? What if they do and then jail him for Zoey's kidnapping ? How did I let things go so wrong ?

"Shit," I mutter, pacing ever faster. "I've messed up. I've messed up !" I stop, crouching on my haunches, and hold my head. "I've lost them both."

Roan glances down at the girl whose is still cowering in her lap. "I have an idea. You can still call the death rope ? Can you use it to call up a soul ? Like you did that night in St Catherine's graveyard ? With the dog ?"

I blink, startled. "You were there ?"

"Can you do it ? The soul is earthbound."

"I . . . I can try. But, why ?"

"I need answers. I need a specific soul."

"Who is it ?"

Roan swallows, a twitch of discomfort in her cheek. "Your father."

I search her eyes, looking for the trick, the joke, the lie. She has never before told me about the man who made me. In our thirty blood-soaked years together, I never wanted to talk. Each time she tried, I left. And eventually, she stopped. I didn't care about anything except Nancy's loss. Now, however . . .

My *father.* The idea is so alien that I wouldn't even know where to look.

"I don't know how . . . I don't know where . . ."

"It's all right. Call for your father, call to him and see if he comes. See if he can. He did once before."

I glance at her sharply. "He did?"

"It's a—"

"Long story? Yeah, right. But still, I don't know my father."

"Family legacy, it seems," Roan mutters.

"How can I call for someone I don't know?"

"I'll help you. I'll use my Conjure to get a location. You just call out to him." She takes a breath, as though steeling herself. "He is called Rapley."

Rapley.

My father's name is Rapley. I am named for a man I have never met, nor ever even thought of.

I take a breath, stilling my mind, banishing my fears over Zoey and Poulton, allowing the cool mists of the other side to reach me. I open my eyes, and there it hangs eerily before me. I watch as my monster closes her eyes and reaches for her own Conjure, the air once again charged with sulphur and brimstone, my skin vibrating with unseen power, nostrils stinging with the caustic stench of her raw ability.

Roan's fingers bleed black once more, Varr radiating into her like poison. I clench my fist around the death rope, and feel Roan's Conjure guiding my own, nudging it forcefully in the direction it chooses.

All at once I see a murky ghost-image rising. A building. A room. Bookcases. A man. He is facing away, reading notes, the walls around him pinned with diagrams and sigils. He stills, sensing something, and begins to turn, to look over his shoulder at me.

"Call now," Roan says, urgency in her voice.

"Father," I call, desperately willing this to work.

Roan murmurs something that sounds like "father" too, or maybe it's "her father", but just as the man is about to turn and see me, the ghostly portal shutters closed in a cloud of mist, and then a different man is in the air before me, suspended, unearthly. He looks like he is blanketed with dust or cooking flour, hair, skin, and eyelashes unnaturally white.

This man is not alive.

I open my mouth to ask who he is, when Roan breathes, "*Father?*"

# ROAN

2019

## Chapter 49
## Factum Corpus

"aughter." His voice is the barest echo. I stare into the eyes of the man who raised me, who trained me and who caged me. The eyes of the man I thought was my father for most of my mortal life. How can this be happening? My mind is whirling with thoughts and questions.

Where is Rapley?

I reach out a trembling hand, unsure this is real, then stop myself. If this is real, then I'm not going to waste a moment. "I have questions."

He nods.

"Why did you send me to Mill House?" Why lead me into all that suffering? To what end? "Tell me quickly."

"Maudley killed me. Forged the letter you took from my hand, which sent you to Meddwyn."

"The letter, forged ? By Maudley ?"

"To get you to Fostos. I did not send you into the lion's den."

I swallow, processing. Can I believe him ? Why would he lie ? "Then why train me in the Conjure ? Why teach me the Devil's Tongue and hide me away ?"

His form flickers, as though it is taking effort to remain, and I sense Raplen straining to keep hold of the death rope. I do not know how far my father has travelled, or how long Raplen can sustain the connection. I must hurry.

"Training you to be a weapon. I was going to use you, Fostos's own creation, to destroy him. Use you, daughter of the devil, to break the chains."

I'm processing this, unsure precisely what it means. I was a weapon. That is all ? Never a daughter ? Never a student or scholar. Only a weapon. But there is no time for my conflicted emotions.

"How can I destroy him ?" I ask quickly. "How do I kill him ?"

"The bones," he says, but his voice is growing faint.

"What bones ? Quickly !"

"When an Unholy deal is made, the mortal body dies. Fostos died on the mountain when he made his bargain. His bones lie somewhere, bound by Conjure. Destroy the bones and the deal is unmade."

Horror fills me like a sudden leap into the void. "What do you mean ?"

"When the deal is done, the body dies. A new form is created from the earth and the evil done to it, in its place.

The mortal form will rot to bones. Destroy the bones and you destroy the bond."

My mind is reeling. "He made his deal centuries ago! The bones will be ash!"

My father shakes his head, growing ever more insubstantial.

"Hold him!" I growl at my daughter. "Be strong!"

"The bones are whole," he says, voice fading. "Bound by Conjure, protected by the Beast to keep the bargain intact. You cannot destroy a relic. The bones become the relic when the bargain is struck."

I feel sick. If this is true . . . if all of this is actually true . . . then the corpse of my own mortal body rotted into the mountain the night I made my own Unholy bargain. Was it not me who left the cave on the last day? Was I something . . . other? Was the real me, the real Roan, dying mere feet behind me in that cave?

Another terrible thought.

Raplen was inside me then. I hadn't known it, but she was. A collection of cells, rapidly dividing, but the beginnings of her. Did my bargain kill my child, only to have her reborn as this . . . creature?

I look at Raplen, straining against the death rope, teeth bared. She is mine. But she is also dead on Devil's Peak in Wales. She is also nothing.

"Destroy the bones," my father says urgently. "And the deal will be unmade."

"How? How can I destroy what cannot be destroyed?"

"A relic can destroy a relic," he says, and his mouth keeps moving, but I can no longer hear him.

"Father—please, wait—"

But he is gone. He is no longer with us.

I stare at the empty space, as my whole world implodes and reforms with this new knowledge. Can this be true ? Can destroying the bones of Fostos unmake his deal ? Make him mortal once more ? Or kill him outright ? Will it unmake his creations ? And if that's true, will destroying my own mortal bones unmake my own deal ? Unmake this thing that I am ? What of Raplen ? Will it unmake her ?

"You've got some explaining to do," Raplen says, panting. Her fist, gripping seemingly thin air, is beginning to tremble. "Calling Rapley was useless. I need to get Zoey and I need to get Poulton back."

"There are more important things—"

"Help me find Zoey," she yells suddenly. "And get my friend back, or I will walk away from you forever !"

Bastard boy, meddling in things not meant for mortals. I don't want to lose Raplen again, but I will if it means keeping her alive. Then again, I have no way of finding another relic. We destroyed The Cross's relic with our combined magic . . . perhaps that will be enough to rid the world of the bones, but without Len's cooperation, I have nothing.

"Fine," I mutter. "We'll go to Gravesend."

"Why ? You said Selene was dead."

"She is. But her descendants remain. And one of them is a powerful Ccugoth Finder. If he can't locate your friend Zoey, then no-one can."

Raplen nods, determination forming in her eyes, pushing out the fatigue.

I haven't even begun to process what has happened tonight. Fostos almost seeing us when Len called the death rope, my father appearing out of thin air, and Emma—my haughty, brilliant Emma O'Brian—popping out of a tear in the world, arriving from who-knows-where, as though today is 1851 and not 2019. I haven't had a chance to think about what the implications are if my father was telling the truth . . . I am dead. The real me has been dead all along.

Emma's hands are like little vices clamped around my neck, her whole body vibrating with shock or terror or both.

"I've got you," I whisper in her ear, and lead the way out of the alley.

DAUGHTER MINE . . .

In my dream, the ram stands before me, tall, proud. Gnarled horns reach for an fathomless sky.

*What do you want?*

THE TIME HAS COME.

*Leave me alone.*

THE TIME HAS COME TO CALL IN YOUR DEBT.

I am cold with terror, hot with fury, paralysed by inevitability.

*Name it.*

BLOOD OF YOUR BLOOD.

An image of Raplen rises between us.

BONE OF YOUR BONE.

Raplen, dancing with a brunette girl, laughing. Happy. In love.

The voice of the Beast cannot be unheard, the terms cannot be rewritten, the debt cannot be uncalled.

DRAIN THE BLOOD OF YOUR BLOOD
BREAK THE BONE OF YOUR BONE
KILL THE FLESH OF YOUR FLESH
THE DEBT IS SO RECALLED.

# Epilogue

BBESS CRANE AND THE sisters pack everything they own into heavy chests and load them into an three ancient Volkswagen Caravelles. They leave Zoey's wooden wheelchair behind, something she finds herself surprisingly saddened by. She is going to miss the creepy squeak of those wheels. As they pull out into the road, she wishes it a fond farewell.

The van is cold, but Sister Wren and Sister Teal have tucked Zoey in with blankets and pillows, and Robin sits beside her the entire journey. Zoey doesn't know how long they drive for, and she doesn't know where they are going. She doesn't care to ask. She closes her eyes and thinks of Len, wondering if she will even notice Zoey gone.

At some point, Zoey falls asleep. When she wakes, they are in a hidden place, far away from London. The light has gone, seeped from the day into a watery blue. They've parked in a small glade surrounded by dense pine trees that loom darkly overhead. They are fingers pointing to a moonless sky. There are no signs and there are no roads. No footpaths either, as far as Zoey can see. It's as though they've simply been transported there.

Already London is draining from Zoey's bones.

They carry her to the edge of the glade and prop her up against a moss-draped boulder.

"Comfortable ?" Robin asks, kneeling by her side.

Zoey closes her eyes and inhales the scent of pine needles. "Yes."

She is allowing my her destiny to come to her.

She is no longer fighting any battles.

She has surrendered to her fate.

They light an enormous bonfire. It takes a long time, but eventually it rages like a beacon in the full dark. The light drapes the women in seductive, muted lambency, sparks rising into the sky like sigils.

They begin to undress, removing black robes and habits, revealing hair and skin and breasts and somehow becoming more and more themselves as Zoey watches.

Robin is unrobed now, her pale hair glowing under the firelight, silken smooth. It is long and luscious and it suits her. She is pale and vibrant like the moon, smiling at Zoey with something like love, something like devotion. Sister Teal, dark and gleaming like oiled mahogany, approaches Zoey where she sits. She is naked too, as are the rest, Wren, Tit, Swallow, Dunnock, Pea—all of the sisters gathered. Zoey is not ashamed. She is not embarrassed. They are all so beautiful.

"Are you ready?" Sister Teal asks.

Zoey nod. "Yes."

They come to her, each one, offering a sip of wine from a goblet she hadn't seen them prepare, but which she recognises from the church. It puts her in mind of Sunday communion. She drinks and tastes the distinctive copper tang of blood.

Sister Wren takes her wrist with gentleness, searches her eyes and asks, "May I?"

Zoey nods. Somehow she knew there would be blood. Blood has tinged her life since she first knew of the Conjure. Why should it not be necessary now? A blood price, but this time she is getting something back. Everything back, she hopes.

The cut is fast, delivered with a small gold blade, but it wouldn't matter if it were slow, since Zoey cannot feel it. Her blood dribbles into the goblet and the sisters all drink. One by one, imbibing her.

"Bound by blood," Abbess Crane calls into the night. "In Unholy union."

She is naked as the day she was born, grey hair long and ragged, down to her knees. She holds up her arms, a dagger in one hand, goblet in the other.

She closes her eyes and begins to speak. Her words are not human.

The sisters pull the blankets off Zoey, the pillows away, they disrobe and unshod her, until she too is sitting naked upon the ground.

Crane yells a call that Zoey cannot understand and lifts a poker she had not before seen from the fire with her right hand. With her left, she dips her fingers into the ash. The poker does not seem to burn her, though it blazes orange with heat. The sisters begin to whisper like little bees, their words blending into a sea of white noise, ululating and hissing with the fire. Abbess Crane approaches Zoey and, though she knows she can't feel a thing, flinches with fear. Crane kneels, eyes blazing. She radiates power, no longer hiding it from anyone.

"*Grotho ti magalori ?*"

And Zoey understands. *Will you join?*

But there is more in the question.

There's : do you wish to be healed ?

There's : do you yearn for family ?

There's : do you want to belong ?

And there is : do you crave power ?

Zoey meets her hungry gaze. "*Yes.*"

Crane brands Zoey in the centre of her chest ; it lands like an excruciating splash of acid. Her skin hisses and bubbles and she shrieks in agony. When Crane pulls the brand back, some of her skin comes away with it. Zoey screams, and screams, and screams, until her cries turn into laughs. Mad, hysterical, insane laughs. Because she felt it.

She felt it.

She *feels* it.

The sisters erupt into shrieks of their own. They scream with laughter, they howl with wild, terrible delight. Zoey had not noticed until now that all of them bear the same sigil, scarred into their chests, circular and angular all at once. All of them, every single one. Even Abbess Crane.

They surround Zoey, and they cry out.

"Sister Magpie ! Sister Magpie ! Sister Magpie !"

Their words turn guttural and harsh, inhuman. They make Zoey's skin hum and vibrate. She joins them, her lips forming the chant, taking on the words that are Conjures, that are Unholy, that are Power.

"Mother of Night ! Beast of Power ! Rise up, we Conjure thee ! We invoke thee mistress of many faces ! Lilith ! Hecate ! Nameless ! Maiden of Sorrow ! Mother of Death ! Crone of Decay ! Rise up !"

Abbess crane rubs the ash from her fingers into Zoey's burn, and she hisses with the pain of it.

"Stand, Sister Magpie," Crane demands in Conjure, and suddenly Zoey knows she can.

She gets to her knees, timid until her body responds to every command. She raises a hand and stares down at it, exultant. Zoey looks up at Crane where she stands.

*What would you give?* That alluring voice seems to come from nowhere and everywhere.

"Anything," Zoey answers, and gets to her feet.

The sisters cackle, raucous with drunken power. Zoey feel it too.

*Cast yourself upon the flames.*

Zoey does not think. She walks into the fire, and lets it burn. Every sinew, every hair, every fiber and nerve is alight with pain. And it is beautiful. And it is unholy.

The fire roars.

The sisters roar.

And as they watch, two proud horns wrench themselves from Zoey's forehead, bone breaking through skin to grow like calcified tree trunks, bending and gnarled until they tower toward the sky. They burn with fire that never scorches.

And as they watch and scream and shriek their unholy cry, they begin to float.

*Just as I always dreamed it*, Zoey thinks.

And from the flames a Horned Goddess rose, terrible and illimitable.

# ACKNOWLEDGMENTS

O THE READERS WHO wrote to me and asked that I write my planned sequel : you are the reason *Blood on the Wind* is here. Thank you ! To the design team at Little, Brown Books for Young Readers for their exemplary work on the *Teeth in the Mist* interiors : thank you for such a gorgeous piece of art ! You truly made the book vibrate off the page !

To Elece Green and Michelle Figueroa, thank you for making such an incredible audiobook version of *Teeth* ! It gives me chills to this day.

To my husband. Without you none of this would be possible, nor half so enjoyable ! You're my person on this wild journey, and I love you.

To my friends, who cheer me on and laugh at my mad ideas. You're brilliant.

To the readers who have found the world of the Conjures : I hope you enjoy !

Photo credits : pg 7-8 (c) Dawn Kurtagich ; pg 10 iStockphoto.com/likazor ID:1186055907 ; pg 20 shutterstock.com/paseven ID:2094068293 ; pg 72 shutterstock.com/paseven ID:1036875328 ; pg 126 iStockphoto/lizakor nID:1135282296 ; pg 142 iStockphoto.com/liligraphie ID:1303382673 ; pg 150 iStockphoto.com/verapetruk ID:824097176 ; pg 178 iStockphoto.com/lizakor ID:1195907904 ; pg 198 iStockphoto.com/likozor ID:1092122860 ; pg 212 iStockphoto.com/likozor ID:1018330940 ; pg 230 iStockphoto.com/likozor ID:1090177480 ; pg 260 iStockphoto.com/likozor ID:1134752203 ; p266 iStockphoto.com/likozor ID:1195907894 ; pg 296 iStockphoto.com/sqback ID:1198829958 ;pg 306 iStockphoto.com/likozor ID:1092122842. Images not listed are in the public domain.

www.ingramcontent.com/pod-product-compliance
Lightning Source LLC
Chambersburg PA
CBHW020306030826
48979CB00029B/2257/J

# Riddle

Amanda Cale



Cover design by Amanda Cale

Book design by Amanda Cale



ISBN-13: 978-0-9895211-2-3

**This book is dedicated first to God, then: my family; my friends (AKA extended family); Will, who has sweetly listened to ramblings about this story and fielded lots of scientific questions for two years while I figured it all out; and Pippa, who steals things from my purse.**

# Chapter 1

*Tick.*

The noise jutted into my thoughts, blocking out the story in the pages that lay open on my lap. Was it him? No, probably not. *A bug hitting the window, that's all.* I let my eyes drift down to the book again.

*Tick.*

Or never mind. What did he find to throw now?

I stacked the book on top of another one I'd been reading. The old table they rested on wobbled at the weight I added as I crossed to the window.

*Tick.*

"Okay, okay, I'm coming. . ."

I pulled the blinds up and looked across the short gap between our homes at the infectious grin of my friend Matt Dobken. He gestured for me to open the window. It hissed softly and squealed as I pushed the wooden frame up, letting in a late spring breeze.

"What are you throwing?"

He shrugged. "I dunno. Beads or something. Found some in the corner of the hallway. I think the vacuum missed them." He paused. "Anyway, what are doing right now?" He leaned out of the window, his hazel eyes glinting pale in the glow of the streetlight, always reflective in the night, exactly like a cat's eyes caught in some wayward beam. I'd never asked him why. Maybe I'd just imagined it.

*I know that look.* "Reading…why?"

"Wanna go do something?"

*Something. Right.* "It's ten o'clock, Matt."

"So?"

"It's…late." *Weak.* No, not weak. *Reading isn't a weak excuse.*

"It's usually late when we do this." He frowned.

*True enough.* "I'm reading." The moon hadn't yet rose up high enough to light us up too much, if we went. *This is a pretty perfect night.*

"Is the book gonna walk away?"

"Hush." I drummed my fingers on the sill. "What you got in mind?"

"Simpson's store."

Simpson's was the shell of a hundred-year-old country store right down the road. It had closed ten years before, when a fire gutted it. Now it just sat empty and half-rotten and probably not even that safe to go into. *Even better.* The night air beckoned me, begged me to head down the stairs and out the door and straight to Matt's truck. "How'd you pick that one?"

"It looks haunted."

"Everywhere we go looks haunted. That's the point of ghost hunting."

He shrugged. "Well, we pass it all the time, and we've never gone there. Figured you'd like it, so what do you say?"

"Just the two of us?"

He shrugged. "Yeah. I don't think Brandon'll mind sitting one out."

*Come on, take your pick. Yes or no.* The answer caught on the tip of my tongue. *He figured I'd like it.* That was nice.

A scream ripped through the air from the woods behind our neighborhood. I jumped, then froze. Guttural and wild, but unmistakably human, the scream lingered for a moment, muffled by distance, before it cut off. Silence reigned. Even the crickets seemed quiet now.

Matt's wide eyes met mine. I slammed my window shut, saw his follow a second later, and rushed for the hallway, knowing he would follow me.

*That had to be a human being, right? What else screams like that?*

Goats. Mountain lions. Stuff that wasn't around here, at least that I knew of.

And where had it come from? Not from right behind my house. It came from the woods, definitely, but how far? I'd run around in those woods with Matt when we were younger. They were deep, and we hadn't even explored the whole of them before his brother Tim had introduced us to more adventurous pursuits. It was part of some land no one had cared to build on, and now the other side of Sanders County, North Carolina was busy with a new shopping center. Our woods lay forgotten by most of the county, so if that was a human scream, then who invaded our playground, and what was happening to them now?

My neighbors' back doors already stood open, and the golden light spilled out of kitchens and living rooms as other citizens of Willow Drive trickled out of their homes. Dad was already outside, talking to Mr. Dobken.

A conversation from inside Matt's house drifted through the open back door and across the short space between our yards.

"Where are you going?"

"Just going to talk to Anya, mom."

"Don't be long."

"It's right next door."

"I know. Don't be long."

"Dad's outside."

"Matthew."

"Okay. I won't be out long."

I waited in the shadows by our back deck as Matt slipped across the strip of grass. His face lifted in half a smile.

Did he know I'd heard what his ever-nervous mother had said? *Guess she's as spooked as anyone else.* "Okay, so what do you think that was?"

He shook his head. "No clue."

A white Salt's Creek Police Department car pulled up and parked on the curb in front of Matt's house. *That was fast. Who called them?* "Pretty sure it was diagonal to the back of your house, but that's just a guess." Goosebumps rose up on my arms. "You know…"

*There's so much more to see.*

"What?"

"I feel like we never really went far enough back there when we were younger." *Better now than never.* Maybe it was just an animal that made that noise, but if we didn't get nosy, then how would we find out?

"You make an excellent point." Matt's gaze moved from the woods to me, his expression hopeful.

"Wish we could go look now." I rubbed my arms.

He tilted his head. "Maybe we should wait and see what's back there." He jerked his head once toward the trees, flicking his eyes the same direction.

*Yes. Perfect.* I nodded. "So…when do you think we will?"

"Probably tomorrow morning. You know. Early."

I held up seven fingers. He glanced at my hands, then nodded.

"Cool." A breeze swept past me, making the hairs on my neck stand up. No fear this time. Plunging into the woods, going after something we weren't even too sure was there. Looking for trouble, as his brother Tim would have said, as if he wasn't the one who got us into stuff like this in the first place. "I better go in."

"See ya tomorrow." He turned away.

"Wait."

"What?"

"Should we call Brandon about this one?"

Matt shrugged. "If you want."

"I doubt he'd want to get up that early on a Saturday for this." I didn't want to exclude him.

"Maybe not."

"He just always comes. I mean, if we already know we're going…"

"Yeah." Matt's face was maddeningly ambivalent.

"Should I call him?"

"Up to you. Doesn't matter." Again, with a shrug.

I bit my lip. "Well, maybe not for this part. If we find something good, I'll call him tomorrow."

"Okay." He smiled again. "See ya early."

"Yeah. 'Night." Back up the wooden steps of our porch, inside to the safe lamp light.

*Forget the store. This is even better.*

***

The misty morning wasn't anywhere near cool enough to worry about wearing a jacket, though the clammy air gave the illusion of a chill. A sweatshirt would have to come off within minutes of our upcoming trek into the woods, if I wore one. Still, the cool metal of the trampoline taunted me, since the dew that soaked the center made it basically useless unless I wanted a second shower. I picked at the elastic around my ponytail, trying to loosen it and relieve the places where hair pulled at my scalp.

Our driveway was empty, Mom and Dad already off to work early. My bed called me back. *This is worth it.* Ghost hunting. Hands-on local study, Tim had called it. It sure wasn't safe, and maybe not legal, depending on where we snuck into. Maybe one day we'd find some juicy secrets hidden in the shadows of Salt's Creek history. Even my family had a story of some crime, committed way back in the past, the details just about hidden beneath ashamed or unsure whispers about a man named Gavin Dupree. Whoever he was in my family, and whatever he'd done, was just something we didn't talk about, and I'd given up asking questions a long time ago, after my inquiries about a newspaper snippet with his name weren't answered.

Matt's back door opened. He ambled over to my yard, his eyes half-closed, still puffy underneath.

"Morning," he mumbled.

"Yes it is." I pushed away from the trampoline. "Shall we?"

"Yeah." He frowned. "Which way did you say it was?"

"It was more behind your house."

Matt shrugged. "Guess we just start walking and see what we find. Evidence, maybe."

My stomach fluttered. *Didn't think about that.* "I really don't want to find a dead body."

"I bet it was just a bobcat," he said.

"Bobcats don't sound like that."

"Well, do you still wanna go?" He paused, turning away from the woods.

*He really should know me better than that.* "Of course I still want to go." I swept past him, aiming for the misty trees. "I was just saying, I don't wanna see anything dead."

"I doubt we will."

The soft rustling of birds and other unseen things hopping around on the ground almost echoed the crunch of our feet on the brush. The mild morning wouldn't be around too much longer, and the cooler mist would turn to hot, sticky air by noon. But for now, the woods were untouched and waiting, towering over us. They had grown here for a long time before a subdivision popped up at the edge, kept years of silent guard, long after the original inhabitants left.

*Wonder what they were like. . . .*

The longer we walked, the less I remembered. None of it jogged my memory after about ten minutes of walking. "I don't think we've ever been back this far before." My voice bounced off the trees, and something in the bushes scampered away.

"Probably not."

I swallowed. Secrets kept themselves here, in untold stories of times long past. "We should probably be marking a trail or something."

"I'll remember." Matt looked back. "I can see my house. Sort of."

"Sort of. Great."

Sunlight glinted off the ground to my right, and whatever it was that reflected the sun shimmered as we moved forward.

"What was that?"

"What?" Matt yawned.

"Something shiny over there." I stepped away from him.

"You're distracted by a shiny object."

"Hush." I let Matt trail behind me. The thing glimmered again as I approached, announcing its location. The rounded end of a reddish metal object, copper probably, peeked out of the dirt. That story my dad had told me came rushing to my mind. There had been a bomber crash, leaving the pieces of a nuclear weapon buried out in Faro, the dangerous parts mostly recovered. They'd told everyone it was safe back then. *This might be another one they didn't want to tell anyone about.* But what really were the odds of that? Goosebumps rose up on my arms as Matt stepped up beside me.

"What is it?"

"I don't know."

"You gonna look?"

"I guess." I moved the toe of my tennis shoe and kicked at it. Dirt flew up from the ground, but the metal didn't budge. Someone had scratched away part of the surface, leaving behind that little part that reflected the sun. I leaned closer, reaching out to touch tiny carvings that ringed the surface.

"Wow."

Nothing from Matt. *Why doesn't he want to check this out?* I peeked at him.

He stared down at the dome, his eyebrows drawn close together in a frown, his eyes wide open. I straightened up and nudged his elbow.

He blinked. "Yeah?"

"What's wrong?"

The worried look on his face smoothed away, and he straightened with a shrug. "Nothing. Just looks weird."

"Yeah…a little." *Not that weird.* I took a step back from it. "I don't know if we can get it out, though."

He just nodded. "So let's keep going." He walked around me, away from me.

I wasn't going to follow until he told me something. "What's with you?"

He stopped. "Huh?"

"You just looked really worried when you were looking at that thing."

"Oh." He glanced at it again, then back to me. "It looked familiar. The markings, I mean. They're pretty rough, though, so I'm probably wrong."

"Where have you seen them?"

"I can't remember." He frowned again. "Or I might not be remembering right. That's what gets me."

"Interesting."

He offered nothing but another nod.

"I'm gonna dig it up, then." I grabbed a stick from the ground. "Wanna help?"

"Okay."

"Let's move the dirt off first so we can see what we have to work with here."

He crouched down. "Allow me."

I watched as his hands clawed into the dirt, breaking it, making it soft. I tossed the stick down and followed his lead, using my hands to tug the soil to a spot beside the metal.

*This might have been why.* . . . "What if whoever screamed last night was trying to take this thing?"

"Maybe someone took it from them."

"So how'd it get buried like this so fast?"

"Good point."

There. Uncovered, and the size of a dinner plate. More copper, but corroded everywhere else, green and rough, and etched with more of those carvings, grouped together. Words that meant something to someone else long ago.

Matt traced the carvings. "This is something."

"And you have no idea what it might be?"

"No clue."

*Can't leave it.* "I think I'll bring it with us."

"Okay." He stood as I picked at the edge of the plate. It pried right up. The edge was only a quarter inch thick, and maybe weighed five pounds, if that. *Not even buried deep.* "Should we keep going?"

Matt narrowed his eyes. "Well, if someone needed to hide, they'd need somewhere to do it."

"Right." I smiled. "So let's find their hiding place." I held the platter close to my side as we walked in the same diagonal path.

We'd only gone maybe a hundred more yards before the gaps between the trees began to widen. The pines were thinner here, and didn't shoot up so far into the air. The broad side of a building hid on the other side of one last thin wall of trunks. I pushed on quicker, gripping the copper plate, feeling it slide a little in the sweat on my fingers. Our feet crunched down loud on the underbrush, and I stepped out past the last of the forest on this side. Matt came to a stop a few feet behind me.

Under the shade of a huge old tree, a two-story house slouched in the morning mist, its side facing us and one window gazing down from the second floor, glass busted out. I approached it, keeping my steps slow and soft. Climbing plants covered a chunk of the porch and reached up to wrap viney fingers around the chimney. It had probably been a white house, but most of the color was chipped off the walls by now, leaving only bits of dirty paint on the wood. The door tilted on barely-clinging hinges, and the insides were all shadow.

A dirt road scarred the field that stretched off away from us to an unseen end. The sound of distant tires hissing over the asphalt reached us. Highway 58.

We stood together staring at it for a few minutes. This had been someone's land, their home. Who'd forgotten about it? Who'd lived here then, and who owned it now? *Probably no one.* Just hidden.

Abandoned. Forgotten. I stepped forward and grabbed Matt's arm, pulling him as I walked towards the house.

"You're not going in, are you?" he asked. He offered no resistance, and his feet thumped along the ground almost in step with mine.

"Not yet. I just want to look around the outside." I dropped his arm.

"Not yet?"

Assuming this house was safe to enter, it was a perfect find. "I blame your brother for getting us into this stuff, you know."

He sighed. "Yeah, so do I."

The house kept quiet. As we circled, I imagined the noises that might be inside. Creaks. Moans. *What stories might you have for us?*

"I bet the porch is gonna get full of bugs this summer," Matt said.

I could see it now. Black spiky bodies and angry buzzing as the wasps would take to the air. Or, instead, the clinging shutter remnants might just be the perfect place for dirt daubers. That would be if hornets didn't claim the overgrowth first.

I gave the climbing vines a wide berth and stood in front of the porch.

"So you want to go inside?" Matt asked.

The morning chill was simmering off even now, and my jeans weighed heavy on my legs. "I forgot to bring a flashlight."

"Me too."

I shook my head. "Honestly…not now." Whatever creature had been in these woods and screamed in the night was gone, and this house was a bonus. Ripe for exploring. The almost fulfilled promise of a hunt, and a reward for our curiosity. "I want to not have to tote this plate around. And we could get Brandon to come with us next time. And I'd like to be able to see once we're inside."

Matt's stomach growled. "That can be your next project."

I hadn't noticed yet how hungry I was getting. "Yeah, me too. I'll call Brandon later."

As we left the clearing where the house stood, I looked back. A flutter of motion in one of the upstairs windows, the one furthest to the right, stopped me. *What* was *that?*

Nothing but the broken panes looked back down.

"What's wrong?" Matt had already walked away, and his raised voice seemed to echo in the forest.

"I saw something move in the window." The weight of the plate at my side tugged down on my wrist. *Does someone know about this thing? Or this house?*

He squinted up at the side of the house. "Let's get out of here, then."

"Agreed." I followed as he walked away again. As we made our way back toward our street, I spared one more glance back at the house.

Nothing that time, either.

"Do you think Tim knows about that house?" I shifted the plate to hold it in front and looked over the markings in the metal. "Or this thing?"

"I'll ask him."

"It'd be cool if he did." The copper plate could go under my bed for now.

Matt yawned. "Yeah."

Nothing chased after us as we walked back under the old trees.

What was this artifact in my hands, and who'd screamed in the night? What if someone or something hid in that house, angry that we'd taken something from it? And what if it did come after us?

*What are these woods hiding?*

# Chapter 2

The video playing at the front of the room should have been more interesting to me, but I barely heard the words droning out of the unseen narrator. It was about space, and normally that would have held my attention.

The screen flared a little brighter with each movement of the pulsar animation. Like that buried thing in the woods, or broken glass glinting in the sun. What had been in that window? Was someone living there? Had they buried the piece of metal? What if they came back and found it so suddenly gone? Maybe what I saw was just the flap of an old curtain, or a torn piece of wallpaper, bothered by any breeze that swept past the broken glass. I realized I'd forgotten to call Brandon. *I'll just bring it up at lunch.*

Something bumped my elbow, and I jumped. Matt leaned away. His arm had hit me. *That's all.*

His eyebrows rose.

I shook my head.

The bell blasted then. Our teacher put down whatever novel he was reading and moved wordlessly towards the TV as our class filed out of the room. The plaid and khaki ranks of Ravenbook Academy students filled the plaster and tile hallway, voices rising and echoing around us.

"What were you thinking so hard about?" Matt asked.

"The house."

"So you definitely still want to go back?"

"Of course." I skirted around a group of gangly middle schoolers. "Don't you?"

"Well…yeah. I've been thinking about that metal thing. The stuff on it."

The cafeteria doors were propped wide open. I stopped and leaned against a polished wood windowsill. "And?"

He slouched next to me. "I haven't figured out why I know I've seen those letters before."

"Oh." *What now?* "Well, I want to get inside the house. And soon."

"Okay. Soon's good."

I hesitated for a moment. "Soon like tonight."

He stared across the hall at a row of brown lockers. "That soon."

"Yep."

He didn't seem to have more than what looked like a slow nod as his answer.

*Yes.* I let my gaze drift around as the stream of students filing past us slowed to a trickle.

A forgotten prom poster on the wall above the lockers caught my eye. The paper was looking rough now, faded and torn at the edges. Up there since January, at least. Prom had been weeks ago, and me and

Matt had gone together.

That was the night we'd gone back to an old middle school in Wilson County. The first place Tim took us, all those years ago. This last time, before prom was even over, we'd left Brandon and his girlfriend at the country club and rushed back home to change. Then we were off, just the two of us, clambering through creaking windows and kicking up dust in the night. The old school was still as spooky as they come.

I blinked. *Weeks ago.* Wow. Tomorrow was the last day of school, something I hadn't even given more than a second's thought before this moment. Preparation for college would overshadow everything in the next year, and what if there was suddenly no more time for our hobby?

"You guys weren't waiting for me, were you?" Brandon White swaggered into my line of vision, his phone loose in his hand. He pocketed it.

I pushed off the windowsill. "Come on, I'm hungry."

"I'll meet y'all. Gotta get my food." Brandon said. He made off for the hot lunch line.

"Me too," Matt added. "You?"

"Naw, I brought mine today. I'll get a table."

"Okay."

He followed Brandon, and I turned to the rest of the cafeteria. Maybe some kid hadn't picked today to claim our usual spot, my favorite corner table, the one where I could keep my back to the wall and my eyes on the door. My eyes landed on it, standing empty, waiting on the other side of the sea of tables, chairs haphazardly pushed away from the table.

*Great.*

Maybe one day Ravenbook would build that expansion they'd been talking about for so long.

The brown paper bag in my backpack had been beaten up by my books, as my flattened sandwich and bruised apple proved. A tray, with a pear and a plastic-wrapped sandwich, slid into my view as Matt sat across from me.

I eyed his tray. "They had sandwiches?"

Matt poked at the plastic wrap. "I don't think they're fresh or anything. Just leftovers."

"Gotta be better than whatever's the main thing today." *Exams are over. This is the next to last school lunch of my junior year.* My stomach took a quick dive downward.

*And why am I so sentimental about it?*

Matt turned his head to one side, then the other. Searching.

"What are you looking for?"

He slouched in his chair. "I think I have a stalker here."

"Who?"

"Some girl that follows me around."

I peered over the top of his head. "Is she in here now?"

He tugged at the sandwich wrapping. "No, I don't see her."

"Well…good?"

He nodded.

I poked at a soft spot on the apple's skin and tugged at the stem, grasping it between my fingers and rotating the apple slowly. The fruit resisted as I turned it until, with a crunchy snap, the stem snapped off in my fingers.

"You okay?" Matt frowned at me over his sandwich.

Did I want to tell him? I shrugged. "Yeah, just feeling weird." *Weird, sad, same difference.*

"It's not contagious, is it?"

"Hush." I pushed down a grin and kicked at him under the table, letting my toe crash into the thick leather of his shoes.

"Seriously, what's wrong?"

A flick of my finger sent the stem scooting across the table and over the edge. "Well…"

"Yeah?"

*We have one more year until we have to grow up and I don't want to lose this, whatever it is that we have.* "It's just that it's the end of the year, and we'll be seniors, and I'll have to do college applications and stuff, and I don't even know if I want to go away or stay here and save some money by taking classes at the tech or something, and on top of it all, we might not have much time for a whole lot of ghost hunting next year, and I just don't want to not be doing that. Salt's Creek is too boring a town without…this." *Keeps us different. Sane. Together.* I drew in a breath, waiting.

He stared at his tray before looking up at me with a half-smile. "We can make time for the ghost hunting."

I shook my head. "It's not just that. It's the change." *It's the weirdness of not doing stuff together all the time.* "In a little over a year, we'll be leaving for college, and…" *And what happens when we don't see each other so much?*

He blinked. *I knew it.* This was ridiculous, this attachment I had to things staying the same, to having my best friend in reach all the time. We had one more year together. I'd have to get used to that idea.

His mouth opened, but before Matt said anything, Brandon slid into a seat, a huge glob of our school's gooey brown barbecued pork heaped on his plate. The greasy odor wafted across the table as Brandon shoveled a huge bite onto a spoon and swallowed, barely chewing.

My stomach turned. "I still can't believe you like that stuff."

Brandon shrugged and opened a bottle of ginger ale. "I've had worse stuff to eat." He spooned more of the mess into his mouth, washing it down with a swallow of his soft drink.

"I think I believe you." *Well, now that my little show is over. . . .* I bit into my apple. The mealy flesh stuck in my mouth. *Ew.* The turkey sandwich had squished some ketchup out into the plastic bag. *Guess I could be stuck with the hot lunch.* "So do y'all wanna do something tonight?"

Matt stared at me, unblinking. *Ignore.* Did he really think I'd want to wait that much longer? That house was ripe for exploration. I'd just told him. Hadn't he nodded in agreement?

*Unless I just didn't see that right.*

"I'm up for it," Brandon said.

I met Matt's gaze. "How about you?" *Come on, say yes.*

"Sure," he said, looking down again at his sandwich.

"Of course." I leaned back in my chair. "We found the perfect place."

"Where?" Brandon asked.

I shoved the apple into my lunch bag. *Giving up on that.* "This house on 58, behind my neighborhood. Old, abandoned, creepy, and right behind where my house is."

Something passed over Brandon's face. A downturn of his mouth, a crease in his forehead, gone after a second. Was it my imagination, or had he turned half a shade paler? "Uh…where on 58?" He spoke fast. "I mean, I'll need directions, right? And I'll have to see if I can go or not. I mean I might have something. Just thought about it. I'll have to find out. Let you know later." He shoved a chunk of barbecue into his mouth and chewed, his mouth working up and down, all stiff.

*That was weird.*

"Like I said, right behind me and Matt's neighborhood. There's a dirt road through a field. Just follow that."

Matt balled up the wrapping from his sandwich. "Yeah, man, you've probably driven by it a few hundred times."

Brandon nodded once, his face smoothing out. "Got it."

*Okay.* "You know, you could just come to my house."

Brandon shook his head. "Nah, I'll drive. So um…what time do I need to meet you there?"

Matt took another bite. *Is he seeing this?* I kicked his foot. He jumped and swallowed, giving Brandon an answer. "I guess…eight-thirty?"

Brandon nodded again, rapidly. "Okay, yeah." He stood up and grabbed his tray. "I uh…I gotta meet with somebody about a thing. I forgot. I'll see you guys tonight." He stepped backwards, turned, and hurried across the cafeteria. His knee collided with a chair, sending it scooting a foot from its table as he kept going through the cafeteria doors.

"That was interesting." Brandon never hurried anywhere.

"Yeah."

I leaned back over the table. "Right after I said where the house was."

Matt shrugged. "Maybe it was the barbecue."

I laughed. "Then I'm glad I never eat any." The brown paper bag crunched as I crumpled it in my hands around the remains of my apple. "He's never acted like that before, though. Really."

"No, he hasn't." Matt's eyebrows were pinched together again. "Hey um…nothing dangerous when we go in there, okay?"

"Who, me?"

The noise in the cafeteria rose.

"Wanna get out of here?" Matt asked, almost yelling.

"Yeah, let's go." The chair knocked against the wall as I shot to my feet.

The night was something to look forward to.

And it might be the last ghost hunt ever.

*Better make it good.*

# Chapter 3

*Come on, Matt. Where are you?* I wanted to get there before Brandon did. *Click-click.* Each flash lit up the backyard like strikes of lightning. *Click-click.*

Matt's back door cracked open, and he hurried out, down the porch steps, and across the yard.

"Sorry," he said. "I know you said 8:15 but…I got sidetracked."

"What time is it now?"

He looked down at his watch. "8:20."

I shrugged and pushed away from the trampoline. "Okay, so not too much off. It's fine. Let's go." The flashlight beam met the dark edge of the woods. *This is gonna be great.*

"Do you remember which way to go?" Matt asked.

"Kind of. Do you?"

He switched his flashlight on. "Um…I know the general direction we went."

"Oh. The general direction. Great."

"How is that worse than 'kind of'?"

*Good point.* "Hush."

He swept the light slowly across the ground as we walked. "I should've marked the trail the other day."

"Probably."

We left the soft glow of the back porch lights and edged into the dark. The moon was at least bright. Crickets chirped and lightning bugs flashed out of the gloom. Our feet crunched over brush and pine straw and leaves, and the night made our steps echo like they never would have under the sun.

Were we alone? Someone might be actually living under these trees, taking refuge for a night in seclusion. If there was anyone, they'd hear us loud and clear.

*No one would notice them if they wanted to hide, that's for sure.*

The minutes passed, our feet mashing down on the pine straw and dead leaves. I let Matt guide me forward. I could still see the glow from our homes, so we weren't too far from them. *Just feels like it.*

I raised the flashlight. "Okay, so we should see the side of the house soon." Or another window. *Or a face staring out of one.* The beam caught a dull flash from a dirty window, a ghostly square in the darkness.

"Good job. You led us right. And in the dark and everything."

"And you thought I'd get us lost," Matt said with a smirk.

I stuck my tongue out, walking past him and standing in front of the porch. "Never said that exactly."

"You didn't have to."

"Well, you didn't mark a trail."

He was silent for a moment. "Point taken."

A pair of headlights illuminated the dirt road and came our way, closer every second.

Brandon's little silver car pulled up under the trees and stopped, kicking up dust around it as he hit the brakes. I kept my flashlight trained on the porch as the car door opened and shut.

Matt walked away from me, getting close to the house, staring at the old structure. "I might be having second thoughts."

"This isn't any creepier than anywhere else we've gone." I turned. "You wimping out on me?"

"I wasn't really thinking about it being creepy." He twirled the light around. "This porch is torn up, and the inside's gotta be no better."

"Then I'll watch where I step."

He rolled his eyes. "At least we have flashlights."

Brandon's voice broke into our discussion. "This is it?" Brandon's voice cracked on his last syllable. He cleared his throat.

I stared at him. "No, we still have to walk a little ways."

He rolled his eyes. "So…this house."

*What's wrong with him?* "Yes." Parts of him looked all wrong. Stiff shoulders, a tightness all over him, instead of the casual slouch I knew.

"How did y'all find it?" he asked.

"Long story," Matt said.

I elbowed Matt. "Not that long."

"Well, yeah."

Brandon raised an eyebrow. Was his forehead shining with sweat? *It's just warm. That's all.*

I shrugged. "Not too much to tell. We heard this scream the other night and went out the next morning to investigate."

Brandon straightened. "And neither of you thought that might have been a bad idea?"

I narrowed my eyes. "Like you haven't broken into half the county with us."

His shoulders dropped, and he took that easy stance back from wherever it had been. "Right." He cleared his throat and stepped closer to the house. "So a scream, huh?"

"Yep."

His flashlight beam rested on the broken window. "We going in?"

"Guess so," Matt said. "Go slow. I doubt this is at all structurally sound." He walked onto the first step and jumped, staring down at his feet.

I poked him. "And you're telling us to be slow."

"No, this is just…pretty interesting here."

I peered over his arm. "What?"

"The steps are new. Ish. Newish."

The wood below made a sharp contrast to rest of the porch. Treated wood. Darkened, unstained, but the screws in the corner gleamed in the flashlight's beam. Definitely new.

"That's…weird." A chill spread over my skin. "This should be…not like that. At all."

"Why not?" Brandon asked.

"No one lives here, and it's pretty obvious that no one has for a long time."

"Maybe somebody's fixing it up." Brandon hopped onto the steps.

"Yeah." Matt's light flipped up to point at the crooked door. "So… the porch is safe, or partly anyway. Should we try the rest?"

"Duh." I slipped by them. "Ladies first."

Matt reached forward. "Oh, at least let me get the door ma'am." He pulled at the edge of it, just enough for me to duck underneath and slip in. The thick darkness inside cleared, and the contrast between it and our lights faded as we stood in the hall. A set of stairs ascended to the pitch black second story. Soft moonlight shone through the left window behind me, filtered through the foliage on the porch.

"Where do you wanna start?" Brandon asked.

"I don't know." I looked back at the two of them. "That way?" I pointed to my right. The flashlight beam caught the edge of a sofa. *A parlor, maybe. That should be interesting.*

"Why there?" Matt asked.

"Seriously? I don't know."

Brandon looked down the hallway. "I could go this way."

Matt held the flashlight under his chin. "You sure we should split up?"

I rolled my eyes. "This isn't the movies. Whatever works. I'm checking this parlor thing."

"Okay." Brandon grimaced. "I'll go this way."

"You sure?"

"Yeah." He stepped away. "Just…keep a little quieter, okay?"

*Jumpy, isn't he?* "Sure." I looked at Matt. "What are you gonna do?"

"Guess I'll go with you."

"Okay." I took another glance up the stairs. "Second floor'll have to wait, then?"

Matt blinked. "Probably indefinitely."

"No fun." The room we entered had a sofa, a stained rug crusted with dust, and a tall piano with a bench stood in the opposite corner. The curtains had long since stopped holding together, but the holey fabric was still draped in front of the dirty glass.

"Not much here," Matt said.

"Yeah." Maybe this would turn out to be one of our more boring outings. "I'll check out the piano."

A sound came from the hallway, feet beating on something.

Someone running. I froze.

"Did you hear that?" Matt whispered.

"Shh!"

The door slammed once against the house. An engine came to life outside, and a beam of white light filled up the room.

"What in the world?" Matt frowned as gravel crunched under tires outside.

I ran to the front window. Brandon's car backed up into a turn and sped down the long road, kicking up dust as the red tail-lights disappeared.

*Why?* "Okay, then."

Matt cleared his throat. "I take it we're not grabbing supper with him later."

"Was he that scared?" What was going on with him?

"Maybe." Matt moved away from the window. "Did you see the way he was acting when he got here?"

"I take it you did, too."

He nodded. "We can ask him later. Do you still want to stay?"

"Of course." Brandon very likely wasn't coming back. "No use waiting for him to change his mind." I grinned, flicking my light at Matt's face. They reflected the beam, bright in the shadows, as he flinched away.

"Thanks. That was just great." He turned back to look at me, one arm raised and shielding his eyes.

"By the way, did you know your eyes glow in the dark?"

"Never thought about it." He blinked hard a few times.

I stared. "So you do know."

Matt looked over quickly, his eyes wide. Had he said more than he intended? "Um…I…sure?"

"So how do they—"

"It's just a weird thing, okay?"

"Okay then." *What's his problem?* At least I knew I wasn't imagining it. "So…then…I'm gonna look around." For something. Anything. Brandon had run away, and now Matt was getting weird. My eyes fell on the piano against the wall. The bench sat sideways, pushed away as if someone had stood up fast from it and not fixed it back like it was supposed to be. What hid underneath the faded striped cushion?

A thick layer of blackened dust coated the keys. How long had it been sitting here, abandoned? What would it sound like now, with no tuning for so many years? I reached out, pressing down the dark ivory.

*Thunk.*

"Beautiful," said Matt.

"Oh yes. Gorgeous." The piano bench nudged at my knee as I stepped aside.

I slipped my fingers underneath and pulled up. The hinges crunched and held the lid firmly open one inch.

"Looks like it might be rusted shut." Matt pulled up at the other side of the lid.

*Probably nothing inside but some old music or something.* "No use in not trying." *Come on, please open.* I put my hand down to hold the bench in place, but didn't brace it. "Okay…one…two…three."

We pulled up together, the hinges squealed, and the lid flew open. The bench, balance thrown off, slipped from my grasp and pitched over, spilling out papers, a thick ratty book, and an old shoebox. The box lost its top and tumbled once, and a stack of envelopes ejected from it and spread across the hardwood floor.

Matt's eyes flicked from the bench, to the shoebox, and up to my face. "Good going."

"That wasn't all me." I bent for the envelope nearest to my foot and shined the beam on it. Matt stepped close, right beside my shoulder, to read the names scrawled on the envelope. Jendra and Rynon Davies, Ocracoke.

"Huh," said Matt.

"What?"

"My mom's family has some Davies in it." He blinked, his frown creasing between his eyebrows. "Plus she's from Ocracoke."

"Really?"

He shrugged. "Yeah."

"Wow." The envelope had definitely been opened, whether it had been by the Davies or someone else, but the folded letter was still inside. "Maybe this house belongs to your family or something."

"Doubt it." He looked down. "Read the letter."

"You don't mind?"

He raised an eyebrow. "Why would I mind?"

"It might be important family business."

"I doubt it."

"Bet this paper's getting fragile." The soft paper hissed as I slid it from the envelope. Stains from ink and time and maybe moisture dotted the spaces between the words. Words from another time. The date scrawled at the top was March 20, 1886, after Sanders County had formed. A chill raced over my skin. *This is amazing.* I moved my flashlight down the page as I read.

> Dear friends,
>
> I hope that my next letter can be longer, but my news for now is this: the riddle is finished and waiting, hidden in light, and I have placed the key where it can be found by those who care to remember. The doors may be locked now, but it is my wish that they never be unlocked, once events are in motion. I trust that you agree, all things considered. I have also hidden the book in Skyrren, so you should be able to find it when you arrive at your destination, should you need it. You may not, but it is there in the spot we agreed upon. It its certainly unfortunate that this all had to occur under such circumstances.
>
> We hope you are well. Maggie and I are. I have some concerns about a neighbor of mine. He is most certainly not a close friend, but a fellow citizen of my town, and I wish to discuss this man with you and see what your thoughts might be concerning him. I hope that we may

meet soon and confer on the matter.

Maggie sends her love. We are expecting our first child to be born in a few months. I hope to arrange a visit, whether we go to you or otherwise.

All the best,
Gavin Dupree

"Whoa." That name. *Can it be the same?*

"What?" Matt looked closer at the letter.

"Gavin Dupree."

"Who?"

Here I stood, in a rotten old house, holding a letter written in his hand to two friends. "I don't know." I swallowed. "Well, I kinda do. I know he's family. I don't know how we're related, but he's definitely… not someone my family will talk about. Ever."

"At all?"

"Nope."

"Why not?"

"Shame or something." I shrugged. "He was apparently a criminal and I'm guessing they just didn't talk about it for a hundred years or so, so now it's habit."

"Interesting."

"Irritating, actually, if you really wanna know where you came from."

Matt stared at the piano and spoke quietly. "Maybe they'd just rather no one think about it too much. Families are like that sometimes."

"Maybe." Another faint round shape showed through from the back as the flashlight lit up the paper. I flipped it over. Just a doodle, in the same black ink as the rest of the letter. Eight lines, rayed out like a ferris wheel, and a circle at the end of each one. "Weird."

Matt tugged softly at the letter again, frowning. "So Gavin Dupree is definitely part of your family?"

"Yeah." A thrill ran through me.

Matt stared at the paper.

"Matt?"

He looked up at me, his eyes for a moment reflecting the light. "He's family? I mean…for you?" He swallowed once.

"I just said that." What had he seen in the letter that I hadn't? "Do you know something I don't?"

Matt frowned. "No just…he's definitely related to you?"

I nodded and considered the rest of the letters, strewn across the floor. "Yes." *What's with him now?* "Do you think—"

*Creeeeeaaak.*

Matt held up his hand. I needed no reminders to be quiet. Another creak followed the first one, from the floor above us. Then a third, and a fourth, all in a rhythm.

Footsteps. My hand tightened around the edge of the letter, gripping the envelope. The crinkling might as well have been a gunshot in my ears. My heart sped up, pounding hard as the footsteps continued. I tried to keep quiet. We'd already made enough noise. Not enough to wake the dead, but apparently just enough to rouse the living.

A sharp tug on my elbow yanked me sideways. "Come on."

Matt pulled me out of the parlor and to the front hall. *Just go for the door. Don't look back.* I didn't dare look back up the stairs to see who haunted this house. He pushed at the door, and I slipped under it after him, dodging as it swung at me. The distressed hinges squealed, and was that the crunch of ruined metal? The door slammed back against the house as we sprinted down the strange new porch steps and straight into the brush, aiming for the warm lights of our neighborhood.

The paper rattled in my hands, now crumpled on one side. Matt kept pace with me.

*Brandon.* "I can't believe Brandon left us there." I slowed. We'd gotten deeper into the woods now. Matt fell into step beside me.

"Me either."

"At least I got a souvenir, right?" *Too bad I didn't have time to grab the others.* I loosened my damp grip on the letter. *Can't ruin this.*

Matt's smile came back, tight at first, but his face relaxed. "Yeah."

I couldn't read it in this low light, but I gazed at the paper as we headed back home. I let Matt lead me. How was it possible for our families to be connected?

We passed under the edge of the trees and into my backyard. Safety. Whoever was hanging out in that house hadn't chased us. "That was intense." Did I tell him how happy I was, despite being scared half to death just five minutes before? I wanted the rest of the letters, but could I get him to go back?

"Yes it was," he said as we paused by the trampoline. "Enough adventure for you tonight?"

"More than enough." *I need the rest of them.*

"But?"

I chewed on the inside of my lip. "I think the letter is a code or something, and the other envelopes…"

"Anya…"

"I didn't mean I want to go back tonight. Just…sometime."

His mouth tightened. "You know, just this once, I don't think it's safe."

"Then I'll go by myself."

His frown came back. "No…don't do that. I'll go with you. Just wait a day. Maybe whoever's in there will leave."

*Better than nothing.* "Deal."

"Okay."

We stared at each other. His eyes shone in the porch light. I backed up. "See you tomorrow then."

"Yep." He strolled to his house, taking his back porch steps two at a time. I hopped onto my back steps and dared a glance backwards into the dark woods.

If anyone had followed us, I sure couldn't see them. A breeze bent the paper in my hand.

*The other letters had better tell the rest of this story.*

# Chapter 4

*The riddle is finished and waiting, hidden in light, and I have hidden the key where it can be found by those who care to remember.*

I frowned at the yellowed paper and leaned back from where it rested on top of the book I'd brought for reading. A riddle, a key. And what was Skyrren? Some code for a real place? *Maybe just a name you've never heard. That's all.*

Who was the neighbor that Gavin worried about? Friend or enemy? *Figure it out*, the letter said. *Read between my lines.* Who was the child they'd been expecting, in relation to me?

*Wish I had the rest of these.* They might have answers.

But if this one was any indication of how the rest of them were written, there wasn't much chance of that.

*This is just the middle chapter. I want the rest of it.* I glanced up at the clock. 2:59. *Time's up for this.* I slid the letter into the paperback.

*Tick. Tick. Tick.* The second hand finished out its minute, and the bell rang.

Miss Whitley spoke over the combination of our noise and the joyful cries from the hallway. "Have a good summer!"

I closed the book carefully and shoved it between the two of my notebooks. *Definitely going back to get the rest of those today. If I have to go by myself, I will.*

Students hollered as I made my way down the hall to where Matt reclined against the plaster wall.

He stood straight as I got near. "Ready to go?"

"Yeah." A familiar profile a few yards ahead crossed my vision, the swagger back in full force. *Better ask him.* "Hey, Brandon!"

He stopped and looked around. I waved. He waited there, shifting from one foot to the other, as I rushed to catch up.

The easy grin was gone, replaced by a tight grimace, and his eyes flicked away and back to us. "Yeah?"

*What's his problem?*

Matt spoke first. "Where'd you go last night?"

"You bailed on us," I added.

Brandon sighed. "I just really wasn't feeling it." He paused. "Changed my mind. Felt like sitting out."

"Why?" The question jerked from my mouth.

*Calm down.*

"I don't know." His eyes narrowed. "You going back?"

Matt nodded. "Yeah, probably."

He strolled backwards. "I might go with you then, but I gotta get going. I'll see y'all around." Without another word, he turned back around and walked away, leaving us standing on the sidewalk.

*I'll see y'all around.*

"Okay." What else could I say?

"Ever seen him like that before?" Matt asked as we walked, pace slower, to the lockers.

"No." *He wasn't feeling it? What did that mean?* "He just…he's never backed out on us before like that. Just suddenly not wanting to go and leaving us in that creepy house—"

Matt grabbed my arm. "Calm down. You're turning red."

I pulled away from Matt's grip. "Well, yeah, whatever. If he didn't want to come the first time he could have just said no. And now he wants to tag along when we go back."

"I really don't think he set out to offend you personally."

"Then what's his problem?" A few other students glanced my way. *Too loud.*

"Maybe something's going on and he just doesn't want to tell us."

*Oh.* "Good point." I took a deep breath. Maybe that was it. *Could be. Pretty likely.* "But even if there is, we're his friends. I still say it's weird." I stopped at my locker. "And I need to clean some trash out of this." *Why do I hate change so much?* I wasn't anywhere near as close to Brandon as Matt. Maybe Brandon did have some stuff going on at home and just simply didn't feel like sharing it with us. I let my mind stick on Matt's words, told myself that it was unlikely for Brandon to be actively trying to offend me. Maybe he'd open up.

"Okay." Matt leaned against an empty one next to mine. I spun the dial on the combination lock. Matt offered no further commentary on why Brandon would act the way he had.

As the ancient locker opened, a ball of paper tumbled out and landed on the floor, leaving behind a pile of fliers, handouts, notebooks, and dried up ink pens.

"Some trash?" Matt said.

"Hush." I poked at the junk, and a pen clattered to the floor. "I swear every year that I'll shake this habit and keep a clean locker with minimal junk."

Matt shook his head and grabbed one of the huge plastic trash cans in the corner. "I think it's best if you just shovel it all in."

"Maybe." I gently tugged at some of it. "Hey wait, there's a notebook in here. Maybe it's still good." I flipped the card stock cover open. The back of it was gone, and the two sheets of paper left inside fluttered uselessly. "Or…no." It scuffed against the trash can's contents. With two more sweeps, the rest of the learning leftovers followed, and Matt pushed the can back to the wall.

"Ready to go?" he asked. "I mean, unless you saw some drink bottles in there you wanted to rescue."

"Hush." Car horns blared from the parking lot as we walked to the doors. I grinned. Three whole months of summer before us, even if it was the last one of high school. A little red-headed boy passed us in the hall, his eyes to the floor. Miss Whitley's son, if I remembered right. One of the double doors at the end of the hall swung open, and a student rushed in, heading our way with her head down, studying a piece of paper in her hand. She looked up at us. I knew her, from some class or other. Gym, maybe. What was her name?

A weight fell across my shoulders suddenly, and Matt pulled me closer. My face blazed hot as blood rushed to my head.

The other girl smirked as she passed, eyes all cool. They rolled once before she dropped her face back down to the paper.

*All right then.*

Matt kept his arm thrown over me until we stepped into the parking lot. I ducked under and turned around to face him, my arms crossed against my chest. "What was that about?"

"Do you know her?" Matt looked back at the building for a moment and loosened his tie.

"We've been in some classes together, I think. Why?" Most of the other cars had cleared out of the lot, thankfully. I cleared my throat. "Again, what was with that…thing you did back there?"

"Can it wait until we're in the truck?" He cast one glance at the school again, then back to me, eyes round. Panicked.

*Oh this must be good*. I let the smile inch onto my face. "I look forward to hearing this." I turned toward his truck. *Let him follow.* My fingers brushed the sun heated metal of a random car I passed. *Air conditioning, please.* The thick fabric of my plaid skirt made the temperature seem even higher as we walked across the sunbaked parking lot. Matt unlocked the passenger side first, letting me climb in, and tossed his backpack into the seat. In two quick motions, he pulled off his tie and tugged the hem of his white button-down shirt out of his pants. Sweat trickled down the side of my face.

"You done undressing yet, or should I step out?"

Matt cranked the ignition, shaking his head. "She's the stalker."

"You have a stalker?"

"I told you about her yesterday."

"When?" I racked my brain.

"At lunch."

"Oh." The way he'd looked around, keeping his head low. "Oh that. I didn't think you were serious."

"Well, I was." Matt backed out of the parking space. "Her name's Samantha."

*Aha.* "That's right. Yeah. I know her."

He kept going. "Samantha was in my Spanish class this year and last year. She always sat either right in front of me or right behind me. Every day. Then she started moving her desk closer. When she wasn't slinging her hair in my face from in front of me, she was behind me and pulling my hair or drumming on my back with a pencil. I kept seeing her everywhere, like when I'd turn corners. I think she even took a couple of pictures of me with her phone."

I stared at him. The laugh started inside, pulling up at the edges of my mouth, then burst out. "You're serious."

"Absolutely." He pulled out onto the road.

"She probably likes you."

"Well, obviously."

"Then give her a chance." He didn't look over as I leaned against the door to face him.

*Wait, do I want him to?* I squirmed. *Stop that. He's not yours.* Why was I even thinking that way?

"Maybe I would if she didn't act like she does." He frowned. "She gives you dirty looks, too, when you're not looking. I've seen it."

"Please."

"I'm serious." He stopped at the red light in an empty intersection. "She's scary."

"Yeah. Terrifying." I flipped the visor down to block the sun. Despite the air conditioning running, the truck was still warm inside. Sweat beaded up on my forehead, the dots of moisture cloudy from the remnants of my face powder. "Seriously, why do I even bother with makeup?"

"I don't know."

*Ouch.* "Thanks a lot."

"What? No, I meant—"

A violent jolt shook the truck, shoving me forward into the visor. I leaned back quickly, pressing into the seat, like the old leather could offer some protection. The truck settled quickly.

Matt's hand moved lightning fast and put the truck in park before he grasped the steering wheel again, his knuckles stark white. He turned to look through the back window.

The car that hit us, a rusted, beat-up, tank of an automobile, backed up with a jerk and pulled around, kicking up gravel dust on the side of the road. As it shot past us, I saw a blank space where there should have been a plate, and any glimpse of the driver got lost in a blur of motion as they sped through the intersection and down the road, faster all the time, racing and disappearing around a curve. Dread bubbled up inside me as I watched it go.

Matt took a deep breath. "Are you okay?"

I nodded. *What was that?*

"You didn't hit your head or anything?"

"No." Dryness clawed at my throat. "How about you?"

"I'm fine." He pushed the door open and climbed out.

*Great way to start summer.* At least it was the bumper, not a head-on collision, not as fast as they'd been going. *This is okay. We are fine.* I watched a speck of dust float through the air in front of me. *We're okay.*

Matt climbed back into the truck and sat for a moment.

"Well?"

He shrugged and shifted into drive. "Not too bad I guess. Just a nice dent. Probably won't even need to be repaired." He pulled forward. "I'll still have to tell my parents. Dad will understand. Mom may freak out." He grimaced.

I took a deep breath. *Calm down.* "At least it's not bad."

He turned right, toward our neighborhood. "Yeah." He patted the wheel. "Good old truck. Just wish I'd caught the plate number."

"There wasn't a plate."

"You're kidding."

"No." Puffy white clouds filled the sky. Was the weather going to turn bad? *I'd better jump on this quick.* "Let's go get the rest of those letters today." There was an urgency in it now, for some reason I couldn't think of.

He frowned for a second, but his face smoothed out. "Okay. We'll do that."

"Really?"

"Yeah. Really."

"Cool." He turned onto Willow Drive. The deep tremble in my hands slowed down. *Just an accident.* I took another deep breath. *Letters now. You have a mystery to solve.*

# Chapter 5

The sun burst out of the thick cloud covering as it moved across the sky, and I closed my eyes as the trampoline pressed warm against my bare legs and arms. The light dimmed again as another bulbous cloud drifted across the sun.

A door popped open, squeaked, and shut again.

*That will be Matt.* I closed my hand around the flashlight at my side.

I sat up. Had his dad been angry? I swung my legs under the metal railing. "So?"

He shrugged. "I explained. Dad's pretty much cool with it. Dent's actually not that bad."

"And your mom?"

He shrugged, a smile playing at the edge of his lips. "Not home."

"How do you think she'll take it?"

"Same as always." He leaned against the trampoline. "Conspiracy theories, talking about being careful, worrying."

"Like when Tim moved?"

"Yeah." He cleared his throat. "I remember that conversation.

'You'll dry up like a piece of leather' were her words, I think. Then she went out and bought him a whole bunch of that thick cream."

"Maybe it won't be that bad in this case."

"Eh, well." He smiled up at me. "You mentioned a certain house?"

"Yes!" I hopped down. "I really just want to go get the letters and leave. Promise."

His face went still. "Yeah. I really think someone's staying there at night."

*Safety lecture.* "It's not night time, and that's why I said we wouldn't be there long. Come on."

"Yes ma'am."

"Hush."

The old trees loomed over us, casting shadows as we hurried through the brush.

*Why have I never poked around back here before?* "So what do you figure the letter meant?"

He kicked a pinecone out of the way. "Well…what do you know about Gavin Dupree?"

"Nothing." I twirled the flashlight in my hand. "I don't even know how he's related to me, just that he's some guy in our family who might've done something really bad."

"Anyone you can ask?"

*No one who'll give me answers.* "I have. My dad was the one who brought up the guy's name when he saw it in some family records, but my granny straight up refuses to say anything about who he was."

"You should check the library."

"Yeah, probably." I shrugged. "I didn't think of that, so…yeah. If it was bad enough, old papers'll have the story, right?"

"I guess."

The second story side window stared down like an empty eye. I pulled my gaze away and edged to the front of the house.

"Coulda been just an animal in there that we heard," I whispered.

*Like the house can hear you? Really?*

"In, out, and home, okay?"

I elbowed Matt softly. "Chicken." I didn't move.

*You'll never do this if you don't do it now.*

I stepped ahead of Matt, but he followed close behind. Up the too-new, impossible front steps, onto the porch. I pulled the door more open than it already was and slipped through.

Sunlight from another window attempted to fill up the still dim house as I stepped through the hall and into the parlor.

The piano keys, so filthy just the night before, gleamed from across the room, and the bench hid halfway into the shadows. Tidy. Goose-bumps on my arm flared up. I moved toward the instrument to touch one of the tooth-white keys.

It thunked quietly. A shadow of a note followed, lingered for a moment before slipping away. *Or maybe I imagined it.* "They're clean." My throat stuck as I swallowed. "That's…weird." My gaze drifted to the other door. *This house is dangerous.*

Matt poked my arm, pulling my mind back. "The letters?"

"Right." I backed away to give the bench room. The wood popped and creaked under the soles of my shoes. *Don't make noise. Don't slide it.* Matt's footsteps creaked on the wooden floor as I closed my fingers around the edges of the bench and lifted it, just a few inches, just enough to get it open. What if the mysterious housekeeper was still here? Matt gripped the other end of the cushion and we pulled together, wrenching it open as he held it steady. With a scream of the hinges, the top opened.

An empty compartment taunted me, the sheets of music, the tattered book, the shoebox, all gone. "No."

BANG! The floor seemed to tremble for just a moment after the crash.

A scream tried to force its way out of me as the entire house echoed with the sudden noise. I clamped my teeth together as my fingers closed around Matt's arm and hung on. We stood there for a long moment in the quiet. Matt grunted once, his face pulled up in a grimace. I still gripped his arm.

"Sorry," I whispered, letting go. *Deep breath.*

He winced. "You're strong."

Nothing else in the house had moved. "What was that?"

"I don't know."

"Should we look?"

He shrugged. "Do you want to?"

"Stop that."

"Stop what?"

"Making me decide." I rolled my eyes. *Keep quiet.* The wood floor let out a long creak under my feet and finished with a pop. I stopped, waited. If someone stood there, listening…what then? I swallowed and peered around the door.

The front door lay flat in the foyer, ruined hinges having finally given up.

"I wondered when that would happen," Matt said in a whisper. "So…the bench is empty and what we came for isn't here."

*But why?* "I'm gonna look in the rest of the house."

"What?"

"Did you not hear me?" I hissed.

"Anya, there's someone living here and they may be insane or—"

"How do you know it's not just some other kids messing around?"

His jaw tensed. "We still should leave."

"You can leave." I moved down the dark hallway, toward another room at the back of the house, passing a door shut most of the way on my left, cracked open enough to see the corner of what might have been a desk.

After a second, I heard his footsteps follow me. A sound from the room at the end of the hall met my ears. Soft, but getting a little louder as I got closer. A rumble, and constant rushing. Rain, unmistakably rain. Somewhere in the house was the sound of a rainstorm while the sun still lit the world beyond the front door. A chill ran right up my spine. It had to be a sound machine, hidden in some nook we couldn't see into. Maybe one of those clocks that made noise. It meant Matt was right, that some crazy person probably made a home here, keeping up appearances of a haunted house, warding off intruders.

I grabbed Matt's wrist and kept walking. *No way am I looking alone.* If we met some nasty surprise, we could always run. *Good thing he didn't actually leave.*

The noise got louder and another rumble beckoned me closer, into the house's kitchen. An old sink rusted under a single window. A wood-burning stove stood against one wall, unmoved and unused. My eyes stayed on it for only a moment, because one of the other walls hung open in a perfect doorway. Chilled wet air flowed out of what had to be a cellar.

"Oh my word." I let go of Matt and stepped closer. The hinges were hidden, and on the other side, the wallpaper was perfectly matched, or at least enough to fool a quick glance once it was actually closed. The sound of the thunderstorm tumbled out of the darkness beyond the wall, too natural, too rhythmless to be from a stereo or sound machine. I reached for the edge of the door. *This isn't…what is this?*

"Anya." Matt's urgent whisper stopped me.

I turned. "What is it now?"

His jaw was set, firm. "Take a look." He pointed out the single window above the sink.

At first, my eyes focused on the trees and dead kudzu and brush. "What?"

"You don't see it?"

"No."

He grabbed my arm and tugged me forward, to the window. "Right there. Covered with a sheet of vines."

I pulled my arm out of his grasp, focused my gaze, and saw it. Hidden, like he'd said, under vines all woven together. The ugly, rusted car that hit his truck was parked firmly under the trees, its rear bumper facing us, with its empty space that was supposed to hold a license plate.

*No way.*

Before either of us said anything, another sound built over the thunderstorm. It was just a soft moan first, then got louder, then lurched into a wail. Loud, and louder and then pitching into a guttural scream. I took one calm, clear moment. *Where's it coming from?* Somewhere distant, not from the parlor or the upstairs. It echoed from behind the wall. I grabbed Matt's hand.

"Okay, now we're leaving!" I towed Matt behind me. My foot landed first on the broken door, and it slid wildly for just a moment before I leapt onto the porch. I jumped over the porch steps and landed on the dry grass. Underbrush, dead stumps, and patches of poison ivy flew by under my feet. *Forget the letters.*

The backs of our houses were just in sight when we finally slowed. I leaned against a tree, shaking and sweating, only half from the heat and the run.

Matt caught his breath first. "No letters."

I shook my head and took in a gulp of air. "Not today." Goosebumps flared up on my arms at the wrongness of it all. Those letters were nothing to anyone else, likely hadn't even been touched for a long time. Why had they disappeared? If the contents of the piano bench were a treasure to some crazy squatter in the home, that was understandable. But the sounds…the thunderstorm, the screaming…the car that slammed so hard into us…they were real, very real and very strange.

Could Gavin Dupree and the strange sounds be connected? Was that why the letters had vanished? The sun darkened; the clouds above us were steadily getting thicker. A thunderstorm would come to Sanders County today.

*Then where was that other storm?*

But the house hadn't scared me away from it yet. "Let's go to the library."

Matt frowned. "The library?"

"The genealogy room."

"Oh." He looked up at the sky. "Okay."

"That was fast."

"The library isn't inhabited by crazy people."

I chewed the inside of my lip for a moment. "I don't think the house is either." I walked past him, heading for my house.

"What?" He followed, crunching over dead old leaves on the forest floor.

"Something's…off about it."

"Well, yeah."

"I mean…" *What is so wrong about it?* "It's Gavin Dupree. His letters."

He kept his gaze focused ahead. "What about them?"

"Letters written by him, probably with more stuff in them about that riddle or whatever it was, just vanished." I swallowed. "Gone. Someone took them. And my family never talks about him. Ever."

"Why not?"

"I don't know!" My voice sounded too loud. "They just don't. Granny changes the subject every time I ask. Like I said, the most I've ever gotten is that he did something that caused a bunch of trouble." I pushed a huff of air out of my lungs. "And what were those noises?"

He blinked. "A haunted house cliché."

"And the car."

"Yeah." His face sobered. "The car."

My knees trembled. “And the…other sounds.” A thunderstorm. That first scream from the other night, and the one that had just run us out of the house so effectively. “What’s in there?”

We stood at the edge of the woods now, close to our homes. Matt’s solemn eyes flicked once back to the woods. “Probably a lot.”

“Well, you know, if walls could talk…” I sighed. “I want to know what he did that’s so secretive, and I’ve never looked before.” The goosebumps rose on my arms again. “Shoot, I’ve never cared before. We were rear-ended by the same car that shows up at a house where stuff written by some family member suddenly goes missing. What if the letters are tied in with whatever reason it is for the way my family acts?” I swallowed. “What if the car…because if they’re trying to hide something…”

*Why try so hard, though? Why Matt’s car?*

Matt tilted his head. “An intriguing idea.’

“I know.” *Let them hide it. I’ll still find the stupid secret.* “So. Library. I’ll drive.”

He hesitated. “Done with the house for today?”

I shrugged. “For today.”

“Okay. Library. If you drive.”

***

The town had built Sanders County Public Library in the early 1900s, and other than repairing the wiring and adding a little paint, the inside had hardly been touched since. Fine with me, though. It was nice inside. Dark wood steps led up to the second floor, and little half-hidden reading nooks lined the wall every five rows or so. The windows looked out onto the tiny, wilted downtown of Salt’s Creek. Beautiful as the building was, a lack of funds kept the library from getting most of the newer book releases, and the times I visited were more spent looking for something worthwhile among all the large-print murder mysteries, random paperback romances, and a few new items here and there.

But I hadn't come here for books this time, just answers. My shoes scuffed on the stairs, echoing off the plaster, as we made our way to the genealogy room.

Laughter from the children's story time filtered through the second floor. The genealogy room sat mostly empty, the desk vacant. The nameplate said "Lukas Simpson" and a paper taped to the front of the desk listed his hours. "Fridays: Out" was the last entry on the list.

"We're on our own, then."

Matt gazed at the printout. "Yeah." He scratched his head before looking back at me. "Lead the way."

A folded card that read "Catalog" perched on the top of a gray CRT monitor in the corner. "Guess we start there."

I pulled the stool out and sat. The stiff gray keys were unwieldy under my fingers as I typed in "Dupree, Gavin" and waited for the results.

A listing, and then another, then a third. The *Salt's Creek Advance* newspaper, from March 30, 1886 to June of the same year, all on microfilm.

*March 30. Right after the letter was written.* "Wow." I grabbed a scrap of paper and a pencil out of the basket beside the computer.

"He must have been famous," Matt said as I scribbled the dates and numbers I needed.

"Salt's Creek famous, anyway." I walked to the drawers where the strips were kept. "Wonder what he did?" Even if it led nowhere, this at least was a finding, something tangible. A way in. *There.* I pulled the reel from the drawer and sat down at the machine. "Need a seat?"

Matt shook his head. "Nah, I'm good."

With the film in, I wound the knob forward, passing through days, weeks, months until my eye caught the name Dupree under the first March 30 headline.

**LOCAL MAN ARRESTED FOR MURDER OF PROMINENT CITIZEN.**

My heart skipped once.

Murder.

The article took up an entire front page. Matt bent lower, his head close to mine, and I read out loud, keeping my voice low.

"Mr. James Abney of Salt's Creek went missing on Thursday evening, and is now presumed to be dead. Mr. Gavin Dupree, age twenty-five, is thought to be the last person to have seen Mr. Abney alive. Mrs. Esther Abney, the widow, claims that her husband visited Mr. Dupree on the night of the school board meeting, after an open disagreement between the two men at the meeting, to settle the matter. There does not seem to have been a previous connection between them. According to his own account and that of Mr. Abney's driver, Mr. Dupree returned to the front of the house, armed with a sword and covered with a substantial amount of blood, saying that James Abney had disappeared. He then asked the driver for help, as both Dupree and Abney had been wounded. The body has not yet been recovered."

*No.*

It couldn't be.

*No, that's wrong.* I let my eyes blur until the screen was just a mass of gray and black little ticks. That was it. I leaned back. *Wow.*

"He…" My throat caught. "So…that's why they don't talk about him." The evil cousin, or whatever he was.

"Aren't there more articles?" Matt reached around me and turned the knob forward.

A shorter note, dated a week later, took up only part of the front page.

"The trial of Mr. Gavin Dupree has begun, despite local authorities not yet having found Mr. Abney's body. Due to the strange circumstances surrounding Mr. Abney's disappearance and the shaky story on which Mr. Dupree's defense relies, there is little doubt of the outcome of this trial."

Smug. I could see the writer now, writing it with a smirk in some sunlit newsroom. Convicted by the media, whatever else had actually happened. Just knowing that…could I believe he might really be guilty?

And how would this connect to that house and the car, and the missing letters?

"Apparently the guys at the paper were pretty big fans of James Abney," Matt said.

I turned the knob forward again. "Then this isn't a neutral source."

"Encouraging?"

I huffed out one quick breath. "I dunno. I mean, I don't really know who he was to me. Just means the newspaper was partial to one version of the story. Doesn't mean he didn't do it, and there's more stuff here."

Day after day of the *Salt's Creek Advance* rolled by, each issue with a tiny snippet on the trial. **CARRIAGE DRIVER TESTIFIES. MRS. ABNEY SPEAKS OUT. EVIDENCE LACKING IN MURDER TRIAL.** Each condemned Gavin Dupree until finally, only one was left, June 25.

**DUPREE TRIAL ENDS.**

This was it. The answer.

"Here goes."

Matt leaned in closer. "Yep."

"The long trial of Gavin Dupree has come to an end, with a verdict of not guilty. Though many of the people of Salt's Creek do believe Dupree to be guilty of the murder of James Abney, little evidence was found to support his guilt. We at the *Advance* hope that the Abney family may find closure in the future and that justice may be served."

I blinked. "Oh."

"Not guilty."

"Looks like the newspaper was disappointed." *Still doesn't mean he didn't do it.* I rewound the film, took it out, and cut the machine off. An empty basket labeled "Place Used Film Here" sat on a table in the corner. I set the film in it and turned to Matt. "So…what now?"

"Anywhere else to check?"

"I dunno." I frowned at the machine. "I don't think we're gonna find much more stuff here."

"Property records?"

"I guess, but I didn't see any." What would I do with those, anyway?

"Right."

As we stepped down the old staircase, a thought struck me. The riddle…the key…worries about a neighbor…not a close one. "The letter."

"Yeah, what about it?"

I swallowed hard. "He said he had worries about a neighbor…and he wrote it right before Abney disappeared."

"Looks like there was a connection between them after all," Matt offered.

"Either way…" What was it then? *How would they have known each other?* I grabbed Matt's arm again and tugged him forward. "Come on."

"What're you thinking now?"

"My house. There's this box in my attic that I know has a bunch of super old pictures in it," I told him as we descended. "I've only looked at it once, but I didn't know what I was looking for then."

"What are the odds of anything being there?"

"I think pretty good in this case." I dropped my voice. "I hope, anyway."

# Chapter 6

The thick string on the attic door swung back and forth, nudged by the air conditioning vent in the ceiling. I caught the end and tugged, and the door opened out of the ceiling with a groan. The ladder let out its nails-on-a-chalkboard squeal when I pulled it down, and warm air poured into the upstairs hallway.

"Where's the light switch?" Matt asked.

"Up there." The ladder creaked as I climbed, and the comforting warmth flowed over me as I ascended into the space and over the top. The rough wood floor scraped softly against my shoes as I stood to flick the switch on. The room filled with a dim, golden light. A soft rattle on the roof and a wet tap at the gray window announced the arrival of what the sky had threatened all afternoon.

Was it raining deep inside that house, too?

On the wall sat a cardboard box, one corner crushed and the word "Pictures" scrawled across the side in black marker. I slid it over and plopped in front of it. Matt eased himself down across from me.

The box wasn't taped together, just held closed by the four panels tucked around each other. I flipped it open, sending dust up into our faces.

He sneezed. "Nice."

I coughed and rubbed my eyes, blinking away the tiny specks that had deposited themselves under my eyelids. "Oops."

A layer of yellowed tissue paper covered whatever rested underneath, and I set the fragile sheets aside.

"Saving the paper?" Matt said.

"Sure." A stack of photo albums took up most of the box, and a newspaper poked out from under all the books. "Might be something on it."

"Probably not."

I narrowed my eyes. "Well, whatever, I'm keeping it." I pulled the leather album, labeled "Photographs" in half-scratched-off gold paint, into my lap. Matt moved over and sat beside me. I pulled the cover open and slid half the book to him. The first page only had one picture.

Just a man and a woman, both older, but not quite elderly, standing in front of a small house. On the page underneath it were the words "Mom and Pop," in faded pencil. An old yellowed card with a picture of flowers on the front rested beside the picture, the envelope long gone. I reached for it. A note in neat black writing took up only a little of the inside, the words so tiny they were almost hard to read.

Elijah,

My parents had this picture of your mother and father at their house. I thought you might like to have it. Please let me know if you find anything else concerning some of the things we discussed. I'll be happy to answer anymore questions if you have them.

Hope to see you soon.

Best,

Mildred Barnes

"Do you know who Elijah is?" Matt lifted the card for a moment, then closed it.

"My great-grandaddy. His name was Elijah." I lifted the corner of the picture. *It might be him*. "Think it'll come off?"

"Give it a try."

I tugged at the corner of the picture, and it came off the page with a soft pop. I flipped it over. Words scribbled on the back identified the people.

Gavin and Maggie, 1923.

The thumping in my chest sped up. Gavin. Gavin Dupree. My great-grandaddy's father.

Then…my Granny's grandfather.

Seeing the man in the sepia-toned picture, his eyes squinted up by a wide smile, made the story sharply concrete. Maybe he was laughing here, in front of that house. Could this guy have killed someone? Self-defense, maybe. *Or he was a psychopathic murderer*. My scalp prickled. "I hope there are more here."

"Keep going."

"Yeah." The thick yellowed page turned stiffly. Granny had these same kinds of photo albums at her house, with still barely tacky adhesive pages that sometimes held onto pictures only for the sake of tradition, but no pictures fell from the pages of this book. Unfamiliar faces at weddings, family dinners, Christmases or maybe Thanksgivings, all passed by until I saw at least one name I knew, though the face was so many years older now. A little girl sat on a porch swing in a frilly dress, the name "Jeannie" penciled in at the bottom. "That's my Granny."

"So Gavin was her grandfather?" Matt leaned back on his hands.

"Looks like it."

"Hmm."

"What are you 'hmming' about?"

Matt shrugged. "Just interesting." He flipped a page towards me. "So, rest of the pictures."

The photos moved forward in time, though still in black and white. More family photos, all in the same house now, and a pattern emerging.

"Hey, I'm starting to see the same thing a lot here," I said. One square object, prominently featured in a lot of the pictures, but the randomness of it meant it might not be a coincidence.

"You mean that thing on the wall, right?"

"Yeah."

"Me too," Matt confirmed.

I flipped back, starting at the first page we'd seen it. Just a simple frame with words, embroidery or something, that showed up on the wall beside a Christmas tree, beside a young and dressed-up version of my Granny with a stiff-backed boy, another of Granny with friends or cousins, and one photo of another Christmas tree, later in time, beside the same frame. In every picture, no matter who was in it, the frame was close to the center of the image, like it was most important.

"It's definitely there a lot." Matt said.

I leaned closer over that last one. "Wish I could see it a little more clearly."

"Any bigger pictures of it?"

"Maybe…" I flicked once, and the page turned over. All of the pictures on these two pages in some way contained the frame again. Family posed under it. Gavin Dupree sitting in his chair, grinning at something out of view. One photo of a stack of presents under a Christmas tree succeeded in actually pushing the frame off to the side, but it was still there, still noticeable, the words just out of reach. The very last picture was a close shot of Gavin Dupree, with his wife perched beside him on an arm of the chair, both smiling at the camera. Whoever took the picture stood closer to them here, and the words in the frame were big enough to be read.

I'll sell you a riddle for a dime
said the bishop at the chime.
With tables and ravens and eggs on a wall,
and diamonds and pennies in keys and all,
the top of the tower pressed down to fall
my riddle is finished sir; what is your call?

*This doesn't make any sense.* "What…"

Matt leaned closer. "What does that mean?"

"I don't know." I flipped the page over. "This is the end."

"It looks like they wanted someone to see it." He paused. "It's everywhere."

"Not necessarily." Could he have been really, truly crazy? I turned back and looked at the photo, read the poem again. Cryptic. Nonsense. "Unless this is a code. Doesn't make much more sense than some of that letter, right?"

"Way less sense."

"What if it's code for something? I mean you could be right…he could have meant it to be found." *The riddle.* "Think this is the riddle he wrote about?"

Matt stared down at the picture again for a long moment. "Maybe."

"But why put it here?" I swallowed. "The pictures just got shoved up here in the attic. He had to have known that."

Matt just shrugged. "Maybe he just counted on whatever is in that frame still hanging on somebody's wall."

"Bet none of the letters would be much help, then," I grumbled. With a sigh, I slid my thumbnail carefully under the edge of the picture, imagining it tearing away, white bits of backing clinging to the sticky page. I pulled carefully.

The photograph came away with a soft *tick* as the paper separated easily from the aged adhesive, and I set it beside me. "Let's check the rest."

Color photographs in this next one. Pictures of my dad's cousins, more family gatherings, but no more of Gavin or the strange picture on the wall. I set the book down beside me.

"So the sampler is only in that one," I said.

Matt peeked into the box. "We've still got a few to go."

"Actually there're like three and they're pretty thin."

"All the more reason to get started."

"You're excited about this, I take it."

He shrugged. "We found something here. I just figure there's gotta be more."

I grabbed the bottom of the stack, dragging the piece of newspaper out with it. "All right. Take one."

"Okay." Matt grabbed the one on top of the new stack, and I took the one under it.

Old pictures, at least to me, but all in color, still the 80s, then the 90s. The last picture in the book I had was of my parents, my mom's belly round under a big, flowing shirt. "Hey, it's a picture of me. Sort of."

Matt peeked over and smiled. "Anything else?"

"Nope."

"Me either."

"Should we bother with the last one?" It was definitely too new. I lifted it into my lap.

Just one picture, of my Granny holding a baby, probably me, beside a table in some house. "I guess mom meant to do a lot more with this. Looks like wherever we lived before we moved here."

"And no sampler."

"Lost to time, I guess." I leaned back on my hands and looked over it all. "Cool old newspaper, though." An old and creased copy of the *Salt's Creek Advance*, folded with the bottom half of the paper visible. It had clearly been folded small before, and the paper had turned yellow and gotten as soft as a cotton ball. I unfolded it. The date in the corner read September 5, 1977.

"**VOYAGER 1 HEADED FOR THE STARS**" proclaimed the headline.

"That is cool." said Matt. His gaze froze on a corner of the page.

"Yeah."

"There's handwriting," he said.

"What?"

"At the bottom."

My eyes went to the end of the article, and a note written there, neat and tiny, in the same handwriting as the card had.

E,

I need you to take note of this day and remember what I said earlier. What we discussed was not insanity. They did find other skies first that this craft will never see.

M.B.

"M.B…" The same initials as the woman who had signed the card. Other skies? "Matt, do you think this is the same M.B.? Mildred Barnes?"

He narrowed his eyes, then nodded. "I think there's a good chance." He read the note again. "What did she mean by other skies?"

"It looks like Elijah was talking to her about something pretty… strange." We'd have to find out somehow, from her, if possible. An idea floated up, crazy, maybe, and hard to pull off if she knew stuff she didn't want to talk about, but if there were more answers. . . . "We should call her if I can find her number listed."

"How do you know she's still living?" He paused. "Or will even be fine with telling us stuff?"

"No harm in trying, right?" I stood, cradling the photo in my hand. "I mean if she's not, then that's it. I'll bug Granny for stuff she might know." *Not that that'll get me anywhere.*

"Fair enough." Matt jumped up as I headed for the attic door. "Want me to get the light?"

"No, leave it on. I'm coming back up." *No one's home yet anyway.*

"Okay."

My feet fell into a rhythm as I ran down the stairs. The thin county phone book sat beside the telephone, just about pristine since we didn't use it too much anymore. Matt's footsteps came up behind me as I flipped the thin gray pages to the Bs and scrolled my finger down. Barnes, Mildred.

"Okay…well…"

"Good luck." Something flashed across Matt's eyes. Eagerness? He was trying to seem casual.

I grinned. "You want to know as much as I do, don't you?"

His eyes stayed trained on the kitchen counter for a moment before he looked up. "Yes, because I know that I've heard Gavin Dupree's name before. So by all means, satisfy my curiosity."

"You can't just ask whoever said something about it?"

One eyebrow arched up. "Let's just say I'm not in a position to say where I heard them talking about him."

"Now that's a story I want to hear." I lifted the receiver, punched the numbers in, and waited. The phone rang once, and again. Then it clicked as someone picked it up.

"Hello?" said a woman.

"Um…" I cleared my throat. "Hi. I'm calling for Mrs. Mildred Barnes. Is she in?"

"She's not here at the moment. May I ask who's calling?"

*Have to make it up*. "My name is Anya McCall. I'm a student at Ravenbook Academy. I'm doing a genealogy project this summer, and Mrs. Barnes' name came up in some of my research. I think she might have known my great-grandfather, and I'd…I'd like to ask her a few questions." *Not too made up…pretty much true.*

"Oh, all right." She coughed. "Well, Anya, I'm her daughter Rebecca. Normally I'd wait for her to get back to ask, but I think since it's a special project, she'd be fine helping you. How about you come by tomorrow afternoon, around one o'clock?"

*Really? That fast?* "Well…okay. That works."

"Good. Now, do you know where Simpson's store is?"

*Boy, do I.* "Yes ma'am."

"Okay, go past the store and down the road about half a mile. There's a little white house with a green metal roof. You can't miss it. That's my mother's house."

*Wow*. "Thank you."

"You're welcome. I'll let her know to expect you at one."

"Thank you so much, again."

"No problem sweetie."

The line clicked. My hand lowered and somehow found the cradle for the phone. Far too easy. Had she been expecting a call?

Matt poking my arm shook me out of the eerie thoughts. "So?"

I looked up, caught his gaze. "One o'clock. Tomorrow. Little white house near Simpson's."

Both eyebrows shot up this time. "Wow. Good."

I shook my head. "It's just weird how fast she agreed."

"Do you still wanna go?"

"Should we?"

Matt shrugged. "I'm following whatever you do in this."

Mildred Barnes was still living and apparently all too willing to provide answers. How could I refuse that? "Yes. I still want to go." Guilt prodded at me inside, from dragging Matt around. "You don't have to, though."

"What did I just say?" That same eagerness flashed across his eyes again, for only a moment.

"I just don't want you to think you have to come along."

He leaned against the counter. "I want to. I'm curious."

*Okay, Mr. Casual.* "So what were you doing when you heard that name?"

"Eavesdropping." His face went solemn. "You know the name on the desk at the library? Lukas Simpson?"

"Yeah?"

"He's friends with my parents. I think. They know him, at any rate. He likes to drop by and they shut themselves up in either the dining room or my dad's office when he comes by, and I heard the name Dupree one time when I was younger." He took a breath. "When I saw Davies and Ocracoke on that one envelope, well…I wanted to know."

"Oh." *How far back does this go?* I remembered the picture in my hand. No one would miss a page from the notebook by the phone. In shaky letters, I copied down Mrs. Barnes' number and the nonsense poem from the photo and stared at the meaningless verse.

Answers. Finally.

Maybe.

## Chapter 7

Sweat dampened my face. I kept my eyes on the dash in front of me, told myself it was from the way the sun streamed into the truck and overwhelmed the air conditioning. The heat was why I was sweating, why I couldn't feel cool. *Liar. You're nervous.*

"Ready?" Matt asked me.

"I guess." I popped the door open, hopped out of the truck, and stopped short. The roof, the windows, the porch, and even the gravel front walk, all the same as the only other place I'd seen it. This was the same house in the photo of Gavin and Maggie. "Um…"

"Looks familiar." Matt's door clunked shut.

"Just a little." *How close were they?* Mildred knew his son, at any rate. A movement in the window, the edge of a curtain falling, caught my eye. Was Mildred watching, since she knew to expect us? "I guess…now or never, right?"

"Right."

I let my breath out and climbed the steps, pressed the doorbell, and waited. Not two seconds passed before the door pulled inward. Mildred

Barnes was short, maybe half a foot shorter than my five feet nine inches, and her dark skin wrinkled along the sides of her face, right where her laugh lines were. She smiled, the creases around her eyes deepening.

"Hello! You must be Anya. Come in, please." She turned around, beckoned me to follow, and kept talking. "Y'all have a seat. Can I get you anything to drink?"

"No thank you." I stepped into the cool house, watching the tiny woman shuffle to her living room. The deep brown shag carpet in her house muffled our steps as we followed along.

"Well all right, then. Sit down, sit down." Photographs of landscapes covered the wall, some new and some obviously old. She smiled widely at Matt. "And what's your name, honey?

He cleared his throat. "Matt Dobken."

She nodded. "Well, nice to meet you."

A photo hung on the wall above a faded armchair. It looked like it might have been Grandfather Mountain, covered in green against a vivid blue sky. "I like that picture there."

She looked back at it and settled down in the chair. "Thank you. My granddaughter does some photography sometimes. She took that one last summer." Then she gestured at the couch again. "Have a seat and go ahead with whatever it was you wanted to ask me."

I lowered myself onto the flowery print sofa, and the cushion sank deep as Matt sat beside me.

Mildred's sharp, dark eyes could have been staring straight through me. She smiled.

*How do I start?* "Well…" A long moment of silence followed as I tried to figure out what to say.

Mildred didn't wait for me to speak. "My daughter told me that you think I knew your great-grandfather."

The answer croaked out of my throat. "Yes." I swallowed. "Elijah Dupree."

Mildred nodded slowly. "I did know him. Quite well, in fact. His father and my parents were good friends, a long time ago, though he was quite a bit older than them."

His father. *Should I fake it?* She didn't know why I was really here. "Who was his father?"

"His name was Gavin Dupree." She coughed. "He owned a lot of land back then, farmed most of it." Her sharp gaze found me again, waiting for me to press further.

*Guess I'll have to ask the right questions.* "What happened to the land?" I was prodding, just like she wanted. Spooky. *She's been waiting to pass all this on, but why?*

"He got rid of it." Her eyes flicked to Matt now, and she stared at his face for a few moments. Did she see what I had seen in Matt's eyes when we stood in the dark the other night? "Mr. Dupree gave the land to my parents on the condition that they follow a particular set of instructions."

Just follow instructions in exchange for free land and a house? *Gavin Dupree was insane. Had to be.* "Where was the land?"

"It was right near here, actually." She pointed out the window. "You know the neighborhood Woodstream, right at the edge of town? Right behind Willow Drive, I think, if I'm remembering right."

My chest tightened up. I took a breath, trying to force myself to relax, to listen. *Don't get excited.* "Who owns the land now?"

Her fingers adjusted a doily on the coffee table. "I do."

*Whoa.* "So what were his instructions?"

Mildred smiled again. It didn't go all the way up to her eyes this time, and she looked down at the table. "What he required when he deeded the land the land to my parents was very strange, which would make following it a perfect payment. Proof he could trust them without any money changing hands or any dealings with the bank, though their friendship had long established that trust. They were not to ever sell the land, in whole or part, and none of their heirs were to do so, either. If they could not agree with the stipulations, then they were not to enter into the contract, and if possible, the land was to be returned to the Dupree family, or their heirs, if there was ever a time when the instructions could not be followed. I have honored the promise my parents made and my daughter will do the same when I pass, though I do prefer to stay on this lot. My husband and I made our home here, after all."

Would an innocent man go so far out of his way to make sure people he didn't trust couldn't have access to the farm? *No, but a crazy man sure would.*

Matt leaned forward, resting an elbow on his knees. "Why didn't he allow them to sell it?"

Mildred Barnes met his question with more silence, longer this time, stretching out the quiet as she studied the floor. *Come on, just tell us.* Then she lifted her gaze straight into my eyes, and laughed softly.

"There is a story behind that." Mildred cleared her throat sharply and shifted in the armchair. "The tale says that Gavin Dupree hid something on his property, a thing close to him and of vast importance. A treasure, you might say."

My stomach fluttered. *I bet it was James Abney's body.* Matt's eyebrows pressed toward each other in a frown. Dare I ask her? *I should.* She'd know. Her parents were there, had seen the events first hand. Yes. "I…I read somewhere that Gavin Dupree was tried for a murder. James Abney was the victim, I think." I swallowed. *This is it, this is what you came for.*

Mildred's eyebrows arched. "The fate of James Abney is still unknown to this day. Completely unsolved."

"Do you know much about the trial?" Matt asked.

She nodded once. "I do. For example, I know that they never found a body to accompany their accusations." Her sentence ended in a hard edge.

That I had known already from the articles we'd read. *Time to get an opinion.* Just the way she said it offered a huge hint as to what she thought of it. "What do you think?"

She moved back a little, shrinking into the chair. I'd caught her by surprise, but she answered this question faster than she had the others. "I personally believe that Gavin Dupree died an innocent man, with the hatred of a town and the distrust of some of his family heaped on him."

*Don't I hope he was innocent.* But believing someone was innocent and him actually being so were two different things.

Matt's voice broke through over my thoughts. "What do you think happened to James Abney, since he vanished?"

"I think that he faked his death and lived out the rest of his life under a different name, somewhere else. He was that kind of man. Got what he wanted out of Salt's Creek and found a neat way to leave."

*Makes for a good story*. "Why would he do that? I thought he was important here or something." *And why would he want to ruin the life of a man he didn't even know?*

Mildred shook her head. "James Abney donated to causes he thought would win him favor here, and all of it's on record, so you could find it at the library if you wanted to. Regardless of what he did, the consensus that he was a slimy old snake was too widespread to ignore, even among those who called themselves his friends. As long as it could do good for them, they'd have put up with anything he did, and he knew that. In the short time they appeared to know each other, Dupree saw right through Abney, and all those bad feelings culminated in their confrontation at the meeting about the graded school." She paused, eyes narrowing. "Now where did you read about the trial?"

"The *Salt's Creek Advance*."

She sneered. "My parents kept those same articles to remind themselves and me of how that newspaper convicted an innocent man and declared him guilty to sway the people. Mr. Dupree may have been innocent, but after the trial and so much fuss in that paper, there was no way to persuade many people otherwise. Lot of shame on that family because of it."

*Wow.* How long had my family dealt with that before not talking about it became habit?

She kept talking. "James Abney would be at a great advantage if he could ruin Gavin Dupree, and I believe Abney faked his death to do just that."

"But why?"

"I told you, honey. They were enemies. Even though there wasn't much chance for them to have met, the version of the story that I know is that they knew each other before James Abney arrived here. From where, well…that's a little mystery to most. Dupree never said, and Abney vanished." She bit her lip. "If James Abney could ruin a man he hated and go on with his life elsewhere, I believe he would have done just that." Her eyes went guarded again. Tight, turned-down lips, cool eyes that revealed nothing and refused to yield. Had Mildred said more than she wanted? In that instant, it became clear I wasn't getting much more out of her, not about the murder anyway. I had to find another question to ask before she decided that we were done.

"Did he really hide a treasure on his land?"

"Anything is possible."

*Not enough of an answer*. "What do you think it is?"

Mildred laughed. "I can't tell you." Another pause. "Because, of course, I was never intended to know that myself." Her face closed up again, but the hint of something in her eyes remained.

My shoulders inched down, drooping. *Don't look so disappointed. She knows things, and you might find out more later.*

A grandmother's warm smile came again to her face. "I suggest you go poking around the old farm yourself, see what you find."

I felt a twinge of guilt. *We already have been.* "You don't mind?"

"Not at all. You certainly can't hurt anything by just looking." She stressed the last two words hard.

I caught Matt's gaze out of the corner of my eye. *We're definitely going back.* I smiled at Mildred. "Well, thank you for the info. You've been a huge help." I stood.

Mildred pushed up out of her chair. "You're welcome."

The three of us moved to the door, silent, until Matt and I waited at the screen door, Mildred facing us, one hand on the heavy front door.

*There's still more she knows.*

"Please come back any time if you have some more questions. I'd be glad to help you some more if you need me to."

"Okay." I pushed the screen out, my mind working. Matt followed me onto the top step. Before I could turn around to thank her again, the door shut.

I stayed there, staring, not making any effort to step off the porch as Matt moved down to the next step.

*A treasure, you might say*. I kept my voice low. "Matt, do you remember the noises we heard in the house? The storm?"

"Of course."

Would he refuse? I'd only said I was done for the day when we'd run. There was more in that house, now that we knew it had been Gavin's. Matt surely had heard how distant the scream was, how it had come from much farther away than logic could ever allow for. *Brandon needs to see this with us.*

"I'm going back in." Slowly I met his gaze. "I think we ought to show it to Brandon. I'll call him tonight. He's gotta check it out with us."

"Okay." He hopped over the two steps and onto the gravel driveway. "I want to see what he hid in that cellar."

What could possibly be down there? Or who? "When should we go back?" What if that car was there again?

"Tomorrow?"

Why put it off? Why wait, when she gave us so much that we didn't even ask for? Access to the land, no questions asked, to look around all we wanted. She wanted us to find something. *But the car.* A chill ran over the back of my neck. "Okay. Tomorrow."

# Chapter 8

"It's been two days," I said. The pine needles and dead leaves crunched as we made our way to meet Brandon. A thorny vine tugged at my jeans for a moment, like a reaching hand, and let go.

"So?"

"What if someone blocked that door off or something?" I hoped not.

"Then it's blocked off."

"Well, yeah, I know that." Something had to be down there.

"Then what's the problem?" Matt asked.

"A missing box of letters we originally found in an apparently still inhabited house that belonged to my great-great grandfather?" I cleared my throat. "Let alone the car that smashed into the back of your truck and then parked at the back of said house. Plus there's something in that cellar, and you want to see what's in it, too."

He nodded.

The wall of siding entered my field of vision. I stopped. Matt waited beside me.

*This is not even close to safe.* "Last time we were here, we weren't exactly alone." Being the newcomers to this house might mean someone had been visiting all the time, every day, long before we got there. "I'm just…why are we even back?"

Matt nudged my arm. "You're crazy enough to push the issue and I'm nuts enough to go along with you."

The tension in my spine eased. "You say that like it's a bad thing."

He smiled. "Not much we can do if it is blocked off."

"True." I cleared my throat, reluctant to step forward. Through the brush I saw Brandon's silver car and him leaning against it, facing the house. I moved, my foot crunched onto a leaf, and Brandon turned around to us, face blank as we approached.

"How long have you been here?" I asked. Sweat made his hairline damp and darkened his hair against skin that I'd never seen quite so pale. Not since the last time, anyway.

Brandon shrugged. "Ten minutes, maybe." He held up a flashlight. "So we still going in?" His gaze rose up the side of the house. Did he feel the empty-eyed windows looking at him too?

Matt answered. "Actually, I wanna check behind it."

Brandon straightened. "Why?"

*I should go with him.* "The last time Matt and I were here, there was a car parked at the back of the house." *One that hit us.*

Matt added to my words. "I don't really wanna chance running into anyone in there."

Brandon's jaw tensed. "It's an empty house."

"Well, it might not have been the last time, so yeah. We should check." *Seriously?*

Matt walked to the corner of the house. "Y'all can stay here. I'll take a look."

I started to move. "I'll go with you."

"I'll literally be right back."

"But—"

"Just hurry up," Brandon said. "I mean, if you really heard someone screaming, I'm not wasting any more time here."

Matt looked at him. "Like I said, I'll be right back." His gaze caught mine for a moment, a smudge of a frown playing there for a split second.

*Yeah, I don't know either, Matt.*

Matt's feet walking away made the only human sound now. I tried to catch Brandon's eye.

He stared at the dirt, kicked it once.

*This is too weird.*

"Nothing there." I jumped as Matt walked around the wall corner. "Y'all ready?"

"Yep." Just Matt. Just my friend. And nothing else. Safe. Kind of.

"So you said you found a door in the wall or something?" Brandon said. He didn't move.

*Is he stalling?* "Pretty much exactly that."

"And you're just gonna go down in this cellar."

"That's the plan," Matt answered.

"What's in it you want so bad?" Brandon asked sharply, leaning back. A trickle of sweat inched down his face.

*Wow.* I forced a laugh out of my mouth. "It's a hidden door in an old house. I think that sums it up pretty well." He was acting weird again, though. *Is there something he knows about it?*

Brandon's shoulders relaxed, but the hard look in his eyes stayed. "Okay."

"So you're really actually going with us and you plan on staying this time?" I asked.

Brandon just stared back, swallowed once, and quirked his shoulder up briefly.

I shook my head. "Let's just do this." I climbed up the steps.

"Door's already open for us," Matt added, kicking at the door. It still laid where it had fallen. Most of it was in the hall and part hung over the threshold. It might mean that no one had been to the house to move the door back, and my foot had been the last human thing to touch it.

*Or they might have just stepped over it like we're doing.*

I paused in the hall. The cool morning light filled up the inside of the house, and it wasn't so ominous this time. Maybe it was knowing that someone in my family had owned it once, had led a life here, that drove away some of the shadows. Whether Gavin was a murderer or not, he was a connection that linked me to this house and softened its presence. His life had changed forever here.

"Lead the way," Matt told me.

"I am." The kitchen looked dimmer from here, since the light didn't quite reach into those windows yet.

Matt asked the same question that raced through my mind. "What do you think's behind the door?"

"I dunno. Maybe something good." And no horrors.

"Probably nothing good," Brandon said. His words shoved the tension ahead of him, blew it up, made it thicker. Prodding at my back, if it had been anything really tangible.

"Thanks for the optimism."

"Look, you two don't know what you're even walking into, other than what you think might be some secret passage."

"What, and you do?" I turned around, stepping backwards into the kitchen. The door still hung halfway open.

His gaze shot to mine, eyes flashing. "No. Of course not."

My pulse sped up. *Yes he does, and he's angry.* "Okay. Then relax."

"I'm always relaxed."

"Not lately," I shot back.

Brandon started to open his mouth. The stress in the air could have been substantial, for all it seemed to be wrapping claws around me.

Matt's words jutted in. "What if we find bones in there or something?" He twirled his metal flashlight in his hands, all casual.

The band around me loosened. *Smack him or thank him for defusing that?* "Ugh, I hope not."

*Settle for neither now, and be grateful later.*

"Don't you have to report that stuff?" Brandon asked. "I mean, in case they're new remains or something?"

"I dunno." I stepped closer to the door. "What do you think, Matt?"

"It's probably a good idea."

Brandon came up beside me. "Then are we sure we wanna be the ones to find something like that?" He spoke faster. "I mean, you really don't what you're walking into here."

I frowned. "I'm walking into a cellar, Brandon."

Matt shined his flashlight into the dark. "We're just going down here. It's probably just a root cellar. Dried up turnips and stuff."

A thrill ran through me. This was it. A rebellion against shame-filled whispers and secrets that were given to my family, unasked for, that still dominated them. *Just try and keep the answers from me.* "There better be more than turnip guts."

"Well, they'd be gone by now anyway," Matt answered.

"Unless there's a current resident with a taste for root vegetables."

I heard the quick huff of air before Brandon spoke. "You know what, you two are on your own here," Brandon said. "I don't think I'm going with you this time."

"What?"

"I'm not going down there." He walked to the kitchen door. "Look, you admit that you don't know anything about it, right?" He sucked in a deep breath, his face white.

"Well, that's why we're going. To find out. Like always, unless you have some information to volunteer."

"No." He shook his head. "You know a dude got straight up murdered at this house, right?"

He knew the story that I hadn't heard before the other day. *Keep it to yourself. See what he says.* "Huh?"

"Way back. Guy named Abney shows up for a visit at this house, and the dude who lived here just…stabbed him out of nowhere with a sword or a knife or something."

"Where'd you hear that?" Matt asked.

Brandon shrugged. "Local legend. Dupree was the killer's name. I looked it up for a project." His voice shook at the end of his sentence.

"What project?" Had Brandon come back and taken the letters?

His face went blank. "Personal."

*Couldn't have. Doesn't make sense. Someone told him.*

"It's a legend, then," Matt said. "That's it." Part of it wasn't though. That was obvious.

Brandon just shook his head again. "Look, you know what? Y'all have fun. I'm not sticking around here." He backed down the hall.

"But—"

"See you later," he called back. "Y'all can stay."

I watched him leave, heard the car start and pull away, and looked at Matt. "What was that all about?"

Matt frowned. "Has he ever been actually afraid to go in any place with us?"

"Not that I can remember." Goosebumps from the cold air rippled over my skin. "What if there is something nasty?"

"Then we'll have a story to tell." He half smiled.

"Should we do this?"

Matt looked back down the hall. "He got you shaken up."

"It's not him exactly…it's more like…" *No way he's afraid of just a cellar.* "This house has brought out that reaction in him since I first suggested coming here."

He looked into the darkness again. "And he knew that story." He paused. "Is that it, that he knew it?"

"Well, I imagine a few old Salt's Creek families might know it, just…"

Matt leaned against the wall. "What?"

*Now I really need to know.* "It's like he was trying to keep us from checking it out."

"I definitely think that's what he's doing," Matt said. "Didn't really give us a good reason as to why, though."

"Maybe he's just afraid he'll get in trouble if anything happens." I rubbed my eyes. "I don't know." *That can't be it.*

Matt raised an eyebrow. "Well, we did come all this way, and he did make such a convincing argument towards going in."

I nodded. "Then it's decided." My stomach fluttered. "You first."

"No problem." He clicked the button on the side of his flashlight.

I shadowed Matt as we stepped across the threshold. The beam of light caught the first of four steps that led down to a dirt floor. There were no windows, no light, really. The air was even colder once we stepped through the opening and away from the sunlight.

"Looks like it really is just a cellar," Matt said.

*There's more to this.* "One with occasional thunderstorms?" The chilled air raised the hair on my neck.

Matt didn't answer, not at first. His mouth quirked, jaw tightening once or twice. "So you're sure about…" His eyes finished the question. After all that had happened here, the creaks and the moans and the strange car and the behavior of an old friend, was I still bent on this, as foolish as that might be?

*Duh.* "Yes." I faltered inside, bolstered myself a second later. "Absolutely." *No matter what's down there.* Even if a bony smile greeted us in some dark corner.

"Excellent."

I grinned. "Come on."

We crept down the steps together, into the pitch black of the cellar.

*This is nothing, just a creepy little room. Gavin Dupree and all the friends he'd ever had were really and truly crazy, and that was why they were friends, and this is nothing.* If I didn't expect anything good, I couldn't be disappointed too much more.

*Normal houses don't have thunderstorms inside.*

It took an instant for another set of steps to loom out of nowhere as the beam of the flashlight reached them. How had we not seen them before? Matt moved the light from the bottom, on up to where the stone twisted left into the dark and out of sight, rendered invisible by the lack of light.

He looked at me. "Stairs."

They went higher than I knew the ceiling in the kitchen to be. Past that point, at least, and the rest hidden. "Why'd he have stairs hidden in his walls?"

"Didn't we pass another room?" he asked.

I shook my head. "That was a study or something. I saw a desk. This is…"

"Something else," he finished.

I let my flashlight beam trail along the stones. "Any ideas where this might go?"

"Nope."

My pulse sped up, pounding against my ribs. My eyes had already adjusted to the poorly lit space, and now I could see that it wasn't just a pitch black void above us. There was a glow, so soft but undoubtedly real, that illuminated the stone steps. "Matt, there's light up there."

"Yeah, I saw it when we came in."

"Oh." *Why didn't he say anything?* "And you didn't tell me?"

"I thought it was obvious."

"Not to me." I sighed. "So do you think we should check it out or not?"

"I like how you're asking my opinion this time around."

I smacked his shoulder. "Hush." Dust floated in front of the light. "Seriously, though."

"I know you won't be satisfied until we do, and I'm pretty curious myself." He held the flashlight under his chin, deepening the shadows on his face and giving his pupils that eerie glow. "So yes."

"Okay." I drew in a deep breath of the chilled air. "Up it is, then."

The sole of my shoe scuffed against the stone as I walked up. The glow didn't waver or flicker or change at all. It just stayed steady as we climbed.

"Think there's a light bulb up there?" I asked Matt.

"Wouldn't be surprised."

But electricity had to come from somewhere.

*What did Dupree build these stairs for, and where's it taking us*? That brought my feet to a stop as I reached the top.

Matt paused on the step. "What's wrong?"

My stomach shuddered. I shoved down the knot in my throat. "No way we're still actually in the house." Did that even make sense? *Then what could this be?* What was I even talking about? Maybe this would just end up in a part of the house. Maybe the structure of this staircase was perfectly logical, only seeming otherwise because we'd entered it in the cellar.

Matt's flashlight beam met the wall where the staircase turned. "Yeah. I don't think we are either." Were we somehow underground?

No, that didn't make sense either, unless there was some trickery in how the cellar was constructed.

"I don't want to go back, though." I gazed up at the light above us. "Houses aren't supposed to have storms inside them. I want answers."

He climbed ahead. "Me too."

We turned the corner. Scattered over the walls around the stairs were tiny lights affixed to the inside, brightening the rest of the staircase and highlighting the bright, hard light of a door's outline at the top.

"Where do you suppose that goes?"

"Any chance it's a second porch?"

*No use not getting closer.* "That would make too much sense." And what were those little bulbs on the wall? I drew closer to the harsh light from the other side, felt the air dampen around me. The little lights covered the back of the wood panels, fading into the inches wider side of the cracked open door. Matt stood in the corner of my vision. I stepped back.

"Well?" he asked.

"Should we go through?" The cool, wet smell of whatever was on the other side reached me, pulled at me, beckoned me farther in.

Matt didn't answer for a long moment. "Climbing all those stairs for nothing probably doesn't appeal to you. Sure doesn't to me."

"Okay." I touched the door. It shuddered half an inch. Hinges squeaked, but only for a second. Was it oiled? A thrill went along my skin. *This door might be in use.* "Then shall we?"

"I'm with you." Matt's eyes gleamed in the light, reflecting it back at me. Maybe my eyes did it too, and I'd just never thought about it.

No. They couldn't. No way possible. Matt's eyeshine was unique to him.

*And he's way eager to find out more about your great-great-grandfather, and his family's mentioned the name before. . . .*

*One weird thing to think about at a time.*

"Okay." I slipped my fingers into the crack and pushed the door away from me, cringing away from the sudden increase in brightness before I opened my eyes. *No more hesitating.* I pushed my eyes open and looked out at what waited on the other side of the door.

Color splashed across my vision, red, orange, yellow, and some green, all half-cloaked by the mist that clung to the trees, the ground, the mountain slopes above and below us. I stepped out onto a wet dirt road that ran off in both directions.

Matt's mouth dropped open.

*Definitely not safe.* "Where are we?"

"Not Sanders County."

The road squished under my shoes as I took another step away from the side of the mountain. "Obviously."

The gray sky, the cold, the stark difference in the seasons, and the obviously different terrain. A hysterical laugh bubbled up and jumped out of my mouth. "Is this it? Is this what Gavin Dupree hid?" *Another place entirely*. My mind grasped it with slippery fingers. *An impossibility.* A whole world hidden in a run-down house.

Matt's eyes dropped to mine. "What else would be?"

Another laugh pushed its way out of me and bounced off the rocky hill. "Did we travel back in time?" *Beautiful. Incredible. These things don't happen. Ever.* How could it? This wasn't real, and it wasn't possible. I stepped away from that mental edge. I could think about the outright strangeness of our find later. It begged to be explored now.

"Maybe." Matt turned slowly. "So what now?"

"Um…I don't know." Something crashed through the brush somewhere above us, an animal probably. Something we'd scared off. *What kinds of things live here?* "Look around?"

"Seriously?"

I faced him. "Yes. Seriously."

"You think that's a good idea."

*He was more than willing to come along before.* "Just for a little bit." *You're not making me turn back now.* "I've said before, you can go home."

Matt shook his head. "I'm not leaving you here alone, especially since we don't know where this is."

"Well, I'm certainly not leaving right now, so you can follow me." The sole of my tennis shoe slipped an inch in the mud as I turned around. *He can't tell me what to do.* I got ten feet before I slowed down. *And I don't know what kind of animals live here*. No wonder Gavin Dupree hid this. Whatever this place and that cellar were, what would other people do with it?

Matt caught up beside me. *Knew he'd do that.*

He spoke, voice solemn. "Can I make a serious request?"

"Okay."

"Don't run off like that again. Please."

Defiance bloomed in my chest as we rounded a curve. "I didn't run off."

"You know what I mean."

"I guess." I stopped walking, briefly aware of the sound of running feet somewhere behind us. *Ignore it. Animals*. "But you need to back off me. You're not my bodyguard, okay?"

"Okay. Fair enough." He sighed. "But you know, since this is not at all a familiar place, then we really don't need to split up."

*Thank you.* "If it makes you happy, sure."

"Good."

How far was the door behind us now? I peeked. It was just around that curve. We could get back, as long as we stayed on the road.

The noise started. Crashing and stomping through the brush in the direction we'd come from filled the forest and echoed off the rocks as a true commotion built up, punctuated by human voices. I froze.

*Uh-oh.*

Matt frowned.

"At least we don't have to worry about animals now," I said.

"Great." He tugged at my elbow, pressing himself against the side of the mountain and pulling me with him. Grit from the dirt dug into my arms as I leaned against the rock.

*Don't find us. Don't see us. We're not here.*

Barked commands, more rustling of dead leaves on the ground. I leaned out, just long enough to see men, a dozen or more, no, many more, all in old-fashioned clothes. Old uniforms, it looked like. They might not have been out of place at a Civil War reenactment, I thought. Each man had a rifle strapped to his back. I leaned back. *We can't get caught.* "What do we do?"

"I don't know."

Fear raced through me. "Figure something out."

"I've never exactly been in this situation before, Anya."

"I noticed." Without a warning, the thick clouds let loose the rain they held, driving it down onto us. "Oh perfect."

"Well, we can't go back that way." Matt's dark hair stuck to his forehead, aiming drops of water down his nose. His eyes narrowed. "Maybe if we circle back or something."

"They'll still be there."

"Not if we lead them away."

"What?"

His teeth ground together. "Lead them away."

"Like be seen on purpose?" *Dumb. Stupid. Bad idea.* "I mean, they might leave, right?" Once more, I leaned forward, peering around Matt, hoping that maybe, please, they'd already started to move on.

Two eyes met mine, though the other pair was far away. A young man froze for a moment as we stared at each other. His arm rose as he looked away, mouthing something at one of the other men. *Get out of his sight, dummy.* I didn't see what he did next, just pressed back against the side of the mountain. "Uh-oh."

"What?"

"One of them saw me."

Matt took a deep breath, then a second one. "Well at least you've got their attention."

"Now what?"

"Run."

No objection there.

Two steps. I didn't even get two steps before another man, not the same who'd seen me, hopped off the mountain and landed in front of us. "Stay right where you are." He reached for my arm. My mind stuck for a long moment on the fact that he had just spoken in English.

My next move came from nowhere, unplanned, thoughtless. As his hand went forward, all slow-motion, I twisted away and drove my other fist into his nose. He shouted, the cry choking off as his nose popped.

"Come on!" My hand found Matt's arm and I pulled him forward, to the side of the road and down the hill, and let go.

Fight and flight. *Good to know that works.*

The man I'd smacked yelled, his voice garbled. "Talbot! We have two intruders!"

*Maybe I broke his nose.*

The slope of the hill gave me plenty of momentum, for all it felt like falling. I just ran, keeping up with Matt, the rain soaking through my clothes, barely staying on my feet in the slick mud. The voices behind us faded, and the rain trickled off. I caught hold of a young tree and leaned against it. "I think we might have lost them."

"Why did you go this way?" Matt asked breathlessly.

"I don't know." My wet jeans clung to my skin as I stepped away from the tree. "Maybe we can circle back now and—" The mud under my feet shifted a second before the ground fell out from under me. I grabbed for Matt, for the tree, for anything, and shrieked as I began a wild, soaking tumble.

My hands grabbed a slick root, and the rest of me slung around, legs suspended over the drop below me. My arm passed over the sharp point of a rock, catching there as I my hands gripped a rain-darkened rope of wood that stuck out of the ground. I squeezed tighter, the wet root slipped under my fingers, and the rock tugged at my skin. I peeked over my shoulder, far as I dared. The drop wasn't too far, ten feet at the most. Not too bad a fall, if I landed right, and if I could guarantee that.

A blur down below. *No.* One of them had caught up. Letting go now would mean…well, something bad, maybe, if they didn't just question us and let us go. I swung my right leg, trying to get one foot back up onto the side, still grasping the slippery root. My shoe just caught the muddy edge and slipped, taking a clump of mud with it. Matt was still yards away. My voice ripped out of my mouth. "Hurry!"

"I'm coming!" He was close, but not close enough to ease the panic racing through me. I couldn't just keep dangling like this. I tried one more swing up.

My foot missed the ledge this time, and the weight of my body jerked my hands free of the root. A sharp pain zinged up my arm where it had rested against the rock as I dropped to the landing below. Maybe at least my knees could absorb this landing. An instant later, the ground hit the soles of my feet, and I landed in a half-crouch before colliding with the shins of whoever had been down there.

He fell back, landing with a grunt. A man. Or a guy, anyway. Young. We looked at each other for a moment. I pushed myself up and backed away. *Need a really big stick.* There. Three feet long, maybe an inch thick. I grabbed it and held it up like a baseball bat. If I landed a blow on him, it would hurt. I was sure enough of that. If the stick didn't just break in half.

The guy was just a boy, probably my age, bent forward, defensive, and watching me with guarded brown eyes, his rain-darkened hair dripping. His clothes were old-fashioned too, a rough brown coat over a tan shirt. Gray pants. Scarred old boots. The nerves in my arm jabbed roughly, blood mixing with mud and running down what was left of the rain on my skin.

"Are you all right?" His eyes went to my arm. "I can bandage that up for you if you want."

*Being nice?* "Don't…just back off. Stay there. I'm…" I swallowed, pulling the stick back into a ready position. "I'm armed."

The side of his mouth lifted. "With a stick."

"Yeah, and whatever you've got, I can still hit you."

He blinked. "What if I had a gun?"

My heart thumped harder. "What do you want?"

"To help." He looked at my arm again. "If you're not going to hit me with that."

I relaxed, just a hair, letting my makeshift bat ease forward and down. "Just don't turn us in or anything."

His eyes narrowed. "What do you mean?"

Something fell from the ledge above me. Matt shoved himself between me and the stranger.

"Matt, seriously?"

He didn't look at me. "Who's this guy?"

I looked at the other boy. He straightened, calm. "Noam."

Matt's gaze landed on the blood oozing from my arm. "You're…"

*Back off.* "I'm good."

"That's blood."

I pushed at his shoulder. "Oh really? I had no idea."

Noam looked down at my shoes, and back up at my face. "You really are a mess."

The heat in my face rose as I looked down. My jeans and t-shirt were caked with the mud I'd slid through, and blood mixed with dirt on my arm. I shivered at the breeze that picked up. "Yeah. Guess I am."

"I can clean and bandage the cut if you want to come with me."

"It's not that bad. Just a scratch." The trembling started in my hands and knees. Cold, pain, realization of what we'd found, the terror of not getting home because of all those men swarming around the door. . . . *Calm down.* "Okay. Yeah, I guess we could come with you." I unwrapped my fingers from around the stick, letting it drop back to the ground. It cracked in half when it landed.

"Anya—" Matt's face relaxed, but the hint of a frown still hovered around his eyes.

*Thought I told him to back off.*

Noam backed up a step. "I'm not making you come. It's just an offer. You don't have to take it."

He sure didn't seem that threatening, but the sounds from up the hill were beginning to carry through the trees to where we stood. "We will, if you promise you're not going to turn us in."

Noam hadn't moved, just listened, but now he spoke again. "To whom would I turn you in?"

I pointed up the slope. "Those guys. The ones in green."

He lifted his chin, understanding dawning in his eyes. "Oh. That's why I heard so much noise." He paused. "Where did you come from?"

"That…the door up there."

He looked back and forth between us. "You really need to come with me, then."

"Why?"

"I'll explain, but not here." He shook his head. "I don't want to leave you here because I can't guarantee you won't be found, and you likely don't want them to find you."

They'd probably start tracking, and I'd left an obvious trail in the mud. They'd find us very quickly. "Okay. We'll go with you."

"Noam, what have you done now?" A girl's voice burst from the trees, loud in the quiet air. "I heard noise—" A girl with braided black hair stepped through the trees, a rifle strapped to her back. "Oh." Her green eyes flicked over me and Matt as the smile faded from her face. "This is new."

"Meris, this is Anya and Matt." He paused. "They've just arrived."

Meris looked up the hill. "I heard the commotion." She looked over to us. "Where did they come from, Noam?"

*Seriously? We're right here.*

He glanced back up. "They said a door in the mountain."

Meris whirled around. "Are you from Earth?"

I blinked. "Yes." *Wait, where is this?*

"We need to go," she said.

*What's going on? Earth?* The note scrawled on the newspaper came back to my mind. *They did find other skies first. . . .*

Noam took a step backwards. "Did he contact you?"

Meris rolled her eyes. "No, he did not, and I'll have a word with dear little Ira the next time I see him. If he's afraid of a little water, then he's of no use to us."

They walked away from where we'd been standing.

"Follow us," Noam said.

*Not really an option here.* I followed them, Matt silent beside me. *What did we fall into?* My elbow throbbed out a beat as we stepped over rocks and roots, heading at a slant upward. There wasn't really anywhere else safe to go except with these two other kids who sure looked like they were alone.

"This area was more guarded today," Noam answered her. "Ira had to have seen it."

"He is not a child, and I know full well that the sneaky little thing can take care of himself."

Noam caught my eye. "At least we found something."

"Two somethings, it would seem." Meris glanced back at us, her face bent in a tight smile.

*She's sure not happy to see us here.*

She spoke again, voice cold. "Welcome to Trenavell."

# Chapter 9

The sound of the leaves crunching under my feet echoed through the forest, bouncing off the trees and rocks, probably alerting anyone who might be on patrol. *Here we are. Come and get us.* After all that, there was bound to be somebody looking for two kids who walked out of the side of a mountain. Noam and Meris didn't speak as we scaled the hills, and neither did I. Matt followed behind me, silent. His face hadn't changed, stayed all pinched in the hint of a frown he wore. Only his hazel eyes were any different, and the fear and worry in them probably mirrored my own. The trees were smaller here, and jutted all crooked out of the bare and rocky ground. Caves dotted the side of the mountain. One phrase flew around inside my head. Brandon knew.

*He couldn't have. No way.*

But that was the only way it made sense for him to act the way he had.

But how could he have known about this? About this world? About who was waiting on the other side? At least he tried to stop us.

*Still wish he was here.* Brandon being here would mean we'd outnumber these other two.

I kept my eyes down on the still muddy ground, just in case, but the rocks and gravel sticking up out of the ground gave the bottom of my tennis shoes some traction.

Much better. Just the sounds of the woods behind us meant there had to be no one following. *Probably still trying to figure out what just happened.* I risked a question. "Where exactly is this camp?"

Meris glanced back. "Noam and I have been camping in one of the caves up here while we wait to meet up with someone to collect some news." She lifted her right hand and pointed to an opening maybe six feet wide and tall in the side of the mountain. "That one, to be precise." Without another word, she walked ahead and disappeared into the entrance. Noam paused at the opening and turned.

"Come in as soon as you can." He gave a half smile and ducked inside.

Matt and I stood together, watching the cave entrance.

"So do we go in?" My elbow still stung, but the bleeding had stopped. *What I wouldn't give right now for soap.* At least the cut wasn't that deep, as far as I could tell.

Matt raised one eyebrow. "Follow two strangers into a cave?"

"Well, either way, the odds are sort of against us here, right?" I took one step closer to the cave. "I just wish we outnumbered them."

"Me too."

"I think Brandon knew."

Matt nodded. "I figured. I just don't know why he would."

"Maybe he guessed." The thought was so surreal. *Guessed what, exactly?* I forced my mind to pull back again. If my mind decided to crash later, then it could, but not yet.

Noam was nice, and Meris didn't seem so bad, just a little intense. Both surprised, to be sure, that we were here at all, and both of them pretty afraid of the soldiers in green. If they lived here, they had to know best. "Regardless, I'd really rather be with those two right now than out here."

"I know, but—"

"Matt." I took a deep breath and braced myself. *Going in. Don't be scared. You can always run.* "It's cold. I'm going in there, and I already know you're gonna follow me. Just…don't be long." I hurried to the cave. *Let him be suspicious.* The ceiling hung just a few inches above my head. My eyes took a moment to adjust to the sudden change, and an orange glow from deeper in the cave drew me forward. The tunnel curved for a few yards, then opened out into a bigger chamber. Matt's shoes scuffed on the tunnel floor a few yards behind me.

Noam looked up from the fire as we walked toward the glow. "Sit down, please," he said. "Get warm." He looked over. "Are you sure I can't at least run some water over your elbow?

"I'm good. Thanks." A sting ran up my arm, as if it was disagreeing with me.

Meris sat beside him. "If either of you are hungry, we have food." Her face had relaxed. Maybe her earlier reaction was just from being outside, with so many hostile people in obvious pursuit and likely headed our way.

*At least right now, they seem a little more okay with us.*

My stomach churned at the mention of food. "No thanks. I um… just ate." That was true, at least. I had eaten breakfast. I settled across from them, my legs still quivering from the hike. Matt sat beside me, tensed and looking ready to spring up again, glaring like this was somehow someone's fault. A thick, awkward silence fell in the cave.

"How is the bleeding?" Noam asked.

"Um..." I looked down. My arm still stung, but blood wasn't leaking out of it anymore. "Looks like it stopped."

He nodded.

Meris' gaze moved from the fire and flicked back and forth between me and Matt. "So...it appears that we need to figure out a few things."

What should I say to that? My mind began to race. *What is this? How are we here?* The words tumbled out of my mouth. "Okay, I'll go first. How are we not in Salt's Creek, North Carolina?" My throat caught.

Meris' eyes narrowed without her giving me an answer, and she stared down at the fire again.

*Well, that's just great.*

Noam broke the quiet tension. "I gather that finding us is quite a surprise for you."

I nodded. "What is this place?"

"Wilderness, in the nation of Trenavell, on the fifth continent of..." Noam poked at the growing flames. "Well, I'd tell you the name of the planet, but no humans here actually know it anymore, and no one's bothered to rename it. It's just...the world." He looked down into the pot.

"Oh." *Humans.* What exactly was the alternative?

"You said you were from Salt's Creek?" Meris asked.

Matt shifted beside me, his face turning impassive in a heartbeat. "Yeah, why?"

"I was only making sure I heard right," Meris answered sharply. She let out one huff of air, rolled her eyes, and looked at me, apparently dismissing Matt. "It appears that you somehow found a gate connecting our worlds and wound up on the main road to our capital city."

Two worlds. *Is this like Narnia or something?* "Gate?"

Noam leaned back from his work on the fire. "This planet and Earth are connected by gates. Hundreds of them. The ones we know of are on this continent, though the exact number is unknown. As for the rest of the planet…" He smiled. "The makers of those gates weren't forthcoming with that information, and there has been no contact with the rest of whoever else might live here for a very long time."

*These people are aliens.*

The fire danced and flickered, larger now. Warmth flowed over my skin and calmed the trembling in my core. Silence dropped over us.

*No use not asking questions.* I breathed in deep, stalling, grasping for any question that might make sense. "Are they all…surrounded like that one?"

Meris and Noam glanced at each other before she looked at me and spoke. "A lot of them are, if they're not old hidden gates or the badly degraded ones. If they're in regular use, they're under guard. The one you found, though…"

What had we done now? "Yeah?"

Meris chewed on her fingernail for a moment. "It presents us with a special situation."

"What do you mean?" Matt asked.

Noam answered him. "It's not a known gate, and that's why you took those men by so much surprise."

"So it's a hidden one?"

Meris shook her head. "No, the actual hidden ones are all known. They're usually ancient, used only if they're confirmed to be safe." She held her hand to the side without looking away. "Noam, let me see your map."

He nodded, stood, and walked over to the wall, dug into the dark, lumpy shape of an old backpack, and came back, a small square of paper in his hand. He passed it to Meris, and she unfolded it.

"Here." She held it out slowly for me to take. "It's a map of Trenavell."

My hand shook as I reached for it. The paper, soft from use, creased gently at right angles. A network of crooked lines, dotted with large and small squares in three different colors, made up the map. A circle near the center of the page was labeled "Compass Hill."

*Okay? So?* I handed the map back. "Those are all gates, right?"

Meris folded the map in a quick motion. "Yes. Every single thing on there is labeled operating, ancient but operating, or dangerous for use. All the gates have been mapped for a hundred years now."

Noam broke in. "The road you walked out onto is called Kings Road, the main way that cuts across, west to east, and runs to Compass Hill, the capital. We're at the most dangerous section of it for traveling, and this particular area has never been used for movement between the worlds. There's too much risk with the terrain like it is. Wagons don't even use that part of the road. They have to go far out of the way."

"What does that mean for us?" Matt asked.

Meris pressed her lips together. "It means that as far as most people know, there were no gates and never have been on this part of that road. Until today."

*More secrets.* Then what had that scream been from? "Oh." It couldn't be completely unknown. Someone knew something about that house. Someone had been there the day that car had smacked into the back of Matt's truck. Someone besides us knew.

*Brandon, impossible as that is.* But who else besides him?

"How did you find it?" Meris pressed.

*Just give me a second to absorb all this stuff.* "Um…" My throat caked up, and I coughed. "We were looking around in this house that belonged to my family a long time ago."

"In Salt's Creek?" Meris asked, once again.

"Yes." Meris and Noam shared another look when I answered. "Why do you keep asking about my town?" My pulse picked up speed.

"There was a man," Meris said, "a friend of Trenavell from Salt's Creek. I know the town's name specifically because it pertains to what Noam and I are waiting for here."

*Thud-thud-thud.* The throbbing in my arm intensified. *Could it be…?* "What was the man's name?"

"Gavin Dupree. Right, Noam?" The boy nodded once, and Meris continued speaking. "He was supposed to have left something behind when he died."

"The riddle." The words jumped from my mouth.

Meris raised her eyebrows. "Yes. His riddle." She paused. "Do you have it?"

"No."

"We don't even know what it is," Matt added. "Do you have any idea?"

Noam cleared his throat. "Just one clue, that the riddle is an object that needs a key to be solved. That's all."

*A key.* The poem, maybe?

More craziness. More cryptic phrases and guessing games. Why was this thing important anyway? "So it's not words. The riddle is a thing."

"Precisely," Noam answered.

Someone was after it, then. "What does it do?"

They both got quiet. Noam answered me. "Seals off all the gates. Keeps anyone from taking shortcuts through those connections."

"I'm guessing the guys back there aren't our friends," Matt said.

Meris' gaze drifted to behind me, at the door of the cave. "No. The soldiers you ran into were not from Trenavell. They are from our neighbor country, Naolon, with whom we are at war."

"We've been at war for twelve years." Noam's voice was quiet. "Truthfully… we lost the first time. It's an occupation now."

A harsh chill raced down my spine. "What does that mean for us, then?"

"Can we get home?" Matt's voice held a hard edge again.

Meris took a moment before answering. "Of course you can. It's just…a little difficult, since they're around a perfectly functioning gate that they just found out about."

The goosebumps spread like a fire over my arms and up the back of my neck. "So if the soldiers weren't expecting two people to walk out of the side of a mountain…"

"Then they'll be guarding it," Noam finished. "They might think you're an invasion force and finding something that no one apparently knew about will really hold their attention for a bit."

*But someone else did know about this.*

Matt leaned forward, his face hardened. "Why would they think we're invading if those gates aren't exactly common knowledge on Earth?"

Noam shook his head. "They don't have to be. Enough friends of Trenavell have allies on the other side. If there were enough people trickling through, then the element of surprise would belong firmly to our nation."

Meris stared down at the fire. "They are also planning the same for Earth and have been for years."

My stomach jerked once. "What?"

Meris kept going. "You can see why they'd be interested in preventing any incidents with Earth people or Trenavellans crossing over so frequently."

"With all the gates they have at their disposal, we don't know what they're stalling for," Noam said. "But we may have time now, since they'll likely be puzzling over this one for a while."

"Why is that going to stall them?" Matt asked.

"It's probably not the only gate no one knew about," Meris said. "It could be, but we don't know. That's why we're so far north now. We were contacted about a possibility of someone knowing where the riddle is."

Noam cut in. "And if we can find the riddle, we can seal off the gates. It would stop Naolon, and perhaps the people of Trenavell can regain control and keep them from forming another front or invading your planet."

Images took shape in my mind. Green uniforms, masses of them, bursting into crowds of people. Would they shoot? What kind of weapons could these people get, knowing the connection between the worlds? Would there be enough police, enough soldiers, enough weapons to hold them back at first? Maybe. Not everywhere. Salt's Creek wouldn't be ready.

Nowhere would be ready.

But the two of us couldn't possibly be the only ones to know. Mildred Barnes with her sharp dark eyes had held back something. There had to be others. *Brandon.* "There have been people, not me or Matt, but other people, around the other side of the gate. Around the house. We heard a scream…that's why we were looking around there…that's how we found this place."

*The letters.* Could I tell them now? *Best to wait.*

"How many others?" Meris asked.

"I don't know." *Don't know a lot of things, it seems.* "But we can help you."

Matt didn't say anything, his eyes troubled. I nudged his shoulder.

He jumped. "I…sure. We can. We will. I guess." His eyes looked into mine for a brief second.

Meris' green eyes narrowed. "How?"

I swallowed. "We know people. A person, anyway. She knew Gavin Dupree. Or his son, actually. Maybe my family could help." *They probably won't. But we can.* "His son was my great-grandaddy. It shouldn't…

See, I'm kind of trying to clear his name, and the lady who told us stuff, she's helped us. A lot."

Time might as well have frozen then as one thought completely took over my mind. *She knew a lot that she didn't tell us. Why should we trust her anymore?*

I started when Meris spoke. She hadn't looked away yet. "Does this person stand a good chance of knowing what we need to know?"

*They did find other skies first.* "There's a pretty good chance we could use what she gave us."

Matt focused on Meris. "I have a question."

"Please ask," she said.

"Why just you?" A good question, at least. "Why are you the only two who are going after this thing?"

Meris raised her chin. "It would seem that only a few of our people are willing to end this the smart way."

A shortcut. They were undermining everyone who'd tried so hard to ignore the root of the problem. "I think I can get behind that."

She tilted her head. "How do we know you'll actually come back?"

*How do you prove yourself to two strangers from another planet?* She had me stuck. Would they keep us here?

Matt's measured answer came. "How do we know you won't just kill us now?" He glanced at the rifle beside Meris.

She followed his gaze and straightened. "Fair enough. Can you return in two days?"

Two days to wrench answers out of a mouth-shut town, some photo albums, and a letter. *Do we even have that time?* Why not get a head start? "How about one day?"

"Just one?" Matt said.

"Sure." I turned to him. "I'll call our friend and then get what we need. One day is plenty if we want to get ahead, right?"

Meris' eyes flicked back and forth between us. Finally, with a nod, she answered. "That sounds fine with me." She leaned forward. "Now, let's see about getting you through the gate, shall we?"

***

Wet dirt stuck to my fingers, shoving up under my nails as I clung to the side of the hill. *This must be what a spider's life is like.* My elbow stung again, a reminder of earlier. The skin still had sticky dried blood on it, and the mud I'd slid through had worked its way through the fabric of my clothes and grated at my skin. *I'm gonna need the world's longest shower.* Out of the corner of my eye, I watched Meris move away from us, up the hill, moving fast.

"I hope no one sees her," I whispered.

Matt shook his head. "They probably will."

We crept up beside Noam, just a few feet down the edge of the road. If I stuck my head over, I probably would be able to see the gate. Probably look right into the face of one of those guys, too. Their voices grumbled low.

Noam began speaking, his voice soft, not quite a whisper. "She plans to shoot two times, at least. Possibly three, to give you time. Do not move until after the second shot goes off."

*Please let me have the self-control to not just go.* "Okay."

Seconds passed. A minute. I stopped counting.

A shot cracked through the trees, echoing. My legs tensed.

Silence fell, for just a moment, before they all started talking at once. "What—"

"Where did that come from?"

"Someone's hunting in these lands again…"

"Just get up there." It was a voice of authority. "Can't have that going on."

Another shot.

"You heard me, get to it!"

Footsteps crashed up the mountain, and for a moment, the world was quiet. I hesitated. *Not yet.* Meris fired once more.

Noam pushed at my heel. "All right, go!"

I scrambled up the hill, digging into the wet ground. My soles slipped but held fast as we dashed across the road to our precious escape. The dim staircase enveloped us, and Matt slammed the entrance closed. *They had to hear that.*

"Quick, lock the door." My knees shook as we pulled on it.

"I need to see if there's a way to even do that."

"Hurry!"

"I am." His hands moved to the side, feeling the wall, I guessed. "Here's a bar for the door." Something heavy dropped into place.

*That wasn't in place when we came through.* "What was it doing unlocked before?"

Matt turned to look at it, his eyes widening in the low light. "Good question."

My hand was around his wrist a second later. "Come on." The glowing lights on the tunnel walls raced by as we ran down, twisting around the bend and plunging into a darkness only broken by the kitchen light. A normal old kitchen, in a run-down house on Earth.

The goosebumps rose up again. On an Earth that could be attacked at any time.

*Please no.*

I slowed my steps, stumbling ahead of Matt into the dim kitchen. My foot caught on the threshold of the door, and I went down on my knees. A puff of dust rose from the sunlit floor. Still morning here, still warm, still home. I pushed to my feet and turned around. We stared at the hidden door in the wall. If it was always here, if he'd made so much effort to hide it, then how often had Dupree used it?

Matt caught his breath. "How do we lock this side?"

"I don't know." *Deep breaths. Don't panic.* "I think the one lock might be good for now…" The wooden bar holding at bay an entire world. What else could we do? I pushed the wall almost closed, open just enough so that we could pull it open when we came back. "Let's get outside. I need some sun."

As I moved down the hallway, I watched the light as it streamed into the house. The day on the other side of the broken front door looked so good, so different now, so warm. We crossed into half-sunlight on the porch, and I dropped onto the top step, staring out at the empty farmland, letting the steam of the humidity roll over my skin.

*An hour ago this was just a creepy house.* The step creaked as Matt lowered himself beside me.

"Are you okay?"

Honestly, I didn't know. "Yes."

He poked my arm. "You need to clean that cut up."

Oh. That. Good. Better dirt than anything else. Soap and water and alcohol. That was how you cleaned a wound. "I know." A telephone. No, that's what I really needed. I pushed up from the step. "Let's go home."

"Right behind you."

We rounded the corner together, and I kept my gaze fixed on the woods. *Not meeting the eyes of the house today.* It kept too many secrets, and too well.

Matt didn't say anything else as we walked, his eyes wide, shocked, and his eyebrows just creased together. Through the trees I saw my trampoline waiting at the back of the house, like nothing had ever changed or ever would. I sped up, knowing the path to the back door, to the mat for the key, through the door and into the duct-cooled living room.

I heard the air conditioning going in the house. Too much, too cold. I looked at the clock. The sun hadn't moved much, but I was no expert. I knew I'd stepped out my back door at 8:00.

The green numbers on the stove cheerfully announced "8:30."

Thirty minutes had passed since I'd left the house. Enough to get us through the woods, into the old home's kitchen, and back.

But not to another world. Not for as long as we'd been there. "Matt…"

"What?"

"The clock. We've only been gone—"

"Thirty minutes." He frowned. "That's…different."

"Just a little." Was it any weirder than anything else? My stomach churned again, queasy. I put the images of war out of my mind. The sheer size of what this had become rattled me to the core.

"You need to wash that cut out."

"I know." *The phone. Need the phone.* "I just really want to make a call first." I grabbed the phone book and flipped the pages, fingers not quite grasping the book. I caught the thin paper with a fingernail when I saw the name Barnes, Mildred.

I reached for the phone and stopped, my hand hovering over it for one, two, three seconds. I let my arm fall back down and pushed the phone book away. It slid an inch before it hit the barrier of the phone.

"What?" Matt asked.

I wet my lips. They'd shriveled up from the cold and they stung now, chapped. *How'd I not notice that?* "Should we trust her?"

"You didn't before?"

The way she'd looked at us the first time we met her…something she wanted to say, maybe nothing she wanted to say but facts that wanted to get out anyway. . . . "What if she's already told people?"

"Told them what?"

"That we came to her house."

He frowned. "Oh. I see."

I took a deep breath. "There's more of this that I don't think she's gonna tell us, but what if she tells someone that we came looking?"

"And we don't know what side she's on."

"Exactly."

He nodded slowly. "And you really think she could be a spy for that other country?"

Did I? I shrugged. "I think if she is, then we walked right into helping her." A car smacking into the back of Matt's truck could be nothing compared to what they might do.

The refrigerator droned.

Matt spoke. "Then what do you want to do?"

*Panic.* "I don't know what to do."

"We did tell them we'd bring information, so where do we get it?"

"I don't know." *The paper. The poem that doesn't make sense. Everything I know.* "We just work with what we've got. I'm sure they'll understand." I shivered in the air conditioning. The goosebumps flared around the cut on my elbow. "Ow."

"You need to wash that out."

"I know, you've said that three times." I looked at the trail of dirt I'd left across the floor and pulled my tennis shoes off. "Think we should try to figure out anything about James Abney?"

"Does it really matter now?"

*To me.* "It might."

"Maybe if it comes up again."

"Okay." The mud on my hands cracked. "I really need a shower."

"I can come back later, then." Matt took a step backwards.

"No."

He frowned. "Don't come back?"

"Don't leave." *Can't be alone. Not until we take care of this.*

The tips of his ears turned pink. "What?"

"I mean, stay downstairs and stuff, because I might punch you if you come upstairs while I'm in the shower, but stay here. Watch TV or something." *Relax before I tell you what we have to do.*

"Okay." He glanced at the floor. "If you're sure."

"I am." I stepped past him, to the hall, to the stairs. "I'll be down really soon."

He answered then. "Wait a second."

I paused on the stairs, aware of the weight of my wet clothes. "What?"

"You've got something in mind, don't you?"

*Busted.* "We've got to go back. Soon."

"When?"

*Today. It has to be today.* "Still early here, isn't it?"

He shook his head. "Anya, those men are still gonna be there."

"Not if Meris did her job right, and I think she did."

"You seriously want to go back today."

"Yeah, I seriously do."

"Why?

*Really?* I stepped back down to the floor and looked up into his face. "You have to ask?"

"The gates, I know, but what good do we do if we go unprepared?" He didn't move. "Besides, they're our best chance for getting around without getting caught, and they're not going to expect us. They'll be at their camp for the night, if they made it back."

*If they made it....* "So we just wait until some guys bust into downtown Salt's Creek and just deal with it?"

Matt sighed. "Didn't look like those guys were ready to invade anything." He paused. "Just...one day. Give it this one day, and we'll go back."

One day. One day stretched out into something that might as well have been two days, or three. But it was time to think. To plan. To gather everything I knew together to offer to them. "Okay. One day. We'll go back tomorrow and we'll take the information we have and see how it works out."

"Sounds good." He stepped away. "I'll still be here. I'll stay until your parents get home, and we can figure it out."

*With nothing. We have so little.* "Okay." I climbed the steps, aware of how loud they squeaked in the quiet.

*What are we getting into here?*

***

I pulled my damp hair back with a ponytail holder. As I wrapped the elastic tighter, droplets of water wove their way down my neck, cooled by the air conditioning. I shivered and rushed down the steps. *Please still be here.*

Matt sat on the couch in my living room, staring at the wall. He looked over as I stepped into the room. He was quiet as I sat beside him.

"Better?" he asked.

"Yeah. A lot." *Still can't warm up.*

A car drove by on the street.

"What did we just agree to?" Matt said. He didn't take his eyes off the other side of our living room.

"Probably something real stupid."

He relaxed and looked at me. "So…we promised to bring them any information we could about this."

"And you're wondering how we're gonna do that in a day."

"Pretty much."

I rubbed my eyes. *Why didn't I think this through?* "Me too." I pulled my knees up and rested my chin on them. "I didn't tell them about the poem in those pictures, though."

"What do you think it has to do with this?"

"I think it's the key they're looking for."

He slouched into the cushion. “Then it’s the best information we could give them with the time we have.”

“Should we go back to the library?”

He shook his head. “And look for what? Gavin Dupree turns up only in those articles, and it’s not like we can go around asking about portals to alien planets or anything.”

I smiled. “Good point.”

“Looks like we’re pretty committed to this thing, then.”

“Yeah.” Still morning. Still early. “I don’t want to sit here all day. Let’s do something.”

Matt half-smiled. “I really don’t think we should start breaking into any more old houses just yet.”

I smacked his arm. “No, I meant…a video game. Your house. Or ours or whatever.”

He tilted his head. “Sure. Let’s go.” He stood up from the couch.

“Okay.” I followed him to my front door. As I stepped onto the porch and pulled the door shut behind me, I was struck how solidly I knew one thing, whatever happened from now on.

*This is the last little bit of normal for us.*

# Chapter 10

The photograph rested beside the scrap of paper for comparison. I leaned over my crossed legs and read it again, read both to make sure I'd written it down right.

> I'll sell you a riddle for a dime
> said the bishop at the chime
> With tables and ravens and eggs on a wall
> and diamonds and pennies in keys and all
> the top of the tower pressed down to fall
> my riddle is finished sir; what is your call?

Stupid. Why did he make sure that no one would find this rhyme for years? Someone had made the sampler, he'd hung it up, and then, with unknown words to his friends, he'd left it buried in time.

But why? If it was so crucial that we find this riddle and figure it out now, why did it have to wait for a hundred years? And was this even important, or was it just someone's embroidery practice?

*I need to stretch.*

I stood and cracked the blinds. The gold-colored square of Matt's window showed his sharp outline.

*How long has he been there?* I tugged on the cord, and the blinds shot open. No words came as I opened the window and leaned out, staring across the gap until my gaze slipped from his and to the tan siding on his house.

His voice, soft as it was, startled me. "What's wrong with you?"

*What's wrong?* He knew. Why would he bother asking? *No. Wait. He didn't do this. You didn't.* "I'm scared."

His gaze held steady. "Me too." I could just barely see his jaw tense in the moonlight.

*Angry, more like it, I bet.* "So what are you thinking about so hard?

"Trenavell."

The thought of that place set my stomach fluttering. "Yeah. Same here." I didn't let my mind touch on how crazy the morning had been. I'd managed not to break yet. I could keep it up for a while.

"I guess we're really going back, right?"

"We have to."

"Yeah."

I set my chin in my hand, staring past him, into his room. I could see his game console and the corner of the old TV he played on. That we'd played on, so many times. *Simpler times.*

"I don't think I still can believe we agreed to this." He shook his head. "I don't even feel like it's real, actually."

*Words out of my mouth.* "Me either."

The sound of tires on the road grew over the cricket sounds and a set of headlights lit up the street. He leaned out his window as a familiar silver car hummed down the street, going slow enough that I could get a good look at it. "That's Brandon."

Matt stared. "Yeah…it is."

*Brandon. The guy who knew everything and wouldn't tell us.*

"Where's he pulling up?"

"He's going past us and turning around, actually." Matt kept his eyes on the street.

"Did he forget where we live?"

"I doubt it." He looked back at me. "Come on out. Maybe he's waiting until he sees us."

*Why would he do that?* "Okay."

More weird behavior. "Think he's coming with another ominous warning?"

"Well, he was right this time." Matt slid his window shut.

*Guess we're checking this out.*

My clock told me eight PM. That wasn't too late, but Brandon knew where we lived, easy. Why would he be driving back and forth like he was lost? Mrs. Dobken's voice floated up from their front porch, too muffled to hear even the tone. It faded and the door shut. I headed downstairs.

My parents were in the living room, watching some crime show on TV, dad's computer open in his lap. I poked my head through the door. "Hey um, I'm gonna go talk to Matt and Brandon really quick, okay? I'll be back soon."

Mom looked up and smiled. "Okay."

I gave them a smile and hurried out my front door, down the steps, and across the quiet yard.

Matt ambled across the yard as I stepped across the cool grass, my bare feet splashing dew onto my shins. Brandon's car slowed as he made another pass around. Matt and I waited, and Brandon parked along the curb. A girl sat in the front passenger seat. His girlfriend Sara, I knew that. She sort of half-waved, then looked at Brandon. She turned back around then, facing the front of the car, and rolled her eyes.

*Totally with you on that one.* What had he said to her, though?

Brandon opened the driver door and swept out, slamming it behind him, almost in one motion. His face was set in a hard expression, not quite a frown, but odd on him. *Like he's been acting normal at all.* He stepped around the front of the car. Was that worry that passed over his face for an instant?

"Hey man," Matt said.

A tight smile found its way onto Brandon's face. He was paler. "So you guys are j-just hanging around here tonight?"

Where had that tremble in his voice come from? He glanced back at his car for a second.

"Yeah," I said. "Just…the usual."

A harsh laugh snapped out of his mouth. "The usual for you isn't exactly hanging out at home, is it?" His face changed then, eyes all cold. I took a half step backwards. He'd been abrupt today, but not like that.

Matt slid a glance my way, shrugged and shoved his hands into his pockets. His shoulders straightened. "Yeah, really." The two guys faced each other.

*Man, if this ain't awkward. . . .*

I jumped in. "So you just stopping by to hang out too, or what?"

Brandon looked over at me. "Nah, just...checking out what y'all are up to tonight." His gaze dropped down to the grass. "And uh...no hard feelings about the house thing?"

*He won't even look up. . . .*

"Naw man, it's good," Matt answered.

"So what are you doing tonight?"

Brandon shrugged and moved backwards. "I dunno. Gonna get something to eat, I guess." He turned, raising his hand in a wave, relief flooding into the frown creases on his face. "I'll see y'all, okay?"

*Another change. Okay.* "'Bye."

He waved again and got into his car. Sara frowned and turned to look at him. As he started the ignition and drove off, she started to speak, completely inaudible through the window. Without another gesture or anything at me or Matt, the car sped off, too fast, away from our homes.

I watched Brandon's taillights disappear around the curve. "That was weird."

"Yes it was."

"It's like he was checking on us." I turned to walk back to my house.

Matt frowned. "Do you think he was?"

"I don't know."

Matt smirked. "Maybe he does care after all."

*Thank goodness that didn't turn into an actual confrontation.*

I watched another car pull into a driveway. One of our neighbors, doing something normal. Like nothing was strange at all about this neighborhood. "He's making it way obvious that he doesn't want us to go in there."

Matt took a step away, toward his house. "Well, there is an entire part of another planet that would probably feel the same way if they knew about us."

I let my shoulders relax. "Got a point there."

My stomach roiled a little. The first lines of the poem ran through my head again. *I'll sell you a riddle. . . .*

"It's good we decided to go back tomorrow." Nausea tensed my jaw up. Panic and urgency bubbled up inside. "We can't wait any longer. We have to take what we know to Meris and Noam."

He took a deep breath. "Tomorrow morning, then."

"When?"

"Does nine o'clock sound like a good time for insanity?"

I couldn't help the laugh that wound its way out. "Nine o'clock sounds fine."

"Meet you out back?"

I smiled. "As always."

He walked backwards. "Okay. Goodnight."

"Yeah. 'Night."

*Morning might change everything.*

# Chapter 11

The dry, heavy denim of my jeans clung to my legs, oppressing my skin and bringing out prickles of sweat on my knees. It would be worth it once we went down that tunnel. So would the dark sweatshirt slung over my arm, an old black one that was just worn and faded enough. I kept pace with Matt as we hurried through the woods to the Dupree house. The fresh piece of notepaper in my pocket crinkled with each step, already shoved in there haphazardly after I'd recopied the rhyme from the picture and the doodle from the one letter I had. I'd shoved the actual letter and picture into one of the drawers in my room.

It wasn't crazy anymore to assume that someone might actually come looking for it, and the letter and picture were both so old. No use messing them up.

I knew what we had to do now, but there was just one question that nagged at my mind. "Wonder what the time difference will be between here and there."

"More than five minutes, I'd guess," Matt answered. "Haven't done the math yet."

There was the house. "Well, what if it's always changing, and we end up being gone for years?"

His eyes narrowed. "I wouldn't worry about that."

"I'm already a little worried, actually."

Matt's face softened. "Sorry." He sighed. "It's just that the way Meris was talking…you're right. Someone might get desperate…and if someone comes after you…" He trailed off, took a long pause. "I dunno. Trenavell's almost safer."

"Not sure I'd agree with that assessment." The house waited. It always would. No matter what happened, it wasn't going anywhere. Just a tool for crossing between worlds, and there wasn't time to wait with it. "But here we go."

"Yep," Matt said, solemn and decisive.

We mounted the too-new steps on the porch, walked over the door, still lying in the hallway, and slowly, as quietly as the creaky floors let us, made our way to the kitchen. The wall was still open just a crack. The tunnel would be cool. I pulled on my sweatshirt. The other world had to begin right at the wall.

*Who even engineered this?* "Ready?" I asked.

"No. Yes." His mouth quirked. "Can I just say I've been ready?"

"I can't hope to match you, oh great one." I eased the door open, just enough to slip in. As Matt followed and pulled the door behind him, I eyed the glow where the steps would be.

I stopped. "Uh-oh."

"What?"

*Stupid.* "Did you forget a flashlight too?"

"Oh." He paused. "Yes."

"Oh."

"We've got a little bit of light, right?"

"Yeah, but I kind of hoped to have a battery operated backup." *No turning back now.* "I guess…let's just go."

We walked, steps slow, not speaking over the crunching of the dirt floor. My toes met the bottom step, just a shadow without the bright beam of a flashlight.

Matt stepped past me. "Coming?"

"Seriously? Can you see in the dark or something?" I put my foot on the bottom step and pushed up. "Give me a second. I'm not super like you apparently are."

"Oh. Sorry." He kept pace with me up the steps, and we rounded the bend together.

The soft gold lights still covered the walls, and there might have even been more of them this time, lighting up the inside of the stairwell as we climbed up to the outline of the door.

Who might be standing on the other side to hear us? We stopped at the door. The bar scraped as Matt lifted it up and into the slot on the wall.

I pressed my face against the crack in the door. Just tree trunks and color showed through. "Do you hear anything?"

"Not yet."

"Should we wait?"

"I think we'd hear someone talking." He frowned. "I think they'd be loud enough. They weren't exactly stealthy last time."

"What do we do?"

Matt yawned. "Well, I don't really feel like going home, so…"

"Okay. Fine." I laid my hand against the door, feeling the grain and the grime, a cool bit of metal just brushing my fingertips. *Did Gavin Dupree build this?*

The road and the forest both stood empty as we inched through the door and closed it behind us. The sun was out today, but the forest grayer at the top. More leaves had fallen already. *In one day?*

Meris and Noam were nowhere to be seen.

"I think we're early," Matt said.

The first hint of panic reared up in my mind, and I stamped it down. "So now what?"

"We should find them."

"How?"

He blinked. "Good point."

"We can't really just stand here." I peered up, trying to see over the hill, but nothing. No noises yet, either. "We could start walking…"

"In what direction?"

My face reddened, remembering. "The way we ran."

His eyebrows rose. "Actually, it's not a bad idea."

"Thanks for the confidence." I swallowed. "Let's go." The absolute quiet of the woods made my footsteps sound louder than they probably were. I saw the curve where we'd first hid that day. "I think we went off the road here."

Matt stepped to the edge of the road. "And down there."

"Sounds right." Maybe I'd grabbed the same rough-skinned tree the other day. The hill looked steeper now that it wasn't clouded by fear, and the leaves under our feet were apparently determined to have every living person here know where we were. I moved sideways down the hill, clinging to roots, rocks, and each skinny tree in reach. How had we even run down this, much less escaped? *All sorts of bad could've happened, so much more than a scratch on my arm.* As my feet crunched down on the leaves under them, another pair of sounds echoed it, almost an instant after, but farther away. I ducked down, clinging to the branch and unable to see around a curve in the hill. *Please just be an actual echo. . . .*

Matt stopped beside me and leaned close. "Did you hear it too?"

I nodded, keeping my mouth shut as the sound continued, footsteps tramping across the crisp leaves, and coming right for us. "What do we do?"

"I...don't know?"

"That's helpful." My heart raced ahead as I tried to catch my breath. Where could we go without getting lost?

*Crunch-crunch...crunch-crunch...crunch-crunch.*

Stand and wait or run from whatever this new threat was?

*Run.*

I rose, took hold of Matt's arm and took one step down, just as two figures stepped into view.

Meris and Noam stared at us, both wide-eyed. I clamped my hand over my mouth to keep the scream inside.

Noam was the first to make any noise, relieved laughter breathed out in a huff. Meris frowned.

"Where have you been?" Her sharp voice was too harsh for this quiet.

Where did she think? "We just came through the gate."

Meris narrowed her eyes. "We expected you a week ago." She

huffed. "We've been coming back every day, just waiting."

"Oh." *Uh-oh.*

"We didn't know that the difference would be that much," Matt continued, impatient.

"That is something we will need to figure later," Noam said.

"So what did you two find out?" Matt asked.

"Nothing we plan to tell you here," Meris said. "It's a good thing we found you so quickly. We need to go back to the shelter."

*Wasn't like y'all were the only ones doing the finding here.* "Okay."

Matt nodded. "We're following you."

"I hope you have something for us," Meris added, smirking and turning as they walked away, back from where they'd come.

"Of course we do," I answered.

"Why else would we come?" Matt snapped.

I smacked him in the shoulder. "Calm down."

As we hiked, keeping a few feet behind the other two, the quiet of the woods weighed down on me. No one had seen us, and that in itself wasn't right.

I cleared my throat. "Meris?"

"Yes?"

"Where are all the soldiers?"

"We believe they were called away." We climbed up a steeper incline now, in the same area as the last time we'd been there. Yesterday, for me and Matt, a week ago for them.

"How long ago?" Matt asked.

Noam answered. "Two days. We don't think they're headed to Compass Hill, but if they are, that would be the least of our worries."

My blood chilled as the cave came into view. "So do you think they're getting ready to go to Earth?"

"Everything's uncertain," Meris said. "But we can speak more inside."

Noam had left a fire burning again, but smaller today. The warmth filled up the cave all the same.

We gathered around the flame, and Noam fed it, them on one side and me on the other side with Matt. *Two worlds meeting.*

Meris broke up the quiet. "Ira finally contacted us." She smirked. "Once the soldiers left, of course."

*Sure doesn't think much of him.* "What did he say?"

"Most of the riddle has been found."

"Where?" Matt asked.

"Up north," Noam said. "It's quite a distance we have to go."

*Oh.*

Meris looked up at me. "What did you find in your search?"

"I think…" The words stuck in my throat as I struggled with what I had to say.

"Yes?" Noam asked.

"I think I found the key to solving the riddle. I think." *I'm sure. Pretty completely sure.*

Meris leaned forward. "Do you know it?"

"I have it with me. Or, what I think might be it."

Noam fed a few dry sticks to the fire. "Did you find anything else about anyone you've seen around the gate?"

"Noam, please," Meris said.

"It's important," he answered. "If they get through, then does the riddle really matter anymore?"

It was quiet as they stared at each other.

*Have to tell them that.* "The answer's actually no. We don't know anything about the people around the gate."

"Oh." Meris' eyes closed for a moment. "Then we don't know what purpose they were using it for, or what side they're on."

*Well, that's one failure.*

Matt ground his teeth. "It's just about impossible to find out all that stuff in one day, and without giving ourselves away."

Meris frowned. "You said you had a friend in this." She shook her head. "I suppose you can't change it now."

"It's my fault," I said. "I didn't know whether we could trust her. She told us stuff, but she also held a lot back." I swallowed. "Like this entire world, for example." I reached into my pocket and pulled the already crumpled paper out. "But I have this. The key." I offered it to Meris. She took it. "I assume."

Her eyes only looked at it for a moment before she thrust it back to me. "Keep that. It..." Her face lit up. "Keep it to yourself, because it if it is key, then you have to keep it safe."

I took the paper. "How?"

Noam held a hand out. "May I see it?"

"Sure." I let him take the paper. He didn't look at it any longer than Meris had before he nodded and handed it back. "Meris is right."

*Isn't this what they wanted?*

"So where's the riddle supposed to go?" Matt asked.

"It's supposed to be assembled in the capital," Meris answered. "The last piece of the device is there."

I looked down, reading the poem again. A list of things, really, hidden in words that might be literal or not. "So this should tell us how to put it together."

"Yes." Meris coughed. "Hopefully."

I held it out again. "Then wouldn't y'all want to read it or take it with you?"

Meris leaned back. "Gavin Dupree meant for only a few to hear and understand it in context." She paused. "At least, that's what we've been told."

"News to us," Matt said.

Noam spoke. "The network of information is structured that way here. That way one person doesn't know every part of an important thing. The less we know that, the better."

"So…you want me and Matt to put it together. Somehow. When you get back."

Noam kept his eyes on the fire in front of him, and Meris answered.

"Yes."

*More waiting around.* "How would we do that?" She'd said most of the riddle. Just most. "Besides…you don't even have all of it."

"We bring it back of course." Meris dropped her gaze into the fire as well.

A few moments of silence passed before Noam spoke again his voice quiet. "The timing is perfect."

Meris frowned at him. "What timing? How?"

Noam's face was solemn. "They came right after what I'd consider a major force movement, with information that we can use to our advantage, while we were planning to leave anyway."

Meris; expression smoothed out. "Oh. I see."

They were headed north, but what did we have to do with that? "You're leaving tonight?"

The other girl's face lit up. "Yes. On the train. It will take us north through mostly wilderness, and we'll come back the same way, with the riddle." She paused. "Do you want to come with us?"

I exchanged a glance with Matt. "Um..." *But my family. . . .*

"Come with us." Meris repeated. "You have the key."

"Well, yeah, but—"

"So come."

Matt leaned back. "We could just tell you what the key says."

Meris put her hands up. "We told you no. Don't share it with anyone until the riddle is...solved."

"Why?"

Noam answered me. "The thought is that if that knowledge is shared, then the people who don't need to have the riddle will be able to find it, identify it, and destroy it."

"So just don't say anything about it and don't lose the paper." *But you know you might find out more about that disappearance. About the murder. About this whole other planet.*

"He's your relative," Noam said. "You can provide greater context."

"I just found out he's that closely related. Why would I know any more than you?"

*You know you want to go.*

"But you know things about him," Meris said. "You know something, at least. More than we do. If you know the key, perhaps you can start working the puzzle pieces before we even get back. It saves time."

"I had no idea about this riddle thing before I met the two of you." Why were they pushing us to go so badly? Didn't matter whether I really did want to go. Their reasoning was pretty weak.

"Couldn't y'all figure it out yourselves? Matt shifted around. "I mean, do you really need us to go with you?"

Meris stared at us.

Matt spoke again. "Well do you?"

No answer appeared to be forthcoming at all. I sighed. "Okay, so what happens if it's destroyed?" *Do I really want to wait around for them to get back, not knowing if someone's gonna come for us?*

Noam answered. "It would leave the gates wide open, and we don't know how Gavin Dupree made it or what went into this device with that kind of power. There wouldn't be a way to seal the gates except individually, by hand. And that presents a problem in itself, beyond taking too long."

Had Dupree even planned anything at all, or just hoped stuff would work out? The fear and frustration, coupled with the sensation of an uncontrolled tumble, rose up in me again. But they asked us to come with them. No waiting to hear or guessing when we might go back and missing the mark by weeks, but moving now, taking this into our own hands, if Matt stayed with me in this alien world. I glanced back and forth between them.

"Matt and I need to discuss it." I stood, pulling at his elbow. He followed without a word, and we walked to the cave entrance. They'd hear us, probably, but it felt private at least.

I tapped my feet for a few seconds, stalling. Matt waited until I finally met his gaze. "I'm going with them. I think we both should." *Please just do it. I'm not waiting.*

"I agree."

"Really?" *That fast?*

He leaned against the wall, crossing his arms. "I'm sticking with you."

"Well yeah, but…obviously that means staying. For however long. Going with them." *Getting a jump on this game.* "You heard that part, right? There's a train or something."

"I figured there was a possibility after we met them." He yawned. "Do you really think Brandon could have known about all this?"

"All this what?" He did know the Dupree story, or at least a version of it.

"This other, inhabited, almost perfectly Earthlike planet, complete with humans who speak English?"

"It's looking like more people back home are aware of it than we could ever know." My stomach clenched at the thought of what Brandon had to know to react the way he did. "Maybe he was trying to keep us safe or something."

"I'd have appreciated a little more information," Matt said dryly.

"Well, I just want a little bit of control in this. That's all. If we go with them, it means we have that at least. No guessing, just action. No sitting around at home and being targets anymore, which I guess we might be now since we've gotten all curious about this." Who might Mildred Barnes tell?

He leaned off the wall. "And the possibility of being gone from home for a really long time, considering how time works?"

The only uncertainty we couldn't get ahead of. "I don't care about the time. If someone in Salt's Creek knew, and if it's so obvious that Gavin Dupree might have been connected to your family, then we should have been prepared for this a long time before now."

He blinked. "Yes, we should have."

"Plus…" I glanced over at the other two. "I trust them. I mean, they're our age and out here alone. They know what they're doing, right?"

"Probably. Maybe. Maybe not."

"Well, at the very least, they likely won't get us killed on purpose or anything."

"I have my doubts about Meris."

"I'm sure she'll calm down eventually." I leaned back against the rock wall. "If this keeps Salt's Creek and our families safe, if this lures someone away from our homes, whoever it is…let's go with Meris and Noam tonight." I could stay here and know this was reality and not break.

"If you're sure…okay."

"Okay." I took a deep breath. "Maybe Brandon will do some stuff for us on that side if he knows where we've gone. We might have some good connections and some help. Since he was so worried…maybe he really does care."

"That's optimistic," Matt said.

"Yeah, well, that's what we've got."

Bad logic and all, what we were about to do was a true and terrifying adventure, far past breaking in old schools back in Sanders County. I pulled at Matt's arm, towing him back to the fire. The orange glow, larger now, cast strange shadows on the faces of our new allies.

"Well?" Meris asked, as Noam just waited, his face impassive.

*Here goes*. "We're going with you."

# Chapter 12

The light took on that gold look of a fall afternoon. It had always meant the days were slowly cooling off, that soon one night it would be time for trick-or-treating, and then Thanksgiving, and then Christmas. Festive. That's how it was supposed to be.

Now it just threw me. Not hours ago had the air been thick and warm, back home. The crisp air and golden light that belonged to autumn now filled me up with dread. *Why'd we do this?*

A chill brushed my ears, and I pulled at my hood, all too aware of my Earth clothing, and Matt's. *Stupid red tennis shoes.*

"Meris?"

"Yes?" *First thing she's said to us since we left the cave.*

"Uh…won't we stand out? I mean, our clothes are…" *Sore thumbs*. A wagon lumbered our way.

Meris turned back to us, smiling, amused. "Just keep your hood up. No one notices, and the ones that do don't take much more time to care." She lowered her voice as the wagon passed. "You're not the first and only folks from Earth to come here."

Matt shrugged and pulled his sweatshirt hood up. I hesitated, then did the same.

The road sloped gently down into the city. Compass Hill hunkered down in the middle of the mountains around it, almost hiding. In the center stood a stone castle that didn't look quite like it had been planned out before it was built.

"Who are we going to meet?" Matt asked.

"You'll see," Meris answered.

"So you can't tell us now?" Matt asked.

Meris didn't even look back. "No names."

There were no closed gates around this city, just openness, and it was busy with people moving about, and carrying food and other stuff. Soldiers in green stood on just about every other street corner, some watching, others obviously lounging. *Definitely keeping the hood up.* I moved up to walk between Meris and Noam.

"I hope she'll have enough," Noam said.

"Enough what?" Matt moved into place beside me.

"Supplies for you two, of course," Meris told him.

*Uh-oh.* The street we'd moved onto was a little quieter, with a few people milling about, some huddled by the sides of the homes. A soldier in green leaned against a wall, his eyes closed and his face tilted into a sliver of sunlight.

*Did we think this through enough?* "Is there a chance she won't?"

Meris rolled her eyes. "She will. Having enough just hasn't been terribly certain in the past. It's been better recently."

Were we the problem? "If us going is gonna give y'all trouble, we don't have to."

Meris shook her head. "Of course it won't. We asked you, didn't we?" She pointed ahead to a rough house squished between two others. The wood siding looked old and chipped and half-gone in some places. "There's Miriam's home."

She led the rest of us up the smooth stone steps and pounded on the door. I cringed, glancing around. There weren't any soldiers popping out to swarm us yet.

The door cracked open. A younger boy, maybe fifteen, if that, leaned out. "Yes?"

Meris glared at him. "Hello, Ira."

Ira smirked right back. "And a fine evening to you, Miss Meris. How can I help you?"

"We're here to see your sister."

The boy didn't budge. "Why such a late visit from you all?"

Meris shoved the door inward, and Ira backed away. "You didn't meet us the first time you were supposed to."

I checked around as I followed the others through the door. By some miracle, we might still be alone in this forgotten neighborhood.

No, that one soldier on the corner was definitely getting a better look at us, and a ragged-looking man crouched across the street stared hard. My heart pounded hard against my ribcage.

Matt pushed the door closed behind him. Ira stood facing us as Meris put her face very close to his own. The side of his mouth quirked. "You know I can't just let you barge in." He still stepped back once, face wavering.

To her credit, Meris was pretty threatening. She shoved her hands against Ira's shoulders. "Go get Miriam, you insufferable little brat."

Ira bowed, bending almost in half. "Yes, ma'am." He sauntered off down the hall, turning a corner.

*I'd have hit him too.* The dim hallway held two lamps and a door on the right.

Meris turned around, rolling her eyes. "My apologies. He's always been like that." She sighed. "Let's go wait in the parlor."

A muffled voice floated down the hall to us, someone snapping Ira's name in a scold. A door closed somewhere. A woman, probably in her twenties, hurried down the hall to us, gathering Meris and Noam in a swift hug before backing away.

"Ira tells me he failed to do as I asked the other day," she said.

Meris nodded. "We were able to make contact eventually."

"All the same, it seems like I'll have to find someone else to run those important errands, then." Miriam's gaze moved to flick back and forth between me and Matt. "Hello."

*Guess no one expected us.* "Hi."

Meris turned to me briefly, her face pulled into a weird expression, nervous maybe. "Matt and Anya have found their way here through a gate we didn't know about before."

Miriam nodded slowly and looked at me. "Was it on Kings Road?"

"Yeah." I swallowed. "We sort of found it by accident."

Miriam frowned. "I heard rumors of that one, but I never knew if they were true or not." She paused. "It's funny that years of searching would lead to you stumbling on it by…accident. And no offense to you or your world, but I've often hoped that gate wasn't real."

Matt's tone came out dry. "No offense taken."

*Maybe I wish it didn't exist, too.* How had I even thought of this as an adventure?

Miriam smiled. "What is it that you need from me?" Her eyes fell on me and Matt again.

"Supplies for a short excursion," Noam answered. "Someone found the…object we discussed."

Miriam's face went neutral. "I see. So you'll be traveling, then?"

Meris nodded. "On the train."

Were the walls that thin? They'd talked about the gate freely enough, but maybe since the soldiers actually knew about that one now. . . .

"You'll need a schedule, then," Miriam said, stepping away. "And a guide to take you to the depot tonight. I think I know who might be perfect for that, since he wasn't exactly completely helpful to you before." She leaned to open the door in the hall and waved us into a well-lit parlor. A couch faced two chairs across the rug. "Please, make yourselves at home. I'll get some things together and remind Ira of his priorities and responsibilities."

She disappeared down the hall.

We stood for a minute, staring around at each other.

I cleared my throat. "So…Ira will be taking us to the train?"

Meris smiled coldly. "Serves him right." She sat on the faded couch. "We have several hours to wait. Look around the house if you want to get familiar with it. I can guarantee you will most definitely be coming back here again."

Grits of dust or dirt or something left grimy trails along my fingers as I touched the back of a chair. Noam and Meris leaned into the couch, probably the only comfortable surface they'd sat on in a while.

What kind of conversation was I supposed to have with two people from another world?

***

Another bedroom. This one looked out onto the street. Better than the one with the view of a stone wall, if you weren't trying to hide. Dust from the street drifted up, and some had coated the window on the outside. The light wasn't reaching this part of the street anymore, and the shadows would be night before the rest of the city. I sat on the bed, legs crossed, playing with a shoestring.

The same man that was there when we'd climbed the steps still sat against the front steps across the street. I saw now, as he shifted and moved his left arm, that his left sleeve was pinned or maybe sewn up, because the arm was gone from the elbow down.

Impossibly, I managed to lock eyes with him. Maybe just a trick of perspective. *He can't see you. Not through the dust, and it's too far.*

I slid over anyway, making myself be out of sight. *Calm down. He probably sees a lot of people come through here every day.*

I didn't know where Matt was. Poking around like me, probably. Sitting, maybe. He'd let me walk off without following for once. That was nice at least. We'd be leaving for the train soon, and headed north to meet whoever it was Meris had spoken with. I needed the time alone.

Did I let myself process this completely? It was insane. Overwhelming. But above all that, it was real. Concrete. This crazy thing was happening, and I should've been more surprised.

All in secrecy. No one had cared who Matt and I were before. Well, they had, but at least it wasn't something I knew about. Now it was obvious and uncomfortable. No telling how many people knew our names and what we looked like, especially since I'd broken that one guy's nose right after he'd gotten a good look at us.

*Did we make this worse by diving in headfirst?*

Oh well. No real turning back now on this, not if I cared whether my family was going to be safe. It would be too dangerous to trek back through the woods and attempt an escape back to our town and our lives there. We would finish this and then we could go back home, if home still remained as I knew it once we got back. *We're committed now.*

***

By the second root I tripped over, I knew I would never take flashlights for granted, ever again. At least we weren't obvious, making our way through the dark woods that only Ira seemed to know. His lantern, partly covered, was the only illumination we had, other than the moon, and thc odd patches of twinkling lights that appeared every so often. They were almost exactly like the ones that lit the staircase, as far as I could tell. I glanced up at the sky again. The moon that orbited whatever planet this was shone orange in the sky. The effect made the shadows deeper in the woods, and the lantern wasn't offering much to counter that.

Meris' harsh whisper was louder in the nighttime quiet. What animals lived here that didn't make any sounds? "Ira, how much longer?"

He didn't bother to whisper, but did speak softly. "We're almost at the depot."

*At least he's not clowning around tonight.* Maybe he just said stuff to get under Meris' skin.

I looked back at Matt. "You ready?"

He tilted his head. "For the train?"

*Deep breath*. "For all this." I rubbed the worn strap of the leather backpack I wore. Miriam had stuffed each with a tightly-rolled blanket, a metal canteen, dense bread, and a whole lot of dried meat. It was a little rugged, I had to admit, but enough. Maybe.

Matt's eyes flashed as a beam of light caught his face. "Not really."

Ira slowed his steps, uncovering his light all the way and letting the glow spread out through the woods. "We're here." A wooden post with a short beam stood by a set of tracks. Ira hung his light up and stepped back. "Shouldn't be long now." It swung slow on the hook, making the shadows of the branches move.

And we waited, silent in the quiet night. The paranoia that we may have been followed washed over me, heightened my senses, made every shift of a shadow into another person and amplified the night sounds of some creature. Patches among the trees glowed with those same little points we'd seen on the staircase. The door had definitely been on this planet then, if those lights were from here, whatever they were.

*Why am I even doing this? Why'd I drag Matt into this? Is this even real?*

It wasn't long before the rumble began to build in the distance, getting closer and growing in volume all the time. The train whistle sounded out in the dark, and a light appeared around a curve, steadily approaching. Brakes squealed long before it reached us, and the train slid to a stop. A dirty window barely let through the glow of a light inside the engine compartment. The door opened.

A man hopped out, a grin on his lined face. "A fine evening to you young folk!" His too loud voice sounded like it just might echo off the trees. "Going north, are you?"

Meris nodded and pulled her backpack around, yanking a loaf of bread out of it. "Miss Miriam sends payment and hopes to receive some of your customers soon."

The man took the bread. "Indeed." He smiled again. "Take your pick of the two front cars. I would advise against the last one, though. It is occupied by someone who paid well to board tonight. Can't help but be pleased at his contribution, but you might just steer clear."

Noam had been quiet for the entire walk, but now he spoke. "Will it be a problem for us?"

"As long as you show some care, likely not," the driver said. "Now, get on quick. We got a schedule to make." He climbed back into the engine car and shut the door.

Ira reached up and pulled his lantern off the beam. "Good luck." He took off the way we'd come, his lantern casting shadows around as he slipped into the dark.

Meris smiled at us. "Well…let us be off."

"Let's get in the first one." Matt walked ahead of Meris. "Sounds like it'll give us a good cushion against whoever is in the last car."

"Good thinking," Noam answered.

*At least those two get along.*

The door and steps on the side meant it had to have been a passenger train once. A single cobweb-coated drape hung from a dirty window inside, frayed fabric barely clinging to the curtain rod. Why wasn't it used anymore? I'd have thought at least one side would make use of it, but instead, both had abandoned it.

It wasn't pitch dark in the car, but the moon's already low light barely reached through the grime coating the glass. A few seats were inside, but most were gone, and the air felt more chilled than it had outside.

"We better get settled," Meris said. "Perhaps we should all gather in one place. For safety."

"Where?" I asked.

"In the corner. It'll be warmer if we're all in that spot." Noam walked to the back and settled down behind a seat. "Come on. I can't light a fire in here." Meris joined him.

Hours traveling, huddled together with two strangers.

*That won't be awkward at all.*

Matt walked to the back, slinging his backpack off. *Well, he's fine with this.*

The thought of warmth won me over, and I followed, settling beside him. No one spoke.

*Wonder if it's as weird for them.* I kept my pack firmly between me and Matt. How were we supposed to sleep if we were all crunched up together?

A minute later, the train lurched forward, gathering speed, going deeper all the time into this strange world.

## Chapter 13

Hours had passed since we'd embarked on the train. I couldn't shake the oddness that spread through my body. Sort of tired, but not quite there. Still wanting to do something, but still too tired. Restless, I guess. That was a close word. Maybe it wouldn't take so long to adjust to this world, then, if I wasn't going to sleep much now. I'd bumped my head too many times to really sleep anyway, so looking out the window was a better option.

The moon wasn't visible through the treetops, so maybe it set already. *Creepy thing.* The patches of twinkling lights that we passed were bright, though, or as much as they could be through the dirt.

Something behind me shuffled, and Matt knelt by me at the window, his face just visible.

"I can't sleep," he said.

"So I didn't wake you?"

"Nope."

For some reason, a laugh popped out of my mouth. Maybe I really was tired. "I've never tried to sleep on a dilapidated train before."

"Me either."

My finger moved in a circle over the window, cleaning a tiny area. "Do you know what those lights we keep passing are?"

He peered through the hole in the grime. "Those things on the ground?"

"Yeah."

He was quiet for a few moments. "My Gramma calls them pixie light bulbs."

"Kind of a mouthful."

He smiled. "Yeah."

"Which Gramma?"

"Mom's mom."

"Oh." I watched another clump of them pass. "She knows about them."

"Yeah." He paused. "My Pop calls them moss lamps."

"I like that better." *This is new.* "Do they grow on Earth somewhere?"

"You mean without help?"

"Well, yeah."

"I don't think so."

I stared at him, and his face changed to some expression I didn't recognize, as if he'd had some realization. He opened his mouth.

The train bumped under us, once, hard, making me lean back.

Another bump, and the world pitched sideways, throwing me against another seat before it stopped.

I stayed still for a second. My lungs felt empty, and my back ached sharply where I'd hit the seat. I just waited. *No panicking. Just got the wind knocked out of you.* I relaxed just enough to suck in a piece of a breath. Where was Matt? The ache traveled up my back again.

*That's gonna bruise.*

The windows across the car looked oddly toward the tops of the trees. Below me, one of the windows gave a close up view of some nicely scarred bark as the train pressed on the tree. Metal groaned. I pushed myself up, forcing air into my chest. "Matt?"

He coughed. He was close, just beside me. "I'm okay. You?"

"Ow." Meris' voice broke through. "What…"

"Did we jump the tracks?" Noam said.

"I think so." Matt leaned back against a seat.

Panic hit me. *What now?* How were we going to get north? What if the train was on fire or something? "We need to get out of here."

"Yes, we do," Meris said. She tossed the pack I'd left in the corner at me. It plunked to the floor at my feet, my hands trembling too hard to catch it. I took a shaky breath and pulled the bag onto my shoulders. It brushed the brand new bruise on my back.

*That really is going to be fun later.*

"Think we can get out through the doors?" Noam asked.

"I think so," Meris said. Her voice held a quiver at the end of her words as her hands adjusted the rifle on her shoulder. "Let's—"

The window nearest to me shattered suddenly. I jumped and moved backwards awkwardly, my foot catching on something. A seat, maybe. The driver of the train poked his head in, his hand firmly gripping whatever it was he'd used to break the glass.

"Out, now," he said. "There may be a fire."

I glanced at Matt and half-slid down the crooked floor to the window. Why had I thought my red tennis shoes would be appropriate for this adventure? The ground wasn't too far down, and it was soft at least. I moved away to give the others room and leaned against the tree. Matt stayed beside me. Blood trickled from a bruising cut on his hand, and I stared, mesmerized by it. The others had marks like that. Two dark spots under Noam's nose and a shadow on Meris' forehead that might not have been anything at all, a smudge of dust maybe.

*We're alive, though.* The sharp, spicy smell of something burning reached my nose. The man had been right.

A motion at the back car drew my eyes. Whoever had been riding back there slid out of a window and ran off into the dark.

The train man frowned. "I hope he won't give us any trouble later. Barely got a look at him to confirm…" He shook his head. "You all seem to be relatively unhurt. I have some suspicion over what hit the train, but I don't know if that's it." He fell silent, frowning again, then looked up at us. "Oh well. You have to go. Run fast and do not stop for anything until you can't go anymore."

Noam swiped at his nose with his sleeve. "Which way?"

"Follow the line of the tracks until it meets Kings Road again, but stay hidden." The man walked to the engine. "Now go. As fast and as far as you can."

Without saying anything, Noam started walking and led us into the trees.

"He said run, Noam," Meris snapped.

"I heard him. I'm trying to get bearings so we can do so the right way." He frowned for a moment. "But if you are so insistent, let us be off."

So we ran. It wasn't sprinting by any means, thankfully. My back jarred with every step as we went fast enough to cover ground, our path guided by those moss lamps, the tracks almost too dark to see in the night and half hidden by the trees. We'd gotten a good distance away from the train already. *Maybe Noam will slow down.* I sure wasn't going to say anything. What if that man in the last car had followed us?

An explosion tore the air around us and ruffled the trees as an orange light lit the forest up. Noam came to a sudden stop, and I pulled up behind him. Sweat prickled under the sweatshirt and gathered around my hairline. A hint of the orange remained where the train had blown up. My heart slammed against my insides. *How close did we come to being right there when it happened?* "Whoa."

"So there was a fire." Matt watched the orange glow as it flickered and danced in the distance.

Meris turned away from our view of the wreckage. "I think he sped it along."

"Why would he do that?" Matt asked her.

"Just think if someone hid sensitive information on a train that's not going anywhere," Noam said. "Anyway, we need to keep moving. I can navigate for a while. There's enough light here to see the compass."

"Yes." Meris took a deep breath. "Though I think we can stop running now."

*That would be nice, but. . . .* "Should we?" *I'd rather be tired than dead.*

Meris face turned unreadable. "Do you two want to go back to your home?"

*Seriously? Where'd that even come from?* "What? No." I hadn't even considered that. Matt caught my gaze and shook his head, just a little.

There wasn't even a good way to get home.

Matt's voice cracked. "We said we'd come with you."

The other girl nodded. "Fine, then."

"Okay, well, if we are going, we need to do it now," Matt said.

No one agreed, and no one dissented. Just a wordless, near simultaneous movement, pushing on into the night with Noam at the lead.

Hours passed as we trekked through the woods. There was really nothing to judge the passage of time here, not for me. Maybe the passage of the moon, but it wasn't my moon. I had no idea how long it took to traverse the sky, and I couldn't see it now anyway. It had probably set. Noam could probably figure it out, and maybe Meris knew. How else had they gotten as far as they had? *Never asked where they came from.*

I didn't even know these people, and now we were off on some stupid grand adventure together. It crossed my mind for a second that now we'd be gone much longer.

*Cannot panic. Not now.*

Noam stopped in a tiny round gap among the trees. "We should sleep while we can. I don't think morning's too far off." His voice wavered.

"Yeah." Matt sat at the base of a tree. "So is here good?"

"It's fine." Meris sat. "Don't even bother with a fire yet."

I eased the backpack off of me and dropped it, missing that square of an extra layer almost immediately.

*It's not that cold. You can deal with it.*

The tree Matt leaned back on looked more comfortable than it was possible for a tree to be, and I settled down beside him, scratching my back on the rough bark. The bruise twinged in protest.

*Forget sitting up*. My pack made a fine pillow as I curled up under the tree, too tired to worry.

***

Rain streamed down my face. My hood had long stopped being effective at keeping me dry, and all it was good for now was holding back the sheer force of the water. The sheets of rain made it impossible to see more than a few yards, or even hear each other well, so we'd stopped somewhere near the side of the road, looking over it for anyone else who might approach. Mud oozed through the fabric of my sopping wet jeans. A soft ache near my spine throbbed every so often, but the bruise wasn't near as bad as I thought it would be.

*At least I didn't pop a lung wide open.*

The rain became a drizzle, then a sprinkle, then nothing. The leaves still left on the trees splashed color against the white sky.

"Finally." Meris stood up.

I stretched and pushed up from the tree. As I pushed it back, my hood sent water streaming down my neck. *Ugh.* "So where are you aiming for, Noam?"

He pulled his pack around. "I'd have to look at the map and see—"

"Shhh." Matt held his hand up. "I hear something."

*Oh no.* Sure enough, close by, enough to hear the sound steadily build as we peered down onto the road, was the jingling of something approaching. A rhythmic thump. Footsteps. Voices.

And a flash of green when the men in front rounded the curve, most walking, a few of them mounted on horses. Naolon's soldiers, all the way out here.

*Like you've gotten far at all.*

"Oh no." Immediately, I clapped my hand over my mouth. That was too loud.

"Come on!" Noam hissed. We followed him up the hill. Would it be far enough? Did they have scouts?

*They saw us. Heard us. We're gonna get caught and then we'll never get home and I'll die here and this was so stupid. . . .*

"Did you see how many there were?" I asked Matt.

"Too many."

I snorted. "Very funny."

"I'm serious!"

"Okay, chill."

Meris glared at us. "Shhh!"

"That isn't helping, Meris." Noam climbed ahead of her.

"At least we weren't seen," Meris said.

"We don't exactly know that, do we?" Matt asked.

My face turned hot. "And they could've heard us." *Stupid. So stupid.*

Noam smiled. "Well, they likely don't know where to look." He pulled the map out of his pack and unfolded it.

At least he was more prepared than Meris to forgive noise. Below us, still far but not at all far enough, the sound of an army passing cut through the silent autumn air.

It struck me that I hadn't heard any birds since we'd been here.

Noam raised his eyebrows, looking up from the map. "There's a tribal settlement very near, maybe a mile. That's encouraging."

*More people.* "Why is that encouraging?"

He refolded the parchment. "It's a human settlement independent of both nations, but sympathetic to Trenavell. They fight with us." He paused. "I think. At least, I don't think they will attack us or turn us in. And it means we're going the right direction."

"Good," Meris said. "It's a good place to be. Perhaps we can acquire more supplies there, since this is going to take longer than we thought."

*Longer.* When would we get home? *We chose this. No use not going along with it.* "Sounds good to me. I mean, y'all live here."

Meris narrowed her eyes. "So you do trust us?"

Matt crossed his arms. "Doesn't seem like we have much of a choice."

I frowned at him and turned to the other two. "I mean…yeah. We have to if we want to get home."

Meris sighed. "It's good, but don't be so quick to trust people here. They get ahead however they can, if they have the means. The camps are about the only place you'll find honest folks." She shook her head. "Let's keep moving."

We crunched through the brush, the jangling of the soldiers growing more distant as we went. At least whoever we were going to meet stood the chance of being on our side.

If the rest of this planet was rough, then this wilderness tribe, just by virtue of everyone leaving them alone, was probably terrifying.

"So why would we be turned in just for walking around?" Matt asked.

"Naolon closely watches the borders and cities, or supposedly does," Noam answered. "They like to pretend at keeping some sort of record, so they will sometimes arrest folks for loitering or something like that."

"By the way," Meris said, "when we get there, one of us should go in alone first."

"Reason being?" Matt said.

Meris narrowed her eyes and opened her mouth.

*He's set her off again.*

Noam spoke before she could. "Caution. Reasonable, I suppose. I can do it."

"Maybe Meris should do it," Matt offered.

She shot him a look, narrowing her eyes.

*Wow, she's testy.* And Matt wasn't helping either. *What's his problem?*

The trees began to thin, and lots of dried up stumps covered the ground, signs that it had been cleared at some point past. A row of squat log houses made a wall through the woods.

"I think that's it. They build like that," Noam said. "But…" The silence of the empty woods and skies was loud enough in itself.

*Why don't we hear anyone?* "It's really way too quiet."

"Yes."

*Well, what now?*

Matt broke the silence. "We don't need to split up here."

Noam shook his head. "No, I'll scout it out. Shouldn't take me long, if this is what I think it is. Just stay close, and I'll come get you." He slipped through the trees, and ducked through a gap in the wall of houses.

The thicker trees offered some shelter as we waited. *This is so creepy.* Meris stared at the back of a house, her face tight, not even acknowledging that we stood with her.

*I'd probably look like that too if Matt went off by himself in this place.*

Noam's voice called back. "You can all come now."

I waited for Meris to move first. She didn't look back as she crept through the same gap Noam had.

"Go ahead." Matt pushed gently at my backpack. "I'll be right behind you." With a nod, I followed Meris. Matt stayed close.

Noam stood in the middle of the dirt street, his forehead creased in a frown. "There's no one here."

"No one?" Meris asked. "Are you sure?"

"It's completely abandoned." Noam took a deep breath. "I don't think it's been like this for long, either."

"Could they all have just evacuated?" Matt asked. "If they were going to be attacked?"

Meris shook her head. "Not like them. They'd stay and fight. They've never abandoned a place if they could fight."

Goosebumps on my arms sent the hairs shooting straight up on end. "Maybe they weren't able to." I let my gaze roll over the town. Just the same buildings and a well with a bunch of arms sticking out, each holding a bucket. Below it was another row of the same, all offset. The buckets were crooked, and one had fallen off. Only thing was, it didn't look like there'd been a battle or anything here. It was just empty.

"Could be…" Meris swallowed. "But where'd they go?"

"No way to know." Noam turned around. "Our best bet is to just leave, cut through here. They left for a reason. I don't think we need to stay here much longer."

Meris grimaced. "We still need supplies."

"We'll get them at the next town," Noam said, turning around.

"We could just loot," Matt suggested. "See if there's anything."

"If being the operative word here," I told him. The tree branches moved as the wind picked up suddenly. Out in the wide open, where everyone could see us. . . . *We're being watched. I know it.*

"We'll look as we go, right Noam?" Meris slung the rifle off her back and walked forward. "It's not as if I'm ill-prepared."

Noam rubbed his eyes. "Very well. If you wish." He followed.

Matt and I followed them as we moved in a line along the dirt road. "If it's all the same, I don't think I'm gonna be poking around in here," Matt said.

"Well, I plan to see what we can find for the benefit of us all," Meris snapped. "The inhabitants would help us if they were here, so I'm going to look."

We didn't get far when the voice floated out between two homes.

"You won't be looking very long."

Meris stopped short and raised her gun. "Who's there?"

A man in his forties, maybe, stepped out from the shadows, head to toe in green, his own pistol aimed at us, gray eyes staring us down. My heart lurched, painfully. *So that's what real fear feels like.*

Fear. Terror. Same thing.

"Just me." His mouth stretched in a tight, cold grimace. "Now put it down, and we'll get you children back to the city. I just need you to answer some questions about that train I saw you all on."

Meris' hold on the gun didn't waver, but her voice came out shaking. "N-no." *Click.*

The other man sobered. "Set your w—"

With the crack of Meris' gun, part of his sleeve seemed to explode, and he cried out, falling to his back on the road.

Meris stared at the man, her eyes wide for just a moment, her mouth open as the guy struggled to get back to his feet.

"Run!" Noam said, grabbing her arm and moving sideways. We all complied, and as we went, Meris slung the rifle over her shoulder in one motion.

*She had it ready. She expected that.* But of course she had. This was their world, and we were the ones not ready for it. I threw a glance back at the man still lying on the ground.

Would he come after us? Would he be able to? More importantly… who was he?

***

"It isn't safe." Noam's voice rang out loud. I flinched. Even if Meris was arguing, did he have to almost yell?

*At least he doesn't seem prone to it.*

I let my backpack rest against my feet and moved back and forth against the bark of the tree behind me, careful not to rub at the bruise. The run had left me itchy. "Man, that feels good."

Matt slouched next to me. "I bet."

Meris still stood on the hill, her gaze fixed on the lights of the town below us. "Noam, we need to get more supplies. Maybe some information about the village or what might have happened to them."

Noam lowered his voice. "We can hunt for food."

"I still need to keep up with events."

"Meris, don't you think it's been pretty well established that we can't be seen after what you did?"

She smirked. "We as a group of four cannot be seen. I am one person, and I intend on coming away with something from this village. All the better if their sympathies lie with Naolon, because they may be too loose with their tongues." The confidence didn't quite reach her eyes as she passed us and started walking down the hill.

Matt lounged against the tree, his face hard. "We could leave you here."

"I don't much care," came her call.

*Too loud. Why is she acting like this?* She put off that air of fearlessness, but this was reckless. Stupid, even.

*Then again, she did shoot a guy this afternoon.* "We need to go after her. She's going to get us seen."

"We definitely will get caught if we go down there." Matt leaned away from the tree.

"No, Anya's right." Noam sighed. "Meris needs a lookout." He walked down the hill. "You can stay here if you'd like. I hope we won't be long."

"I'm not waiting around back here," Matt muttered, stepping away from the tree. "Coming?"

I tilted my head to the side. "You don't think it would be better to stay back?" *To stay still, to stay put, to not scream for someone to get a real good look?*

He shrugged. "I know it would be better, but I also think it's better to stay together. I don't know what Meris is thinking, but those two stand the best chance of getting us through this alive."

I ground my teeth together at the wave of nerves that traveled through me. "Okay. Sure. You first." I kept my eyes on the back of Matt's shoes as we made our way down the hill. *Really don't ever want to roll down a mountain again.* Noam had already covered a fair distance and pushed ahead. The land flattened, and another lamp was lit in the town, brightening the dusk. A low wall ran around the town, broken by a cobblestone road off to the side.

What I could see of the buildings in the town looked similar to how they'd built the capital city, as if they'd been built at the same time. This town didn't have the thrown together look, though. Most of it looked newer.

*Must've tried to be a bigger city at some point.*

Without warning, two voices shouted from somewhere in the town, and a figure sprinted down the street toward the wall, a long shape making a strange extension beside its head. The rifle glinted in the light. Meris.

"Uh-oh." Matt tensed beside me.

A group of men and boys chased her, but none were as fast. Meris leapt and cleared the wall and reached Noam, and the pair ran past us.

I sure didn't need directions then.

Our feet crashed over the brush as we ran up the mountain. I couldn't see the men who were chasing us, but I could hear them, shouting to each other as they prepared to go after us. *They're slow, we're fast, we're ahead, it's okay. . . .*

"Where?" Matt stayed behind me.

*Where what?*

A wild moment of fear left me hoping those men wouldn't shoot at us. Feet running over brush confirmed that they'd started the chase for real now. If they were running, then they weren't shooting, so at least there was that.

"Caves." Noam's answer was quick and decisive.

The hill got steeper then, and we ran half-crouched like animals, grabbing the roots and rocks as we climbed. My mouth dried up, and a cramp pulled at my right side.

"This way." Noam disappeared into the side of the mountain. A root grabbed at the toe of my shoe. I pulled back, cracking the root in half, as Matt yanked at my arm. We followed Noam's path straight into the pitch black hole.

The other two sat on the floor of the cavern, pressed against a wall. I let my legs fold up under me and yanked the canteen out of my backpack. There wasn't enough water in the world, not at all, and certainly not in that little metal container. *Can't waste it.* I pulled it away from me, drawing in deep, ragged breaths. Matt knelt down beside me.

Voices. I froze, trying to keep my breath quiet as my lungs worked to pull in air at a furious rate.

"They disappeared."

"They came this way, I saw the eyeshine from one. Went into one of the caves."

*Eyeshine?* Matt was just a shadow beside me, barely visible in the golden light from the back of the cave. His eyes weren't reflecting now. *Did he give us away?* There was light behind me in the cave. I turned.

More little twinkling lights were scattered all over the cave walls at the back.

*At least we can see.* The voices outside kept grumbling on.

"And that girl we found, you heard the description of the shooter…"

"Is that coming along well?"

"A simple bullet removal, not bad. The king will recover."

*The king…?*

"Well, they're gone now, and I don't suppose they'll trouble us. And I hate the thought of crossing the swamp folk. I don't care who we serve."

*Swamp folk?*

"Well, they have to come out sometime. We'll return tomorrow. Get one of the men to come back up here and patrol this area in case they do turn up."

We were trapped.

The grumble of voices faded, and no one spoke for a few long minutes, until there wasn't any evidence of people outside.

Noam spoke first. "You shot the king of Naolon."

Meris didn't say anything at first, and the silence swelled until she finally answered. "Good. He deserved it."

Noam looked at her for a moment, his face as calm as usual under the golden light. "Did you find anything for your trouble?

She shook her head. "No." She sighed. "We need fuel to light a fire now. We should have plenty of supplies and we can get information somewhere else."

"I'll get it." Noam stood and slipped into the dark. I watched him go, wondering how someone could end up so selfless in this world that, by all appearances, was full of spies in every corner. Shouldn't a place like this be every man or woman for themselves?

It would have made me that way if I'd grown up here, no question.

"So it appears we will need to be more careful now." Meris stood and stretched. Neither of us replied. She knew she'd acted too soon. What point would there be in continuing the discussion?

My eyes adjusted to the darkness quicker, helped by the mass of gently twinkling lights that seemed to grow in number as I stared at them, all trailing to the back of the cave.

"Matt."

"Hm?"

I crawled to the wall. "Convenient, right?"

"Hmm?" He looked around. "Oh those. Yeah." His eyes picked up the glow from them and shone softly.

*Still so spooky.*

"I wonder where they end up?" I stood, testing the height of the cavern. Maybe a foot of clearance hung between my skull and the rock. I made my way back to where I'd been sitting. "I'll have to check it out later." A flash lit the back of the cave wall, and the rumble of thunder followed a second later. For a second, a round patch of darkness, sprinkled with those tiny lights, showed stark against the lit up stone. *Another tunnel.* As rain began to sheet down, Noam dashed in, his hair damp and a bundle of sticks clutched in one hand.

"This amount of kindling isn't a good start," Noam said. "If it goes out…I don't know what then."

"At least we have shelter tonight," Meris answered.

Noam went to work on building the fire. The rushing of the rain outside calmed me, and my eyelids dragged downward. The moss lamps caught my attention. Was it just me, or were they moving?

A soft *tick* came from Noam's hands, and the rustle of a tiny flame signaled the arrival of the orange light. He sat back on his heels as it grew.

*Days of travel and I know nothing about them.* They hadn't talked much, and I hadn't known how to start a conversation with them, let alone ask what made them go after what they were looking for.

I cleared the gunk out of my throat. "So…where exactly are y'all from?"

Noam settled back. "We came this way from one of the refugee settlements down south."

"It's a camp, not a settlement," Meris corrected him. "Just a camp."

Noam gave a shake of his head that I almost didn't notice. "It's where we were raised, though our families are from Compass Hill originally."

Matt leaned forward, setting his chin in his right hand. "What did the two of you do before coming up here?"

"Noam's a doctor," Meris said.

His brown eyes flicked her way for a second. "Apprentice, really." He frowned. "For now."

*Whoa.* "Then you could perform surgery or something?"

"Technically, yes. I'd know what to do." He paused. "I'm better at stitching than cutting, though."

*No wonder he's so patient.* "And you're how old?"

Meris lifted her chin. "We're both seventeen."

"So what about you, Meris?" Matt asked. "What do you do?"

"I work where I can. Hunt sometimes." She didn't say anything else.

*Okay.* "So who sent you after the riddle?"

Meris smirked. "As I said before, some folks weren't interested in ending this war the smart way. The right pieces came into play, and we deemed it necessary to act without further input."

"In other words, she talked me into sneaking away from the camp,"

Noam added, smiling.

"I did not."

He shrugged. "If we win, all the better." He stared into the flame, forehead creasing.

Meris watched him. "You're not going to lose the apprenticeship. You have far too much skill."

"I hope so." Noam dug into his pack, pulling out one of the rough wool blankets. "Think I'll turn in. Goodnight, everyone." He reclined onto the leather pack, his hands behind his head.

Matt and Meris both murmured replies, but my eyes were on the fire as I tried not to start staring at Noam.

They had risked their futures for this.

They were raised in a refugee camp that this war had shoved them in. How had everything gotten started anyway? I intended to find that out. There was one thing I did know, though. Coming here wasn't a stupid decision for the other two. It was everything to them.

*And now it's the same for us...*

Meris soon followed after Noam. Just Matt and I sat up now, him staring into the flame and my eyes wandering over to the lights strung across the wall. Why were they here, in this cave? How did they thrive in the dark? Maybe they were more than plants. I'd have to ask one of the others. Maybe they'd know. Noam seemed like he would.

A noise from the back of the cave caught my ear. No. Not a noise. A voice. A human voice, singing. Low, but loud enough to hear the notes. It beckoned me closer. I held back. *Not a good idea.*

But who was singing? I got up.

The cave opening in the back swerved to the right in a long tunnel.

The lights continued down there, far off until they disappeared somewhere out of sight. The only difference was a lighter glow on one wall, waist high. The voices came from there. I stepped closer, pressed my hands to it. They reached into empty air, and I looked down into the wide opening.

It was like the world had turned upside down. The lights were everywhere, making the whole thing look like a star field. Matt appeared in the side of my vision, staring with me into the beauty below.

"I know that song." There was no puzzle in his whisper.

It wasn't one I'd heard before. "From where?"

He pressed his lips together, briefly. "My grandmother, I think." He leaned back. "Careful."

"I'm not gonna fall in." I took a half-step back from the opening.

He shook his head. "No…it's just that…" More notes punctuated the silence.

"Just that what?"

His jaw tightened, and he let out a puff of air. "There are a lot of people down there. I don't think they've seen us yet, but be careful."

How was he able to tell that? I squinted, leaning over again. Yes. Movement. Here and there, a shadow would break up the lights. One of them made a sharp motion in the gloom, and a small spark sprang up. "Oh."

"Yeah." He huffed out a single laugh. "Don't let them see you."

*Really? In this light?* "I don't see how they could. That fire's too tiny."

"Trust me. They can see."

"How?"

A long moment passed. I couldn't look away from the lights, didn't when he started speaking. "Because they're like me. They can see in the dark. Some call them frog people, or swamp folk, or moon-eyes." He cleared his throat. "If you saw one up close, you'd see their eyes glow. Like a cat's."

Glow? I lifted my gaze from the view and turned to him, confused. "What…"

He met my gaze. In the soft light of the moss lamps, Matt's eyes shone back that subtle green.

The way the light from my window made his eyes glow in the dark. The way my flashlight had made his eyes light right up in the dark house. Something we both knew but that he said he'd never thought much about.

I jumped back from him. "You're…"

"Yep, sure am." His hand closed around my elbow, pulled me to the main room. I let him. *Why should I let him?* He was something else, not human. What did this mean? How much did he really know, and why was I fine being yanked around to another room?

*This isn't okay.*

With a twist, I wrenched out of his grip and faced him, glaring with all I had in me.

"Anya—"

"Uh, no." My voice shook as I struggled to keep it low. "You're going to let me talk, and first of all, you won't grab me like that ever again. Second…" Why did my voice have to crack? "What are you?"

He frowned, emotions racing through his hazel eyes, now maybe back to normal, as they moved from sad to confused to sad again and finally accepting. "I'm half-human."

I could feel the eyes of the other two on us. "Well…what's the other half?"

"Mostly…that." He pointed at the back of the cave.

"Like those people down there?"

"Yes."

I let my face stay hard. Acting like he didn't know anything about this. Nice. "Why didn't you tell me?"

He sat heavily by the fire, his jaw set in a hard line, his eyes cold. "Because I consider myself to be human, and I didn't think it mattered much anyway."

*Is he lying now?* My feet took me closer to the fire, where I'd been sitting before. Next to my liar of a best friend. "So you're really from here?"

He rubbed his eyes. "I spent my entire life in Salt's Creek, just like you." He looked up at me, desperation filling his face. "I didn't even know this place existed. I swear."

Nothing I could verify, not really. We were four when my parents moved next to each other. Before that. . . . "What about your parents?"

"You know their story already."

"So?" *Dare you to lie again.*

He exhaled quickly. "Dad's from Charlotte. He's the human one, by the way. Some Cherokee ancestry, if that matters at all to you. Mom, the non-human, is from Ocracoke. Remember my grandparents' house?"

My eyelids drooped. *So tired.* I leaned back against the wall. "I thought you didn't know anything about this war."

"I didn't."

"But your family—"

He jutted in, cutting me off, meeting my eyes. "I actively avoid getting involved in whatever it is my relatives get themselves tangled up in and argue about during Thanksgiving dinner." His gaze never wavered. "And honestly, there was never much they told me, anyway. Just…I found some old books in our house and figured some things out. Mom only told me when I actually asked her, and she wouldn't say anything else other than that her kind of people were rare and that I should keep it to myself. We were twelve. I figured it was pretty lame and not that important, so I stopped caring."

One of the sticks in the fire finally succumbed to the flame, cracked, and fell deeper in. The image of his face when he'd seen Dupree's name on the letter. "But you've heard of Gavin Dupree."

"I heard his name once." He sighed. "I guess it didn't stick or something, other than being familiar."

"So if there's that connection…"

He shrugged. "It would explain a lot about my Aunt Della." His gaze turned to me again, a smile inching onto his face. "I promise I won't ever let her get her claws into you."

His supposedly crazy aunt with normal kids like his cousin Danny. They lived in Michigan, but Matt was close to him, and I thought of Danny as a good friend. *Danny's just like Matt, too.* I had to squelch the exhaustion fueled laugh that wanted to explode out. "Anything else?"

"That's it." He looked right into my eyes, his own reflecting the light of the fire. "Nothing. I promise."

"You knew about those moss lamp things."

"My grandmother tried to grow them little while back." He rested his head on the wall behind us.

"I guess it didn't work."

"It did for a little while." He glanced at them. "They're actually a bug or something that lives inside the plant. No idea what they eat. Whatever it is doesn't grow in North Carolina."

"I don't care about the plants." *Really?* "Why didn't you tell me about you?"

"Would you have believed me?"

I bit down on my tongue. Would I have? "Maybe. Especially now."

It wasn't a conversation I'd ever expected to have.

"Well, if it took coming here to offer the possibility of you believing me now, then you probably wouldn't have then." He poked at my shoulder. "You should get some sleep."

"Okay." At least we hadn't disturbed the other two much. A yawn forced its way out. "Within reason…you can tell me anything."

He nodded. "Okay."

A leather backpack full of dried meat and bread had probably never felt as soft as it did when I curled up on it. "Goodnight."

"'Night."

*Can I trust him?*

***

*I'll sell you a riddle. . . .*

The lines of the poem floated around in my half-asleep mind, falling out of order and repeating the first phrase.

The skittering noise that echoed softly in the cave trailed over the last edge of a dream. My body woke suddenly and fully, and I pushed up, my heart racing.

Had I dreamed it?

The fire was long dead, and the chill made the darkness feel like a solid thing. The moss lamps looked different, too, now running in three thick lines on the wall, heading to the back of the cave, back to where we'd heard the singing. *How is that possible?*

The cave entrance made a gray smudge in the dark. Morning would come soon. Something else about the leftovers of the fire picked at my brain. Its shape had changed in some way I couldn't determine. I crawled closer, seeing its shape become more definite in the sparse light.

A long knife was stuck down into the wood, a piece of paper impaled on it. The air caught in my throat as I crawled back to Matt, banging my knees and shins along the rock floor. I shook his shoulder frantically.

I felt him jump under my hand. "What?" His voice sounded thick with sleep.

"The fire." I pointed back to it. "There's a knife in it."

He sat up, eyes opening fully, and looked, then tilted his head.

"Can you see it?" *Of course he can. He's got night vision.*

"Yeah..."

He crept to the remains of the pile. I heard some still intact wood crack as he pulled the knife up and unfolded the note.

"What does it say?"

He held it closer to the glow on the wall. "I can't read it."

"Too dark?"

He shook his head. "No...it's...it's not..."

"It's not what?"

"In English." He took a breath. "I think it's whatever language those…people speak, which I can't read."

"Oh."

"Yeah." He walked back to where he'd been sleeping. "I've seen it before, but I have no idea how to read it."

*They did see us.* "What do we do?"

"Wait until morning, I guess."

*Maybe I can doze off.* Not likely, though, and did I want to? "This is creepy."

"A little bit."

My eyes couldn't look away from the spot where they'd invaded our peace and shoved the knife into the fire. "They saw us, didn't they? When we were looking?"

"They did a good job of hiding it."

"Yeah, because spy techniques would be completely out of place herc."

Matt laughed softly.

*I wish the sun would hurry up and rise.* I shivered. Another sun, so much like Earth's. What really was this place?

This sun took its sweet time in lifting up from the horizon as the time dragged on by. Finally, the gray smudge at the entrance brightened, and the cold morning light came into the cave.

Meris sat up, rubbing her eyes, and stared at me and Matt. "You're already up."

"Yeah. We had some visitors last night." Matt held the note up.

"What?" Meris jumped to her feet. Her voice sharpened. "Noam, get up."

The pulled the paper out of Matt's hand and studied it, her mouth working slowly as she stared down at the paper. The blanket rustled where Noam had slept.

Could she read it, if we couldn't?

"That was stuck on a knife in the firewood," Matt said. Noam appeared over Meris' shoulder. She pushed the note towards him.

"What?" he asked.

"You're better at reading the swamp folk's words."

"Oh." He took it, yawning, and turned away toward the growing daylight.

Meris looked a little paler. "We might have been attacked."

Noam came back over. "Actually, we probably wouldn't have been." He handed the note to Matt. "It's says 'be good, nephew, and follow the lights we leave.'"

*Lights?* The lines on the wall. "The lines lead deeper into the caverns."

Matt looked to the back and took the note, his eyes slipping down to it. "Nephew?"

Meris looked Matt up and down and smirked. "I knew I had you picked out, moon-eye. Who do you know here? Who have you been in contact with?"

Matt glared at her. "No one. How do you know it isn't for one of you?"

"Who else could it be for?" The other girl's green eyes darkened as she turned away, walking to the entrance of the cave. "We're human, and I saw your eyes glowing at me on the train."

"I can't read this," Matt snapped, getting to his feet. "You two can."

"Maybe it's someone who hopes you might be able to," Noam said, evenly.

Matt rubbed his eyes with one hand. "Oh, man."

"What is it?" I asked. Meris was hovering over near the cave entrance. *Did she not learn anything last night?*

"Nephew," Matt said. "I bet this was written by my Aunt Della. Or at least she sent it."

*How would she know we're here?* My eyes found those thick glowing lines again. "So…should we follow what it says?"

"Yes." Meris hurried to her backpack. "There are men fairly close to this cave now." Fear covered her face as she stared at the lines. "I don't relish the idea of going into the darkness." She frowned at Matt. "Especially on the instructions of a phantom people who haven't shown their faces in far too long, despite this being their planet."

"That's not my fault." Matt grabbed the knife off the floor of the cave. "Anyone want this? I'm bringing it."

I ran my finger carefully over the blade. "It's dull." But could I use it? "I'll take it."

"Sure?" Matt asked.

"Yes. It can be sharpened." *Back off.* I tugged at the handle, and his grip tightened.

"You got it?"

"Yes. Thank you." His grip loosened and I pulled it to me, shoved it into the backpack. Somehow, having a weapon bolstered me. "So…we going?" A sharp voice from outside sounded in the woods.

"Yes." Meris turned to Matt. "I think anyone who can see in the dark should go first." Her tone invited an argument.

*Are those two gonna be like this the rest of the time we're here?*

His face stayed neutral. "Fine." He faced me, not even sparing a glance at Meris or Noam. "Just follow me. Hold on if you have to, and we'll take it slow."

I grabbed ahold of part of his backpack. More voices from outside came in. "Lead on."

We stepped, all in a line, into the dark. It swallowed me as we went, with nothing to hold me out of it except for the sparse bulbs on my left and the thick lines on my right. Whoever had made them had squished a bunch of the lights and smeared them on the walls to lead us.

*Ew.* How had Matt's aunt figured out where we were? Was she there, somewhere, in that cave, or had word about the incident in the village traveled that quickly?

The shuffling of our feet echoed off the walls, soft and all out of rhythm, keeping some indeterminate time. Noam's voice rose over the noise. "The lines behind us are fading."

Matt didn't answer for a moment. "Anya, do you still have hold of my backpack?"

"Yeah?"

"Don't let go. I'm not sure how long the glow lasts, and I won't be able to see without it. Just hold on." Panic crept into his voice and bled out a little to me.

*If they fade, we'll be blind.*

He sped up. I felt Meris' hand close down on my pack as we went, and I knew Noam would have done the same with hers.

*At least we're all in agreement about this.*

How could we measure time here? The lines faded behind us more as we turned corners, and my stomach started to growl. Past time for breakfast. Was that the dried meat in the backpack I was smelling, or just hunger making me imagine things? The only sound that followed us was that of our footsteps in the close tunnel.

We'd probably entered the tunnel hours ago. I'd lost count of the seconds somewhere after three hundred. Why hadn't Matt's aunt waited around for us to wake up, or gotten us up herself?

*Maybe she didn't have much time herself.*

Then again, he had said the woman was crazy. Matt and Danny had always pulled me away to play outside, so I didn't really know Della.

It had been much longer than the first five minutes I counted, and it was only getting darker. The lines were dimming, still so steadily, and the ones behind us had gone dark long ago.

Then Matt turned his head to look back.

I could see him.

The outline of his head wasn't a stark contrast, but the cavern was deep gray now, not pitch black as it had been. His pace sped up as we turned a curve and a bright light illuminated the cavern somewhere ahead of us.

I let out a deep breath and pulled my cramped hand away from him. "Finally."

"Thank goodness," Meris added.

Matt led us out of the tunnel and into a tiny entrance chamber with a ceiling just a little bit over our heads, close enough to reach easily and dotted with more lights.

*Should I be this relieved?* We'd escaped, but to where? My stomach grumbled. “Anyone else hungry?”

# Chapter 14

Whatever kind of trees it was that grew here still rustled in the breeze. Colors. Moving. *Even here it's beautiful.* Fall was disarming, always. Comforting. I couldn't let it do that.

Noam stared hard at the map in his hands. "I…I'm not too sure where we are."

Two days after emerging from the cavern, we stood in the middle of thick woods, near some road that might or might not have been the main road. It was beautiful here, but if even Noam didn't know where we were. . . . *Lost.* Should we have followed those directions on the note? If someone knew Matt's aunt, then they might know her connection to him and to this place. We might have been tricked into taking that detour.

*Can't turn back now.*

Matt answered him. "But we're still headed north, right?"

"Well, yes." Noam lowered the parchment. "It's just…as far as finding where exactly we might be…the detour through the caverns did throw us off."

"I knew it would." Meris smirked at Matt. He rolled his eyes.

*Really could do without them constantly baiting each other.* I scratched under the strap of my backpack. "So what now?"

Noam glanced at the other girl. "Meris, it's Brightleaf Manor, correct?"

"Yes." She looked out over the trees below us. "That's what Barney's message said."

Brightleaf. It sounded like something I would have heard at home.

Maybe if we could just wander along the road in a general direction, we'd have a break from the running.

*That's one benefit of getting lost.*

But I hadn't been able to ignore the snuffling I'd heard last night, and the one before. Something, off in the dark, hunting us, growling every so often. It had to be the same, or a pack of them, whatever it was, going along behind and waiting for the right moment for us to slip, or fall, or somehow be helpless. Whatever this animal was, it was obviously intelligent.

"Matt?"

"What?"

"What do you think that thing is we keep hearing at night?"

He shrugged. "Curious animal?"

"Must be real curious if it's followed us for two nights." *No way that's the right explanation.* It might not have even been the same thing. The wildlife here didn't seem like it wanted to be found.

Noam folded his map back up. "I have to confess that when we're this far off course and nowhere near anything, I'm not very good at reading maps. We could be on any of the roads. I can basically pick a direction."

*Great.*

Meris nodded. "Well if we do find our way again, maybe we can stay on course this time."

Matt rolled his eyes. "Just drop it Meris. That might have saved your life."

She lifted her chin. "If you say so." She looked around. "I'll return shortly." She hurried down the path and disappeared.

"And there she goes." I pulled my backpack off and leaned into the tree, scratching back and forth. The bruised area didn't hurt as much anymore. Too bad there weren't any mirrors to get a good look. How much longer would my ponytail holder last? I felt the thick dryness of my hair at the ends and the waxy oil gathering at the roots.

*Bet I look just great.* My skin itched with the grime that had gathered on it, and my legs barely cooperated. My teeth even felt fuzzy. I was so tired it barely registered that I'd gone days without my basic routines.

Noam stretched. "She'll be back."

Matt snorted. "Maybe she won't be followed by a bunch of angry men this time."

The brush crashed near us, someone running through the woods. I spun around. "Oh no."

Meris burst through the trees, her face lit up. "We're not lost!"

Noam went still. "What?"

She grinned. "You will not believe where we are."

"We might if you tell us," Matt said.

She narrowed her eyes, but kept speaking. "We're near Skyrren, very near. I can see it from over there."

My heart thumped hard and I looked at Matt. Skyrren. The book. *How did I almost forget about that?*

A smile grew on Noam's face as he pulled out his map again. "Then…that's good. That's very good. We should be able to go around it to reach that fort. Let's get on with it."

A fort now? Avoiding the city made sense, but we had to get in there, especially if there was any chance of getting to look for the book. "Why only go around it?"

*Way to ask the obvious question.*

Meris answered. "There was a time when we might have been able to go through it, blend in. Not anymore."

*Uh-oh.* "Why?"

"Something happened there, about thirty years ago," Meris said. "Skyrren was connected to Earth. Still is. One day, there was an incident in one of the cities it connected to. Something poisoned the air and water and ground in that city. It wasn't a problem here until the poison began to leak through a gate here, and they couldn't seal it. People got sick. Many died. The rest left, and they walled it off."

"And Skyrren's still abandoned?" *Which Earth city?*

"People are afraid to go back." Noam took a place beside me. "With good reason, though it might be fine."

An incident. Poison leaking through, soaking everything. Killing slowly as it arrived. All the marks of a power plant meltdown, somewhere on Earth. I felt a chill at how connected the two planets must be.

Right out in the open, just out of sight.

How many incidents could have done that? "What Earth city was it?"

Meris answered. "I'm not sure. I believe it started with a 'P.'"

The chill ran up my back. *Was it…?* "Oh." I didn't dare confirm, but one city matched. Prypiat, assuming the years passed the same way. Websites and documentaries and pictures had told me that story, and I remembered old conversations between me and Matt. How we'd said in the future, when we were older, maybe we'd go there. The ultimate ghost hunt.

Noam tilted his head. "You've heard of things like this happening."

"Oh yeah." Matt grimaced. "We have."

They didn't ask.

Stuff that happened on Earth, the devastating disasters that emptied whole towns, also affected Trenavell. It had to work in reverse.

If Gavin Dupree had created some device to seal the gates, would it even work? And why hadn't he used it back then, when he made it? What if it broke something, or contaminated Earth? Anything powerful enough to spread around to more than one gate might have a pretty terrible set of side effects. It was risky, and he was either brave or crazy.

I settled on crazy. This connection got shoved into the forefront. The original reason we even started poking around in my family's history was the search for proving his innocence, which did seem doubtful if he was insane.

But poison or not, at some point, we had to get into that city.

*That book might tell us everything.*

***

I caught glimpses of Skyrren as we went along, more of wall than anything. High walls with words scratched into them. I shivered.

Noam stopped us at a weird, vine-covered wall, like a fence, with one hole where I guessed there must have been a gate at some point.

"What's this wall for?" Meris asked.

Noam frowned. "I think we'll have to go through this area to get to the edge." He pointed. "I can see it from here."

And there it stood. Far off, across the enclosed area, a dark wood expanse blocked any further view of Skyrren. In between was so much undergrowth that no hint remained of what this area might have been.

Meris took one step into the paddock. "There should be a path around it, then. Come on."

"And if there isn't, we come back," Noam added.

"Of course," Meris said.

We stepped under the twisted arch. Would there be a way to get through the wall? Would the other two come with us? Probably not. If they believed it was still poisoned, then they definitely wouldn't be joining us. This opportunity probably wouldn't arise again. Time crunched down a little, and brought panic in with it.

*Have to find that book. We could lose them. Leave them. Pretend to see something and run ahead. They won't want to go in, not if it's so bad.*

And by running away, what would that tell them?

*This is a mess, but I need that book.* It wouldn't be right to leave, though.

The vines covered the inside of the paddock in a thinner layer than the one that consumed the fence. Uneven circles dotted the ground here and there, and the vines seemed especially thick in those spots. Bleached white bones from huge animals littered the ground, and rising up above the ropey coating on the ground were skulls in an alien shape I'd never seen before.

"What are these bones from?" I asked Matt. My voice came out softer and shakier than I meant it to. *Think.*

Noam and Meris hadn't heard me. They kept going. *That gives us time.*

Matt shrugged and edged across the paddock floor, approaching one of the circles. I watched him.

*Little too casual there, buddy.*

I stepped closer. Maybe the circles were a way in. I followed, getting right up to the edge of one of them. They were larger than I'd figured, maybe ten feet across. What had they been for? Did the vines cover up a hatch, or a cellar? Noam and Meris weren't paying attention as we stood with our toes at the edge of a circle.

Matt stared down at it. "I almost want to see if I can open it."

"We could wait and see if there's another way in." My resolve faltered. I hesitated. *This isn't safe. We can't leave them.* "If we can get away and come back. You know, later. If we get a chance."

He nodded. "Let's catch up."

I turned, faster than I'd intended, and stumbled, bumping into him. He put one foot forward to steady the both of us, planting down right into the vines.

His tennis shoe shot straight through, and without a warning, we tumbled through the hole, dead vines shredding under us. A shriek ripped out of my throat as I slammed into the inside of the hole.

We half-rolled, half-fell, for minutes or hours. The world got still abruptly. I found myself sprawled breathlessly somewhere very dark, my head the only thing still spinning. *Ow.* I'd inhaled dirt at some point, and it scraped at my throat as I coughed it out. Something glowed somewhere, but it didn't offer enough light for me to see by.

"Matt?" The word croaked out. I coughed again, pushing the dirt out of my throat. "Matt?" At least my voice was audible this time, broken and cracked as it was.

"I'm right here." Just a few feet away. There wasn't enough light in this hole, not enough for me, anyway. I lurched over the ground, shaking, my hands reaching out for where I'd heard him last. They met his, and I grabbed on, throwing my arms around him.

"Are you okay?" My voice was rough and choked. *Literally gravelly.* The thought made me want to laugh for one hysterical moment.

"I'm fine." He pushed me away, his hands still on my shoulders. "Are you?"

*Can he see me?* "Yeah. My head hurts." I backed away from him, took of my backpack, and reached inside. *Water.* The cool metal canteen bumped against my hand. I freed it from the stuff piled on top of it, yanked the stopper out and gulped it down. "Where...where are we?" More coughs, and a gag threatened to leave me heaving out the food we'd eaten.

"I don't know." He sighed. "I don't know how to get back out. I can barely see down here." Distantly, I could hear two voices calling, muffled, but it was impossible to tell where it might have come from.

How far had we fallen? "I can't see much."

He tugged at my elbow. "I can now, some. I saw some light. Let's try to follow it. It might be the surface." I followed him, glad I had actually seen something. We rounded a corner, and the glow's source popped into view.

More moss lamps on the wall, but my heart leaped at what they looked like. Growth had blurred the edges a little, but it was clearly a wheel, with eight spokes around it. First time I'd seen it here. We stopped, staring, studying this same picture that Gavin Dupree had doodled on the back of a letter so long ago.

"Matt…do you think that means anything?" Dumb question. Nothing was random here. The rest of this tunnel stretched on into the dark.

"Probably does." He looked around us. "I think this might be just a light, though. I don't see any doors or whatever."

More deep darkness. "So we keep going." *Stop shaking. Stop. You're alive.*

"I can use the light for a little bit. After that, we'll have to feel our way unless there's something else to see."

"Okay."

We walked, in silence. But who was gonna hear us? Why not risk talking?

"Matt?"

"Mmm?"

"Do you know what those animals were?" *Would this make him lie?*

He was quiet for a long moment. "I've heard a story about them. I think they're called burrow-beasts, and they're supposed to be really fast at digging, and you really wouldn't want to get caught in front of one." He shook his head. "I never thought they were real."

"Oh." *They burrowed.* "What if there's one here?"

"We'd probably know about it before it got here."

"I hope so." We rounded another corner, and a soft light ahead let me at least see his outline more. The source came into focus, and I saw now that the light was in a sharp rectangle shape. A door. Our feet hurried together as we climbed the sloping floor. I couldn't reach it fast enough. It was some way out. No more of this tunnel. Matt grabbed the doorknob.

*Please don't let it be locked.*

It inched open, pushing inward, and the light of the day spilled through as we rushed into the room and shut the door behind us.

No one greeted us. Bolts of faded fabric filled up the shelves beside needles and spools of thread, all covered with a layer of dust. A shop once, probably. A seamstress or a tailor had done business here, before sickness had driven the whole city away.

"Where are we?" My headache sharpened. "I mean, Skyrren, obviously…"

Matt's hazel eyes were wary. "Yeah, but where in it?" He rubbed at his face.

This was what I wanted, but knowing that Skyrren had been contaminated with enough radiation to empty the city…that was a different story.

*I'm an idiot.* "I guess…" My voice cracked again. "We could look for the book."

*Like we'd know where to start.*

Matt just smiled. "Can't hurt, right?"

"Guess not." It was better here in the light. The ache still pressed on in my head. "But how do we find Meris and Noam again?"

"Start walking, look for the wall and hope for the best, I guess."

My pulse pounded in my head, sharp and persistent. "Lead on."

"Yeah, like I know where I'm going…"

"Hush." I rubbed my eyes.

Matt frowned. "How big do you think Skyrren is?"

"No idea."

He nodded. "Okay." We slipped out the door and into the deserted city. A brick sidewalk ran in front of the other buildings, with gaps in some places to allow the dirt roads to go through. Tiny round bulbs clung to everything, buzzing faintly, but not lit up. If they could live here, maybe the air wasn't so bad anymore.

*Or maybe they really can just live anywhere.*

And still, I half expected something horrible to come lurching out of the weathered doors of the shops. "Think Meris and Noam will come after us?"

Matt looked into a well as we passed it. "I hope not, but Meris might try."

"You hope not?"

"No use in all of us getting stuck here," he answered.

I could see them now, her diving down the hole and Noam following, his mouth set in a hard line, following after her so persistently. "So how do we find them again?"

He got serious. "That I don't know. Maybe they'll find a way through the wall."

"Maybe we can get out of here, look for that fort and wait there."

"Sounds good."

"I'm still going to search for the book if we can find it." *Not that there's a good chance of that.*

The first gap was just a hundred yards away, if that at all. We stepped to the edge of the sidewalk and peered to the right. The giant wall that surrounded the city loomed even taller than it had seemed when we were just approaching the city.

"We're on the outer edge, I think."

"That's encouraging," Matt said. "For when we leave, I mean."

*The edge.* Twice now I'd seen that eight-spoked wheel. It was a long shot to assume that the cities were round, but it did make sense, maybe. "Matt...do you think the book might be somewhere in the walls? I mean, if Gavin had friends who were able to hide things and they hid it out here?"

His eyes scanned the stained wood. "It's a long shot."

I gritted my teeth. "I know, but why not try while we're here?" *My head hurts way too much for him to be difficult.*

He shrugged, a jerky motion. "Whatever. It can't hurt."

"Okay." I swallowed. "Thank you."

We kept our pace slow as we moved down the sidewalk. Most of the empty windows were too much like eyes. To duck into any of those places was daunting now, and my head was still throbbing.

"You gonna look any?" Matt asked.

"Yeah, it's just...they're creepy. The windows." I rubbed at my temple.

"You okay?"

"Yeah. I'm good." I clamped my jaw against the hint of nausea swirling around in my stomach.

When the city began to darken, and the moss lamps began to illuminate the streets, I gave up pretending I actually intended to look around in any of the places we stopped. We had no lights for any good searching, and the headache pounded even harder now. What good would it do, anyway? To look here for that book would just be a lot of guessing.

*I feel watched anyway.* Too quickly, the sun slipped below the horizon, giving out one last orange ribbon of light before it disappeared. *Stupid sun. Stupid planet.* I knew I should be caught up in some sort of wonder that this place even existed. For me, though, the reality of it waited just at the edge of the throbbing in my head. I couldn't think of it now. Even without a raging headache, it was too overwhelming.

We stopped in front of one of the close-together buildings here, another business, probably. The sign had long ago fallen off, gone who knows where, leaving two rusted chains hanging from a pole. Matt climbed the steps and put his hand on the doorknob. It came open easily.

"Well, we're not without shelter." He smiled, hopeful, but I saw the weariness tighten the corners of his eyes.

"Yeah."

The few tables inside had chairs stacked on top, as if the owner had left it clean. A bar along the wall stood before a bunch of empty shelves. I hoped whoever had left this place, some stranger, hadn't left sick. At least they might have had some warning of that poison. Maybe they thought they'd come back one day. Maybe they were just hopeful.

The chill was deeper in here. "Should we light a fire or something?"

"I might." Matt peeked out of the front window. "I guess we could break a chair or something, but I almost don't want to take the chance."

I imagined something bearing down on us in the night, drawn to our fire, if someone was living in this city. Or soldiers. We probably weren't the only ones here, if someone had discovered it was actually safer than originally thought. "I think I know what you mean."

*Not risking that.*

Matt narrowed his eyes. "Will you be fine without one?"

"Well, we have blankets and we're inside." *In the dark.* "We don't have to have a fire."

"Then I guess we could sleep behind the bar." He crossed the room to it.

It sounded pretty comfortable already. I followed, my steps slow. "Okay."

He frowned. "What's wrong?"

*Whiner. Complainer.* "Nothing."

"Yes there is."

I stepped around the bar. *Nosy.* "How do you know? You're hardly a mind-reader."

"Well, you have the most obvious face I've ever seen."

I flopped down and yanked the blanket out of my backpack, each movement making my head hurt worse. I felt irritated with myself for feeling so bad and so scared and so not up to any of this. "Back off." I wrapped the stiff wool around me and pulled dug a chunk of bread out of the nest of squished and broken crumbs. It at least had survived the fall. My stomach turned.

His face didn't change. "Whatever. You just look like you don't feel good."

"I don't. My head hurts." Suddenly the uneven bundle under my head didn't sound like such a good pillow. I forced myself to chew.

"So does mine."

A laugh bubbled up, unwelcome and wild. "Then I guess this is a tie." He wasn't complaining. I didn't want to, if he wasn't.

His face relaxed into half of a smile then.

With a sigh, I pulled the rhyme out of my pocket. "So what I was thinking about the wall earlier..." I held the paper over to show him the words. "Maybe the wheel has something to do with points on a map that Gavin thought up, and if Skyrren is round, which it could be, then..."

He nodded slowly. "Then the spokes might mean something."

"And the book might be on the edge, if this is a code."

"I didn't think about that before." He squinted at me. "How did you come up with that?"

I settled into the corner. "Well...there would have to be eight points around the city that meant something."

"You think that animal pen was one of them?"

"Not necessarily, but...I dunno. I just feel like it's important, especially if there's more than one, but he didn't leave behind any instructions so I can't rule out anything." *Okay. Dead end.* The logic didn't hold up. Gavin Dupree was writing to friends. He didn't have to be specific in a letter if they already had an agreement.

"And you think it might be in the book?"

"Of course." *Grrr.* "I guess he assumed someone would pass this information down but..."

"Yes?"

"They'd know." I swallowed. "The Davies would know what he was talking about. Maybe Skyrren wasn't really an instruction. They probably already had an agreement." I folded the paper and shoved it back into my pocket. I should be more careful with it. "Was he crazy, Matt?"

The blanket was rough in my hands as I pulled it up higher around me.

"Maybe a little." He yawned. "Let's get some sleep while we can."

"Okay."

We didn't speak any after that. My thoughts fell into a wondering rhythm of questioning why I had agreed to do this, why we were here, how could I have been so stupid. If this whole thing we were doing was always supposed to be some grand secret, then I should have figured that Matt and I could disappear for days at a time without our parents knowing the real reason. It would be hard to believe, unless they lived it themselves. What was the point of trying to tell them once we got back?

*If we get back.*

My hands ached from how hard I gripped the blanket, imagining all the things that had already happened to us. The car, the tumble down a mountain, a train crash, and now a separation from the only two people we really knew and trusted here.

At least from behind the bar, I didn't have to feel the empty windows watching.

***

"I swear, if I stick my hand into another hidden compartment…"

I backed away from the shelf at the back of this shop as Matt leaned up from the drawer he'd been searching. He sighed. "Yeah, I don't think it's in here."

"I didn't actually think we'd find anything." The book hadn't turned up, and I felt foolish now for being so eager to get into the city. There was nothing for us to find. My stomach grumbled. With the rest of the bread all crumbs, and the dried meat running low, breakfast was starting to seem like a long time ago. *Cinnamon rolls would be amazing right now. . . .*

"Whoever owned this shop took everything with them." It wasn't obvious anymore what it had been. The only things in here were a huge trunk behind me and a wardrobe against the wall that hung halfway open. The other door had been nailed shut. I walked to it and played with the open side. "Did you ever imagine we'd pretty much find Narnia?"

"I think I'd take it over pioneer-land any day." He looked out the door. "Should we look anywhere else?"

The deserted emptiness was bland now, not even frightening anymore. "I'm kinda getting Skyrren burnout. Maybe we should just try to get back to the outside."

*No book. So much for that.* If Dupree had spent enough time in this world, someone would know stuff. *Just wish I'd been able to get it firsthand.* Giving up on this pointless search was the only option we had, if we wanted to find Meris and Noam again.

A noise built, feet running on hard-packed streets. I froze for a second. A group, if I was hearing right, two male voices leading, almost yelling back and forth. I half-crouched, ready to run or hide or anything that might let us stay unnoticed.

"I saw something come down this street."

"Well if the rumors are true, they'll know what we need to know."

The conversation didn't go on any further. One of them yelled, and gunfire followed.

Matt sounded panicked. "Hide."

The trunk. It was open, and I could just fit in if I curled up. I jumped in, cramped but secure, and pulled the lid down, leaving it cracked open an inch. The outside got louder now, with the sounds of guns covering everything. What was happening? Had Matt found a decent place to hide?

Heavy footsteps rattled the floor under the trunk.

*Please don't check in here, walk away, there's nothing. . . .*

There was a sharp crack from outside, and something fell across the trunk, hitting the lid hard, forcing it closed, and sliding off to land heavily beside it on the floor. I didn't dare move.

Then the quiet fell. I waited, counting the seconds slowly. Two minutes. Five. My arms tingled, and I couldn't really feel my fingers. *What just fell on this trunk…?* The quiet outside had to be safe now, and the trunk was closing in on me.

I reached one hand up to push on the trunk lid.

It didn't budge.

My heart started to race. Had Matt seen me jump in here? Was I trapped? If I was locked in, how was I going to get out? Horror stories of people locked in trunks and left to turn to skeletons blazed through my mind. No one would hear me. *They're just stories. Stupid stories.* I pushed again.

But I'd have to break out of it somehow. The lid wasn't going to move.

I shifted back and forth, making the trunk rock until it tipped onto one edge. With a heave, it pitched over and crashed to the floor. Wood snapped and splintered as the trunk fell awkwardly. The open lid left me with a big enough gap to crawl out of on the side.

I froze. A pair of feet made a silhouette against the daylight. The gap was big enough to slip out of. I could knock this guy down and find Matt, couldn't I? *Please let him be okay.* . . . We'd have to run, but wasn't that all we'd been doing lately anyway?

With one awkward lunge, I pushed myself out of the trunk and into the shins of the almost attacker. He cried out and tipped forward, falling over me into the wall. I sprang to my feet, ready to run.

Matt pushed himself away from the wall, one sleeve of his sweatshirt at his nose. He moved it away, smirking, leaving behind a red smudge. "Good move."

The tips of my ears turned hot. "I'm so sorry."

He held a hand up. "It's okay. Really."

"It's not broken, is it?"

"Don't think so." He grinned. "You got me pretty good. I'd keep practicing that if I were you."

My gaze went down to the trunk. That was one thing I'd definitely broken. To the left of it, a pair of boots at the end of green pants stuck out from the shadows.

"Is he…" My stomach roiled.

Matt pulled me away. "Yeah, he is. Don't look. Let's just go."

*No argument there.*

The street was empty, except for a few arrows on the ground, and blood, but no people. The stillness now wasn't boring, or quiet, or safe. A guarded air hung over the city, as if the buildings were aware of our presence. Someone was definitely watching, and they'd left little evidence of what just happened.

*They're after the guys from Naolon, and at least they haven't attacked us.*

The gap in the sidewalk a few yards ahead of us meant we were about to run across a road. "Let's get out of here."

"No problem."

We walked faster, almost breaking into a run, for no reason other than knowing that eyes watched us as we ran for a gap in the wall. The tiny, broken slot had once been splintered, but the splinters protruded, smooth, from the edges.

People had been coming here while the rest of the world assumed they couldn't. We slipped through without a snag and paused. A smooth, packed dirt path ran alongside the wall, flanked by forest and vines. Just a thin pathway, but clear of anyone.

"Which way?" Matt asked.

"Left, I guess, if we were traveling toward the center of the city."

"Okay." Matt nodded. "Left it is."

Matt walked on the outside, between me and the woods. "Well, I'm glad to be out of there."

"Me too." The sky wasn't giving up its secrets about directions. "Still don't know which way's north."

"We'll figure it out." He scratched at his nose. "When the sun sets or something."

"Noam did say the fort was on the other side…I guess we could try to find that."

"If those people trust us," Matt said.

"Yeah." *Why did we ever step into that pen?* "If."

We walked the same unchanging path until the sun began to sink in the sky. There weren't any more gaps in the walls, but plenty of graffiti had been applied. Carvings covered the wood, some in that moon-eye language, some in English. Words like "poison," "keep out," and "no passage." If it wasn't gouged into the wood, it was smeared with something that might have once been sticky, now coated with dirt and just a shade lighter than the wall. Probably goo from the little glowing plants, to warn anyone traveling at night that might not have heard.

It was almost truly dark now. "We need to stop." Matt stared at the vines that covered the trees at the edge of the woods. "We're outside. We need a fire tonight."

"Do you have the same thing Noam uses?"

Matt shook his head. "I don't think so."

Another cold night. "Can you start one without it?"

"I don't know. Maybe. Might take a while, but theoretically, yes. I could."

"I can keep watch. We've got time." I swallowed.

"True." He walked a few feet into the woods and gathered some of the vines. I kept myself planted against the wall. No one was coming, not yet anyway. And if whoever guarded the empty insides had anything to do with it, there wouldn't be many more shortcuts taken through it.

Matt went to work, bent over the vines and sticks, working at starting a fire. I only caught glimpses of what he did as I watched over the road. After a while I smelled the sharpness of a new fire, saw a soft mist coming from his hands. He bent over it, working some more, and the smoke got thicker. As I settled down under a tree near him, the vines caught more, and the fire jumped up.

The flames burned purple.

Matt backed away and sat beside me. "Whoa."

The warmth soaked into me. "It's kind of pretty."

"Must be something in the plants."

A yawn forced my mouth open. "Yeah."

"You can take a nap if you want."

"You sure?" I folded my arms on my drawn-up knees. *That sure sounds good.*

"Go ahead."

I let my forehead rest in the gap between my arms. I knew my neck would be stiff later, but I really just wanted to shut my eyes. *Where do we go if we don't meet the others?*

My thoughts dissolved into a dream. Ravenbook Academy. That's what I knew the growing, shrinking, stretching place I found myself in was, even though it looked different. Six floors and a weird spiral staircase raced by in my vision. Next I was in a classroom, and a teacher I didn't know stood at the front of the room, droning on and on about chalk and barbecue, all matter of fact. Was that the lesson? Something shuffled behind me. I couldn't turn, dared not to, and the snuffling got louder all the time. I called Matt's name, and there wasn't an answer. The shuffling, more a dragging now, something sniffing, came closer, inching to the back of my desk…a snarl.

I jumped. My heart pounded hard. The purple fire had shrunk. Matt dozed beside me.

*Did I really just hear that?*

Something still shuffled in the woods, nearby, but out of my sight. *I did hear it.* I dug my elbow into Matt's side. He opened his eyes, obviously confused for a moment, then went still as he heard the noise. The only thing I knew to do was spook the thing.

I grabbed a handful of the vines and threw them on the flame. It sputtered and jumped higher. A black shadow in the woods scooted away.

"Sorry." Matt's eyes opened wide now. "I tried to stay awake, I promise."

"It's okay." *Stop shaking.* "Let's…let's just rest but try not to sleep."

"Fine with me." He looked back up at me. "What did you hear?"

"Same thing."

"The sniffing?"

"It might have growled, too." *Wish that knife was sharp.* My pack didn't have anything to fix that problem.

"Oh." He stared at the flame.

I set my chin on my knees again and stared out into the woods. Whatever creature it was that decided to hunt us had to be waiting for us to fall asleep again.

*That's not happening.*

# Chapter 15

My eyelids scraped against dry eyeballs as I blinked. *Why again did we stay up?* I rubbed at them.

Matt stirred some dirt into what was left of our fire as I rolled my blanket up tight.

*Well I definitely don't regret not being eaten.*

A steady ache and a heaviness weighed my legs down. "I guess we'll try to reach that fort today, right?"

"Try to," Matt said. "Wish I'd asked for a map for us or something."

"Well if it helps, I didn't think about it either."

He shrugged. "Doubt they'd have had an extra one anyway."

Breakfast was the jumbled up contents of our backpacks. The dried meat left my jaw sore as I chewed. It hadn't before, but the fatigue that soaked my limbs sharpened every discomfort. Whatever other animals lived in the woods could probably hear us smacking on it as we followed the dirt road around Skyrren. *At least it ought to scare them off.*

It was all wall to the left, as far as I could see, the only points of interest being the eerie and frequent warnings carved into the wall every few yards. The forest on the right went on forever, thick and wild.

Matt looked up at the wall. "Man, when these people abandon things, they really get serious."

"Yeah, just a bit." No one to give us directions. No one to ask if they'd seen our friends. "What if Meris and Noam are behind us?" My voice rasped from an hours-long silence. "I mean, what if we end up walking in circles trying to reach each other?"

"If we can find Kings Road again, then we can just wait somewhere around there, right?" Matt turned his head, as if he might see the two somewhere behind us.

"I just hope they're not looking for us back there."

Matt cleared his throat. "Let's just keep going to the fort."

"If it means I can maybe sit down for a second, of course." I chewed on my lip. "And I can get the knife sharpened. That way we're actually armed." I couldn't even convince myself to actually be scared. The big realities, of war and survival, were now coated with a thick film of simply being too tired to care or think too hard.

Matt ground his teeth together. "Nice of my aunt to hand us a weapon that won't even work."

*What did she ever do get him so mad?*

"Like I said. We'll get it sharpened." The trees ahead thinned on the right. Another road, maybe? "Calm down."

"Yeah, whatever."

"Matt." I stopped walking.

He turned around, eyes blazing. "What?"

"Your aunt's not here."

Matt's shoulders relaxed, just enough to show me how tense he'd been. "Guess you're right."

"I am right." My eyes wandered to the gap ahead to the right as I walked past him.

He caught up quick. "You know, all the comments she's made about my dad, and about me, suddenly make sense." He took a deep breath. "She wanted us to come here."

This was getting ridiculous. "Okay, well, so did a lot of people, apparently."

"Yeah, well, they weren't family and they never told me I look too much like my dad or said I should stop hanging around with those foolish and nearsighted humans."

A low sound built over our conversation, far away for now, as we got nearer to a drop off ahead. There had to be something Matt wasn't telling me. "Matt, what is your problem?"

He opened his mouth, once, twice, and swallowed hard, and stared at me. "I hate the secrets my family keeps. If Aunt Della knows all this stuff…then the rest of them might. We didn't have to just stumble into this. They had to know, and I hate that the way they keep secrets might mean that you'll get hurt."

His intensity made me squirm. "Oh."

He looked down at his shoes, then ahead, and didn't say anything else.

Until now, I hadn't known an awkward silence with my best friend. The rhythmic scuffling of our feet on the dirt road seemed to mark the time as we walked, not speaking.

*Well, I sure don't know what to say.*

The noise from ahead of us was louder, but not by much, as we passed that gap in the trees. The only way to see what was making that noise was to hang on and lean out over the cliff.

"Should we take a look?" I asked Matt.

"Do you really think it's safe?"

"Of course I don't." I grabbed the trunk of a young tree. "But we might be able to get something useful out of this."

"I guess we can risk it, then."

I nodded and peered over, my stomach flipping at the height. I tightened the grip on the tree, taking in the strange comfort of the bark digging into my skin. The tree didn't bend or budge as Matt grabbed a part and peeked out.

A camp. No green anywhere, thankfully, but who were all the men and women milling about? There were tents, and horses, and I definitely saw weapons. It wasn't large, maybe a hundred people or so, and it had an obviously temporary status. These people were going somewhere, and if these were enemy soldiers, then they were undercover.

Where were they headed? I pushed away from the tree and retreated back to the security of the wall. They might not be from Naolon, but why risk just being out in the open? I liked the anonymity we had gained by falling down that hole.

Matt followed me, his mouth in a half-smile. "Wanna introduce ourselves?"

I smacked his arm, hiding a smile of my own. "Hilarious." We went on, staying close to the dark wall, still quiet. They maybe hadn't seen us, and maybe we'd been in a good position not to be seen, but still. I shivered.

The clouds began moving in, a slow covering of the sky over a few hours. They weren't heavy-looking, just thick enough to white out the sky above us. And still the silence went on. *I can at least do something about that.*

"Matt...um..." What should I say, though? Why would it make me feel so awkward for him to be afraid his family secrets would hurt me? I felt the same way; he was my best friend and I didn't want anything to happen to him.

He cut in. "I'm sorry. I mean, for getting mad."

*Oh.* "It's...fine. I get it." *I think.* Matt was fairly even-tempered. Was his Aunt Della really that bad?

We rounded another curve and stopped.

In foot-high letters filled with the remnants of paint, a very final etching on the wall twenty feet above us said only, "Keep out. Here Skyrren died."

Matt stepped back, going over the text again. "Must've been the main gate."

"Must have." *What a way to announce things.* A wide road ended abruptly at the barrier and led off away from it, branching into the woods ahead of us. A post a few yards away had some pointed signs nailed up, all weathered, but the letters had been carved deep into the wood. One had the name of the capital city. The other more obviously pointed back to Skyrren. The top one, not pointing anywhere, I thought, just said "Kings Road."

Relief poured over my tight shoulders. "Finally." We'd only been around part of the huge curve that had to make up the border of the city.

Matt stepped closer to the sign. "Yeah, but where do we go?"

The other two hadn't said anything about the fort being along the road. Or the manor. Or much of anything. *Wish I'd asked them more questions.* The main road wasn't getting us anywhere, but that wide forest trail just might. "That way. Maybe."

"Why that way?"

The map Noam had showed us, with all the gate markers, floated into my memory. "Kings Road runs east to west, so that one…must go north."

Matt studied the signs. "Worth a shot."

Something farther down the road kicked up dust. We were definitely out in the open here. "Come on." *Whoever they are, they're moving fast.* "Stay under the trees." We dashed across the road, heading for that little path under the thick cover.

It was better under here. More places and deeper shadows to hide in.

With a pang, one fact became obvious. Trenavell was changing me, even in the little time I'd been here. Fear made me seek out any shadow and avoid any other people we came across. It wasn't normal for me, and it didn't look like that change would work in reverse.

*Why'd I ever leave home?*

***

The root felt like it reached up out of the ground to grab my toes as I saw the glow of torches ahead in the darkness. I stumbled and caught myself on the side of a tree.

"Careful." Matt's voice was strained.

"Stupid root." *Can't even yawn. Too tired.* "I think that's the fort."

"Yeah, I think so."

We moved forward, my limbs just following directions, but protesting all the way. *Just want to sleep. That's all.* Slowly, the fort moved into view. It looked like all the frontier forts we'd seen pictures of in books, or at least what I could see of it did. Thick logs made up the looming walls, and lanterns glowed on the outside of a huge gate, with a few torches along the top.

"I think we can get down on the road now." Maybe it was the golden light, but the fort looked so warm, even comfortable. We climbed down the embankment, and my tennis shoes slid a little. Fatigue didn't even let me flinch. *I've fallen worse lately*. I didn't register the noise behind me all the way, but it was far, sounded like maybe something rumbling over the dirt road as the fort grew larger in my view.

The gates stood open to the night, and a bunch of men stood around. A note of panic struck, just for a moment. *Run.* But I didn't see any green.

*This place is seriously messing with me.*

The rumble behind us was louder, and someone shouted. "Clear the road!"

Matt tugged at my arm. I stumbled with him into a ditch just as a wagon gained on us. A shred of a scream leaked out as the wagon passed us.

I watched it, numb, wondering. *Why is he in so much pain?*

Matt's hand pulled at my arm. "Come on, there might be more coming."

We kept going forward, together. One hundred yards. One hundred feet. A few more steps, and we stood at the gate.

The guard, a guy not too much older, stared back at us as we stood dumbly before him. His eyebrows rose and he opened his mouth.

And he didn't get a word out. A shriek cut him off and punctured the air. "Anya! Matt!"

Meris launched herself through the gate and hugged both of us, then stepped away. Noam appeared behind her, solemn. "We thought you might have been dead." The relief was clear on his face. "We've been here a few hours, just…hoping you'd come."

"We kept calling for you," Meris said. "We didn't hear an answer at all."

"Yeah, we wound up in the dark," Matt said. "You just went on ahead, though?"

"Yes," Meris said. "We thought we heard something going on inside the walls, so we hurried away."

They had gone on ahead. *Better in the long run. We weren't caught.* But if they thought we were lost, what was the point of waiting? They had a goal, and for all purposes, we were along for the ride. "Something did happen."

"What was it?" Noam asked.

I shrugged. "A fight. It wasn't long, but it looked like some soldiers from Naolon got ambushed by some folks hiding in the city."

"You were inside?" Meris stepped back. "Is Skyrren…?" I knew what she'd ask. *Is it still poisoned, and did you bring poison clinging to you?* We'd have to tell them that someone was hiding in there.

Matt looked past her into the fort. "There're a lot of moss lamps there. I think the city's safe to live in." He sighed. "Can we go in?"

Noam pulled my arm. "Yes. We've been waiting right here, but we thought we'd seek sanctuary at the chapel for the rest of the night."

I followed the other two, glad this time to know that Matt walked so close behind me. We passed long structures, barracks, I guessed, and more plain buildings, always heading to what appeared to be the center of the fort.

We stopped at a little box of a building with double doors on the front. They were mostly closed, just cracked open a little bit. Meris yanked the right door towards her and led us inside.

The inner part of the chapel held a few lit candles, a couple of benches, and one little table at the front. A man at the front, the chaplain I guessed, rose and turned to us.

His face went from benign and welcoming to completely surprised. "Meris?"

"Cargan!" She ran to the man, throwing her arms around him, then stepped away. "I didn't know you were the chaplain."

Cargan stared at her. "Meris, why are you away from the camp? Does Mother know you're here?" He looked at me and Matt and frowned. "Who—"

"Brother, you have trust me." Meris straightened her back. "Matt and Anya two are friends of ours. They're helping us, but…" She trailed off as Cargan kept staring at her. With a quick sigh, Meris kept talking. "No, Mother doesn't know."

His mouth quirked. "Then I suppose I can't make you go back there," he said.

"No." She lifted her chin. "I have no intention of returning."

His eyes wandered over us again. "I'd heard rumors of four…" He smirked. "What are you up to, Meris?"

"Only a good errand that I can't share with you at the moment."

Cargan shrugged. "I expect only good from my little sister." He frowned. "I'm afraid you can't sleep here. Too many arrivals expected tonight."

*Rumors of four…the king…need to sleep. . . .* "Is there anywhere we can stay?" I asked.

Cargan looked at me. "Come with me. I'll let you all use my quarters."

He stepped around us to the doors of the little chapel, pushed them open, and led us out and across the fort.

"You've made a name for yourselves," Cargan said as we walked. "You managed to shoot King Iacomus at close range and get away. You're lucky there aren't too many folks out in this part of the country."

The chill settled in my core. "So he's definitely still alive?"

Cargan nodded. "Of course. Meris hit him in the arm, but he was alone at the time, the idiot." He paused. "By all our accounts, he is mostly recovered, but awaiting more men before moving again. He hasn't been seen in public."

He stopped in front of an even smaller shack than the chapel. Cargan pushed the door open, showing us just one little table, a rough bed, and a tiny stone fireplace along one wall. He held the door as we went in.

"This is where I'm staying, for the time being." He backed out. "I'll probably be back fairly late, if at all, but you should be safe here. Goodnight." He pulled the door shut after him.

I shrugged off the straps of my pack, let it drop to the floor, and plopped beside it. "I've never been so glad to sit down in my life."

Meris sat across from me, her back against the bed. "You two don't look like you slept much."

Matt yawned. "We didn't last night."

"Where did you camp?" Noam pulled his blanket out.

"In the woods outside the wall." I wrapped my own blanket around my shoulders. "We actually heard a huge animal sniffing around us."

Meris frowned. "Just an animal?"

I felt my face redden as I pillowed my head into the backpack. *Chicken.* "Yeah. Just…we were just not sure what it was. It ran off." *Stupid. Probably was just something small.* "Spooked us, though."

"I can imagine," Meris said.

"Let them get some rest, Meris," Noam said.

I barely heard her retort to him as I drifted off.

***

*Creeeeak.*

The sound broke into my dreams. Maybe Cargan was returning. There were voices outside, far away, some singing, some laughing. I forced my eyelids open, barely cracking them. *What now…?*

A man stood in the doorway, a dark shape against the torches. One of his arms looked strange, the end of it pointing down at a harsh angle, ending in a sharp point.

*That's not an arm.*

Fear froze me to the core. Would it work to scare him off like the other thing? I sat up. *Loud. Be loud.* "Who are you?" It wasn't quite a scream. Matt sat bolt upright beside me. *All I have is that stupid dull knife.*

"Hey, man, get out of here," Matt said, standing. "This ain't the place you want."

The man grunted roughly and seemed to hesitate. In the darkness I could hear one of the others moving around, and the sound of a gun being cocked.

Then the man started to lunge, and a gunshot rang out. He crumpled, heavily, the knife skittering across the floor and coming to rest by my foot. I stared. The blade was black in the dim light, painted or covered with tar or something.

Cargan stepped into his shack, rifle in hand, the smell of gunpowder following close behind him. Now there were voices in the fort, no longer singing, but shouting, and people running. I looked at the blade again and kicked it away.

*That could've been in me right now. Or Matt, or Meris or Noam.* My imagination lurched dangerously toward panic mode.

*No. I'm not going down that road. We're okay.*

"This man was Trenavellan." Cargan frowned. "I thought, anyway. Apparently not."

An older man ran up to the door. "Chaplain, do you know who this man was after?"

Cargan swept his hand around. "One of them, I suppose. He might have been drunk."

The guy frowned. "And now we can't find out."

Cargan's face turned fierce. "Would you rather I had paused to ask him politely?"

No answer. The man ducked back out.

Cargan stood up straighter. "Come. All of you. You'll sleep in the chapel tonight."

Meris sat back. "But—"

"No." Cargan stayed in the doorway. "Now."

At least someone could boss Meris around. Didn't matter, I'd be wide awake for a while, the way my adrenaline pumped now. Without another word, we packed up our blankets and stood. Meris' brother looked troubled.

She broke the silence. "It's not your fault, Cargan."

He shook his head, once. "I assumed you'd be safe, and I was wrong." He marched out the door, and we followed.

There were men up, all armed, staring at us as Cargan led us back to the chapel. I kept my eyes to the ground as we went inside. *Let them stare. Did they even do their job?* My knees trembled.

It wasn't so dark in here, with all the candles. Cargan shut the doors.

"What troubles me," he said, "is that that man prayed here tonight. He wasn't wounded or drunk. He was a traitor, if he was Trenavellan at all. How many of their ranks are hiding in ours?" He rubbed at his eyes. "We've never had an assassin to attack children before."

"I am not a child," Meris snapped.

"Well to me you are, little sister." Cargan stepped backwards. "I don't think I'll be very busy tonight. The men are celebrating, so we shouldn't be bothered. There might be an investigation into this." He lifted the rifle again. "I'll be outside. Sleep well."

The doors shut with a soft thump, and we all stared at each other. An assassin. Maybe he wasn't looking for us. Maybe he had the wrong place. He'd meant to kill somebody, that was for sure, and if it was us, there could be only one reason, stemming from one moment on that road.

*We aren't faceless anymore.*

# Chapter 16

"I do wish you'd stay here." Cargan's voice was quiet. "I won't force you, though." The deep color of the sky was slowly becoming morning.

"We're already behind," Meris said. "We have to leave now."

*Why stick around long enough for another attempt on our lives?*

Cargan shook his head, but his mouth lifted in a not-quite smile. "If you're going to be this foolish, then good luck."

We stepped through the entrance on the other side of the fort. The road stretched on in front of us, but from what I could tell, this was still wilderness. The gate swung shut, muffling the quiet movement inside. At one time, I imagined, it might have been busier along this road, before Skyrren was lost.

*Lost to most of them, anyway.*

The gray sky lightened, and the sun gave us more warmth as it rose in the sky. It was pretty, that much was true, and I'd taken for granted the fact that the trees were like the ones back home, if not just the same. It would be nice if one day I could pay closer attention to this planet.

*Just wish we weren't being hunted. Another planet might be a little more wonderful.* Maybe some day I'd get to take a closer look.

Noam spoke suddenly. "We're almost there, I think."

"Almost where?" Meris asked.

"Brightleaf Manor."

*That was fast.* "You're kidding."

Noam smiled. "I'll check the map later, but I am certain that we're very near it. It's possible that we'll arrive later afternoon. We overestimated the journey."

"And how late are we?" Matt asked.

Meris' face went blank. "A few days, I'm sure." Her tone was light, almost forcibly so.

What did she have to hide? "Well, do you think your friend will still be there with the pieces?"

"I'm sure of it." There was a strange note in her voice, something uneasy, too cheerful. Whatever it was tipped Noam off, and he turned to face her.

"Meris…how are you so sure of it?"

She drew up, for just a moment, but the girl's eyes darted around to the rest of us, like a cornered animal. "He's part of a work crew. The manor is being repaired as Iacomus' summer home."

*A crew.* "He's not just there alone?" At least the king wouldn't be here. People working for him, however. . . .

Meris dropped her eyes to the ground. "It's a way he can keep watch on the riddle pieces and gain information that we need."

Noam's eyes hardened. "You had me thinking it was abandoned."

"I never said what it was. You merely assumed." She looked annoyed.

"Meris, why did you keep that to yourself?"

She rolled her eyes. "Because, Noam, we aren't going to be there for long. Barney is just going to bring us the pieces, and we will leave and go back to the capital."

"It's a good idea, actually," said Matt.

Matt? Agreeing with Meris?

*Huh.*

"Thank you, Matthew." The sarcasm in her voice contrasted with the moment of surprise on her face. "It—"

The ground shook under us, hard, a steady rumble. I planted my feet. Had there even been any tremors before? *Is this an earthquake?*

Yards ahead of us, dirt and rocks exploded out of the ground. A huge creature burst out, all legs, or tentacles, smacking the trees around it and flinging bark through the woods. It moved too fast to see well, and in another few seconds, dove down again and burrowed into the earth. We stood, quietly, as the ground grew still again, leaving two gaping holes where the creature had passed by us.

*What did we just see?*

"They've awakened," Meris said, in a horrified whisper.

"What?" Matt asked. His face took on a shade paler than normal. "Is it the burrow-beasts?"

Noam answered. "We thought they'd been extinct for years. They're supposed to be, but…I suppose that report was wrong."

Matt blinked. "Oh."

What if more came? "Any more details about those, Matt?"

"No." He blinked. "It was just a story my grandmother told me."

I edged to the hole in front of us. If there was another one coming, then we'd feel it long before it got here, I hoped. "So what woke them up?"

"The war, probably." Meris said. "So much movement. Cannon fire, if there was any." She looked confused. "I suppose there have been more battles that aren't near us. That's reasonable to assume."

The things burrowed deep. I knew that firsthand. Why would people moving around on the surface make them surge upward? "So what does this mean?"

Meris looked down into the hole. "They could take our troops or a village by surprise. There would many injuries just from one of these things tearing out of the ground. More than one, or a whole herd, driven from their home by any sort of violence elsewhere."

The hair stood up on my neck. What if we'd walked just a few yards more?

Matt skirted the edge of the hole. "Well, if there are more, we gotta go now. You saw how they moved."

"Agreed," Meris said.

As I passed it, I looked down into the jagged-edged opening. Meris' explanation for the sudden reappearance of these things wasn't convincing. They were too big and all the people were so, so small. I sure hadn't heard any cannon fire near us since we arrived, though Meris did say it could be distant. That was fair enough. Still. They were huge, and apparently not as long-dead as everyone had thought. Between those creatures and whatever that thing was that could get so close and stay so quiet, would we even have the time to defend ourselves from other humans?

And what had woken these creatures up?

***

The rough tree I waited behind felt like a refuge, from the front anyway. I couldn't help but glance backwards every few seconds, just to check, though the shadows between the trees were swiftly growing deeper as evening came. The sounds of hammers and saws came through the woods, echoing and broken up some. I didn't dare to take a peek at the grounds of Brightleaf Manor yet. Maybe I should. I looked at Matt, but he was already watching, tense.

*We're way too close.*

As soon as I'd leaned around the tree, a bell rang out. The bunch of men gathered around their work moved away, heading to a long shack nearby. All except for one of them. This particular guy yelled something inaudible at the men behind him, and started walking our way. No one moved, and my heart started up its pounding.

Why weren't the other two reacting?

Matt looked at the other two, panic etched into his eyes.

He cleared his throat and whispered. "Meris."

She frowned, her eyes still on the steadily approaching man. I wanted to run. "What?"

Matt pointed. "He's gonna see us." I hadn't seen Matt so panicky yet; maybe we'd been too tired before. "Do you want me to take him out?"

"Don't you dare." Her eyes finally tore away from the guy. "That's Barney."

Frustration chased away the brief moment of relief I had. "Why didn't you say that before?"

She kept her eyes on Barney. "I thought it was obvious."

*She's gonna get us caught.* "To who?" I asked.

"Shhhh!" Noam leaned forward.

Barney was whistling, some barely audible and unfamiliar tune. I let myself calm down as Meris leaned forward and whistled sharply.

I watched as Barney threw a glance our way and turned, ambling to stand near where we hid. He crossed in front of a tree just a few yards away and slipped around it to face us, leaning back on the trunk. Meris slipped out from her hiding place, beckoning the rest of us to follow.

I looked over at the two boys. Should we? Noam lifted one shoulder in a shrug and followed Meris.

Matt kept his voice low. "I guess…we really should get a look at the riddle pieces, right?"

"Hopefully this won't take long." The other two were already talking to Barney in low whispers. *We're going to get it, and put it together, and go home. Home. Almost there.*

"We were delayed," Meris said. "A problem with the train."

Barney kept a smile on his face. "Do you expect it'll be fixed before long?"

"No." Noam didn't return the smile. "It will take some time before that is resolved, if at all."

"That may be a worry later." Barney's glance landed on us. "We'll need to act a little faster, then, for today."

Meris nodded. "Yes we will." She straightened. "Now…where is it?"

Barney blinked. "The riddle?"

"Of course."

Barney's eyes flicked away for a moment.

*Uh-oh.* Something inside me crumbled.

"Barney?" Meris' fist clenched up.

"I don't exactly have it with me," he said.

Meris struck quickly, her hands shoving Barney back against the tree. He grunted at the impact. "What do you mean you don't have it?"

"It's in the house."

Meris was about to explode with rage, I was sure of it, from the way her face turned red. She shoved him harder against the tree.

*Whoa.*

Barney put his hands up. "It'll be easy to get, I promise."

This was my task, too. *Might as well ask him.* "How easy?"

Barney smiled tightly. "Just walk right in. The house is empty, because they're all at a meal now in that dining hall over there. We have to move fast, though. They'll be expecting me back soon."

Meris pulled a knife from her belt. She didn't lift it, but just held it there. Her voice came out shrill. "You said you'd have it. Why don't you?"

Noam stepped toward her. "Meris, calm down."

Barney eyed the knife. "Because I haven't been able to get into the house alone."

"So we get to do your dirty work." The weapon in her hand glinted, but she still didn't move it.

*This isn't helping.* "Barney, we really need the pieces now. Just…tell us where they are." My stomach flipped. *Can't believe we're going in.*

"I can get it for you." He looked down at Meris, the sweat on his forehead gathering. She backed away from him, sheathing the knife.

"No." Meris crossed her arms.

"What?" Matt stepped forward. "Meris, he just offered to do what you asked him to do in the first place."

"And what we needed wasn't here, was it?" Meris smirked.

I already knew Matt wasn't Meris' biggest fan, but I didn't really feel like watching them get into it again. I let my eyes roam over the manor and looked at him. "Okay, Barney. Take us."

His eyes shifted around. "I'll take one of you. The rest may follow if you wish to risk it. We'll be back." He turned, Meris trailing closely after him.

"We will not be separating again," Noam said. "I, at least, am going."

"Okay." *We're definitely going to get caught this time.* I looked at Matt. He shrugged. *That's helpful.* "I don't want to stay behind either."

"Lead on."

As I made the way through the woods and over the even ground, the manor loomed over us. Iacomus' summer home, or it would be. What if he came while we were here? *He knows us. That's the worst part.*

I kept my eyes on the long shacks the crew went in, sure that someone was going to come out of them. It would only take one to see us and sound the alarm. A few to hold us in wait. And one more to identify us. *Please let this be a really long meal for them.* Ahead, Barney dashed up a short set of stairs and through a door, Meris close behind him.

After ten more awful, exposed, too loud and sure to be heard steps, we shot up after them and through the door.

My eyes took a second to adjust to the dim hallway. This wasn't the front of the house, that was for sure.

Barney didn't waste time. "Right this way." Our footsteps still sounded through the house much louder than I liked as he led us down the hall to a door on the right. No voices or sounds of other people upstairs or hidden in another room.

*At least the house is empty.*

White cloths, layered with a shadow of dust on each one, covered the furniture in the room. Shelves on either side of the fireplace stood empty, and a door across the room was the only way out. The heavy drapes half covered the windows, leaving the room dim and gloomy.

Barney crossed the room to the fireplace, reaching for the small chest on top of the mantle with a smug smile. He pulled the latch and reached inside.

Dread trickled into my gut as his face went white.

The silence stretched on for a few moments. Meris stared at the man, saying just one word. "Barney?"

"It…it's gone." He swallowed. "It was supposed to be here."

The thick silence hung in the air, almost itself audible. Meris was the first one to speak. "You were wrong." Her voice shook with barely controlled rage. Or maybe it was fear combined with her anger. What were we supposed to do now?

Barney nodded, once. "I will admit to that."

A creak of the floor in the hallway made me freeze in a single terrifying moment of realization.

We hadn't closed the door behind us.

I turned.

A little boy, not more than eight years old I figured, stood staring, his too-big hat pushed down over his light hair. He met my eyes, and I met his, numb.

*Oh no.*

He took off running, hollering as his feet pounded down the hallway. "Somebody broke in!"

"This way!" Barney dashed to the other door across the room. The golden flicker of gas lamps lit a dark hallway. Barney ducked into it. Meris was closest behind him, but she didn't appear to be moving toward the door, just staring into it.

It clicked then, her reaction in the cave. How she'd been so unsettled by it.

Her fear of the dark might have been funny in any other situation.

Noam pushed at her back. "Meris, go!"

She hesitated for one more too-long second before her face set and she followed Barney. I ducked into the doorway behind Noam, Matt close behind me.

Barney led us down the hall, through what looked like an endless line of lanterns that shone down on a bunch of closed doors.

*How well used is this place?* The end of the hallway looked like it was just a wall, that maybe this was some central servant's hallway, but there wasn't dust on everything. People had been here recently. *Probably just the crew.* Barney stopped and pressed both of his hands against the wall. With a click, it popped open, revealing an even darker space beyond.

He turned back as he slipped into the door. "This way, down the stairs! Pull it closed behind you!" Were those footsteps behind us? I ducked through the door, but Matt stopped, staring through the opening, as the voices came closer.

I turned. "Matt, what are you doing?"

He grabbed one of the lanterns off of a hook, and the footsteps following us got louder. A second passed. Matt slung the lantern as hard as he could down the hall. I backed up, letting him in, as the lantern struck its target with a crash. Matt pulled the door closed, and a muffled *wumph* came through the door, orange light blazing in the gap underneath. Cries from the other side came through.

I felt frozen as I stared up at him. His eyes stood wide open.

"It'll slow them down," he said, in a voice that cracked at the end.

*He…what did he just do?*

I turned, barely getting my legs to move, and stumbled ahead. There were the other three, moving in the glow of a single lantern, shadows as they disappeared down that stairway.

*You can think about what he did later, just go.*

I hurried down the spiral staircase, keeping my hands pressed into the wall, trying to grip where there were no railings or handholds. More light waited at the bottom, the flicker of a flame. Barney, Meris and Noam waited, faces just visible.

"What was that noise?" Meris, for once, didn't sound angry, but alarmed.

"Broke a lantern." Matt didn't add anything else.

*I could pinch him.* But he had given us time.

Barney's voice broke in cheerfully. "Well, we're all here now, so if you'll just follow me…" He walked to the wall and pushed open a door there, one I hadn't seen before. The steady, strange, tell-tale illumination from the moss lamps came through. "This way." His voice echoed as he stepped under the threshold.

How much time had Matt bought us? I shuddered at what had to happen to those men. They weren't soldiers, and we did just walk in. *It'll help us. And maybe they weren't all that hurt.* Matt's eyes still stood wide open, reflecting the lights on the walls around us.

"What now, Barney?" Meris asked.

Barney took a deep breath, slowly, in and out. "Something very dangerous."

Meris reacted immediately, shoving Barney against the wall, yanking out her knife and this time, holding it under his throat.

No one dared move. Meris might as well have been a cornered animal in the dark like this. Barney swallowed.

"I'm quite serious." His face had gone all solemn now.

"Why is it dangerous?" Meris' voice bordered on a shriek.

Fear for Barney, and all of us, bloomed up inside me. "Meris, please. Calm down." She glared at me, but the expression wasn't all anger. I could see the fear searing through when she looked back at Barney.

His gaze flicked to mine. He couldn't move, not with that knife at his throat, but he looked down at Meris again. "We'll have to split up now. Head in different directions. I can't go back there, and there are some folks who need to know what I've heard while I've been working here."

"How is that dangerous?" The deadly calm in the other girl's voice chilled my spine.

Barney looked all around him, as much as he could with just his eyes. "I don't see any evidence of a recent passage, but these tunnels were made by the burrow-beasts and may still be in use. Humans who use them know to be cautious because being run down by one is a very real possibility here."

If we were in the way, those things would be on us before we could do anything about it.

"Which way do we go?" Noam looked like he was about to pull Meris away, but didn't want to move yet. *Don't blame him.* Not with that knife in her hand, and not the way she reacted.

Barney pointed to his left. "This way. It's not complicated. You will pass three tunnels, on your right. Go through the fourth one, also on the right. Stay on the path until it divides, then take the left path. Before long, you'll reach an exit through the ground. Nothing's there, so you'll be able to pass through safely."

Meris lowered her knife. "Fine, then."

Then she slapped him, the sound reverberating in the tiny space.

His mouth fell open. "Wha—"

"For lying." She sheathed her knife again.

Barney's halfway smile found its way onto his face again. "I won't argue with you. Maybe we'll meet again soon." He nodded once and jogged into the darkness.

Meris let out a quick breath. "I hope he wasn't lying this time."

Matt snorted. "You did have a knife to his throat."

She didn't answer, just rolled her eyes and looked down the tunnel, the fear crawling back onto her face. Noam stepped forward. "We need to go. And I suggest perhaps we hurry."

More running through near total darkness, but being crushed by one of those things didn't appeal to me, either. "Lead on, Noam." No way was Meris going to. *She lives in a country turned upside-down by war, and she's afraid of the dark.*

For a little while, none of the tunnels showed themselves. Had Barney lied again?

No. There was the first one, a dark hole, surrounded by the moss lamps. And after twenty yards or so, the second. Close behind it, the third, with no footsteps following behind. Matt's method had been effective.

A splotch of light streaming from the surface revealed the fourth one, and Noam turned into it.

"We go left, do we not?" Meris asked. Her voice shook a little.

"That's what he told us." Noam led us steadily, though it was a little darker here, and fewer of those little lights clung to the walls. At least Matt could see.

And before us, with little warning, the path split. One went left, and one went right, as Barney had said. We didn't pause, just plunged into the tunnel on the left.

"Matthew, is there any light ahead?" Meris' hand clutched Noam's backpack. "We're going to run out soon."

He didn't answer for a minute. Then, with an intake of breath, "Not really."

"Oh."

Was this a dead end, then?

The ground trembled, and something scraped and crashed behind us, tearing into the earth. Was it coming this way? The rumbling grew louder as we started to run. The wall curved, and then there was a light. It was dull, but it was a light, shining down through a square shape in the ceiling above. The rumble got louder, and the ground trembled.

Noam reached the light first. A ladder stuck down from what probably was a hatch. As the ground jumped and trembled under our feet, he clambered up the ladder, and Meris followed him.

*Wish I could see.* A glance backwards told me nothing about what might be chasing us, but I could guess well enough. I scrambled up. Blazing fast motion flew past in the corner of my eye. The earth shook crumbs of rock down from the wall in sheets. I pushed myself up into the night, throwing half my body onto the ground and crawling away from the opening as Matt scrambled out behind me. I stared at the ground in front of me, taking in the soft grass and letting it brush my face as I laid my head on the ground. *They have grass here, and we're alive.* Another rumble, a gentle shake of the ground, and the burrow-beast was gone on its way. The trapdoor we'd come through thumped closed.

I filled my lungs and sat back against something that scratched against my neck. I felt for it. Branches and leaves from a hedge tickled my hand. We'd ended up in a little divide between two rows of rough bushes, and I could just see over the top. A clever hiding place for the trap door, whatever else it functioned as. Our path must have sloped up gently as we ran. Not that I'd taken the time to notice. *Hope Barney gets where he's going.* I peeked over the hedge, and my eyes registered the flickering lights ahead of me.

Torches. A lot of them. And tents. So many tents. For all the people weaving around the camp, one color dominated.

"I am seeing a lot of green here." Matt's voice sounded tight.

My stomach dropped. "I thought this place was supposed to be deserted."

The raw anger crept onto Meris' voice again. "It was."

"Well, what now?" Matt hissed.

"We could wait until later," Noam said, "but someone will still be up on watch, and I don't want to risk waiting until they move on in the morning."

"And they'd probably find us by then anyway." *Way to be optimistic, Anya.*

"Very likely," Noam said with a nod.

"Then we run now," Meris said. "We might be fast enough."

"Might," Matt said.

"Where would we run?" I asked.

"Well, past them," Meris said. "Then disappear if we're seen. We are four, and they might forget us."

"They're also looking for four traveling together and they know what we look like," Matt replied. "The king did get a real good look at us."

Silence fell. Something, one of the fires I guessed, crackled loud enough to be heard all the way from where we crouched.

Honestly, I liked Meris' idea, more out of panic than anything. We weren't laden down with swords, and none of us was by any means slow. These men would move on, though, so why not stay here? *Why can't we just stop and hide for once, instead of running?*

Noam peered over the hedge once. "Trenavellan forces tend toward stealth."

A grin curled onto Meris' face. "Precisely."

"We're also not as well armed," Matt told her. "I mean, a gun and a couple of knives isn't gonna do much."

My face turned hot. "Then why don't the both of you tough guys figure out what to do, huh?"

"We could go back into the tunnels," Matt offered. "It might be —"

"No," Meris said. "We truly shouldn't go backwards. We need to keep moving, and Barney only gave us directions on how to get out."

*No surprise there.* I turned my attention back to the camp and watched one of the figures pause, then run to another man, both of them still for a moment. Within seconds, the second guy was in motion. My heart thudded against my ribs. "Well, somebody think of something quick because I'm pretty sure those guys just saw us."

"Looks like your idea's it, Meris," Matt said as he stood.

I followed him, keeping my eyes on the rest of the camp, not looking ahead of me. With a jolt, I ran into something solid and stepped backwards.

Matt faced away from me, both hands in the air. A rifle barrel was pointed straight at us.

*Please no.*

"Step from behind him," the young man holding the gun ordered. "Now."

I stood beside Matt and raised my hands. They trembled violently. A clash of footsteps sounded behind us, and the man spoke again. "And you two aren't going anywhere, either. Face me, packs off. On your knees. "

My legs trembled. *Move.* My knees were on their way to buckling anyway, so I folded them and got down, slinging my backpack down on the grass. The cool dampness seeped through my jeans as I stared at the soldier's feet. A lump grew in my throat. All that way. All that stealth and secrecy and creeping underground like ants. For nothing.

We'd still gotten caught. I spared a glance at Matt from the side. His jaw flexed.

A strange calm filled me. The voices around muffled and one thought filled up my head.

*I don't have to give in like this.*

Rage welled up inside me, anger at Salt's Creek and all its stupid secrets, at the people who watched from the sidelines, waiting for something to happen to me and Matt, never telling us anything.

I couldn't give my next move any thought. I lunged at the pair of legs man nearest and felt the man topple over my back. Someone barked an order, and other pairs of feet ran to me as I swung and tackled wildly. A wordless shriek ripped from my mouth as I tried to stand up.

A crushing weight shoved me down onto the ground, pressing me flat on my stomach and forcing air out of my lungs as my face scraped against a root. I fought wildly for a few moments as strong hands grabbed my limbs and held them still. Something warm burned on the side of my face, and a wet drip tickled my skin. Then the weight on my back lifted and strong arms yanked me back up.

"Told you I'd seen movement over here, sir," said the first man who caught us, the one I'd knocked over.

"Stop bragging, Addison," answered an older man. "Get them to a cage. Lady Hestia will hardly appreciate being disturbed this late at night. We'll have to wait until morning. Someone get the packs." His hand clutched Meris' rifle. He spat something goopy and brown at Noam's feet. "Lock 'em up."

***

*So thirsty.* My canteen had gone with my backpack. I could see the lump it made a few yards away, taunting me, waiting to be turned in to this Hestia. I ran my fingers over the worn wood underneath me. The boards thumped every time I hit one of the cracks between them. I fell into the hypnotic rhythm, relishing the harsh feeling on my fingertips, the noise growing louder.

"Anya, stop, please." Matt looked up across from me.

"Make me." I pulled my hand up and nibbled on my fingernails, snapping as I chewed each one. *Why did I ever come?*

"Stop that, too."

"Matthew Dobken, you are not my daddy." I crossed my arms over my stomach with a glare.

He didn't answer.

*So why am I even listening to him?*

"At least she tried to fight back," Meris told him.

Noam sighed. "Meris—"

Meris cut him off. "Noam, this is one time when you—"

Matt's answer interrupted Meris. "I didn't fight back because he had a rifle pointed at her head. I didn't exactly have a way to challenge that."

*I can take care of myself.* Heat traveled from my neck to my forehead. *Next target.* "Meris, you had a gun."

"Not by then, I didn't."

"You're willing enough to brandish it when it's not needed, but not ready to use it at the most crucial of moments." Noam sounded disgusted.

"At least I carry one!" Meris' voice bordered on shrill. That was the cue that she was as scared as me.

Noam narrowed his eyes, eyeing Meris coldly. "Congratulations. You've managed to make us fugitives with a twitchy trigger finger."

Meris turned red. "I did not!"

"Stop screaming," Matt said, his eyes rolling.

"Be quiet, Matthew," Meris snapped at him.

"And what are you going to do if I don't?"

I kicked his foot hard. "Shut up, Matt."

"Then why don't you look at all this you got started, Anya," he spat as he met my eyes.

*What?* I felt the anger rise up inside. "I didn't start this."

A deafening click sounded behind my head. I turned, slowly. The guard had a revolver pointed into the cage, and it wasn't obvious what he aimed at.

"All of you will shut up," he said. "I'm on watch instead of in bed because of you bickering little spies, and I'd be more than pleased to endure the wrath of this military in addition to that of whatever shrieking harpy lives in the manor if ending this business right now would let me sleep tonight." He lowered his weapon. "So not another word, if you don't mind."

I sat back against the cage walls and stared at my hands. They hadn't stopped trembling yet. I had no desire to meet this Hestia. Shrieking harpy, he'd said.

We'd been running and hiding for long enough that I'd almost forgotten why Matt and I had even come here, had even agreed to come with Noam and Meris. *I'll sell you a riddle. . . .* The stupid poem mocked me now. No riddle, and no way out of this. The lump in my throat swelled.

*I just want to go home.*

# Chapter 17

*Tables and ravens and eggs. . . .*

What could that possibly mean? Not that it mattered now. The sun edged over the horizon.

*What if Barney did this on purpose?*

The image of Matt's face after he'd thrown the lantern down that hallway flitted through my mind. Scared, almost. Like he'd done it without thinking it through all the way. I'd wanted to ask him about it at some point, but that didn't seem likely now. *What's Hestia going to do with us?* I heard the door to our cage open, and pulled my head away from where it rested on my knees. My neck creaked.

"Out." The man in charge last night stood in front of the cage. "Today, we will be seeing what happens to you." If the presence of the other four or five men around him were any indication, there wouldn't be a chance for us to run. Two of them shoved Meris and Noam in front, and filled the gap between me and Matt and them with more soldiers. We were completely surrounded.

*Do they think we're dangerous or something?*

"Head out," said the man in front. One of them behind me prodded my back, and I walked forward.

The scream. That stupid scream, probably just a noise from someone's TV turned up way too loud, and we'd mistaken it for some grand mystery. *Wish I'd never stepped foot in those woods.* Never gone poking around for the answers to family secrets. There was a reason they were kept so quiet, right? If I hadn't gone looking for answers so stubbornly, we wouldn't be in this mess.

*No. That's not true. You were never in control of any of this. Something would have happened sooner or later.*

The house moved into view ahead as we marched on the dirt path. This one wasn't near as big as Brightleaf, but it was still a mansion, stiff and imposing, surrounded by trees on all sides. Maybe those troops we'd seen outside Skyrren were nearby. Maybe they'd help us.

*Who am I kidding?*

I watched the hypnotic flashes of red on my shoes, peeking out through whatever wasn't covered with grime. Thinking of the washing machine at home bought tears prickling at the corners of my eyes. *Get a grip. You chose this.*

I stepped onto a stone walkway that wound to an entrance way at the mansion's front. Was the door getting bigger? No way it was actually frowning at me. The man in front pounded on the door. A minute passed with no answer.

Then the door cracked open and a man, dressed in what was probably a gray uniform, stuck his head out of the opening. He looked down his nose at the soldier who'd knocked at the door.

"Is this important?" he asked, his voice drawling out with a note of impatience, one eyebrow raised.

"Prisoners," was all the answer he got.

The man at the door did nothing for a moment. "And what significance might that have for me?"

The leader of the soldiers squirmed. "We found these four lurking around on Lady Hestia's land. Just following her orders to bring any intruders we might find her way, since we're using this area."

The butler, if that's what he was, rolled his eyes and stepped back, pulling the door farther open. "Wait in the hall," he said, turning away.

A rough hand shoved me over the threshold. The butler disappeared up a wide, curved set of stairs in the middle of the hall. The soldiers stayed quiet. Coughs and feet shuffling echoed off the marble floor and white walls.

I barely kept a huge yawn down. A clock ticked, somewhere, and now that I'd noticed it, I couldn't un-hear it. The noise grew, echoing off the dark wood around us as I studied my dirty shoelaces, letting my eyes blur. A third noise, off-rhythm, intruded on the steady ticking. *What is that?* I looked up as the butler descended the stairs and stopped halfway down.

"Lady Hestia will see you in her private study. Please follow me." He turned and climbed back up the stairs.

"Get up there," the captain said.

One of the men grabbed my arm. *Oh, no way*. I yanked it from his grip. "I'm going."

How much damage could I inflict, if it came to that kind of desperation?

We climbed the stairs and turned right. The butler watched us, sighed, and knocked on a pair of doors.

*Looks like he loves his job.*

"In please," a woman's clipped tone answered from inside. The man opened the doors and another hand pushed me forward.

*Do they really get that much of a kick out of all the shoving?*

A wide window in front of a huge desk let in the morning light, flanked by bookshelves and two heavy, drawn-back curtains. A woman in a plain dress stood facing us, just watching us, neutral and cool.

"Captain, why are you bothering me at this hour?" she asked. Hestia's eyes went around to each of us, moved down for a moment to her shoes before they flicked back to the captain. My mouth dried up.

The captain cleared his throat. "We found these four snooping at the edges of our camp, on your land. They match the descriptions of four individuals charged with—"

Hestia blinked and cut in. "You brought me children."

The captain paused.

She wasn't looking at us, but her words were hope, even if she might be awful.

The guy behind Noam spoke. "These four are accused of shooting and wounding Iacomus, king of Naolon, and were seen attempting to steal food some days back, in a town south of here."

"Hungry children, then." Hestia raised an eyebrow as the captain shifted uncomfortably.

"Yes, well—" The captain straightened his back. "There's the matter of the assault on the king—"

The woman interrupted. "Captain, please place the items you confiscated from them on my floor and leave them here. I do not care for your special gift of capturing traveling seventeen-year-olds." She exhaled in a huff. "I've seen the representations of the accused. These four are not it, I am most certain. You've wasted my time with your error. Leave us."

*She's going to set us free.*

For a second, relief filled me up, but the men began to gather around us again.

"Captain," Hestia said.

He turned around. Hestia continued to speak. "When I said 'leave us,' I included the children in that. Go back to your work, and leave them here. Is that understood, or do I need to find some way of making it clearer?"

The captain stared at her. "Yes, ma'am," he grumbled.

"Their belongings as well, as I asked."

I eyed the leader. He had my knife. He kept glaring at Hestia, his face turning steadily redder. Something flashed through his eyes, but he signaled. One of his men stepped forward and laid the weapons on the floor, along with our backpacks. He tossed my knife down. I let my eyes focus on the dull blade as it clattered and lay still. *Don't lunge for it. Just wait.*

No more waiting afterwards, though. It had to be sharpened.

*Why is she letting us go?*

The men stepped back. "Anything else, my lady?" the captain asked.

"Just that you are out of my home as soon as possible."

*No wonder they don't like to deal with her.*

The men filed out, closing the door behind them with a thud. Hestia walked to the window and held a mirror up briefly, twisting her hand side to side. After a second, something flashed back. A reflection. I caught Noam's eye, but he only shook his head once.

Hestia then pulled the curtains shut and turned to the servant who'd led us up here. "Cephas, you are dismissed for your holiday."

"Yes ma'am." The butler exited through the door he'd brought us in, boots echoing back down the hallway and fading out.

The room was silent for another minute.

Hestia sighed and leaned against the desk. "Why are you here?"

It didn't seem like anyone was going to answer, which made us seem even more suspicious.

Noam opened his mouth.

"We were taken captive—"

Hestia cut him off. "And why did you allow that to happen?"

"It was unintentional," Meris answered.

Hestia rubbed her eyes. "I am quite sure that it was." She paused. "Do you have it, then?"

My heart raced. *She knows. Don't answer. Don't react.*

"I don't know what you speak of," Meris said, her voice quivering at the end.

Hestia laughed bitterly. "Meris, you are a bad liar, just like your father."

Meris' face went white. "My father...?"

"You look like your mother, though," the woman continued. "Just like her, I swear." There was a pause. "Tell me, how is Margaret?"

Meris just stared wordlessly back.

Noam cleared his throat. "How do you know who we are?"

Hestia smiled. "Meris I know from her childhood, though she won't remember me. As for the rest of you, well, Barnabas is a young man I have long been in contact with. He did direct you in error this time, though it wasn't his fault, I can assure you. He did intend for you to escape. Cephas has a son who was in that very same camp, just last night, and you're very fortunate for that." She paused. "So…where is it really?"

The words blurted out of my mouth before I could stop them. "It wasn't where Barney said it would be." Meris shot me a hard look.

Alarm crossed Hestia's face. "You truly don't have it?"

*And now our world won't be safe, ever.*

"No, we don't." Matt took a deep breath. "We never did." The woman's piercing eyes stared into his, and seemed distracted all of a sudden.

"How do two children of Earth come here, so eagerly seeking the work of Gavin Dupree?" She began to pace. "Never mind. If Barney was given bad or old information…" She stopped and looked across the room. "You have to leave. Gather your things and come with me." She rushed to a door off to the side and opened it, disappearing into what looked like a closet.

Matt spoke softly. "Should we?"

Meris still looked pale and disturbed. "I think we can trust her."

Hestia's muffled voice interrupted us. "Now, please!"

The first thing I grabbed was the knife. I stuffed it into my backpack. If we were able to get away, I'd sharpen it, most definitely. Maybe I'd take it home if I had to. If it helped solve anything, and maybe it would.

Home. Now, impossibly, after the night was past, it was starting to look like we'd really get back there. I shoved the blade down into my backpack and kept close to Matt as we passed through the door.

Hestia stood in the inside, by another door that opened into a smaller room. "Get in here."

"What is that?" Meris asked.

"It will take you out of the house and off my property the safest way I know how." The woman pulled on Noam's arm, guiding him into the space. "Please get in. I find that I will be needing to leave as well."

We squeezed in, and I was the last before Hestia closed the door. A muffled "good luck," a shuddering creak, and the box lurched, then steadied, moving slowly downward.

*Please be sturdy, please be sturdy. . . .*

It kept going, far past the point it should have. We'd only been on the second story of the house, and it seemed like the elevator had moved us far past that now, as best as I could figure.

Noam groaned. "Where is she sending us?"

Meris answered, her voice shaking. "It will be fine."

Had she not noticed what Hestia had done at the window? "You know she signaled someone, right?"

"I saw that, too," said Matt.

"I did see it." Meris didn't sound so sure of herself this time. Could've been because we were in a tiny box in the pitch dark.

*Why don't these people like lights?*

The car came to a stop with a soft jolt, and nothing happened for a minute.

What had she wanted us to do?

"Are we supposed to wait for somebody?" Matt asked.

"She didn't say," Meris told him.

"So are we just gonna wait in here?"

Noam spoke next. "Maybe we should, just for a few—"

The door opened, pulled by some unseen force, and a dark figure moved into the doorway, a dark shape against a lot of light behind him.

*Oh no. What do we do? Run? Fight?*

"Finally! Thought you guys would never get here."

The voice was unmistakable and so familiar. "Danny?"

Without warning, I was wrapped in a bear hug, too stunned to do anything.

*What's he doing here? Is Matt's aunt here too? His whole family?* His parents weren't mine, but I'd take seeing anyone from home. *How long has it been there?*

"Who is this, Matthew?" Meris' voice was sharp.

"My cousin Danny." Matt met my glance, and the smile slid from his face.

The cousins stood side by side, both pairs of eyes glowing in the dark.

"You're a moon-eye too," Meris said.

Danny laughed.

Noam coughed. "That was rude."

"No, it's all good." Danny smiled again. "I'm supposed to get you all out of here, apparently. That was the suggestion, anyway."

My eyes adjusted to the low light in the room, and I saw stoves and trays and pots. A kitchen.

And people, staring for a moment as they went by. I sucked in a breath and took a step backwards. Matt stayed where he was as the staff of this house bustled around us. Danny sure didn't seem to be in a hurry.

"They're ignoring you. Just wait for a second," he whispered.

"Why?" Meris hissed.

Danny grinned. "You'll see."

Everyone else in the room paused, as if on cue, and all stared up at a clock on the wall, stopping as one and standing still.

Without another warning, a bell began to clang from upstairs, fast and frantic. Everyone who was gathered around in the kitchen began to move again, running now, and a voice yelled out from above us. "Breach! Evacuate!"

"Okay, let's go!" Danny took off through the kitchen, pulling me and Matt after him, leaving the other two to follow him through the door and into the hallway. He turned sharply left, and I could see the staircase ahead.

"Up there?" Matt asked him.

"Yep!"

Sounds filled the air, crashes and people running, even some screaming now and then. About halfway from us and the stairs, a grate in the floor showed off a golden glow.

"What's that thing in the floor go to?"

Danny glanced at it was we passed. "Underground, I guess. Another exit."

The inside of it rumbled louder as we got closer to the stairs, and right after Noam passed the grate, flames shot out and touched the other wall.

We crashed up the stairs, keeping to the right as more people dashed down and others ran past us. Why had Hestia sent us all the way downstairs if we were just going to come up again?

*What is going on?* Had it suddenly become more than some distraction?

We ran into a light, airy hallway that stretched all the way to a smaller door. Just barely, I could see a rough old building in the distance outside. With one last burst, we were at the end, but Danny pulled up short and stopped us.

"Okay, do you guys see that barn?" He pointed at the building.

"Yeah," Matt said, panting.

Danny nodded, inhaling deep. "Okay, you're gonna run for that. There's a compartment inside where you can bunk down for a while if you need to." He stepped to the side to let us all through.

*Where's he going?* "Aren't you coming with us?"

"Nope." He smiled. "I gotta get somewhere else for now. I'll see you all soon, but you have to go. This evacuation got their attention down at the camp, I'm pretty sure. Trust me when I say you don't want to stick around much longer." His face got serious. "Good luck."

And without another word, he was off down the hallway again.

Matt looked around at us, pausing longest on me. "I guess we should go there, then."

"Well it's that or stay in the house, Matthew." Meris pushed by him. A second after she stepped out of the door, she looked left and set her face in a hard expression. "And the barn is my preference."

Matt ran out the door, and I followed, feeling the spongy grass give under my feet. The barn was close, getting closer.

One cry echoed across the fields from the men gathered in front of the manor. "Stop right there!"

The barn stood empty, welcoming us as the shouts started up from all over Hestia's land and servants streamed out of the house. Matt pushed the doors closed and slid the bar down to lock it, for now. Until someone broke in, which they'd probably do.

"There's a compartment here somewhere," Noam said. I scanned the floor.

There. A weird inconsistency, a perfect square shape. I took a step, sweeping my foot back and forth, and some of the straw on it didn't move. *Clever.* "Here it is."

It opened easily enough, and I climbed down first. It wasn't tall enough to stand in here, but there was more than enough space to sit down, and just enough room for all of us to fit. My knees shook as I bent them and lowered myself into the corner of the cold, dark hole. Noam came down the ladder last, pulling the hatch with him, and shutting us off from the daylight.

We waited. I knew better than to talk. A muffled crash came as someone broke through the door of the barn. Footsteps entered, thumping on the floor above us. Something heavy stopped on one edge of the hatch. It was still thin enough to hear the loud voices grumbling through.

"…know I saw them come in here."

"Don't know where Lady Hestia went, but she's apparently gone."

Disgust wrapped up the third voice. "More tunnels, I bet. Moon-eyes."

"Must be a hatch here, and if that's the case, we'll just plan on marching. They're long gone, and I'm not heading down into the dark to go looking for them."

*Are all people here afraid of the dark?* Were people like Matt and Danny the reason?

The footsteps trooped back out, heading away from us and taking the voices with them.

*That's the second time we've gotten away because they don't want to cross whoever lives underground.*

Once it was clear that they were gone, I let out a sigh, daring a whisper. "So I guess we're just gonna relax in here a while."

"It would probably be best." Noam yawned.

I leaned forward and put my backpack at my feet, huddling closer to Matt. "Fine with me."

Meris' voice held a strain at the edges. "How long should we hide?"

Matt shifted next to me. "Long as we need to. Until it gets completely quiet out there."

Why were all these people helping us so much? They were ready to, it was clear. Why, then, hadn't they done everything before?

I told myself it was just because they didn't have the key to solving the riddle, like we did.

*Oh well.*

There was no more discussion. *Too tired to move.* The air was warmer now. *Don't even need a blanket.*

# Chapter 18

The discomfort on the side of my head started slowly, slipping into my dream. I was swimming, trying my best to stay at the bottom of the pool, looking for something Matt had thrown in there, free of the popping in my ears that would have come if this was real. The discomfort throbbed once, hard, and I jerked my head away from Matt's shoulder, blinking and dazed at being woken up right in the middle of the dream.

He grunted, clothes rustling as he shifted.

"What time is it?" His voice was barely a grumble.

No way to tell. The edges of the door above us were now bright. "Dunno. Forgot my watch."

He laughed quietly. "Good point."

The other two were starting to move around, I could hear, as little as we could here. Maybe we'd be able to leave, but all our wanderings seemed so pointless now. We were without the one thing we'd come for.

*If it was ever real at all.*

I didn't want to entertain that thought.

"Who wants to check?" Matt stretched, I thought, his hand brushing the ceiling.

"I will." Meris' boots scuffed across the floor while she crawled to one side of the compartment. The daylight flooded into the hiding spot as the hatch opened up.

"Ow," Matt said.

I blinked hard, my eyes watering, and forced my eyelids fully apart.

Meris called down from the inside of the barn. "All clear."

I eyed Matt and Noam, my hand around the strap of my backpack. "Ladies first," said Matt.

I stuck my tongue out at him and went up the tiny ladder after Meris. My spine creaked as I straightened up. Meris already stood by the bright window facing the sun. The boys climbed out, and Noam replaced thc hatch.

"You sure it's all clear?" Matt stretched.

Meris nodded. "There is no one around."

"Good." Noam pulled his backpack on. "I'm tired of running."

Between the barn and the nearest thick woods lay an empty field. "Yeah, well, the problem is we'll be out in the open."

"If there's really no one here, then that won't be a problem." Matt crossed the floor of the barn, to the door. It was halfway opened. "And if anyone was gonna see us, they would have done it already."

Goosebumps spread over my arms. I hadn't even looked. "Yeah. Probably." *Dumb mistake.* Not one I'd make again.

We marched across the field under sunlight and a perfect periwinkle sky. Refreshing, even. We'd been walking around underground for too long, always running. Now it was back to just going, even if that wound up being short-lived.

Still. Out in the open, wanted fugitives that had barely just escaped. The trees closing over us brought some relief. *Is it gonna be like this for the rest of my life?* I didn't want to fear the sky. A soft rushing sound reached us, far away.

Noam frowned. "We're near a river." He shrugged out of his backpack.

"Noam, can't you keep that map somewhere more accessible?" Meris leaned against a tree. "We have to stop every time you pull it out."

He unfolded it. "Then where else should I keep it?"

Meris blinked. "Your coat pocket."

Noam's ears turned pink. "Of course," he said. His attention went right back to the map. "The river…so…we're near a town." He looked up, brown eyes brighter. "We could get the supplies we need. Find out what's going on down in the capital."

Meris tilted her head to the side. "Must we again go into a town and be seen?"

Noam folded his map and shoved it into a pocket on his coat. "I'll go."

Did Meris really expect him to go alone? I guessed it was smart. He could get away easier, if it came to that. But two was better. I counted Noam as a friend now, and he shouldn't go by himself. "I'll go with you."

Matt's head snapped up. "What?"

Was he feeling protective all of a sudden? After all we'd done, what did he have to be shocked about? "I said, I'm going with Noam."

His mouth opened and closed once. "Then I'll—"

Meris cut him off. "We can't all go. It's not safe."

Matt looked at her for a moment, speaking one word like it was being forced out of him. "True."

*Thought he liked to argue with Meris.* "Okay so…we going, Noam?" *Maybe they won't be at each other's throats when we get back.*

He nodded. "We won't be long."

We set off. The thick trees hid us, but what else? These woods had a lot of places for spying eyes to peek out of, and the sensation of being watched hovered over me. Whoever might be looking, if there was anyone, wasn't making a sound.

The crunch of the leaves under our feet was starting to seem awfully loud.

"Think we'll be recognized?" I asked.

"Might be," Noam said. "I wouldn't worry since we're in Trenavell."

"You don't think there's anyone loyal to Naolon in this village?"

Noam shook his head. "Not somewhere this remote. I've heard these towns barely paid any attention to the war and were taken over suddenly by a nation they never bothered nor owed anything to." He smiled. "These are the kinds of places you want on your side."

The soft wind got faster, raising up goosebumps on the back of my neck. "Let's get on the road. I don't want to look too sneaky." *Especially if these people could be allies.*

"Good idea," Noam said. He angled down and hopped onto the dirt road, then turned and held his hand up. I grabbed it and jumped down beside him.

"Thanks."

"Anytime."

My nerves started going wild, fluttering through my stomach and tightening my jaw. I chewed the inside of my mouth as we walked down the dirt road. The trees became sparser, widening the road. Two fat, rough-hewn posts acted as a gate to what seemed to be a busy town.

"Good morning!" Noam called as we approached. If he was nervous, he was hiding it pretty well. *Hope I don't look like a sweaty wreck.*

"Morning to you," the man answered. "What's your business here?"

"Supply purchase." The gate man nodded and waved us in. I kept my hands in my pockets. *Good thing my shoes are so dirty.* At least that would keep some eyes off part of my clothes, but fitting in didn't seem like that much of a priority anymore. People hurried around us as we passed houses with boards over the windows. Three or four families rushed past us, loaded down with bags and backpacks and sacks of food.

What was going on here?

"Excuse me, sir," Noam said, stepping in front of one of the families. The man stopped, his eyes flicking to me before turning back to Noam.

"Yes?"

"Could you point us the way to the store?" Noam continued. "My friend and I are very much in need of it."

The man nodded. "Keep on this street. It's down on the right. You might want to hurry though, as he's about to leave town." He continued on his way.

"Let's get there if we can," Noam said. His face flinched with panic for a moment.

The dark soil in the trampled street kicked up as we hurried. In the distance, a wagon, filled with people, rolled down a hill and out of sight. A man and woman, the latter with two young children clinging to her hands, locked the door of a small house as we passed. They walked down the street, heads down and eyes on the dirt road.

"Where do you think they're all going?" I asked. *And why?*

Noam looked behind us. "I don't know. Here's the store."

The double doors were shut against the near chaos in the town. I tried to peek through one of the windows as Noam pulled on the door handle. Heavy curtains covered the glass.

The door rattled, but didn't budge open. Through a part in the drapes, I saw someone move in the dim room. The figure whirled around to look at the door.

"I'm closed!" came the man's muffled yell.

I put my face close to the door and spoke loudly. "Please sir? We really need some stuff. We won't be long."

Footsteps pounded across the floor inside, the lock clicked, and the door swung inward a few inches. The shop owner glared at us through the gap.

"I don't have anything for you," he said. "I sold it or gave it away, and I am leaving soon. I recommend you do the same and head south with all the others before something happens to you too. Good day." He slammed the door shut.

For a moment, I watched him move around inside. "Great. What now?"

Noam shrugged. "We'll just have to wait." He swallowed. "We can get plenty of food for now, if we run out, but animals have little to say in regards to current events."

I leaned against the wall. "What's south, other than the capital?"

"Wilderness. More camps, I suppose," he answered. "The people here could all be going south to the camp where Meris and I grew up. It's the largest one."

I started chewing on my lip again, felt a sting, and tasted the saltiness of blood. "What's happening here, then?"

"It might be just a precaution," Noam said as we stepped back down into the street. "Leave rather than be attacked, if things are intensifying near Compass Hill. There's been so much troop movement lately, I wouldn't be surprised if this is just a reaction."

I kept my eyes down, watching as my shoes hit a pebble and sent the projectile flying.

*What are we walking into?* "Well, if anything's going to happen, it'll be soon, I guess."

"Very likely," Noam said.

A motion out of the corner of my left eye was my only warning before I felt myself being pushed to the side, taking Noam along with me. We stumbled together into an alleyway, pushed someone much bigger than me. I caught my footing and turned around, yanking the knife out of my pack. Noam held a shorter knife. His would be much more effective, but at least I could pretend I was armed.

The shop owner pulled out a revolver. "I highly suggest you don't go the way you were headed."

Noam brushed his coat off with one hand, lowered his knife an inch. "Why?"

I swallowed. My hands were sweating now. The hilt of the knife slipped around in my hands.

The man smirked. "The king and a sizable group of his soldiers were headed here from a very long way, down this road, according to a bit of gossip."

My heart gave a wild leap. "How long until they're here?"

"Not long," he said. "You seem to have timed your visit badly."

"Where do we go?" Noam asked.

"Around there." The man pointed behind us, to where the alleyway continued on, meeting the woods. "Take this little side street. You'll end up in the woods again, but if you're going back that way, you'll circle around and lose them." The man put his gun down and smiled. "Good luck. Maybe if we make a big enough commotion here, it'll will keep him distracted long enough." He stepped away and disappeared into the crowd of the town.

"Come on," Noam said. He led the way down the side street, headed for the woods again. The town behind us became more frenzied, if the frantic yelling was any indication. As the shadows of the trees fell over us, the village fell completely silent. Noam stopped, and I waited with him, both of us listening. The thump of footsteps and horses' hooves filled up the air. I pressed against the building behind us, wishing I could flatten into it.

One man spoke loudly. "Four prisoners were set loose by a traitor to Naolon. They wounded me and now seek to commit high treason. They are young, and we believe two of them may have some place on Earth as their country of origin. Now…"

*That's him. He's alive, and he knows us.*

"Has anyone seen four individuals, perhaps around seventeen years of age, pass through this place?"

Run or wait? What if that shop owner betrayed us? It was just us two. Suddenly I couldn't see the use of not bringing Matt and Meris, but there wasn't any point now to worrying. I couldn't outrun a horse. Could we get back to them?

*Stick with Noam. Just stay close, you'll be fine, he's a smart guy.*

"Look elsewhere," came another voice, gruff and angry. "Leave us alone."

There was silence for another moment.

Then a gunshot rang out into the air. Someone started screaming, and more shots echoed around us. My limbs froze and I looked at Noam. The horror in his eyes shone through. He glanced back, obviously shaking, and I was afraid for a moment he'd want to help anyone who was hurt.

*We've got to go*. A lump built in my throat, and I stifled a sob to yell over the noise. "Let's go, Noam!"

We crashed into the trees together, letting go of each other. The cold wind chilled the wetness on my face, and I wiped away the tears roughly, feeling the grime from my sleeve scrape my skin.

*Those people.* . . . How many were dead now?

I didn't—couldn't—let my mind finish the thought. The sounds seemed like they were following us, the yelling and the gunfire and the screams, as the underbrush crumpled beneath our feet. Cold sweat beaded up on my forehead.

We crashed into the place we'd left Matt and Meris. I leaned over, hands on my knees, gasping for air. A gray tennis shoe stepped into view, and I looked up as Matt stepped from behind a tree.

"What happened?" he asked. "We saw a bunch of soldiers go that way and heard some stuff, so we hid."

I swallowed. "I think they just shot up a whole village." My breath calmed slowly, but my stomach still rocked unsteadily. My jaw tightened, the normal sign that I was about to throw up. I shuddered. *There were kids there.*

"Iacomus is with them," Noam added.

"We can't go back that way." *What have they done to them?*

"Of course." Meris' face was gray.

"We can't just wait," Matt said. They fell into silence.

Now I'd seen that Iacomus was undoubtedly the vengeful kind.

A horse snorted nearby. A rider's gear jingled, and the hoof beats grew louder on the road below.

"The river." Meris said. "They might have dogs. We can throw off the scent." We followed the sound of the water, still too far away to feel good about.

*Please let us make it.*

# Chapter 19

The rushing of the water was definitely louder now. The trees began to thin, giving way to a riverbank ahead, and calmer waters here. At least we wouldn't be trying to cross rough waters, though they were close by.

"Wait." Noam held up a hand. "I hear something else."

We stopped. Just over the sounds of the river, something creaked and water slapped against some surface. I crouched against the nearest tree.

*Like this'll help if someone comes up behind us.* The back of my neck prickled. What if the person on horseback had followed us this far? I glanced back.

Nothing visible, as usual. No use trying to see the invisible creature that had hunted us, though, not now. I turned back around, trying to ignore the feeling that maybe I should pay attention and try and hear any snuffling coming through the trees. I pushed that thought away. Scaring myself wasn't going to help.

A small ship slid into view, the wooden hull gliding smooth over the water. It was unremarkable, except for a small shape at the stern of the boat, carved into the wood and splashed with white paint. The same shape I'd seen a few other times, a wheel with eight spokes. Three canoes were roped to the side, and the deck looked empty. Two other boats were close behind it.

Meris stared at the boat. "We need to get on one."

Matt raised an eyebrow. "How?"

Meris kept her eyes on the boat. "Swim to it and climb on."

Noam reached out. "Meris—"

She cut him off. "I doubt they'll see us."

*Or they might.* "I doubt they'd appreciate us just showing up on their boats."

Noam moved forward. "Why don't we just hail them?"

"No," Meris said. "We need to get on one of those canoes." Before anyone else could protest, she waded into the river.

Noam headed wordlessly toward the bank, splashing as he entered the river and swam after her.

"We're gonna freeze," I said.

"We don't really have a choice," Matt said.

He was right. Another separation from them would be deadly. "Okay." *And this is just as risky, regardless of what's on the side of that boat.*

The water flowed over my shoes, soaking my feet instantly and splashing up as I went deeper into the current. Moving fast helped a little, but I couldn't ignore the stark cold cutting through me as the river got too deep for wading. The boat was too far away. The river hadn't seemed that fast when I'd been looking at it; why was it rushing in such a hurry now? A ripple of water broke on the top of my head. *Faster!* I surged, trying to remember all the stuff me and Matt taught ourselves at the pool in the summers. *Closer now. Just a few feet, just a few strokes. You can get there.*

My hands closed down on the side of the life boat, and I was tumbling in, impossibly cold, but out of the water. *I need a blanket now.* The blankets would be soaked, though. Matt climbed in. Meris didn't look as confident about her idea now, not as we all sat shivering in what I thought had been a light breeze before.

"Keep your heads down," Noam said, a tremble in his voice. "Stay out of the wind."

*No problem there.* I curled up on my side, trying to keep my teeth from clacking together so loud. Thoughts of summer back home, of steaming air and heavy humidity, tumbled around in my head.

The sky moved by over us, and I dozed off, fighting down the fear of hypothermia or being caught. What if the folks on this boat weren't too friendly? It didn't matter what was carved on the hull if this boat was stolen. I'd realized that possibility too late.

*Can't get too worked up.* The sky dimmed after hours of quiet. Sunset. Panic gripped me hard, squeezing my chest, forcing out a shudder. We might freeze overnight, if we didn't find a way to bail out now. The chill still crept through my bones. We'd be dangerously cold soon, if we weren't already.

A scrape over wood, a shiver through the boat, and a lurch came right before the sky above us slowed. No. Not the sky. Us. I was just too cold to think straight.

*Is this worse or better?*

The boat rocked as we drifted to the side. "Stay still," Meris whispered, voice barely audible.

There were sounds coming through the woods now, voices and the crunch of gravel as people moved onto the shore. They were disembarking.

I leaned up and peered over the edge at the people walking down ramps and onto the shore. Maybe ten men patrolled along, close to the edge, watching the woods beside a wide road along the river. I ducked back down into the boat.

"We'll have to wait." I hated the tremble in my voice and what it meant. "They're still hanging around."

"How many?" Noam asked.

"I can't tell."

Frustration crossed over Meris' face. "We can't move until they do." In the next moment, her eyes widened.

Something heavy knocked twice against the side of the boat we hid in, making me jump. I twisted around.

"Well, a fine evening to you folks!" The man spoke loudly, almost cheerful, from a few yards away, and I turned, heart thumping. He couldn't have been that old, probably older than us, but not by much. His beard just gave the impression of age. He kept talking. "Come on out, then. You look cold." His face stayed merry, but his eyes were solemn. This was no invitation.

I unfolded myself to wade onto shore. The wind we'd managed to stay out of cut through me as it met my wet clothes. One side of me was a little drier than the other, but I'd half been lying in a puddle all day. Matt followed me, grinding his teeth together. I let him catch up and stuck close to him. He pushed his shoulder against mine. The man watched us all huddled there for a few moments, a crease between his eyebrows.

He stepped forward. "I'm Abner. Come on to the fire." He walked ahead.

*Fire.* The word was beautiful to hear. "Well, we aren't gonna get far like we are now, y'all. I don't think I can run."

"I agree," Noam said. "Freezing will hurt us worse than going with him."

Abner led us through the trees, passing a bunch of other people, men, women, and children. Tents rose and fires dotted the woods here and there. He stopped at an already growing fire. A woman with baby in her arms eyed us from inside a tent nearby, but didn't say anything.

"Have a seat," Abner said. He gestured at the woman. "My wife, Lillian, is in the tent if you need help." He paused, taking us all in. "I won't ask for more than one thing in exchange for our hospitality."

"Of course," Noam replied.

I knelt by the fire, feeling the warmth soak through me, fighting down the shaking that rattled my core.

Abner smiled. "Just a short patrol tonight. There've been some reports of some sort of animal stalking traveling groups lately. No one's got a real good look at it yet, but we just need to check the perimeter of our camp after dark, make sure it or them or however many there are aren't here. Won't take long."

An animal. Was it the same thing that had followed us? The same species, maybe?

*Herds and herds of them*. Why would an animal native to this country be a problem?

Meris scooted closer to the fire. "Agreed."

Abner nodded. "Then enjoy the fire." He stepped away, then paused. "And don't go anywhere for a bit. I think one of our number might want to talk with you."

I watched him leave. "Bet he knew we were there the whole time."

Matt nodded. "Probably." His eyes met mine. "How you feeling after that swim?"

"Better." I yawned. "Tired."

"Me too."

I rubbed my eyes. "We didn't even do anything."

Noam cut in to our conversation. "We did almost freeze." He stared at Meris for a long moment.

She rolled her eyes. "You must admit I was right this time. These people are friendly, and we got a lot farther than we would have on foot. I dare say we all got some rest as well."

"Something like that," Matt said.

But she was right. She'd been right a lot, actually, even if it didn't look like she was always thinking through her decisions very much.

My clothes started to stiffen up, probably full of dirt and other stuff from the river, as the fire dried us. As night fell, more of the fires became obvious, and larger. Probably every family had their own fire, however many families there had been. So many fires, in combination with the moss lamps that clung to the trees, made the whole camp bright. They didn't seem too interested in trying to hide themselves. How did they expect anything to sneak up on us with all this illumination?

*You're just scared. Gotta pay up. He could've turned all of us away.* Should have, after the village, if they were allies. *All that's our fault.*

"And we meet again." I jumped at the sudden voice behind us, then relaxed. Warm and familiar. I barely turned my head.

"Hey, Danny."

Matt's cousin settled beside me and poked at me with an elbow. "So how was your trip here?"

The sounds of the guns going off in that village…the screams. *What did we cause?* "Terrifying."

Danny frowned, opening his mouth. "What—"

Matt cut him off. "What are you doing here?"

Danny blinked. "On my way to the capital."

Would it hurt to ask him along? "Come with us."

He shook his head. "I can't. I'm not even staying here much longer. I have a lot of information to pass on, including a report of an attack on a town near here. Lots of dead."

I looked at Noam. He returned my gaze, his eyes sad.

*Lots of dead.*

"How many?" he asked.

For the first time, ever, since I'd known him, anger took over Danny's face. "Most of the inhabitants."

The fire crackled for a few seconds. *Because they didn't have information. Because they resisted.*

"We should've gone back," Noam murmured.

The shaking started up again. "We couldn't have changed it, Noam."

"Well if I could have helped one person, then…"

The horror was rising up in me again, fresh and awful, and the lump in my throat built.

*This can't logically be our fault, but yet it is.* "Noam—"

Danny cut in. "You were there?"

*I'm gonna be sick.* "We got away. This one guy helped us." *Which is hazardous to one's health, apparently.*

"Oh." Danny paused. "Well, you should know that a few did survive, and they're on their way somewhere safe. A lot of fatalities. Mostly untreatable wounds."

*A few survived.* "Maybe if we'd—"

Matt sighed. "Anya, you can't do anything now. It's done."

Danny nodded. "That's why you're here. To keep it from happening anywhere else. The shooting would've happened whether or not you were there."

He was right. One man had noticed us. That was all.

And Noam couldn't have treated more than one person at a time. But if we hadn't gone through the abandoned village, if Meris hadn't shot the king, if we were never here in the first place. . . .

*I want to go home.*

Just then Abner walked up to the fire, his hands shoved into his pants pockets. "Well, you all certainly look like you've warmed up."

"We have," Meris answered him. "Thank you."

He grinned. "Since you're ready, it's time to pay up for my hospitality. We're off to patrol."

We stood. Meris' eyes went down to her rifle. "What about Matt and Anya? They don't have any weapons."

*Stupid knife. Still haven't sharpened it. Why did Della think that would be a good idea?*

Abner narrowed his eyes. "I'll lend you my pistol since you'll be pairing off." He pulled the weapon out of its holster and passed it to Matt, then clapped his hands together. "Let's get going. Shouldn't take more than an hour."

I stood and watched Danny stand out of the corner of my eye as he moved backwards. Matt's head turned just a little bit to look. Danny lifted his hand and backed away. In a few seconds, he faded into the trees and was gone.

*Spooky how he does that.*

Why couldn't he stay?

*What's he even here for?*

I shuddered to think of a whole hour wandering in the dark to look for that thing. What if we did find it? Matt stared down at the gun in his hand.

*Hope he doesn't have to use it.*

We followed the fires past the last one, separating from Meris and Noam. They moved off, leaving the two of us alone.

"Matt?"

"Yeah?"

"What do you think that animal could be?"

He shrugged. "A wolf?"

"I don't think they have those here."

"I'm sure they have dogs, then." There was doubt in his voice.

"And those could have been brought over from Earth." I swallowed the nervousness that was building up.

"Oh. True."

"Yeah. I don't think they're native." I wiped a hand on my jeans.

At least I wasn't the one holding the weapon, or else it might slip out of my hands. The orange light of the moon made everything spookier, deepening every shadow around us as we got away from the fires. The leaves crunched under our feet. *At least we'll hear that thing coming.* We passed spots of the little lights, then one place where they grew in a solid ring around a dark hole. More burrow-beasts, but if the lights could grow there safely, then the hole probably wasn't new. *At least there's that.*

"How are we supposed to measure an hour?"

"The moon, maybe?" was Matt's answer. "I don't know how to do that." His eyes flicked up to the sky. "Especially not here."

"Great." My shoestring caught on a root and pulled loose. "Hang on just a second. I gotta tie my shoe."

He stopped, standing over me as I knelt and squinted down at the laces.

"When we get home, our moon's gonna seem too bright." I grinned up at his dim shape.

He smiled back and started to open his mouth.

The floor of the forest rustled. In the darkness, just a few feet beyond, something breathed loud and snorted. I stood straight, moving slow. If it was that close, it had already seen us. *How'd we miss it before? How'd it move so quietly?*

"Matt?"

"I hear it," he whispered.

Two eyes shone in the moonlight, low to the ground, a tiny part of a huge body that crouched low. It was the most I'd seen of this kind of creature since we first had heard it. The animal snarled, then let out some cross between a bark and a roar, teeth shining under the lights.

I started backing up, wishing now that I had the weapon. *Matt, you better know how to work that thing. . . .* Another snarl. Matt fumbled with the gun.

Voices. All around us, feet running, and a single loud gunshot, close enough to us to tell its direction.

The thing snarled again, and the eyes flicked away, paws beating on the ground as it took off. I let my breath out as Abner's voice boomed nearby.

"All right, let's head back to camp. Looks like we scared it off."

I let out a trembling breath. "I don't think that was a wolf."

Matt looked just as shaken. "Yeah," he answered. "Me either."

We hurried back through the brush, and I tried not to let the panic overtake me. That creature was the exact same thing I'd heard so many times before. *And now we've seen how big it really is.* It could have been on us in an instant.

So why did it hesitate? Why did it stop to just look at us? Intimidation, maybe?

Maybe it was particularly territorial.

Thankfully, sooner than I thought we'd reach it, we stood in front of Abner's fire again. Meris and Noam trailed behind us. Matt gave the gun back to Abner, and I plopped down in front of the fire. The flap to the tent was already closed, I saw.

*Wish I could sleep like that baby.*

Meris stared back and forth between me and Matt.

"So I gather you're headed south too." Abner smiled amiably. Like nothing at all had just happened.

"Yes," Noam answered. "Meeting some friends in the capital."

And we'd be empty-handed.

Abner nodded slowly. "Quite a place to be these days. Dangerous that we're only a few hundred yards away from Kings Road, too, but with what's happening soon, it's the best place to be."

I glanced at Matt out of the corner of my eye. "What do you mean?"

Abner took a glance around, then just smiled knowingly. "Maybe you'll hear about it. Or see it. Up to you." He stood. "And now, if you don't mind, I'll be turning in for the night."

None of us said anything until he was inside the tent. *So we are near Kings Road after all.*

Matt leaned forward. "So, now we need to figure out what's happening in the capital."

Meris looked around. "Well, we're near the main road, he said." She sighed. "I'm just glad we're not lost."

Noam put a hand around his backpack. "We should go."

"Why?" Meris asked.

He slipped the pack on. "Well, I doubt anyone here's going to tell us right out what's going to happen in the capital. Looks like everyone knows about us. Abner does. If word's spread, we don't know who else might be a traitor, and if there is something being planned, I'd rather find some folks who will tell us what it is."

That smile Abner had given us. Like we should know what he meant. Maybe Noam was right. Maybe they were counting on us, but why? We didn't have what we came for, but were we endangering these people by staying? If a single animal had followed us, people could. *A whole town got shot up for us.* And the entire country knew what we were up to. Noam was right.

"Well we need to move fast if we're going," I said as I stood up, careful to keep quiet, knowing Abner was probably hearing us anyway. It could be that the riddle pieces were somewhere else, with someone. Abner might have been trying to tell us that. Meris and Matt got to their feet as well, and almost moving as one, we ran away from the camp and plunged into the darkness.

# Chapter 20

My jeans were stiff with grime two mornings later as we kicked up dirt on our path beside the road. "Why no one is around is what I want to know." The quiet had lost its eeriness.

Noam pulled his compass out. "The whole nation's coming to a standstill over this."

*And for what?* "Like we have anything to show for our trouble." At this point, heading to the capital just meant hurrying some bad news.

"I just wonder where Barney got his information from." Meris sighed. "What he knew was just so completely wrong, and that really isn't his fault."

*Guess she regrets almost cutting his throat.*

"It's not, but still, what are we supposed to do?" Matt asked.

*Good question.* I stretched. "Well, Barney couldn't have been the only person who knew, right?"

Meris rolled her eyes. "I suppose not."

"We have to do something." My stomach flipped over at the mental image of Naolon forces marching through Salt's Creek. "Our home's in trouble, too."

"I wish we had a clearer idea of where to look," Noam said. "Dupree wasn't…" He trailed off.

*Too polite as always.* "He wasn't super clear on what he was talking about. His clues were obscure and I really don't think the riddle was meant to go this long without being found."

"And it's not like we had a plan for not having something you were told was available," Matt added.

"Well, regardless of what we do next, we don't need to stay out in the open much longer." Noam looked up the side of the road at a shack perched on the hill, just as a soft sound came down the road. Footsteps. Hooves pounding the ground and jingling, still far enough off, but getting louder. "Good timing, once again."

"Is that an outhouse?" Matt asked, squinting at the shack as we hurried up the hill.

"Is that really important, Matthew?" Meris huffed once, but her voice held an edge of fear that was getting pretty familiar from her.

He didn't answer for a moment. "It might be."

Hope bloomed inside. *What if…?*

Noam got to the door first and flung it open. We pressed in, close, and a green uniform caught the edge of my vision as I pulled the door shut.

Matt's harsh whisper broke the silence. "Is the door locked?"

A little switch looking thing, like the deadbolt on my front door at home, stuck out about halfway up the door. I turned it, and the bolt slid into place. It hadn't stuck. Someone had used it recently, or was keeping it oiled. "It is now."

*But for how long?* The sounds of horses and footsteps got louder, and I knew they were just down that little ridge.

*Please keep going, please keep going . . .*

The muffled command came then, and all the noises stopped.

None of us dared speak as two men began a conversation outside. My heart jumped hard as the unmistakable crunching gait of someone climbing a leaf-covered hill reached us.

*Have to do something.* My eyes, adjusted to the dim now, frantically searched the inside of the shack for anything. Another trap door, into a compartment or more caves, I didn't care. The footsteps got closer, heavy in the leaves. *What was Matt thinking about this shack?* I couldn't ask him, but I might as well look.

And then, a difference along the back wall, something I hadn't seen before. The light. Not the gray-green light of branch-filtered sun, but harsh. I edged closer. A definite temperature change, much warmer. *It might be. . . .* I studied the wall. To one side, just visible and gouged into the wood, an eight-spoked wheel the size of a quarter, caught my attention. *So obvious.* So welcome. I tore my eyes away from it and dared a whisper.

"Look at this." The others turned as the footsteps crunched over the leaves and steadily approached the door of the shack. "The light's different. I think this might help us." Meris' face lit up, and maybe she had the same idea. A gate. Another one, to Earth, somewhere to hide temporarily. *Please let this be right.* The footfalls stopped outside the shack, and a hand pounded on the door.

"Come out of there," said the man. Alarm shot through my chest. *Did he hear me?*

No more time to waste. Meris pushed open the side of the outhouse gate, and the shack vibrated as the pounding on the front door started up. Noam closed the door behind us, sliding it into the frame.

Immediately, the heat of the sun pressed down on me. I scrabbled for my backpack straps and pulled it off, throwing it to the ground and shrugging out of the sweatshirt. As the black knit slid off my arms, the relief was immediate. Noam and Meris were both removing their coats, and Matt tossed his sweatshirt on the ground as we moved into the shade. *Time to get some bearings.*

The shack, probably supposed to be disguised as an outhouse on this side too, appeared to be the only thing around, except for another little structure off in the distance. A highway, two lanes along faded yellow markings, went off in either direction, visible for miles across the brown land. The rectangular black and white speed limit sign, far ahead and impossible to read from here, stood beside the highway, shadowed by mountains in the background.

A wooden sign across the road caught my gaze. I stared at the faded green on white paint. Moon-eye, 7 miles.

I glanced at Matt. He faced the sign, red-faced, sweat running down his face. His eyes met mine.

*Moon-eye. That can't be right.*

Meris was the first to speak. "Where is this?"

Hot, dry desert. But that speed limit sign was the same as every other one where I came from. "I think we're in the United States."

"Ah," she said. "Your country." A pause. "It's hot."

I laid my head against the rough wooden wall. "We must be out west somewhere. It's almost summer here." *Water.* I dug around in the backpack, rifling through the stiff blanket and empty burlap food wrappings. My hand closed down on the cool metal of my canteen.

"It looks like part of New Mexico." Matt took a drink.

The distant rush of wheels on asphalt came through the air. "How do you know?"

"I've been here." He put the canteen down. "Camping with my troop, remember?" He huffed a breath out. "This area looks pretty familiar, actually."

"Oh." I gulped a mouthful of water down, then another.

"How long should we wait here?" Noam asked.

A car on the road kept approaching us, and out of the corner of my eye I saw the glint of the sun off its windshield. "I guess maybe an hour. Make sure they're gone." *If we don't melt first.*

"They might follow us," Meris suggested.

Matt shook his head. "Well, if they haven't by now, I doubt they'd waste their time. They don't know what's on this side. I think finding us woulda been convenient for them. They'll move on if they need to, I bet."

The outline of the car was clear now. A truck, actually. Maybe the driver wouldn't see us. Maybe we'd just look like four kids waiting for a ride from our parents.

*Like that's not suspicious enough this far from town.*

Closer. Old and blue and completely hiding the driver. None of us moved.

*Just look comfortable. Casual.*

The rushing sound slowed, lowered in pitch, as the roaring engine drove behind us. Meris' grip tightened on her rifle.

*Keep driving. We're unimportant.*

It swept past, and the road was quiet again.

"We need to do something," Matt said. "We can't just sit here baking in the sun."

"Well we can't go back that way," Meris said.

"And why not, Meris?" Matt's jaw flexed.

*Not this again.*

"Because they'll probably search it, and I don't think we've given it long enough yet."

I rubbed my eyes. "So I guess we're just gonna sit here." My eyes fell on the other building. *Weird place for anything to be built.* Was that white paint on the side? I squinted.

Yes. White paint, in straight lines and circles, with letters painted above and below the shape, too faded to read from here. *How did I not see that before?* I got to my feet. "I think we need to check out that other building over there."

"What?" Meris asked. "Why?"

Matt followed my gaze, and his eyebrows rose. "Yeah. I think so too. Definitely."

"What do you see?" Meris asked.

I took another swallow of water. "The wheel painted on the side. Same thing was on the inside of the shack."

Noam stared at it. "I knew some of our people used it, but I never knew why. It does make more sense."

Matt looked back at the outhouse. "Well, that would explain this."

"What?" I turned. I'd missed it when we'd come through; we all had, I guessed. Another wheel, white on the wood. The paint had chipped, but it was the same. "Oh."

"It's a signal, then," Meris said. "And if it is used for transit between worlds…then the other one may be a gate as well."

"Or a drop-off point for supplies," Noam added.

*Where would we end up if it's a gate?* "Either way, it won't hurt to check it out," I said. "If it's empty or doesn't do anything, we'll just cool off there and come back. There's shade, at the very least."

"Works for me," Matt said. He glanced at the road sign to Moon-eye again, then looked back to me.

"Then we'll go there," Meris said.

*Please let this be something.* We crunched across the dirt. I let my sweat-shirt trail behind me, kicking up a stream of dust. *Like it could get any nastier.* The sun pressed down on my skin. We'd get sunburned if we were out too much longer.

The shadow of whatever this second place was stretched out sideways as we reached it. "Guess it wasn't that far," I said. The letters painted on the side were clear now, as much as was left of them. "Two Moons Café" stretched across the top of the wheel, "Open 24 hours" below it.

*Why isn't it closer to the road?* "How far did you think it was?" Matt asked me, his gaze lingering on the letters.

"I dunno." I shrugged. "Farther than this. It's hard to tell." I touched the cracked paint of the symbol. *Now to find a door. . . .*

Noam pressed on the wall. "This is a good system for quick escapes."

"It's probably been in place forever," I told him. *So the wheel does mean something.* Two Moons Café. The well in that abandoned village, so long forgotten, flashed through my mind. It was weird, with arms and a bunch of buckets…and no way to look at it from above. *What if it is something?*

"Possibly." Meris stepped up beside Noam. "Now how do we get in here?"

"There's a door over here," Matt called. He peeked around the corner. "Y'all coming?"

*Something easy for once.* I followed his path around. "Guess I was thinking too much."

Matt shrugged. "Well, Gavin Dupree's game seems to require overthinking."

*Game. Got that right.* The entrance stood beside a larger garage door with painted over windows. Not subtle, but this garage probably didn't attract much attention anyway, not this far out.

The cool air on the inside of the garage flowed over my skin and cooled the sweat on my face. Junk towered high on the inside, complete with two columns of old pots flanking another door at the other end. Farm equipment was slung in the corner on top of chunks of metal and what might have been car parts. A pair of headlights shone dully under that particular pile.

Noam kicked at a pile of rusted metal. "I admire the extent to which this was disguised."

*Unless you're from Trenavell.* "Yeah, except for the obvious signs on the side of the building, it's pretty well done." *Too obvious.*

"Might as well look around for a minute, right?" Matt pulled open the door of a safe that balanced on a creaking shelf.

Meris lifted a pot and shook it. "I don't suppose that would be harmful. Perhaps even fun." She smiled.

*Guess we have her approval.*

Under a tiny, filthy window stood a desk, cluttered with books, papers, maps, and a haphazard stack of pamphlets. The top one had all but the year "1958" bleached out, probably from any sun that might have snuck through the window. A half-full bottle of rubbing alcohol sat on the edge of the desk. *That we can use.* "Noam?"

"Yes?"

I held the bottle up. "Wanna hold onto this?"

He came closer. "What is it?"

"Rubbing alcohol." I tossed it to him. "Might come in handy, if it's still good."

"A good find," he said, stuffing it down in his backpack. "See if there's anything else we can use."

I turned back to the desk. *Maybe we will find something.* I lifted the faded papers to reveal an ancient road map. I unfolded it, revealing the state of California. *Is this random, or is all of this stuff relevant?* No way could I take it all with me. I wanted to. Even if it had nothing to do with the riddle or Trenavell at all, they were pieces of one life, or several, left behind in this garage, maybe just to lighten a load of a traveler passing through. I slid my finger under the road map and picked it up. A yellowed sheet of paper stuck to it for a moment, then fluttered down onto the desk.

It was an older map, almost identical to the one of the gate system that Meris had shown me. The stains and browned edges showed its age, and the hand drawn details of swirling lines and scrawled words in tiny writing set it apart from the printed scrap that littered this piece of furniture. Nothing on the desk was necessarily scrap paper, considering what this place was, but the lone sheet of parchment was clearly meant to be more. I held it closer to the window, hoping that could provide more light.

Squares littered the paper, like on the other map. But there were differences, all over it. Nothing to indicate anything broken or damaged or functioning. Just the squares that might symbolize gates. There was Kings Road, and there was the capital. In a point on the road where it twisted the most, was one lone square. A gate, on a part of the road where nothing else stood, with others around it in places that perhaps they weren't meant to be.

*Is that ours?* My gaze fell on the tiny black signature at the bottom.

Gavin Dupree.

The world froze for a moment. My heart began to race as I recognized all the other marks littered on it, many more than on the other. *A separate map.* Did they really not know about this?

Another, separate network of gates. A map of them drawn up by Gavin Dupree.

*What does this mean for using the riddle? How many people know about that gate?*

Me, and Matt, and very possibly Brandon. Now Noam and Meris, and the men who'd greeted us the first time Matt and I had crossed over. How many more, if this map was what it appeared to be?

*If he made this map of all these gates, then what's the point of the riddle?*

Noam's voice shook me out of my thoughts. "We should keep moving."

"Indeed," Meris agreed. "Is there a gate in here too?"

*Is this place on the map too?* I folded the paper and shoved it into the back pocket of my jeans. I'd have to find a way to compare the two maps, if I could. I wasn't likely to get a moment alone very soon. I heard the sound of a door opening, squeaking just a little bit. The well in the village came to mind, with its odd shape and all the buckets attached around it. If I could just see it more closely, compare it to the same shape we kept seeing everywhere, then maybe it might give us something, if only to send us in the right direction again.

"Yes," Noam said. "Looks like it's set in a hill. Comes right out on a road."

I forced myself to step away from the desk. "Then let's get out of here." My voice pitched up high. *Calm down*. "I…I think there's one more place we could check for the riddle pieces."

"Where?" Meris asked.

*This might be the stupidest idea ever.* "That first village. The abandoned one."

"Why there?" Meris asked.

"The well." I swallowed. "It looks weird, and I don't know. I didn't think about it until now and seeing that wheel on so many things. Maybe it's nothing, but…I think we should check."

The silence stretched out. Finally, Meris, with one glance at Noam, answered. "I suppose we could try."

"We should be on our way then," Noam said.

They stepped through the door and into the gray sunshine on the other side. A breeze cooled the sweat on my face, but I knew it would get cold fast. I pulled my sweatshirt back on quickly as my friends hurried on.

The map shifted in my back pocket. I'd have to move it soon. *Did they see me take it?*

Only Matt's iron stare stayed on me. "Coming?"

"Yeah." His footsteps fell in with mine.

*He's not asking. Thank goodness.*

I'd have to find a way to tell them, or him at the very least.

And if this map was secret, there was no way I could ever let it get found.

*No pressure.*

# Chapter 21

"Is this it?" I asked.

We hid behind the homes at the edge of that same abandoned village. It looked the same, but we couldn't be sure. There weren't any sounds of living people, though.

*And how many villages are like that now?*

"Should be." Noam didn't move forward. "I think we're far south enough, but it's hard to figure since the train took us so far." Three days had passed since we'd crossed onto Earth and back again. We'd pressed forward as we dared and slept little. "I think that gate shaved a little time off our trip, so that was good."

The corner of the fold in the map poked me inside my jeans pocket. *Not luck though. Can't be that.* When we stopped I could put the map somewhere much safer.

Meris thumped her fist on the wall. "It will take us much longer to reach the capital than I thought."

*Please let this be it.* "It's not like we could do much about that." My hunch had to be right. We couldn't help someone feeding Barney some bad information, especially if the riddle pieces were never there to begin with. The worst part was not knowing whether it had been intentional or just a wrong guess.

"So are we going in or not?" Matt asked.

"Yes." I pushed away from the back of the cabin and stepped into the short passage to the street. "I think I might know what we're looking for."

"If I might ask," Noam said, "will you please explain again why you feel so strongly that we should look in the well?"

Frustration blazed through me. *They live here and they can't even pay attention.* "It just doesn't look like a very efficient well. From what I remember, it also might be a wheel with eight arms, like we've been seeing on all that other stuff." I sighed. "Didn't you notice that pattern everywhere?"

They didn't answer. They had.

*Calm down.* "Sorry. Let's go. If I'm wrong, then we'll have to figure something else out."

Noam cleared his throat. "You wouldn't be the first one wrong. It is worth trying."

As I led my friends toward the sunny street, I could hear the rustling around us in the woods, the noises of unseen animals. Why hadn't we seen any besides those burrow-beasts and whatever it was that approached Abner's camp? As odd as that struck me, it was good to hear living things around us, whatever they might be. Maybe it was a sign that the village, so completely silent when Iacomus confronted us, really was empty this time around. We stepped out into the sun, and no one greeted us. The well stood on the left, its shape casting strange shadows on the road as we approached, the familiar sign etched into the side. A wheel with eight points.

*Yes.* "The letter that Gavin Dupree wrote said that the riddle was hidden in light."

Noam looked up. "The wheel does look like a star."

"It's a good clue, I guess." I walked around it. Two rows of arms, casting weird shadows that stretched out from the ground, all eight spokes distorted by the position of the sun. The actual pieces were about a foot long and stuck out around the lip of the opening. I peeked over the side. The bottom of the well was maybe six feet down.

*That's weird.*

Light. *Maybe.* A big maybe. A huge one. This might be it, this might be the reason we were even here. But it could be nothing, a trick of the light or a false alarm. Another part of this insane puzzle.

Matt walked around the well. "If it's hidden in light…"

"Maybe there's a piece in each of the arms," Meris offered.

"Be nice if it was that simple," I said. Why did everything have to be a puzzle? "But Gavin Dupree really, really liked things complicated."

Noam put his hand on one of the points. It shuddered. "At least we know it's probably still there."

"Yeah." *Why'd it move?* I stepped closer to it and looked down at the shadows again. "Hidden in light…maybe…something here has to line up." *Like in a movie or something.* I grabbed the end of the spoke and pushed. With a crunch and a clang of something deep inside the metal, the lip of the well began to move. Something started grinding inside it, brick scraping on brick.

"There's movement," Matt said. "Keep going." He got behind one of the other arms, and Meris and Noam followed. A minute passed as we pushed, and the ends of the arms lined up with the shadows and brought us to an abrupt stop.

We hesitated, all looking at each other. But this was my idea. "Guess I'll take a look, then." My wild imagination shoved forth one image of something leaping out of the well, and I pushed back. *Stop being ridiculous.* I peered over the edge.

A ladder of long brick stones that hadn't been there before now stuck out of the wall. And how had the whole thing even worked? If it had been the wrong time of day...we'd probably still have kept pushing. Dupree logic. Did the shadows even matter? Maybe the arms just had to line up right.

*Great. A ladder going down into the dark.* "Hidden in light."

"Nice irony." Matt leaned over the side. "Should we try it out?"

"Well, it's obviously probably supposed to be down there." I glanced back at Noam and Meris. "Y'all can stay up here if you want."

"No, we'll go with you," Meris said. "No use splitting up now, is there?"

"Guess not." I eyed the top of the ladder, went to that edge, and swung a leg over the lip.

"Wait." Matt stepped forward.

I clung to the side, quivering, my knuckles blazing white. If he kept me back a second longer, I would fall. "What?"

"Let me go first."

"What? No. I'm already halfway in." My foot found the ladder.

"Anya—"

"Hush. Just follow me." I lowered myself down, climbing slowly. Looking down wasn't a problem. There wasn't anything to see, just a soft ring of illumination that didn't bother to light up the actual bottom of the well.

Matt's shadow blocked the sun for a moment, and I held on tight to the rung. *Keep going. Just keep going*. Down and down and down, separated from my friends by at least a yard, and nothing to tell me when this would stop. I was Alice falling into Wonderland, except hanging on to a ladder that felt more slippery by the second. Gravity wouldn't allow me to settle softly at the bottom.

*Stupid Gavin Dupree and his stupid riddles.*

And then something solid met the bottom of my feet. Rough and uneven, like brick, but hard and substantial at least. S*weet, sweet solid ground.* I stepped away from the dim column of light, waiting for my friends. We stood, staring at each other, the other three faces just pale shapes across from me.

"So what now?" Matt asked. "This is the place, but…"

But another cryptic puzzle. A game that might be the scariest one ever, full of all kinds of nice things shivering in the darkness and waiting for you to stumble into their slimy hands, but none of the escapism. Just the shadows and a real failure if we didn't find those pieces. "I don't know." I turned and put my hand on the wall, following the roughness into the dark. What had Dupree been thinking? All fun and games for him, probably, especially if he didn't have to worry about it then.

My shoulder collided with something solid. "Ow."

"What?" Matt was maybe a foot behind me, too close as the bones in my arm throbbed.

"I hit something on the wall." I let my hand drift to it, felt the second of give it had. *A lever?* I pulled down and heard the crunch of a long-unused machine.

It ground once, stuck, then moved on without another catch. Light grew from the center of the floor as stone scraped against stone. A shadow, round and solid, slid away from the light, like the end of a solar eclipse, revealing part of a circle, then half, then the whole of that and half of another, and straight lines meeting them.

That same shape, the wheel with eight arms, shone up from the floor, neater than I'd seen it. The end of each arm bloomed out in a circle of moss lamps.

"Wow," Matt said.

Meris stepped into the center of the circle. "Is this a map, then? To the next puzzle?"

The lights showed only more brick walls and no doors. My stomach shuddered a little. The ladder was the only way out. Finally. *Something that makes sense*. "No. This…this has to be it." I stuck out a toe towards one of the circles on the edge, setting it dead in the center. It rattled.

I couldn't stop the grin that inched up onto my face. "I bet the pieces are stuck in here." I knelt beside one of them and pushed. With another crunchy squeal, it swung open. I paused.

Who was keeping these little plants alive, and did I really want to stick my hands into any part of it without being completely sure what it was?

*No, but I want to go home.*

I reached slowly down into the center, brushing the sides of the hole, moving cautiously so I didn't meet the bottom so suddenly. Five inches down, a cold, flat object met my fingertips. I grabbed it and pulled my hand out before something nasty could scurry over my fingers.

In the dim, I could barely make out the thing in my hand, but the outline at least was visible in the light. I lowered it closer to the light source.

It was a key, old fashioned, like a skeleton key. A tiny square of some stone was set in it.

*Is this it?* "There has to be more."

Matt leaned over one of the other circles. "Start looking."

I turned to the next circle over and shoved at the edge as Meris and Noam stepped into the circle. The cover flipped on its side like the first one had.

Another key. My friends were quick as me, and it took only a few seconds, maybe a minute, before all the keys were out of the holes.

Matt looked down at his hands. "Are all the stones different colors?"

I looked at the two I had. "Yeah. That's got to mean something." All that stuff listed out in the poem…maybe this was it.

Meris backed toward the ladder. "So we have them. Might we get back into the sunlight now?"

Nothing was keeping us here, not now. No more secret passages in the dark, just an empty puzzle in the floor, and what we came for finally in reach. "Yeah. Let's do that." I moved back to the lever. "Should we cover the lights?"

Noam answered. "Maybe we shouldn't."

"Why not?" I let my hand rest on the lever. Meris was already clinging to the ladder, watching us, and inching up to the next rung.

"To tell whoever comes this way that the riddle is on its way to the capital." A smile played at the edge of his eyes, triumph growing on his face.

It was contagious. *We have it.*

Matt spoke. "Well, they already all know we're here, so why not rub it in a little more?"

*And I'm as ready to get out of here as Meris.* "Okay. Let's go." I felt a thrill move through me. That stupid, stupid riddle that left so much trouble in its wake, even as it rested underground in another world. After so long, we had it, and all we had to do now was use it.

*And how are we supposed to do that?* It didn't matter. It was real and in our hands.

Matt waved at the ladder. "Ladies first."

Meris apparently took that to heart, and disappeared quickly into the daylight. I climbed after her, two keys in my jeans pocket. The rest I could get later, when we could stop in the light and think about them and what they meant. The hard metal edges in my pocket gave too much solid evidence that Gavin Dupree had made something, whatever it did. That this thing waited exactly where he'd led us. That maybe he wasn't crazy.

And maybe that meant he wasn't a murderer, either.

***

The overhang next to me created a nice little pocket where maybe we could sleep tonight. "What do y'all think?" I asked, pointing at it.

"For what?" Matt asked me.

"For shelter."

He shrugged. "Maybe. Might be a little exposed."

"It should be fine all the way out here," Noam said. "I still need to sharpen that knife for you by the way, Anya."

"Take your time." My legs dragged, even as much as I coaxed them to keep going. Matt could have a point. Maybe that wasn't the best place for the packs. *Can't get too closed in.* I yawned.

Meris called from a few yards away. "I set my things down in that clump of trees, if you all want to take a look." She gestured with her thumb. "Now I want to see if I can get any food." She slipped off into the woods.

Noam's ears turned red. "I should have looked more thoroughly. Set your gear in there."

I followed the direction she'd pointed and ducked under a low branch. A layer of green moss coated the ground, and tiny round bulbs ringed the roots and climbed up the trunks around me. I wondered if it wasn't too perfect. It was a gift. One last nice, possibly safe place to maybe get some rest before we headed into the city. I closed my hand around the knife.

*This is the home stretch.*

Matt stood nearby as I stepped back out of the little place. Maybe the blade could do a little like it was. A memory came back, something Matt said a long time ago, unimportant then as I'd watched him rasping his little pocketknife while we sat on the trampoline. *A sharp blade is safer than a dull one.* It would have to be sharpened.

I remembered yelling that he'd cut the trampoline if he wasn't careful. I approached slowly. "Hey."

He turned to face me, his eyes going down to the blade in my hand.

"I should have sharpened that for you. I know how to do it, if you let me."

*Um. What?* "I just haven't been thinking about it that much. It's fine."

Matt was teetering on the edge of full-blown angst mode. He shook his head. "No, you need something to defend yourself with, and I should have tried at least. I owe you that, right?"

*Owe?* "Really?" I swallowed, my heart pounding, fatigue making me more frustrated than I might have been otherwise. Enough with the guilt over not telling me stuff he didn't even know. I brushed past him, smacking his shoulder hard. "You don't owe me stuff and I'm not helpless." My face flushed anyway. "I'm gonna get some sticks for a fire."

He stared. "Okay."

"I'll meet you back here."

How could I get away to clear my head a little, though? My eyes wandered up the hill. Let him be intense here for a minute. Let him freak out, just as long as I had some space for a moment. I climbed the slope. There had to be enough dry fuel around here, if the ground wasn't too wet.

*Why is it weird with him all of a sudden?* Probably because we'd just been in quarters way too close for the last little bit. *That's it.* We'd get home, to our own spaces, back to normal, and it would be fine. Everything would be okay.

*It won't be normal again. Can't be. Not after all this.* I crested the slope and clambered to stand on top, facing out over the place below me, and whistled. The noise was weak in the chilled air.

Matt stared up at me. "Don't fall."

"I'll do my best." The same old spooky feeling crept over me. We'd become too casual in not meeting anyone along the road. I wouldn't be so loud again.

Something rustled behind me, rattling the leaves. The chill raced up my back, half freezing me. *Please be a bird, please be a bird. . . .* I spun, pivoting on one foot, feeling my forehead break out into a sweat.

The creature, even on four legs, stood as high as my head, all shaggy dark fur, lanky legs, claws as long as my fingers. A snarl cracked the air as it bared its teeth.

It was the same creature that had been in the camp those few nights before. That was all I had time to process as it lunged, and I couldn't get out of its way in time before its body slammed into me. For a moment I was flying, then falling, my grasp still tight around the knife. The ground came faster, and why was that a surprise? It wasn't high. The air rushed out of my lungs on impact. Voices, shouting something around me. The creature crept to me, stalking closer, relishing the kill it was about to have.

*My knife. I need my knife.* Maybe it would punch through the thing's hide. My arm was lead as I lifted the only weapon I had. *Why didn't I sharpen it before now?* If I could just punch a hole in its side, maybe I'd do enough damage.

Weight landed on my right leg, and the claws sunk in. Fire raced up my leg, and I barely could squeeze out a choking scream as it dragged me a yard across the ground. A root jabbed into my back, and a dark beastly face blocked out the sun over me.

*Knife! Knife! Come on!*

Matt's voice broke through everything. "No, Meris don't—!"

A gunshot snapped through the air. It yelped and backed away, and another shot sounded. Then with another half-snarl, half-yelp, the creature bounded up the hill and was gone.

My lungs finally gave in and expanded the rest of the way. I pushed myself up.

Matt was suddenly beside me. "Can you move?"

"Seriously?" I swallowed the nausea that welled up inside. "I'm sitting up." I moved my left leg to push it up under me. No use waiting for that thing to come back.

Meris walked into my line of sight then. "I didn't hit you, did I?"

My stomach shuddered. Something warm and wet inched its way down my shin. My jeans had to be ripped, but I didn't dare look. "No, it…the thing clawed me. I think it's just scratched or something."

Matt pulled me up to my feet. The burning knifed down my leg again, lighting up the panic that was already brewing.

"Let go of me!" I leaned away, frantic, and pulled my arm away from him.

"Anya, please."

I took a deep breath, calming, feeling the lump in my throat. Nothing else had ever hurt this much. "I can walk. It's fine." I moved away from him.

"Let's go back to where we dumped our stuff." His face hardened, intense and focused, angry.

"After you." My voice cracked. *Don't cry. Don't cry. Don't break now. You're so close to home.*

Noam already crouched by the backpacks, digging through his and pulling stuff out and spreading it over the ground, his hands just about flying as he put things in front of him.

I let my left leg fold and plopped down, gritting my teeth. Dark spots already splotched the hem of my jeans around the jagged rips.

*That'll be fun to explain.* I put my fingers on the hem and rolled it up, gritting my teeth at the shivers of pain that followed my fingers up. The cold autumn air reached my skin, soothing the spot. I hadn't realized I was sweating until my forehead cooled. Then I dared to look down.

Three jagged gashes bled halfway up my shin, one wrapping around to the calf. My jeans had absorbed blood, and as far as wounds went, they were shallow. Should they hurt as much as they did?

*Jagged claws instead of a clean blade. Of course it hurts.*

Noam lifted his canteen. "They're not bad at all." He frowned. "Let me just get them clear of anything."

I stiffened when he poured the cool water in, then relaxed. "Actually, that's better."

Noam set the canteen down, his eyes following the jagged red lines up and down. "It's clean, but it looks strange."

I leaned forward, studying the cuts. They still oozed a little, and Noam was unrolling some strips of cloth right now, but they burned, deep inside, an ache, and now an itch, clear on up to my knee now. The skin around the wounds puffed out, all red, swollen, and tight, with what looked like a rash starting to spread. Trauma, I guessed. *I hope.* Alarm shot through me as the wounds throbbed. Noam swallowed.

"It didn't bite you, did it?" he asked.

"No." I looked down again. The rash had spread. "Why?"

"Just asking." He started pulling strips of rag from his pack. "It looks swollen. As if…"

Meris walked in circles around us, her rifle ready. "Is it the same thing as at Abner's camp?"

"Yeah," Matt answered.

"And before that. Outside of Skyrren." I tried to keep still. The urge to claw at the wound grew. "I think it's been following us."

"Do the scratches feel strange at all?" Noam asked, holding the bandage end suspended above my leg.

*What I wouldn't give for some itch cream.* "They itch."

He nodded. "Well, it's not bleeding as much." He rolled the strips of cloth. "If you don't mind, I'll just leave it uncovered for now. I'd like to keep an eye on it."

"Fine." *The itching's gonna drive me insane, anyway.* The less bandages there were to claw at, the better.

He pulled the rubbing alcohol out of his pack. "And this?"

I stared at the bottle. It would sting, but I wasn't afraid of that. It was way less than half-full. Slowly, I shook my head. "Save it. There's not much."

He frowned. "You have a point, but I'd still like to."

I bit the inside of my mouth. "Okay, but don't use much. We don't know when it might come more in handy later." I gritted my teeth.

Noam unscrewed the cap. "Not much. I promise."

I looked up at Matt and Meris. The cold trickle came just a second before the harsh burn of the alcohol flowed through my skin. I tensed, but focused on my friends.

"So that thing's been following us," Meris said.

"Maybe." I leaned back on my hands. "I've heard something sniffing around us at night sometimes. Is it some kind of animal you only have here?"

"I can't tell you what it was," Noam said. "If it's native to this planet, then it's not from this area. I don't know of anything like it." His forehead creased into a frown. "Looking at those wounds makes me wonder if it could have been venomous."

"It looked like a wolf or something," Matt said.

My stomach quivered, and I wanted to heave. "Well, a platypus is venomous, and obviously this thing is pretty unique too, right? We don't know what it can do." I coaxed the lump in my throat back. *This isn't Earth, as similar as they look.*

Meris resumed her pacing. "Or how many there are."

"Doesn't seem like they travel in packs." Matt smirked. "At least there's that. We've just heard one."

A laugh slid out of my mouth. It was getting dark now. "Yeah, guess we're lucky."

Noam shoved his things into his backpack. "I'll have to keep a watch on that rash. I meant to ask…does it hurt anywhere else?"

"Just there." I rubbed my knee. "It aches a little further up, but… dunno, that could be a bruise, right?"

He rubbed his eyes. "We'll find out, I suppose." He looked around again. "Better get the fire going for tonight. Come on, Meris." He stood and stepped out of the thicket. Meris followed without a word, her rifle still in hand.

*She actually followed someone's directions. Wow.*

Matt stared down at the blood, his eyes round. Ignoring the shooting pains, I jerked on the hem, rolling my ripped jeans down over it again.

*Guess that's not much better.* "You can go, too."

"I'm not leaving."

"Okay." And for once, it was. The itch persisted. What was this? Noam's words, so full of doubt and fear and uncertainty, rose up in my mind.

*We'll find out.*

***

*Stupid orange moon. Stupid Trenavell. Stupid Gavin Dupree. Stupid me for even going looking in the first place.* The pieces were wrapped up at the bottom of my backpack now, the map slipped into an inner pocket.

My leg throbbed every time my heart thumped. I sighed. Meris and Noam were already asleep, and so was Matt for all I knew.

*Stupid Matt for following me and getting himself into this.*

"Didn't think you were sleeping yet." I could hear the dry edge in Matt's whisper.

I pulled the stiff wool tighter around me. "And why aren't you?"

"'Cause I can hear you making noise over there." Something shifted around. "It still hurts?"

"Not really." The itch had spread to my knee now, but it didn't feel any worse than it had earlier. More like chiggers or poison ivy. Itching, though, that was minor. A little thing, though Noam would want to hear about it if there was a rash or something that popped up.

"I wish I'd known."

*Huh?* "About that thing?"

"No." He looked at me, his reflective eyes spooky in the firelight. "This world. Being what I am…it means I should have known. I should have been like you, asking questions."

“Please stop already.”

“Why?”

“Because all this stuff was hidden pretty well from both of us.” I yawned. At least I was tired now. “It’s not your fault and it’s not my fault. It’s anyone’s who decided they’d hide the whole story from us and then expect us to do something about it.” Who’d dropped the ball along the way?

The tightness in his face relaxed. “I guess.” He looked down toward my feet again. “I just wish—”

“Believe me, so do I.” I rubbed near the stains on my jeans. *Ugh.*

He smiled. “Then, if you’re okay, goodnight.”

“Stop asking me if I’m okay. I’m as fine as I’m gonna be. Promise. Just stop emoting over everything that happens.”

He raised his eyebrows for just a moment and said nothing else.

*Hope he calms down a little now.* A thin cloud, just a wisp and nothing much else, drifted across the strange and creepy and beautiful moon above me. I let the fact sink in that I was camping right now on a whole other planet, under no familiar stars, fine with it if I didn’t think too hard about that, enchanted with the presence of some other place where life thrived. Where people like me lived.

*Maybe Gavin Dupree wasn’t so stupid.*

# Chapter 22

We climbed the ridge and stood, still concealed by trees, looking out at the edge of the capital city. Had we really moved that fast? A breeze pushed up against me, making goosebumps prickle all over. Just an ache in my spine remained from the tumble off the hill, and all the itching was done with. *Thank goodness.*

Matt's elbow bumped my arm. "How are you feeling?"

*So maybe he didn't calm down any*. "If that thing did have any venom, then it's not exactly doing its job. I'm good."

Meris' face was pale white again, and looked damp. Just final confirmation that the other two weren't all that fearless. It was a comfort. "Is everyone ready?" she said.

"Whenever y'all are." I swallowed hard as we climbed down.

Matt cleared his throat. "Remember the huge camp we saw near Skyrren?"

"Yeah." If only I'd gotten a better look, but risking a climb down there on the hunch that they weren't from Naolon…no. No regrets that we didn't look a little closer.

"Well, where have they been?"

Meris looked back at us. "They could have just gone elsewhere. Wasn't too much shared with us, remember."

"It looked like a military camp to me."

I'd forgotten what we'd seen, after all that happened since then. "Maybe they've already reached the city." The eerie calm was firmly settled over the capital. Something was about to break and change in the city, and we stuck to the woods, stopping in a thicker patch of trees.

"We'll need to avoid the main gates," Meris said. "There's a hole in the wall somewhere around this part, I think. We've used it before."

The only gate I could see had two Naolon soldiers standing on either side. Not too weird, but the part of the city I could see came through what looked like a filter of green covering everything. That, at least, explained the troop movements. They expected something.

"Do you remember where the entrance is?" Noam asked.

Meris squinted, frowning. "It's there." She pointed. "That wooden patch on the side. We're near Miriam's house."

"If we can just get there, then…" Noam trailed off.

*Then maybe I can figure out how the poem and the pieces are supposed to have anything to do with each other.* "Good jumping off point, even though the city's packed with those guys."

Meris straightened her back. "We'll just have to keep being stealthy, I suppose."

Matt snorted. "That wasn't exactly helpful after Barney's directions, was it?"

I shook my head. "Nice optimism."

"I'm being realistic."

"You're being gloomy." I looked at the other two, paused for a moment. *They're my friends now, even if I don't know much about them.* A hard knot formed in my stomach. Would we all make it past this? Images came, of blood and death and one of them, or two, or all three, not being there anymore as a result of anything they might do, or any action I took. Noam stubbornly refusing to stop treating someone, Meris rushing forward without thinking, Matt being stupid and pushing himself in front of me. *No. Don't think about that.* "Let's go. Now or never."

Meris nodded. "Off we go." She stopped, looked around, and sprinted across the short gap between the trees and the wall. No use waiting for her to actually reach it. I ran after. Just a few yards now, and a few feet, and I was there, clinging to the brick like my life depended on it. Meris pulled the patch away and ducked through the opening. *Just give me one second. One more moment before I have to do this, before there's no turning back.* I ducked, bending my knees to crouch under the broken stone. I kept my eyes closed against the possibility of slipping so furtively out into somewhere busy.

*Please let us be safe.*

But who was I kidding? I emerged into a cluttered and dusty alleyway behind a row of homes. A quiet tension flowed from the rest of the city.

Matt and Noam slipped in behind us, and Noam pulled the patch back over the hole. I peeked through to the street. It looked almost normal, peaceful, the citizens still bustling around and doing things as they had the first time we came through here.

The color drained from Meris' face. "Oh no."

"What?" Noam asked. He glanced around. "Wait. This isn't…"

My heart thumped hard once. "This isn't the right place."

Meris shook her head. "We'll have to cross this street farther up, I think. Not far, but..." She blinked, staring across at the soldier who stood on the corner there, his head craning around. Hadn't they all been a little more relaxed the last time? That guy was looking for something.

My heart seemed to skip a beat. He was looking for us.

I could hear Matt's teeth grind together. "We're definitely going to be seen, Meris."

"I should have judged the distance better," Meris said, her face reddening, eyes narrowing. "My apologies."

Noam started walking down the passage behind the homes. "We can go this way for now. Keep moving."

*Most sense I've heard all day*. I followed Noam. "You heard the man." Let Matt and Meris work out whatever issue they had with each other now.

Meris caught up to us, taking a place in front of Noam. "As I said, it's not far. I just forgot about that one row of houses. We haven't used that hole in a long time."

We passed through the shadows, under windows that all had been covered with drapes. Wouldn't they want to be able to see any kind of threat? People were still moving around as we passed the few gaps between our hidden entrance and our destination. At a second look, their movements were slow and guarded, not lively.

*Maybe they're trying to look busy.*

Meris stopped. "This way. There's the crossing." She turned between two brick houses, creeping to the street. My heart began to pound. We'd been so long traveling in the shadows, the thought of walking out into the open, right in the capital, in front of all these people brought that frozen feeling in my gut and a steady trembling that started at my knees and moved up to the rest of me. Voices in a conversation drifted to us.

"King's supposed to be visiting the city today."

"Word spread then. No wonder they're well-behaved."

The first man laughed. "Sounds like he's healed up just fine, too."

My throat clicked as I swallowed hard. Iacomus. Maybe our timing would be okay. Maybe we could be in and out and done and gone, back to some safe place. Miriam's house, or a hidden slot in a castle wall.

But had it ever been that simple in the past few weeks?

Meris peered around the edge of the wall, smiled and scooted around.

Bold. *Great.* I followed, wordless. The men stood a few yards away, but maybe they wouldn't glance over. Never had I been more thankful for the grime and dried mud that coated my shoes. My footsteps echoed loud in my ears. Our movements were going to attract attention, that was for sure. Meris stood at the corner, waiting. We bunched together. *There are eyes right on us.* A slow green figure in the corner of my eye. Good posture. Attentive, and coming right for us. Would he even speak?

Meris hesitated. She looked first left, then right. Seconds ticked, too long. The movements on the streets and sidewalks seemed to slow. The posture of the men and women passing on the streets changed, straightened.

The crack of a pistol down the street broke through the city, and as one, the people moved, quickly, pulling out guns and knives and swords and striking at any soldier in green that stood near them.

*What just happened?*

It took a few moments for a reaction, for a real fight to begin, and then noise filled the air, metal, screams, gunfire.

"This is perfect," Meris said. "Run!"

We took off across the street. Bullets snapped the ground around us and people were falling and the quiet had dissolved into cries and sounds of real battle. Scary, and real. A sob stuck at the back of my throat.

*I don't want to die here.*

The brick walkway met the bottom of my feet, and we were across the street, and running up the steps to the house we'd departed from so peacefully, how long ago now? Meris fiddled with the knob, and it swung open.

*Why is it unlocked?*

We rushed into the hallway and Noam shut the door behind us.

No one and nothing greeted us.

"That was insane." Matt leaned on the wall.

I caught my breath. "Wow." *How in the world are we still alive?*

Noam raised his eyebrows. "That might explain what happened to the camp you two saw."

A smile inched onto Meris' face. "If they arrived slowly…and joined with the citizens, knowing the king was coming…"

"Good plan." I looked down the hall. And why in all of thirteen years hadn't they tried it before?

*Guess knowing your enemy can't escape to another planet helps.*

"Doesn't look like anyone's here," Matt said.

Meris answered. "Miriam might be off fighting or being ready to treat wounded. There will no doubt be many."

"There already are," Noam told her.

"This is a good distraction if we want to go do what we came for," I said, before I thought all the way about it. Did I want to venture back outside? We could wait it out, right?

Noam walked down the hall. "It is. I'm going to look for supplies before we set out again."

"Be careful." I looked back at the door. "Whoever was here didn't lock the house back up."

Meris frowned. "I'll go with Noam and look around. Miriam possibly expected us."

"Hope so," Matt told her.

She didn't answer him and stepped away. I leaned against the wall. Quiet filled the house, and maybe it was left alone, unnoticed. Someone had been here.

My heart hammered. I'd just suggested something that might have been a good idea if not for the absolutely sure danger of getting killed on the way there. Dying wasn't going to help anyone. I could tell my friends the key, but what if, worst case, we were all killed? Then who'd seal the gates?

And how would my family find out what happened?

Surely Miriam had left something. I pulled Matt's hand. "Let's go this way. See what we can find, if there's anything." We crossed the parlor to another short hallway with three doors that came to a fourth door. The floor creaked under my feet as I led the way. "Let's look in that last room and work our way back."

"Okay." Matt stayed behind me, just a few feet.

*Good. Space is nice.* No hovering, just walking the empty halls, there, but not so close behind me. The house screamed emptiness, like it waited. But for whom?

Shelter. It was always that. Somewhere for anyone traveling with news or information or help or reinforcements to wait out. Miriam left the door unlocked for that purpose. To let it wait for anyone who sought shelter inside, at the risk of someone snooping around.

The door nearest me burst open with no warning, and the person inside jumped out screaming and lunging forward. I hardly saw the long object clutched in his hands as he swung it towards me, all in a second. Something hard collided with my right side, and a sharp, blinding pain exploded there. I yelped and fell to my hands and knees, saw the jagged rip in my sweatshirt and felt something wet ooze onto my skin. I wrapped arms around myself, covering my side, protecting it, my fear transforming, becoming instinct and reaction now.

*No…No no no. . . .*

Matt yelled, all rage and anger and strength as he pressed the attacker into the wall. The weapon thudded to the floor, a yard away from me, maybe. I stared, fixated on the glinting metal. An ax, and the edge looked nice and sharp. *The map. . . .*

No. It was safe in my backpack. *Good. At least there's that.*

"I'll kill you for that!" I'd never heard Matt so angry. He slammed the guy's head against the wall, once, twice.

"I'm sorry!" That voice was familiar. "I didn't look, I'm sorry. I didn't mean to."

I dared take a look at the attacker, lifting my face. Ira stood against the wall, his face gray and Matt's fists lurking dangerously close to the kid's throat.

"Matt..." My voice choked. "Back off a second. Please."

His gaze went down to my shaking hands. The hardness in his face crumbled, fell away, and he shoved Ira into the wall one more time before he knelt beside me. I didn't move, didn't sit back or lay down or move my hands. I just crouched. *Can't be alone. Don't want to be.* I forced words out. "I'm good. I'm fine."

*I'm not good. I'm not fine.* There was more wetness soaking my side now, but it was hidden under my sweatshirt, somewhere between my hip and the bottom of my ribs.

Ira stammered. "M-my sister's in the city somewhere. She told me to just stay here and guard the house." His face shone with sweat. "I'm really sorry. I didn't know who you were."

The attitude he'd displayed when we'd first met him, the overconfident arrogance, was gone. It was like he'd shrunk. My head buzzed, and I didn't dare breathe in too much. "It's okay." *Those scratches were nothing compared to this.*

Footsteps clattered over the floor as Meris and Noam ran to us. Noam looked down at me, his eyes going to the ax once. Matt backed away, too fast.

"What happened?"

Matt's mouth opened.

*No, you're too angry.* I cut him off. "An accident. Kind of."

He kept talking anyway. "Little punk attacked."

"Matt, shut up." *It hurts*. "He thought we were the bad guys." *Air. Need air. Please.* "It's fine." Panic inched into my chest. The riddle. We had to finish it. My backpack still weighed down on me. If I said anything…if I let them know now how bad it was. . . . "We need to get to the castle now." *Or we never will.*

"Don't we need to make sure nothing's broken?" Matt stepped forward.

*Something's broken all right.* "I have to put the keys together."

"Can you?"

*I ought to slap him*. "Yes." Noam and Meris weren't speaking, and I could still feel the stinging at my side. It was only going to get worse, and we were running out of time. It was a miracle that it wasn't raging pain, that that was still at bay at least. *For now.* Did I even know how to think straight anymore? I pushed up, moving my feet, trying to get them under me. *Why are they so heavy?* "I just…I'm good. Really. Just a little breathless."

I stood. I could see Matt's hand there, but I didn't take it as I straightened, didn't look into his eyes.

I had to get home, and that was all that was keeping me standing right now. *Don't look. Don't even think about it.* The room wobbled, though, no denying that. *Don't think about it.*

Ira slipped to the side, halfway through the door he'd burst out of. "I'll be right back." A moment later, he returned with a rifle in his hand.

*Thankfully he didn't use that.*

"I'll help you get there," Ira said. "If you'll let me."

"Of course," Meris said. "But we need to go now."

Ira walked ahead. "We'll go out the back way. Follow me."

Ira led us through a kitchen, and out the back door. We faced the back of a second house, and Ira set off, heading in some direction he knew. The fighting in the surrounding streets was still loud. Moans reached my ears, and weeping sometimes, but more often there were gunshots and a clatter of metal on metal.

We made our way down alleyways, and side streets, and past hidden alcoves where wounded men and woman lay, bleeding and being hovered over, for I don't know how long. Maybe a long time, maybe short, but in the hypnotic monotony and fatigue that crept over me, time softened at the edges, and everything around me seemed muffled and stretched or too quick or too loud. I couldn't hide it for much longer. I pulled my sweatshirt down lower. Blood was already soaking through. I wiped my hand on my jeans, leaving a smudge there.

The sounds of battle dropped off. Ira stopped and turned around. "We're near the castle. We'll take the servant's entrance and passages to the old throne room. Behind it—"

"The chapel," Meris said. "I remember that. That's where the rest of the mechanism is."

*So close.*

"Are you ready?" Ira asked.

"Yes," Meris said. She shoved at his back. "Go."

His lip quirked up at the side, a shadow of his personality back, and aimed for a door across the narrow passage, leading us.

Something roared, off to the right, ending in a snarl. I chanced a look.

The creature that had attacked us stood down the street, not right up on us but close, too close, one of its sides matted with blood where

Meris shot it. Its gaze found me, and it made some motion like it was sniffing. It stalked forward, eyes always in my direction, cold and far too intelligent, bent on finishing its botched job.

*How did it find us?*

"In here!" Ira held the door open. Why wasn't that creature running? It came to us, casually, still approaching, but in no apparent hurry. It stopped to sniff again as we slipped into a torch-lit hallway and slammed the door after us.

*It let us go.* "Matt…that thing just—"

"Yeah."

Relief should have been moving through me, even as my head spun, but those eyes were the only thing in my mind, those big black eyes watching me with a fierce, frightening intelligence.

People bustled around us, talking loud, some sounding panicked, but I couldn't make out their words. Ira walked around Meris, pointing to his left. "This way."

A few of the folks back here smiled and nodded at Ira as we went along, but the rest ignored us.

*Do they know we're here?* My feet fumbled around each other. I kept my hand on the wall. *Keep it together just a little bit longer.* I could feel Matt's eyes on me, but I didn't look back.

Ira stopped at a door and opened it, peeking out. "It's clear. Come on."

*How much time do we have? What if this reaches the castle?*

He stepped through, leading us into an open space, keeping close to the wall. My heart did that funny jump again, making my vision wobble. The ceiling hung high above us, and the long room led up to two thrones at the wall. The double doors at the end stood tall and very much closed, but there was some weird buzzing sound coming from nearby. What was it? Maybe it was me, maybe the dizziness and the cool sweat that built on my forehead, or the sticky dampness that soaked the inside of my sweatshirt. The air felt thin in my lungs.

This was bad. Matt would know soon enough, if I kept leaking like this.

Ira pointed towards the thrones. "Meris knows where the chapel is, behind the wall. There's a door." He hefted his gun, and his eyes drifted to mine. "I'm going to go where I can actually help someone."

I couldn't help it. "It's okay, Ira." I had to make it look okay, for now, or Matt would never help me get to the chapel.

He nodded. "Good luck." Then he slipped through the door again, and his footsteps pounded away, fading as he went.

The doors to the hall burst open then, and bodies, all green and gray and shooting and swinging swords, filled the hall, pushed backwards. We didn't move, though we had to. *Have to go, have to move out.* The battle had followed on our heels and reached us, just taking a different direction than we had, that was all.

One man charged in, on a horse, waving a sword with his right arm, the left one gone and the reins hooked around the remains of his elbow. His familiar face caught my eye. It had been so drawn then, so sad looking when those sharp eyes had seen me through that window at Miriam's house, but now it was the opposite, alive again and thriving as he led the men, even as he sat like a target on top of the horse, clinging with just his knees.

One of the soldiers in green turned around, facing us directly.

Something about his shape, the way he moved, the light brown hair. The eyes that looked straight up into mine, the face that held so much shock.

*Brandon.*

Then he was gone, vanishing again into the crowd.

*He's with them.*

We crept toward the thrones. A vase exploded nearby. *We're gonna get hit.* The only clear thing I knew was how stupid it was to be out in the open like this. I bent lower, feeling the movement of torn skin and fighting the nausea. It was a miracle that we hadn't been hit yet. The thrones were so close, just yards away, the door behind them almost blending with the wall. *So close.*

We reached the shadows. The door stood just yards away. *Made it.* I looked back in time to watch as Meris' gaze landed on the one-armed man. She froze, turned, and lunged in that direction. "Father!" Her scream echoed across the hall, and heads turned to look.

*What is she doing?* My thoughts muddled together. *Brandon's here. The riddle. No. Focus. Don't. . . .*

"No, Meris!" Noam went after her, grabbing one of her arms and pulling her back. My legs were heavier now. The waistband and pocket of my jeans were wet now. A dark splotch on my jeans peeked out under the hem of my sweatshirt. *Too slow, we waited too long…now I have to tell him.*

I had to put the pieces together, and I had to do it now, but there was no way I'd get there without help. I gripped Matt's arm, my head and stomach whirling. "Matt…"

He looked at my face, then down at the rip in my sweatshirt, and the dark spot under it. His face turned whiter than I'd ever seen it, and the horror on it made the thrones ahead of us tilt to the side. *Can anyone else see the way they move…?* We had to go now, he was wasting time staring at me. The fighting was moving in slow motion.

"We've got to get out of here," he said, looping my left arm over his shoulder.

Someone shrieked. A fist thunked on flesh, and Noam stumbled away from Meris as she swung her rifle around and took off, into the battle.

Noam turned to us, anger at the edges of his face. One eye was red underneath, and already swelling. "Go. I'll be there soon." He froze when he looked at my face. "What happened?"

I swallowed. "Ira got me pretty good."

"Where?"

*I don't have time for this.* "Doesn't matter right now."

He looked back and forth between us and the direction Meris had run. "I'll join you as soon as I can."

"By all means, please go." I tightened my hand on Matt's shoulder. "We have something to do anyway, right?"

Noam gave one sharp nod and hurried off.

*Please let them be safe.*

My thoughts were coming fast now as I tried to map out what I had to do. The door. The chapel. The riddle pieces, safe in my backpack. Matt grabbed onto my arm tighter, making the other side stretch. A yelp jerked out of my mouth as a fresh warmth spread down the side.

*I'm gonna throw up.*

"I'm sorry." He didn't stop, but his voice broke.

"It's okay." The words to the key ran through my mind. *I'll sell you a riddle for a dime. . . come on, think.*

My knees threatened to fold as we ducked into the room through one half of the double doors. Matt closed it, shutting off the sounds of battle. The air here was cool. Dust swirled up from the floor.

"This hasn't been used in a while." My voice held no force behind it anymore, robbed of air.

"Occupation will do that, right?" Matt guided me around to the back of a huge cabinet at the front. An odd wooden box was stuck to the back of what I guessed was an altar. I could just see the outline of a rifle set on a shelf built into the back of the wood. *Even here.* Matt lowered me to the ground, and I pulled off the backpack. *It's almost done.* The dizziness and pain radiated through my torso. I touched the wet stain on my sweatshirt. My stomach tightened, and I pulled my hand away. *Ignore it, just finish.* There. The keys, and the square of notebook paper, slick and so much of a piece of Earth here, so far from home. I pulled it out, praying the ink had survived our dip in the river, though I'd been afraid to even check before now. I spread it, hands shaking, on the floor. My fingers left bloody trails on the paper, but the ink, though faded and blurred from the contact with water, remained.

I'll sell you a riddle for a dime
said the bishop at the chime.
With tables and ravens and eggs on a wall,
and diamonds and pennies in keys and all,
the top of the tower pressed down to fall

my riddle is finished sir; what is your call?

I spread them out on the floor, staring down at the colored stones glittering up at me.

Shining silver, blood red, a smooth royal blue piece, wood of all things, some dark shiny stone, gold or brass maybe, a translucent piece, and copper. *In keys and all. . . .*

These were so definitely it. Relief. *I'm almost finished. Almost done. Almost to the end.*

Matt lifted the box away. I'd thought it was part of the cabinet, but it wasn't. Just a clever cover for the squat, round piece of metal that rose up out of the floor. Eight holes dotted the top, and a seam ran around under them. It was like the well.

"Why didn't you tell me you were hurt before now?"

I shook my head, hoping maybe the fog would clear, but all it did was make me dizzier. "We have to figure out what the order is…" I drew in a breath, deep as I could. "I think the colors go along with the words in the key."

Matt ignored me. "You're losing a lot of blood." He scooted closer and tugged the tear in my sweatshirt open. "You need to lay down."

*No.* "I have to finish this."

"Anya…"

"Matt, for once, just please." The irritation brought me clarity. "Just help me figure this out first." I sucked in a breath. "You can't protect me right now. Just help me."

He stared at me for a long moment, swallowed, and bent over the key. "So you're thinking about the objects in the key, and the colors…

this could be the order they go in."

I nodded. "And I figure the first one is silver, since the first thing mentioned after a riddle is a dime."

He nodded. "Good start. And the color red pops up in churches…so bishop." He laid that piece down.

*What's the next one, what is it. . . .* "Chime. That one's hard."

"We can come back to it." His voice was soft, and fear teased at the edges. "Tables. That's easily the one with the wooden piece."

"Ravens are black." *Don't think about it. Don't throw up.* "Eggs are yellow when you cook them, and that brass or gold or whatever's the only thing that matches."

Matt held up the one with the clear stone. "Diamonds."

"Then that leaves pennies." I set the copper one down.

"Chime is all that's left." Matt frowned down at it. "Water is blue… time moves like a stream…so…chime is that blue one." It was dizzying logic. He put it in its place between the red and brown. "Now let's get to work."

I gave him the best smile I could and leaned over the device, scared of the soft trickle I felt on my side. "How do we know where they go in?" *Panic.*

"We'll have to test each one."

*Oh.* "Worth a try." How long would that take? I felt Matt's hand rest on my shoulder as I tested the silver piece and found its spot. It slipped in and clicked softly. Then the red went in, after a couple of tries. Each piece fit perfectly into the slot designed for it, and soon it was as simple as elimination until all of them were in.

The wheel sat there, quiet. What had I been expecting?

Matt blinked. "It's not doing anything."

A thought swam up, murky. *It's a wheel, genius.* "Wait…I think…" I put both hands on the keys and turned. It went around, once, and again, and one more time before I heard a crack inside.

A burst of energy, like a static shock, made me jerk my hands away, and the metal began to put off heat. I scooted away and looked down. The side of my jeans was dark and soaked. The world spun around me.

"We did it."

Matt pulled on my arm. "We need to—"

The doors to the chapel burst open, and green uniforms filled my vision. "Oh please, no…"

Had Trenavell lost, after all that trouble? No, it didn't have to mean that. Not at all.

Matt grabbed the rifle out of the cabinet. I had been leaning against the altar piece, but I couldn't let him confront them. No. Couldn't happen. "No, Matt, don't!"

They hadn't even seen us until now. What was he doing? I got to my knees as a gunshot cracked off. Matt yelled and stumbled backwards, and the gun he had clattered to the floor. "Matt!" I had to go to him. He was moving still, now sitting up. Had he just tripped? My thoughts took on a razor sharpness as I heard more shots and saw the men in green fall, replaced by two men wearing shabby clothing and armed with rifles. *Get to him now*. I lurched his way.

Arms were suddenly around me, pulling me back. My side stretched as I went backwards, and I screamed, half in pain, half in fear for my friend. "No, let me go!" I couldn't struggle much more. All of my fight was pouring out the side of my body. More blood, more warmth and damp and fire that spread over me, and it would cut me right in half soon.

Noam's voice was in my ear. "I'm sorry, Anya." He pulled me back to a shadowy corner and set me down, letting me lie on the floor. I bit my lip against the sobs tearing through me and tried to see the door. Men were still coming into the room, none of them wearing the green of Naolon. Maybe they were ignoring us. Noam crouched, still standing over me, as Matt ran to us.

"Why did you pull on her?" His voice was too loud, cracking at its own edges of volume as he shoved Noam against the wall.

Noam pushed Matt away, his own voice loud as he knelt down. "I had to, she was chasing after you."

Matt yelled again, his pitch nearly hysterical. "She's bleeding more now!"

I slapped at his knee, anger giving me one final push. "Matt, shut up and let him do his job." I let my head move back down to the floor again, stared at the ceiling as it swirled overhead.

Noam frowned. "First, I need you to sit up a little. Lift your arms so we can get the sweatshirt off."

My head didn't feel quite so fuzzy laying down. "I might need your help."

"Took you long enough to ask for it," Matt said. He slipped a hand under me.

"Hush." I let them push me up, losing myself in a few whirling moments of pain and a buzzing in my head as the sweatshirt came off. They let me down. I was sweating still, and this room was too hot. My stomach swirled and my jaw tightened up, ready to expel whatever was in my stomach.

There was quiet then as Noam bent over me for a few moments, then his hands pressed against the wound. He looked into my face. "This is really bad. Why didn't you say anything?"

"I tried the same question," Matt told him.

"I have to stitch it up," Noam told me.

*Stitches. Oh.* "Go ahead." I didn't care. Maybe I'd get home now. The room was filling up with people, all apparently ignoring us as we huddled in the corner. It didn't matter. We'd won this round. I smiled.

# Chapter 23

I let the icy floor push its coolness into my skin and kept my eyes squeezed closed. *Not looking down.* So much was happening around us. Voices and yelled orders echoed off the walls, but I didn't care right now about any of it. The nausea started to ease, and the battle outside seemed to have gone silent, or at least much more quiet than it had been.

I heard Noam's voice closest. "Anya, this isn't going to feel good, but I've got to clean the wound and wipe the blood away so I can see."

My throat was dry. "Okay. Just get it over with." I squelched a gag.

"Be careful," Matt said.

"I will," Noam said. "I do this, remember?" One of them took in a sharp breath.

Something fiery filled up one side of my body, the sharp smell of alcohol reaching my nose as the cold liquid splashed onto my side. A rough thing pulled on the nerves as it trailed across my skin. Another splash of the liquid fire. I dug my fingertips into the floor, barely hearing the soft squeal as grits of dust wedged themselves under my fingernails.

A squeak inched out of my mouth, and it was over. I dragged air into my mouth. Had I been holding my breath? I popped my eyelids open and looked up at Noam.

"Matt, if you could hold that tight," he said.

Matt nodded. Something pressed against me where Noam had cleaned, but it was steady, unmoving, and didn't hurt like it had.

Noam kept talking. "This next part isn't going to be too much better, but I think that might have been the worst," he said, his face strained. Matt crouched beside him, his hands out of my line of sight.

"It's fine," I said. "Just get this over with." Even now I could feel a warm trickle work down my skin. I shut my eyes hard again and felt the pressure lift from my side. Someone bent closer and I fought the urge to push them away in the closed-in terror that came over me. *Just Noam. That's all.*

They started then. Sharp little pains, a few seconds apart, and a thing that dragged and pulled after each hard note. Sweat prickled up on my forehead, and I let my mind drift. Time passed, I thought. There was a draft now, and orange light somewhere irritatingly close to my eyelids, and the smell of wood burning from somewhere nearby. When had that been lit? Voices grumbled in the background, but I hadn't heard Noam or Matt say a thing. For a moment, cold air flowed over my side, and I shivered. If my eyes wanted to stay closed against the light, then that would be just fine. I cracked my eyelids open.

A hand pressed against my forehead. *Who's that?*

I slapped it away and opened my eyes wide.

The side of Matt's mouth lifted in a smile. "Hello."

Dry throat still. My voice croaked out. "Hi." I shifted, trying to get up onto my elbows.

Both of Matt's hands came down on my shoulders, pressing me into a hard floor. "Don't."

*Telling me what to do again*. "Why?"

Matt's teeth ground together. "You're gonna make it worse. The… thing." His throat bobbed, and I saw something I hadn't noticed yet, or ever. His hazel eyes rimmed in red, and just that edge of swollen.

Had he been crying? "Oh. Yeah."

Noam hovered on my other side. "I'm done for now." He paused, mouth quirking. "If you keep still and let me put the dressing on it."

Dressing. To go over the stitching that held me together. "Okay." I chewed my lip. "Can I sit up?"

Matt answered quickly, his hands pressing firmer. "No."

I narrowed my eyes. "You are not the boss of me." I twisted a little. Something stabbed up my side, and the pain buzzed through my head a second later. "Ow."

Matt smiled, but it was bitter. "Thought so."

My hands still worked, and that was still fast. I didn't think, just reached up for Matt's wrist and pinched, hard as I could, and held on.

"Ouch!" He jerked his hand away. "You're mean when you're hurt."

"I'm mean when you're bossy, that's when I'm mean." Only Matt and Noam were with me here. "Where's Meris?" I remembered her charging off into the battle.

Matt's eyes traveled to where Noam had been working. "She's taking care of some personal things."

*Her father, I bet.* I didn't press any further.

Noam held up a roll of bandages. "I do need you to sit up again, just for a little bit."

I smirked at Matt. "Fine with me." Then I tried to push up. The pain lanced through again, harder this time. "Ick." Matt pushed up until I was halfway sitting, and held me there, leaning back against him.

The room rocked back and forth. Over all that, though, was one thought that echoed as I became all too aware of being pressed up against my best friend. *This is weird.* My hands got clammy. *This is really weird.*

Finally, mercifully, Noam tugged once and sat back. "Finished."

I pulled away from Matt, and he set me back down, but slow. Now it was hurting good.

Noam set his hand on the side that was covered with the dressing and looked toward the door. "Hate to say this, but I think we will need to move soon."

"To where?" Matt asked.

Noam frowned. "I'll find a room. I don't think there was much fighting upstairs. I'll stay with you, but I have a feeling there's about to be quite a bit of commotion in here."

I took a deep, slow breath. "Let's do it, then."

"How?" Matt asked. "Don't we need a stretcher or something?"

"No." I pushed my elbows under me and leaned up on them. "I think I can walk." The words choked off as the burn spread up my side.

"Don't do that, either," Noam said. He lifted me the rest of the way. "I worked so hard on those stitches. Wouldn't want you to ruin them." He smiled.

"My mistake." I propped on my hands, but my arms quivered wildly. This wasn't going to hold for long. "So how we gonna do this?"

Matt pulled my left arm over his shoulder. "Like this. Come on, Noam."

The other boy nodded once and slowly did the same as Matt. "Okay. Brace for it, Anya. We'll move together, good and slow."

I swallowed. "Ready."

"All right." Noam took a deep breath. "Now."

They stood, carefully, as one, and I helped as much as I could, feeling only a soft tug under the steady burning. I snuck a glance behind me, through the wide open doors of the chapel. It was calm, for all the figures lying on the floor, or walking around, or kneeling. A mix of green uniforms and worn out clothes filled up the hall, but it was obvious who the victors were. The green was all to one side, lined against the wall, just sitting and waiting there, maybe twenty men altogether.

I took a peek, but I didn't see if Brandon was there. There was no way, then, to be sure that it was him I'd seen. If it was, if he was on the other side of this, I still hoped he was still alive, somewhere in here. Or maybe he'd escaped. But I couldn't know now, and I was tired. Focusing on getting to our next destination was my main thought.

"We won," I said.

"Yeah." Matt's smile grew slowly.

"For today," Noam answered. "Now, let's find a place to settle down."

We edged into the dark hallway, shadows made deeper by the burnt out torches.

*Whatever happens now, we won the day.*

***

*Tick tick tick.*

Did I hear that before?

*Tick tick tick.*

I moved my bare feet under the blanket, and the mattress shuffled quietly under me.

I pushed myself up, and something knifed through my side, same thing as before. A choked cry forced its way out at that agony.

Matt's hands were at my shoulders again, shoving me back down onto something soft. "Seriously, Anya?" He lifted the edge of my shirt, just enough to see the very edge of the bandage. He didn't move from the wooden chair he sat in.

I didn't fight him, just looked around the room. Drapes covered windows, a fire was lit, and a few candles burned. The orange moonlight streamed through the curtains, the only trace of an idea of what time of day it might be. The clock ticked on. People passed the open door, hurrying through the hallway.

I patted the mattress. "Haven't seen one of these in a while." *We really did this.*

Matt nodded. "I think we got out of the chapel just in time."

"Who's using it now?"

He sighed. "Well, what's left of the government of Trenavell was hunkering down there for a while, last I heard."

"Oh." My head spun, and the energy I'd had drained away.

He held up a canteen. "Thirsty?"

My throat was dry. "Yeah." I reached for the metal container and pulled it close, drinking one mouthful. My stomach roiled, protesting at the little bit I put in.

"Were you hit?"

Matt half-smiled. "I slipped, actually."

"Good." I gulped down another mouthful of water. "I legitimately thought you got shot."

He shrugged. "Guess it's okay. I could've hit someone else I wasn't aiming for."

Relief, distant but so real, cleared my head a little more. "Can I sit up some, at least?"

He didn't answer for a long minute, forehead all creased up.

"I mean, I sorta half-walked here, right?" The image of his swollen and red eyes came back. *Don't think about that.* "Please? I can lean against something." My eyes wandered to a lump of brown leather across the room. My shoes were beside it. "Like my backpack. Please."

"Okay." He got up and walked to the dim corner I pushed myself straight up again, careful not to move so fast this time as Matt came back. I held still, arms quivering, as he did something with the pillow and the backpack together. "There you go. Noam told me not for long, though. It's only been a few hours since…well."

*Wow.* I settled back. "Thanks." I tugged at the blanket, let it rest under my chin. "Hours?" How could it possibly be so quiet? "So everything is really over?"

"Uh, mostly." Matt set the canteen down in my lap. "Drink some more. They don't have IVs here, and you really need fluids."

"Yes, sir." I took another mouthful in. So many questions. "So the city is back in Trenavell's hands, right?"

"Along with a few other large towns, since so many of Naolon's troops were here." He yawned. "You saw Meris' dad."

The man on horseback, who I'd seen huddled across from Miriam's house weeks ago. "So is he a general or something like that?"

"Kind of. Now, anyway." Matt paused. "He was the king."

The surprise couldn't quite register yet, and my dry throat took over my attention. *Another drink can't hurt.* "So he's the king again, right?"

Matt shook his head. "It's a little more complicated than that. I didn't get much out of Noam, but it seems that Meris' dad actually stepped down right before the war began."

"Why?"

He shrugged. "We got off the topic when Noam decided to go see where else he could help." He paused. "After he made sure you weren't gonna start bleeding again or anything."

My stomach turned. "Oh." I reached for the edge of the blanket that hid my shirt's hem.

Matt's hand caught mine. "Don't."

"Why?" I didn't struggle with him, but we froze, each of us staring into the other's eyes, the same old conflict between us that had begun this whole mess.

"Do you really need to see them?"

"No, not really, but what, besides you, is stopping me?"

He waited, just a second, before moving his hand away. "Nothing, I guess."

I let go of my shirt and stared at my blanket-coated knees. It would be time to face them soon enough. "Okay. Didn't want to see them anyway." *Just quit bossing me around.*

Neither one of us spoke for a few minutes. That clock, wherever it was, ticked louder and louder. I had to stop the noise from building more, from overcoming everything in this room.

"So." I gulped down another swallow of water. "Stitches."

"Yep."

*First time for everything.* "How am I supposed to hide that?"

Matt rubbed his eyes. "I don't know. Noam's hoping we can stay until he can take them out."

"Well, what's another few days here?"

"Weeks, actually."

"What's the difference anymore?" What if someone had gotten to my family while we were here? There hadn't been a way to lock the gate, and now that it was common knowledge. . . .

"As long as we get home." Matt leaned his head on the palm of his hand, his eyes fixed on the wool blanket. "Also, it looks like the claw marks are healing up well."

"Good." One other thing. One more nightmare I'd seen when we'd fled into the castle. "That creature was there."

Matt nodded. "I know."

Oh good. "So I didn't imagine that?"

"Nope." He frowned. "It was really there in the street."

I could almost see it now, the claws, the teeth bared at us. "Did it get anyone?"

"A few bites."

"Bites?" Getting clawed was bad enough.

Matt nodded. "Yeah. Turns out you were pretty lucky." He paused. "They still think it's venomous, but it's hard to tell when he got ahold of one guy's throat. The other guy got bit in the arm, but he didn't last long."

"Oh." Cold sweat broke out on my forehead. "Did they catch it?"

"It disappeared, actually." Matt frowned. "The attacks were after we got in. After the riddle was put together. Like it was running away."

*And what if it comes back?*

"But it let us go."

"Yep."

"And they still don't know what it is?"

"Nope." He leaned back in the chair. "Sure looked intelligent, though."

*The eyes.* "Yeah." I rubbed at my own eyes, fighting the yawn that came. "I bet it'll be back." Why had it run away?

"Now we know what to expect."

"Mhmm." *Just accept it. You don't have control.* My vision began a soft spin. *Just want to go home.*

"Do you still want to keep looking for the book?"

"Yes." I couldn't stop, not now. "I mean, where did those letters go? Just because we came here and did what we did doesn't mean the riddle was all there was for us to find out. We knew nothing about any of this and there were still people slamming into your car…and Brandon…"

"What about him?"

"He's here."

Matt went completely still. "What?"

"We saw each other." The horror in his face when we'd locked eyes. . . . "He knew it was me."

Someone calling down the hall outside broke up the pressing silence.

Matt looked away from me. "I'm tired. I know you are."

*Don't you dare change the subject.* "Promise me we'll keep looking. If there's someone watching us close enough to come behind us, clean up, and take those letters, then this is more than just the riddle." Had the map been stained or damaged? Maybe it would be for the best, if it covered up the gates and hid them from other eyes.

There was little chance of soldiers in green invading Salt's Creek now, but I couldn't help but feel like part of this was personal. Bad old blood between Gavin Dupree and James Abney, welling up again from dead men.

Matt nodded. "Okay."

I relaxed against the backpack. *No more speeches tonight.* I'd have to tell him about the map, but not now.

The clock ticked.

***

I probably needed a shower really bad, but clean clothes were an improvement at least. The pants were too long and the sleeves of the shirt covered most of my hands, but someone had offered to try and wash the stains out of my regular clothes. I'd just about jumped at the chance to get rid of that stiff burgundy stain on my jeans.

The hallway stayed empty, good enough for me as I hid up here, my knees curled under my chin. Probably a bad idea. I leaned against the railing and peeked out at the scene down below me, stretching my spine slowly. Pain in my side stopped me before I got too far. There were so many busy people in this castle, most of them tending to anyone who had been wounded the day before, and there were a lot of those.

*So many worse than me.* At least I could walk, if not very fast. At least I was alive.

I saw the back of Noam's head, hurrying somewhere, and leaned away from sight in case he turned around. I'd broken his one rule: stay put. It had only been a day. He ducked into another doorway.

*I'm really gonna hear about this later.* At least he'd be nice about it, if a little frustrated.

The scuff of a footstep made me tense my spine up. *You're not bothering anyone. You're fine where you are. Stop being jumpy.* Matt stepped into view.

"Why are you up here?"

*Because you and Noam are bugging me, that's why*. "I got bored."

He sat across from me. "I guess you feel better."

"It'd be nice if you could convince Noam of that."

Matt smirked. "Actually, he's looking for you."

I rolled my eyes. "Thought that might be the case."

"To be fair, I think he was a little surprised that you disappeared."

I scraped the brick floor with my bare toes. "And you weren't?"

Matt shrugged. "Not really."

"You still came looking."

He looked down at his shoes, and his face was neutral the next second. "Just wanted to see where you went." His jaw went rigid. "I can leave."

What was one more escape today? "Okay." I pushed myself up, straightening and trying not to make a sound as the wound in my side protested. "Tell Noam I'm fine and that he needs to get some sleep. I was headed to the chapel anyway."

Matt tensed, like he was about to get up. "Why?"

*The entire reason we even did all this.* "I want to look at the mechanism again. I didn't exactly have time to figure it out yesterday, okay? I really think it means something, since the shape of it wound up being plastered all over this country as well as a random garage in New Mexico."

"Wait." He stood. "It hasn't been cleaned yet."

That almost got me. The floor, still stained, and probably not just with my blood. Squeamishness wasn't going to get us anywhere. "Well, you can stay here if you don't want to look at it. I'm going."

I swept past him, quicker than I should, back down the corridor. The dizziness inched back, not as bad, but there. Most of the hallways led straight to the thrones, and the chapel was easy to find after that. Only my bare footsteps echoed off the walls. No one had followed me.

*Good.* Alone. I needed that. *Just give me some air, some time to think, some time where no one's hovering over me and checking on me.*

The riddle. Eight spokes, eight pieces, eight keys, and still no way of knowing for sure what had actually happened to James Abney all those years ago. It was weird to think of how that had even led to us coming here. Except for knowing Gavin Dupree was mixed up in all of it, our adventures and that murder mystery felt disconnected.

I took the same path we had yesterday, slinking along the wall of the throne room to the back, to the double doors. One was closed all the way, the other cracked partly inward. I pushed, hearing the soft squeak of the hinges, keeping my eyes off the smudged floor. *Just pretend they look like that anyway.*

A dark figure sat on the pew at the front.

I couldn't be alone even here. I approached the front. He might leave, and until then, I'd just be one more person seeking quiet. The light hit the guy's face as I got closer to the front. He spoke.

"I'm sorry, but I will not be offering counsel today." The familiar voice held a sharp edge I'd heard before, too. "You'll have to see another chaplain."

"Cargan?" I lowered myself onto the pew across the aisle from him. The whirling in my head eased.

He looked up. "Anya." He cleared his throat. "You seem to be feeling much better than Meris and Noam described yesterday."

"I guess." Had he fought too? "I'm not here for counsel, though. Just…for quiet."

He nodded.

I stayed still, staring up at the front of the room. Matt was sure some horror waited up there. My stomach wobbled. *Maybe I'll just wait. Just sit and breathe for a while and not go have a look yet.*

Cargan spoke. "I am not sure that my father fully thought about what repercussions might come as a result of his sudden abdication."

*What do you say to that?* "I'm sure he knows now."

"I suppose." The man sighed.

"Are you happy that he's alive?"

Cargan's mouth quirked, but his gaze stayed on the floor. "I was a boy when he was first presumed dead. My family spent all these years in a camp, watching as this nation fell and stayed down, with no word from him, nothing to say he even survived, and no hope." His eyes flicked up to mine. "I'm am happy that my family is whole again. What I am not looking forward to is this nation picking up a fledgling representative government where they left off and fighting a war at the same time. It will not be easy, and yet some continue to think it is."

I didn't offer any words, but Cargan didn't need a reply. He just kept on speaking.

"My father created a situation thirteen years ago that gave our enemies an opening. He is wiser for it, I hope." He stared back at the altar. "This has always been so much more complicated than two nations warring, and you being here, Anya, is proof of that." Cargan stood, a bitter half-smile on his face. "I'm going to see about getting some food."

"Okay." *That was intense.*

"Best wishes on your healing." A kinder expression took over his face.

"Thanks."

He nodded and walked back up the aisle, his boots thumping away until the sound faded. The door squealed, and I was alone.

*Always more complicated.* Of course. Gavin Dupree was a man who'd loved complication. That was easy enough to guess. Even back then, back before this war, before the government changed, Trenavell had to be like candy to him. A problem, with a solution, a puzzle to burden all of us with later. But why? What had happened in the 1880s to draw him to it?

And who was I kidding? *I'm like him.* Solving everything came with too good a thrill to pass up.

*Time to take another look. There has to be more in this room.* I pushed myself off the bench and approached the altar, circled around, and looked down at the mechanism. A dark smudge on the floor near it turned my stomach. *Don't think about it.* I didn't dare look at the other place where Noam had worked. The metal circle hadn't changed, and the keys still stuck out of the center piece, all still in place. *I'm blessed to be alive.*

Where was Brandon now? *Is he even still alive?* Even if he was the enemy, the thought of him dying was awful. *Maybe he got pulled into this too.*

"That's all yours, you know." Matt's voice startled me. "The blood."

"I figured." I knelt, slow, letting one knee thunk on the floor.

Matt was suddenly beside me, sitting and staring, his eyes at turns angry and sad, his voice not saying anything.

*Still?* I swallowed, my throat feeling thick again. "What's wrong now? I'm still here."

"You'll just laugh."

"I will not." *Please.*

"It scares me to think of what could have happened to you."

"Well, yeah. I lived it." I pushed at his shoulder. "Why would that make me laugh?"

He shrugged.

*Fine then.* "Well, I'm here, and we're going home soon…ish." And now what? Try to pretend everything could be regular again? "I have to look for more of that symbol. He left it for us. Gavin, I mean."

"Then I'll help."

I pushed half a smile onto my face. "Of course you will."

My fingers found the keys on the mechanism. Dupree had made it so complex, banking on the hope that someone would understand it, even after he was long gone.

*This is just going to get bigger, no doubt about that.* "Cargan said us being here is proof that this whole thing was always more complicated than two countries at war."

Matt's eyes looked at each of the keys. "When I'm faced with everything we've found out while we've been here, I know he's right. We didn't have any reason to become involved in this. Not from this side."

My heart sped up. "Why didn't Dupree just do all this then? Why'd he wait?" My head refused to wrap around this, to figure it out. *I'm missing something. That's got to be why.*

"Anya."

"What?"

"Calm down."

"Stop saying that."

"You're asking questions I can't answer." He sat back. "We'll find the answers. But right now…" He looked down at my side. "Just calm down."

I drew a deep breath in through my nose, expanded my lungs. The skin at my side stretched, not painfully, but oddly. Pulling against the stitches that held me together. "Okay. Fine. I'm calm." I pressed my fingers into my eyes, rubbing them. Now we had to deal with a bigger problem than I'd ever expected, an old friend fighting as an enemy soldier, and no answers yet.

***

"Why do we need to be here, Meris?" I kept my voice low as we leaned back on the walls in the quickly filling room.

She stared at the table near us. "My father requested it."

Noam jumped in. "Your father ordered it."

She moved quickly. I heard the thunk of an elbow on flesh and a grunt of pain. "He said if I am to make the sort of truly adult decisions that brought me and Noam to the capital, I am expected to pay attention to the details so that I can make informed choices."

"Just don't break Noam," I told her. "He's the best doctor we have."

"Well, if he hadn't spoken so freely around certain people, perhaps I wouldn't have to be so frustrated."

Noam stretched away from her. "I merely provided the details about these past weeks. You can't blame me for the conclusions drawn."

Meris glared at him and turned to the front of the room.

It didn't take knowing Meris long to figure out that she wasn't prone to thinking through stuff carefully. But her father hadn't been there, at all. Not since she was little. *Guess he needed to hear from Noam.*

Meris' father stood, cleared his throat, and the room fell quiet. His mouth quirked, not in humor I guessed, because that wasn't in his eyes. Surprise, maybe, like there was some chance that the people gathered here weren't going to listen. "We've taken this city back, but our work isn't done. Naolon and Iacomus are not defeated, but we've weakened them and we do have new information from a few sources in regards to this war." His eyes flicked out into the crowd. "Hestia, if you'd please share with us what you've learned." He kept standing as footsteps padded across the room, and Hestia stepped into view. *Didn't think we'd see her again.*

She nodded at Meris' father. "Thank you, general." He took his seat.

Hestia began talking. "It's very apparent, from multiple reports throughout the city, that Iacomus never made an appearance, and that is contrary to what we know are his preferences. He sees this city as his, and has been staying here half of each year. I know from personal experiences that he considers himself to have conquered the capitol on his own, and often said that he would defend it against anyone who tried to take it from his grasp."

"Why does that matter?" came another voice from somewhere near.

Hestia's sharp eyes found the man. "It is bothersome because he could be elsewhere. We know that Naolon has many more forces and not all of them were here or in the other areas that were taken. Our people have been mainly concerned with the takeover of the capital, so it was a surprise to take the number of places we did. If Iacomus is not here, defending his greatest conquest or killed in battle, then where is he, and what is he planning?" She paused. "And why did he allow so much to slip from his grasp?"

The room stayed quiet for a moment.

She continued. "There are four other continents on this planet, all unknown and unexplored by our people." A pause. "We must consider it extremely likely that he is only waiting, and that he might have made allies elsewhere."

Waiting. Hiding. The same guy who saw us, looked right into our faces before Meris dared to shoot him, would be back. For us, probably, since he was that kind of person.

Another man stood up. "What about the rumors of his uncanny longevity?"

"They are proving true," Hestia answered him.

The rumble of voices started up then.

"There's no way it's possible," Noam said.

Hestia's gaze shot to where we stood. "It is possible." Her voice raised. "Iacomus has always been interested in using the gates for something other than transportation, and we've always been aware of their strange qualities."

Meris looked paler, but spoke up over the noise. "So he's the same one."

Hestia nodded. "Yes, Meris. We have reason to believe that this Iacomus is the same man who drove the moon-eyed people away one hundred and thirty years ago and who was thought dead at the hands of Jendra Davies. We've gathered that the people of Naolon believed his supposed death was unjust, and were willing to wait for vengeance."

Matt's mouth dropped open, just for a second.

Jendra Davies. The letters. *That's why they were taken.* Goosebumps rippled over my skin, pricking at my stitches and making the hair on my neck stand straight up.

"Why would the gates let him be able to do that?" The words snapped out of my mouth before I could stop them.

A familiar voice spoke up as Matt's cousin Danny stood.

*When did he get here?*

"The gates," he said. "He'd have to hide inside one, with both ends closed and hidden, and just wait. Time doesn't pass normally inside a gate, so he wouldn't age. Once he'd proven that he'd be unharmed, it's an infinite resource if he wanted to spend time in some sort of stasis."

And he'd just waited. *All that time.*

The king looked over at Hestia. "When did you confirm this information?"

"Only in the past two months." Hestia crossed her arms. "And the creature we've been witnessing…it appeared again in the capital." Her face stilled. "If there are more, and if Iacomus is bringing allies from another part of our world, along with what unknown creatures they have there…then we must act. The seal on the gates is not permanent."

My heart thumped. *What?*

Meris' father spoke then. "And all this would explain why Naolon has so consistently been trouble for our nation."

*The seal isn't permanent. It's going to break, and what then?*

The voices faded into an indistinguishable grumble, the noise unable to push through the loud thoughts in my head.

*If the seals aren't permanent, then what good are they?*

I stared at Matt. His face had gone pale. *Not for nothing…but this isn't over.* Finding the letters and the book, and keeping that map safe, had never been more important.

***

Five torn pieces of the hard chunk of bread spread across the table in front of me.

Five continents.

*This place is crazy.*

I put one of the flavorless hunks in my mouth, crunching down.

*Not as crazy as Gavin Dupree.*

I sipped water and pushed the mush down my throat.

*He probably was a murderer too, and how are we even gonna get home now?*

Danny's voice broke in. "What are you so intense about, Anya?"

"Huh?" The dry bread had crumbled a little on the table. "Oh." I forced another piece down and shrugged. "Just…this is all a lot to think about."

"Well, whenever you want to get home, we think the gate that you guys used to get here isn't part of the network." Danny sobered.

"Figured that," Matt said.

*The map.* I rubbed my eyes. "Good secret." *Can't talk about that here.*

Meris frowned. "What if there are more like that?"

I kept my eyes down on the bread. *The less they know, the better, until we get this figured out.*

"Not a very good secret, then," Noam answered. "It would take a lot of moon-eyes to accomplish that. To our knowledge, he only had the willing help of Jendra Davies."

Matt nodded. "So that's who he was writing to. The only other people who knew. Her and her husband."

*At least that we know about. Stranger and stranger. More complications, and for what?* "The book."

"What?" Meris asked.

We'd never found it in Skyrren, but that didn't mean it hadn't been there, or wasn't still. It might have just been moved, or still hid amid the poison. "Gavin Dupree mentioned some book in one of his letters. He said that he put it in Skyrren. That's why we stuck around in there."

Matt took a deep breath. "We think it would be a big help, if we could find it."

And the rest of the letters. *Like we'll ever see them again.* "I think this goes pretty far beyond that mechanism in the chapel."

Meris blinked once. "Then keep looking."

Matt just stared at her, for once without some snap of a reply. "We will."

"We'll find out whatever it is we need to," I added.

But what if James Abney had been trying to do that very thing? *What if that's why he was murdered?*

No. Gavin Dupree was crazy, but he couldn't be a murderer.

It just couldn't all be about the riddle anymore.

***

Seven days. Seven days of being here and learning nothing at all useful. More troop movements, whispers of beast creatures that lurked in the dark. And still the eerie knowledge that this might not have been a true victory, that Iacomus was planning something much bigger, hung over everything in the capital. No celebrations. No parades.

I stood in a pretty small room with my friends, Danny included. Sunlight blazed into the otherwise cool spot, giving us plenty of light to see by. Noam held up a pair of scissors.

"Ready?"

"Of course." I smiled and moved into the sunlight. "I'm ready to stretch again without feeling like I'm gonna rip a seam open."

His brown eyes widened. "I wouldn't recommend that for a little while. You have to—"

Matt interrupted him. "She's joking, man."

Noam's ears reddened, followed by his face. "Oh. Right."

Meris laughed.

I grabbed the hem of my old t-shirt, now ripped on the one side, still stained. Some of the stain on my jeans was still there. *Hope I can get that out.* As I rolled the hem up, my eyes fixed on the dark stitches, the first time I'd dared to take a good look. Neat, and straight, and not much different from any sort of stitching back home. Noam's skill showcased across my side.

*Wow. He is good.*

Noam knelt beside me, his ears still red, but his eyes absolutely focused. I tensed, expecting it to hurt. *My first stitches*. I locked eyes with Matt across the room. His eyes flicked down to where the wound had been, and back up as he swallowed.

Noam leaned away. "I can't take these out."

*Oh no.* "Why?"

Noam sighed. "It's not ready." He looked up at me. "I'll be honest, I didn't think it would be healed all the way yet."

I'd be taking them home with me. *Need to move, have to, can't.* Itching. Why did it itch now?

"Ira should be here for this," Matt said with an edge in his voice.

*Please*. "I think he learned his lesson."

Danny settled against the wall. "He's actually been pretty useful lately. Too bad it took maiming someone to straighten him out."

"Where is he now?" He had helped us that day, and all that time before when he'd led us to the train.

"I don't know," Meris answered. "Miriam said he was off on an errand, but she was evasive concerning that." She frowned. "I feel like I should be worried."

Noam stood. "If anything, the way he acts will help us. I trust him." He fished in his pocket and handed me a small jar.

Meris snorted. "You're likely the only one, Noam."

"Better that than constant suspicion." The red in his face had calmed by now, and he pointed at the jar in my hand. "Put some of that on the wound site now, and once you get home, keep it covered with some sort of balm until you can have them removed."

"Okay." *Guess I'll be picking up some cocoa butter.* I rubbed the thick cream in and let my shirt drop. The soft material stuck to the glob for a moment. *Yuck.*

Noam tilted his head. "I suppose you could have someone remove them on Earth."

I shook my head, feeling the panic spread. "No, we can't."

"Why not?" Meris asked.

"No one knows we're here," Matt answered. "Going to a family doctor for a mysterious suture removal just might attract a little attention."

I looked down at Noam. "Is it okay if we come back here?"

He blinked. "Of course. Yes."

We stood, all quiet. Not awkward, not now, not anymore.

Time was short. I met Matt's gaze.

"We better be getting home, Matt."

His eyes swept the room. "Yeah. Let's do that."

# Chapter 24

It was just five of us there, but eyes unseen watched us through the woods, guarding this gate. Meris and Noam stood across from me and Matt, and Danny stood between, his eyes on the gate as if he didn't trust it.

*Guess he knows all about it.* I fidgeted, feeling the edges of the knife and map  in my sweatshirt pocket. I dared not touch the map, not here.

Danny spoke first. "I'm gonna stick around here for a while, find out what I can before I head back."

"Let us know what you find, okay?" My eyes drifted to the door in the side of the hill. I'd never stopped to consider what his route would be.

"Sure thing." He grinned. "I'll give you a call in a couple Earth days."

*And how long will that be on this side?*

"You'll both be coming back here, won't you?" Meris asked.

"Of course. We've still got a lot of work to do." *Assuming home is still there.*

"Take care of those stitches until I can remove them," Noam said.

"I will." *But how do I hide them?*

I chewed on the inside of my lip as we stood there. The tiny edge of a breeze snuck through the rip in my sweatshirt. I'd have to fix it.

What would happen to my friends if Hestia was right and Iacomus was only waiting? What if the capital was attacked? Earth would be safe, as far as I knew, but would anyone on this side of the gate?

I lurched forward and hugged them both, quickly, then backed off. Surprise took over their faces.

"We'll try and be back in two days Earth time," I told them as I looked at our exit.

Matt stepped forward and shook Noam's hand. "Thanks," was all he said.

Noam raised his eyebrows. "Of course."

Matt stopped in front of Meris, and both gave a formal nod.

*Okay, well. Progress, I guess.*

Danny approached the gate just behind us. "I won't lock it from here, but you might want to take that precaution on your side. Just in case."

*Your side.* Had Danny adopted Trenavell as his home? *Shake that off. He's trying to help.*

With another glance at the three, I stepped through the gate, Matt still close on my heels. As soon as we were through, he pushed it shut, and we stood at the top of the dimly lit staircase.

"We made it back," I said.

Matt poked my arm. "Almost." He stepped around me. "Going

home should be interesting."

I descended after him, just following the points of light above us, rounding the corner into the dark cellar.

*Or whatever it is.*

The door stood just as we left it, only a little open and having no indication that it had been moved.

*These people are sneaky, not careless. They could have just set it exactly as we left it.* Someone else might have used it. We stepped through. I closed it almost all the way behind us. I didn't stop to dwell on what it meant, because there was no way to stop anything now.

Home. Back on Earth, back in that dirty old kitchen in an abandoned house. The heavy air still filled up the room with sticky, thick humidity, but the light was dimmer.

I faced Matt and threw my arms around him, letting myself indulge a little in the fears I hadn't yet allowed since we'd stepped through that gate the first time. The trembling started in my knees, not violent, just there. At first, Matt didn't move, just stood there and let me keep my arms around him. Then, finally, his arms moved and wrapped around me, not tight. *He's still being careful.* A flash of irritation came, just for a moment. *I'm not going to break.* But still we held on, a minute, then two.

The sweat broke out on my forehead, and now the neck of my sweatshirt pressed up, choking me. I pulled away from Matt, peeling at the hem of the sweatshirt. "I've never been so glad to feel this humid weather." I pulled the heavy knit off and felt liberated, thrilled even. *Home, and it's summer, and that might mean. . . .*

Matt smirked. "Same old Salt's Creek."

I moved to the hallway, kicking up thick dust, covering my nose against the smell of mold. At least Trenavell had felt fresh. "Assuming we haven't been gone like three hundred years or something."

He laughed. "I'm gonna guess more like three hours, if previous trips are any good indication."

"And what if they aren't?" What in the world would our parents think? Maybe that we'd run off together, or had some accident, or worse. My foot hit the porch, and I sat on the top step. The shin-high grass waved in a mockery of a breeze that didn't deliver on its promise. The dirt path led away from the house, straight to Highway 58, off to a little world full of people who'd never known, would never if I could do this right, the secret that wound up buried in this house.

*Not buried. Hidden. Waiting.*

Matt descended the steps and moved into my line of sight. "Well, regardless…I'm ready to go home."

"Yeah. Guess we should."

I walked down after him. The tension in my shoulders eased as the pine shadows stretched over us. Why should I be surprised at that?

"Think that copper thing is still in your room?"

"I'm sure it is." I could see the details in my mind, the strange carvings ringing the surface. "It had that moon-eye language all over it."

Matt inhaled. "Yes."

"Then what do you want to do with it?"

He shrugged. "If I can, I'll translate it, once I get it home. For now…just keep it hidden." He sighed.

"Honestly, how likely is that?"

He breathed out a laugh. "Good point, if your parents go poking around."

But I knew they wouldn't.

"We never found out if Dupree was innocent." Maybe he was still alive. Maybe he was Iacomus. The thought stood the hairs on my neck straight up. *That would be a cruel twist.* If Gavin Dupree was still alive, if he preserved himself and remade himself as King Iacomus of Naolon, then cruelty wouldn't be out of his reach. I tried to shut out the scene that played on in my head, of underbrush crashing away under my feet, the screams of men, women, and children ripping the air behind me. I didn't want to face the possibility of someone in my family being responsible for that.

"We'll figure out the connection," Matt said.

"I know we will." I ground my teeth together. "It just seems like there's no answer, and I want to know this one before anything else." I didn't dare voice my fears.

"Believe me, I know the feeling." Matt smiled, a hint of bitterness clinging.

*No, you don't.* This wasn't like having reflective eyes. This was different. This was all about my family and about how one man had changed everything, how he might still be one of the worst people alive. An answer snapped back and paused at my lips.

But it wasn't so different. Matt's life was affected deeply by people he'd never met, who had no idea what effect they'd have years after they were dead and buried. Those people lived the same story, and anger at the dead wouldn't help us any.

I took in the scene before us. Our homes, our neighborhood, so quiet in the muggy air. Some kids down the street, unintelligible words, laughter. All unchanged, even the position of the cars in the driveways, except for the golden light. Our parents' cars and ours waited there. They were all home. Could I walk into my house like nothing had changed?

Matt stared at his house for a long moment. "I'm not ready to go there yet."

*Fine with me*. "Then come to my house." *Admit it. You're scared.*

"Sure."

The trampoline still stood where it had before, grass brown underneath it where the sun couldn't get through. A detail I'd never cared about before. Was it a new instinct? The living grass still needed cutting, as it had the day we'd left. We climbed onto the back deck. The blue flower pot was set in the corner by the door. My heart jumped a little, and I rushed forward. The back door swung open. Mrs. Dobken stepped through and stopped, staring at her son.

"Matthew Dobken, where have you been?"

*Uh-oh.*

"Hi, Mom."

My parents stood in the door, their faces going back and forth from relief and anger as Matt's mom pushed us forward.

*Oh no.*

"I think we all need to have a little talk," Mrs. Dobken said.

***

I stared at the green numbers on the cable box. 7:37. Matt sat two feet away from me, keeping a distance between us as we prepared to face all the parents at once. They'd already spent an agonizing ten minutes in our kitchen while we sat, coated with dirt, on the couch. I kept my sweatshirt on my lap, pushed up against the rip in my t-shirt, and listened to the quiet conversation hit a swift end. Chairs scraped the linoleum.

*Here goes.*

The hissed whispers ended, and they all filed in to stand in front of the couch, looking down at us. My dad and Mr. Dobken stood behind our moms, silent.

"Now that we're all in here," my mother began, "I'm sure you'd like to tell us where in the world you two have been, alone, and why exactly you were so unreachable."

*I dunno Mom, it's a long story. . . .* "We were messing around in the woods." *And why is it a problem to be alone all of a sudden?*

"All day?" Mom asked.

"No…well…I guess—"

"We got lost," Matt said. The adults all looked at him. "Neither of us had our phones, so we couldn't really call you."

I stared at the carpet. *Don't look at him.* But it was all true. We didn't have phones, and we did get lost more than once.

Mr. Dobken narrowed his eyes. "How did you manage to get lost back there?"

"It all looks the same sometimes," Matt answered. "It gets pretty thick back there, and we couldn't find the trail back once we left it."

*Yeah, right.* Matt could have navigated without a compass, and he would have marked a trail. He knew better, and his mom was well aware of that. *He's gonna incriminate us.*

Mrs. Dobken stared at him, her eyes suspicious. "Why did you both take sweatshirts?"

I couldn't answer that.

*Great. You're looking real strong here.*

She didn't back down from our flimsy excuses.

*She's figured something out.*

But she didn't say anything.

It would probably blow her cover and ruin all those secrets they worked so hard to keep.

Mom rubbed at her eyes with one hand. "Jen, they're home now," she said. *Bless her.* "They can't help if they were lost, right?" If Mom did see something out of the ordinary, she sure wasn't saying anything. Matt's excuse was good enough for her. Why would she have any reason to worry as much as Matt's mom did? If anything, my mother seemed confused by Mrs. Dobken's reaction to this.

Mrs. Dobken nodded. "Right." Her eyes bored into me once. "Matt, it's a warning for this offense. I don't want you to be doing this ever again. You go out, you tell us where you are and you keep in contact. You're not as grown as you think you are."

He dropped his eyes. "Yes ma'am."

I looked up at my parents. "What about me?"

"The same," Dad said. "But no more hiking back there unless you have a way to get in touch with us, just like Matt. You don't know who hangs out back there."

I squelched the laugh that pushed its way up. *I'd say we do.* I straightened my face up and nodded. Just an acknowledgment. There was no way I could promise that.

Mr. Dobken stepped forward. "And we better get going. I think we're gonna have to talk a little more once we're home. Come on,

Matt."

Matt pushed himself off the couch, shooting a glance at me.

*Better slip out myself.* The skin in my side stung as I stood up. "I think I'm gonna go take a shower." I looked over at Matt.

He nodded. *They let us just get away with this. If they only knew. . . .* But really, our offense had been minor to them. For all my mom and dad knew, I'd just been unreachable for an afternoon. Matt was in trouble, but his mother maybe knew more than mine did, even if she wasn't planning on letting him know anything.

The doorbell rang and echoed through the hallway. A jolt ran through my body as my heart sped up. *Calm down. You're just jumpy.* It was safe. We were home, and with our parents. Nothing could happen here. *Just answer the door.*

"I'll get it." *Might as well be casual.* It didn't ring a second time. *Maybe just a delivery guy.* I pulled the door inward.

Empty. Not a soul stood there to have rung the doorbell. The sound of tires on pavement came from the street as a burgundy car sped off, its driver invisible from this angle. I watched as it vanished out of the neighborhood. A splash of pale pink coaxed my eyes downward.

The pink shoebox rested on the welcome mat. I gazed at its faded plainness and black pinstripes for a long minute.

*They're right in your reach, and you're just staring.* I edged the glass door open, grabbed the box, and scooted back, away from the sunlight, away from sight of the door and the living room, and closed the heavy wooden door after me as I cradled the box.

My mom appeared in the doorway. "Who was that?"

I lifted the box. "Someone from school." I swallowed. "It's a thing for a project."

Matt eyed the box in my arms, his eyebrows going up. He held my gaze as his family walked by me and for the door. I retreated up the stairs again. Mrs. Dobkens' voice traveled up the stairs. "We'll see y'all later."

*Maybe she won't ask him anything.*

The envelopes clattered softly against the sides of the shoebox.

*Who left this?*

***

A too loud cricket song drifted up to my window. Not that they ever bothered me, and they shouldn't now. But tonight the little singers, so absent in the past weeks, intruded.

*Just want some quiet.*

The letters rested on my bed, fanned out a little. Most of them had an actual address, but a few older looking ones didn't, like they'd been hand-delivered. Jendra Davies had once lived in Trenavell. At some point, they'd thought she'd gotten rid of the king of Naolon. How had she and her husband ended up on Ocracoke Island? It had to matter as much as the content of the letters.

*One thing at a time.*

I reached out my hand for one of the envelopes.

*Thwack!*

Thrown with a purpose, aimed just right, the object smacked hard into its target. *Not going to ignore that this time*. I stood and cracked the blinds, and saw the gold-colored square of Matt's window with him in the middle of it.

The metal blinds rattled, hissing as I pulled on the cord. I fumbled with the window lock, pulling on it twice before finally it slid around right and let me shove the bottom of the window up. Noise. More noise. *Stupid crickets.*

I didn't say anything over them, just listened to the chirping and stared across the gap until my gaze slipped from his and down to the tan siding on his house.

His voice, soft as it was in the night, startled me. "What's wrong?"

What's wrong? He knew. How dare he ask? I rounded up the ammunition in my mouth, ready to let it loose on him. *No. Wait. He didn't do this. You didn't.* Someone did, and even the question I must ask, knowing what I knew, was hard to force out.

"Do you think your mom and dad have something to do with… with this?" I swallowed. "I mean, with that kind of connection…"

His gaze held steady. "Honestly, I'm afraid to find out myself."

"Me too."

He yawned. "She just yelled at me some more about me not having my phone with me. Didn't ask me anything else about where we'd been."

"Good."

"Why good?"

*Because then I can pretend that a family I knew almost as well as my own wasn't keeping things from us on purpose.* "I dunno. Just…good."

He nodded, slowly, confused, and didn't say anything else.

*Man, this is awkward.*

The sound of tires on the road grew over the cricket sounds and a set of headlights lit up Matt's front yard. He leaned farther out his window as a small dark blue car pulled into his driveway and disappeared behind the corner of the house.

His fist slammed down on his windowsill and he looked back at me. "Quick, what did that car look like?"

"Little. Blue. Why?"

His face brightened. "Okay. Wait one minute, and then come over to my house." Without another word, he slid the window shut. The thunk echoed.

*Okay.*

My clock told me 12:00 AM. Everything was weird about someone showing up at Matt's house. Voices floated up from the Dobkens' front porch, too muffled, but friendly, maybe. They faded and the door shut. What were his parents doing up this late, and who was visiting them at midnight?

It had been one minute. Of course it had. The house was quiet now, at the late hour. My parents were in bed. Maybe I wouldn't wake them by creaking down the stairs.

*Matt's a neighbor. They won't mind. I'll just slip out.*

Hadn't I just slipped to another world, after all?

Out the door, down the steps, and across the quiet yard. The porch light went on as I passed the motion sensor and mounted the steps. Before my hand could even reach to knock, the door opened. Matt stood on the other side of the glass. I smiled, hesitating, and he pushed the door towards me. I took it and pulled it the rest of the way open.

"Matt, what—"

"Shhhh!" His hand closed over my wrist and yanked me inside. "Upstairs!" he hissed. I followed, passing the closed dining room door, trying to keep my steps much quieter than his pounding feet as we made our way to the second floor landing. Some secret operation this was.

I shook my hand away from his. “Okay, seriously, what is going on?”

His mouth was a tight line. “Lukas Simpson is here.”

The name pinged in my head, on the very tip of memory. “Who?”

Matt let out a quick breath. “Remember? He works at the library downtown, in the genealogy room.”

That was it. The name on the plaque, the absent employee. “Why is he here?”

“I don’t know.” He looked down the stairs. “They shut themselves up in the dining room again.”

“Oh.”

“Yeah.”

“So?”

“I told you, he’s the one I heard talk about Gavin Dupree a long time ago. I want to know why they shut themselves in there, and I need a second person to confirm what they’re talking about.”

“How?”

“Listen in.”

“What?”

He smiled. “The dining room door’s pretty thin.” He stepped down. “Come on.”

His bare feet clumped down a few steps. What did I have to lose now? I followed.

He stood beside the doorway, leaning against the wall. I took a place opposite and moved so my ear just brushed the door. The quiet voices came through the thin wooden filter.

A man's deep voice grumbled, one I didn't recognize. "We didn't know it existed before, but there appears to have been traffic for a while now."

"How long?" Matt's mom.

Silence, for just a few moments. "A week. That is the definite length of time that we know of. The screaming you heard the other night might mean it's been happening for longer. We don't know who that was or what happened, and we're looking into it. Recent events aren't making that easy."

*Uh-oh.*

The next voice was Matt's dad. "How did you find out?"

"Rebecca called me last week to tell me that a teenager contacted her mother to ask some questions about the Dupree family. Your son and that girl he hangs around with showed up at Mildred Barnes' home around the same time."

Another few moments of quiet followed, punctuated only by the rough pounding in my chest. Had we been watched our whole lives? Every day?

Matt's mom spoke again. "What about the…subject we discussed before?"

"Most of the network has been shut down, and things are at a standstill there and here. We'll need to act soon, and no one is sure why the delay, but it's a blessing to be sure. Rebecca would disagree, but their age isn't right."

Mrs. Dobken again. "Are the kids in any danger?"

"Right now, no."

A lie. He had to know. Why the network of gates suddenly wasn't working, who was behind it, that it had even happened at all.

*Unless.* . . . The gates not working meant news would be slower now.

Mr. Dobken spoke. "But?"

"But they're beginning to figure things out and poke around, and who knows when they'll start asking the wrong people. I do not know Mrs. Barnes' stance on this issue, but just keep a close eye on the two of them from now on. Rebecca is eager to push this through."

"And they've been gone and unreachable for most of the day." Mrs. Dobken's voice was softer.

My gaze met Matt's. They knew about us. Others were watching, whoever they were. Mr. Simpson and Mildred Barnes and her daughter, and who knows how many others? Could my parents know anything about this, or were they kept in the dark too?

The chairs scraped roughly on the floor. Matt pointed towards the back of his house, and we rushed away from the dining room, down the hall, and out his back door. I forced my feet to a stop on the deck and grabbed the railing. Matt sat on the steps, facing into the dark back yard. Into those woods. I approached his side slowly and lowered myself to sit on the step.

My voice felt rough. "Think we heard enough to figure that out?"

"Yep."

His parents. They did know, always had. About the riddle, the network of gates, how they all, all of them, every last adult just wanted us to do a job for them that they should have done. And what did Matt know about all this?

I glared, ready to rip into him again, because if they knew, then he had to.

Wide eyes, not staring at the woods, but at empty space in front of them. The bundle of his dark hair bunched up in his fist, the other hand clutching the back of his neck, a look of fear all over his face.

"You promise they never told you?"

He shook his head, just a twitch side to side. "No."

They knew, just like Danny's mom. Matt's aunt. Mrs. Dobken's sister.

We had access to a valuable secret that most people on either side of that gate had no knowledge of. "We're sort of at a disadvantage here."

Matt frowned as he looked my way. "How do you figure?"

"We don't know if the people who were in the house before us are on our side or not. We don't know who they are, and apparently we're not supposed to know what we do." I swallowed hard. "We're not supposed to have found out yet." Even if Rebecca Davis was pushing for it. All they knew was that the gate network was shut down, not who did it. Not yet.

*I guess I called right on not visiting Mildred a second time.*

Just me and Matt, stranded, isolated, unable to trust anyone, at least when we were on Earth. No one else but each other amid a void of black sky and dark water in the place that should have been safest. Matt's face changed, rapidly, from angry to worried, and back to angry.

"We played right into the game," Matt said. "Me and you and Meris and Noam."

That was true enough. "I guess. Maybe." *But if they'd wanted to control our actions, they should have moved sooner.* "But…we're ahead, though. Right?" I bit my lip. "And we do have friends in this."

Matt nodded. "Yeah." He rubbed his eyes. "I just always knew my aunt was into weird stuff. Never thought my mom was."

"Didn't sound like she was all that happy."

"No, but she knew." Matt looked over at me. "She knew the whole time. Her and my dad."

"So did a lot of other people, Matt."

"I don't think even Tim knew," he said.

"Maybe that's for the best." I looked up at the stars. Barely visible through the trees, just a patch above his backyard. If we shared a universe, which of those suns lit up the skies on Trenavell's planet? "A lot of other people put this off until now, and we're involved, and now someone wants to do something about it."

"I know." He shook his head. "Now they're panicking."

"And the network's down." *This could all be a secret until someone delivers the news.* "A lot could happen while we're waiting."

"True."

"Are you gonna tell your parents what we did?"

"No." He followed my gaze to the sky. "Better they don't know exactly how much we've done. Safer for your family, too. Might be why Mr. Simpson didn't tell them exactly who shut the gates down, if he even knows."

More secrets. More sneaking, but at least our secrets had reason. Why advertise, especially when we already knew there were people watching us on this side of the gate, who maybe weren't all that interested in our well-being? "Okay."

All that remained was to find that book. Figure out what Gavin Dupree had done on that night so many years ago, or what any of it had to do with Matt's ancestors and their absence, the king of Naolon, and the network of gates that connected two planets half a universe away from each other. And the map, with all those gates that no one knew about, or the copper plate still stowed in my room. I let the goose-bumps roll up over my arms. In whatever form they came, answers waited for us, hiding, somewhere up ahead in the dark. All we needed was enough light to see by.

If they wanted secrets uncovered, fine, we'd do that. All those weird nights with the flashlights, peering into dark, abandoned corners, had shaped me and Matt for this, given us what we needed to see this through to the finish.

*Bring it on. We're ready.*

## About the Author

Amanda Cale has had the *Riddle* universe under construction since 2001. In her spare time she enjoys running, reading, and keeping her eyes on the stars. She currently resides in North Carolina.

Want to know more about Riddle? Visit WorldofRiddle.wordpress.com for news, info, and bonus content!

Follow her on Instagram @amanda_cale_author

www.ingramcontent.com/pod-product-compliance
Lightning Source LLC
Chambersburg PA
CBHW030549310726
48979CB00010B/2083/J

* 9 7 8 0 9 8 9 5 2 1 1 2 3 *